Scion

by

Murray McDonald

First Published by Kennedy Mack publishing

Scion

ISBN 978-0-9574871-3-0

Copyright © Murray McDonald 2013

The right of Murray McDonald to be identified as the author of this work has been asserted by him in accordance with the Copyright, Designs and Patents act 1988.

This book is a work of fiction. Names, characters, places and incidents are the product of the author's imagination or are used fictitiously. Any resemblance to actual events, locations, or persons, living or dead, is purely coincidental.

Part One

Chapter 1

He was lost in a world of pain. Where he was, who he was, why he was there, unimportant. His only goal was stopping the pain. And he was failing.

Just when he thought the pounding in his head would never stop, it did.

"Police! Throw your weapons down and come out with your hands up!" came the shout from behind the door.

His mind struggled to understand what was happening. Had the pounding been in his head or not? Where was the shout coming from? Was he imagining it or was it real?

"This is the police! Open the door or we'll break it down!"

The fuzziness began to clear. He opened his eyes. The light seared his brain. Pain pulsed as each vein expanded and contracted. The room was spinning or was he spinning? He snapped his eyes shut but the room kept moving. It wasn't him, it was the room. He tried to focus. What had happened? From the glimpse he had caught of the room, he knew it wasn't his room. He'd arrived and gone for a meal. He'd had one pint but after that, he couldn't remember a thing. The words began to make sense. Police, open up, break it down.

"You have ten seconds or we'll break the door down!"

Each word assaulted him like a baseball bat in the face, the shockwaves of sound blasting him one by one. After a few seconds, the words began to come together, ten seconds, break door. What did they want?

"Put your weapons down!!!"

Weapons? What the hell? His mind began to focus. He didn't have any weapons. He was in Cambridge, on the university campus. He was a student. Scott the assassin had been left behind. He was Scott the student now or at least he hoped he was.

As the door crashed open, he tried to move, his mind intuitively reacting to the assault. However, his stomach had other ideas and Scott the student deposited its contents all over the floor. Scott the assassin had most definitely been left behind.

Chapter 2

Detective Sergeant Kelly was second into the room and realised instantly something was very wrong.

"Cuff him!" screamed Detective Chief Inspector Harris, her superior who was kneeling on the suspect's back.

"Sir, he's not going anywhere," she replied ignoring her superior's call for cuffs.

Harris turned away from her angrily and barked at the officer behind her. "Officer, cuff him," he ordered.

Kelly surveyed the small room as Harris and the officer restrained the already incapacitated suspect. It was clinical. A bed, a table, a chair, nothing else. No stash of weapons, no sign of any personal belongings, just a drunken comatose student being manhandled by the police. She walked across to the small window and looked down at the chaos below. Police expert shooters, temporary barriers, news crews, floodlights, crowds of students waiting impatiently in varying degrees of undress, huddling to stay warm in the chill of the autumn night and desperate to get back to their beds. She looked back at Harris yanking the suspect from the bed and doing his best to keep him upright. The young man swayed erratically. She had waited ten months to catch this bastard. Five girls raped, the first four almost beaten to death but it just didn't feel right.

"Don't just stand there gawping, woman. Give me a hand!" he shouted.

Kelly walked across and helped Harris stabilise the suspect. It was obvious he wanted to be seen escorting the suspect from the block.

"Sir, this isn't right. It just doesn't fit."

"Rubbish, this is the room the victim pinpointed and here he is, exactly where she said he'd be."

"But look at him. Are you telling me this guy just raped someone? Look at him, he can't stand up never mind stand to attention if you know what I mean."

"He knew he was cornered and drank himself stupid."

"With what? The room's empty. There's nothing in here and where are the weapons?"

"She was brutally raped, she may just have imagined them."

"Imagined them? We've been here for three hours, we've had people believe we've got a crazed gunman in here. It's Virginia Tech in Cambridge. We're being beamed live across the world and she may have fucking imagined the guns and him being deranged?!"

Harris paused as the implications of the level of response he had ordered began to register. The evacuation of the accommodation blocks, the request for specialist marksmen from neighbouring police forces, the news crews that had grown by the minute, the interviews confirming the Cambridge Ripper was trapped in the building, heavily armed and in a psychotic state. The links to Virginia Tech were instantly made and Cambridge was number one news across the globe.

Kelly looked at the suspect again.

"How would you describe him?" she asked angrily.

"Six foot, slim and dark hair."

"I'm a woman like the victim and I would not describe this guy like that. He's the original diet coke guy, tall dark, and drop dead fucking gorgeous."

"So what are you saying, he's not the rapist?"

"I seriously doubt it."

With that thought ringing in his ears, Harris began to pull the suspect towards the door and with Kelly's help, manoeuvred him downstairs towards the waiting press.

Scott was struggling to understand a single word they were saying. All his energies and thoughts were focussed on holding onto the remainder of his stomach, something the motion was making difficult. At the bottom of the stairs, a door opened and a wall of light hit him like a sledgehammer. His concentration went from preventing sickness to covering his eyeballs but, with his hands cuffed, the manoeuvre looked more like a wild jerk than a defensive motion.

As Harris opened the door, the suspect struggled wildly. Any thoughts of innocence evaporated as the suspect fought against Harris and head butted him in the stomach. Harris, not one for modern political correctness, responded automatically and punched the suspect hard in the stomach sending him crashing to the floor head first. With no hands to protect him, the suspect thudded onto the concrete floor. Vomit spewed from his mouth as his body spasmed uncontrollably.

Kelly looked on in horror as the news media caught every gruesome detail. After a second of stunned silence, she jumped into action, waving wildly for a police van and bundled the suspect and Harris into the back. They left the news crews with a final comment, a tyre squeal, as they got the hell out of there.

Chapter 3

"Shut the door," he barked as the girl walked into his office.

Darius was not impressed. The girl had been in his house for four days and hadn't turned a single trick. He ran the best whorehouse in Washington D.C.. His girls were some of the hardest working in the State. Open twenty-four hours a day, seven days a week, three hundred and sixty five days a year, they never missed a trick, never.

"Well?" he asked without raising his head from the papers on his desk.

"Well, what?" asked Rosie cheerily, opting for the smaller chair rather than the large lounge chair as she sat down.

Darius raised his head slowly from his papers and fixed Rosie with a stare that did not leave any doubt as to his demeanour.

Rosie squirmed in her seat. Darius had always been a perfect gentleman to her. Of course, she had heard stories from the other girls of what could happen if you got on his wrong side but up until that point, they had not really sunk in.

"I've not been feeling well," stammered Rosie, understanding exactly why Darius was pissed off.

Darius flicked a sheet of paper across the desk without breaking his stare. Rosie saw the sheet flash below her and land on her lap but did not look down. Her eyes were transfixed. She felt like a rabbit caught in the headlights of a freight train. Something bad was about to happen and there was nothing she could do about it but watch as the inevitability of the event unfolded.

"What's that?" she asked, her voice beginning to tremble.

"That," responded Darius forcefully as he reached for his lighter. "Is how much money I should have made on your scrawny little ass over the last four days."

Rosie dropped her gaze towards the paper and instantly knew she had made a mistake. Darius' motion to retrieve his lighter was nothing more than a deliberate distraction. As Rosie's eyes moved towards the paper, his left hand hit her like a sledgehammer, her cheek and jaw bearing the full brunt of the blow. She fell backwards in her chair and landed unceremoniously on the floor and immediately rolled into a tight foetal position. The left side of her face exploding with pain.

Darius stood up slowly, walked around his desk and towards the cowering Rosie, towering over her, at 6' 4" and over 250 lbs. Rosie curled up even tighter, anticipating further blows. She was left with no doubt that every story she had heard about him was true. Had she been sitting in the high backed chair to her right, rather than the flimsy wooden one she had chosen, she would not have been thrown back and the full force of the punch would have had nowhere to go but into her skull and would have surely killed her. She did not think for a second that Darius had taken this into consideration when he had thrown his punch.

"Get up," he commanded angrily.

Rosie shook her still aching head in defiance, she was not going to give up her defensive position lightly.

"Get up, I'm not going to hit you again," he said in a softer tone, adding as he walked back to his seat. "I'd have to charge less if you had too many bruises."

Rosie watched through a gap in her arms as he retreated behind the desk, sat down and catching her eye, motioned for her to get up. She tentatively stood up, her right hand held her face while she desperately tried to steady herself with her left. Her first attempt failed as her legs gave way and she crumbled back to the floor. Darius rose from his seat.

"It's OK, I'll manage," said Rosie proudly.

Darius shrugged his shoulders and sat back down, relaxing in his seat as he watched Rosie stagger to her feet, pick up the small chair and sit down.

Rosie was groggy but it was not the first time she had been punched and was certain it would not be the last.

Four days. Rosie could hardly believe she had been there that long. She had heard of 'The Palace', more recently referred to as 'Darius" in honour of its relatively new owner. Whatever your sexual preference, The Palace catered for you, so long as it was legal. However, recent rumours were beginning to suggest that the new owner was more lax with what was legal. Rosie had been introduced to Darius through a mutual acquaintance and on seeing the young beauty, he had wasted no time in offering her a place at The Palace with a significant increase on her current percentage.

Darius eyed Rosie as she sat back down. He was beginning to have second thoughts about this girl. He had thought she was too good to be true when he was introduced to her. Nobody who looked as good as she did was on the game and if they were, they worked privately charging thousands of dollars per night. She was too skinny for him, he preferred his woman with a bit more meat but it didn't mean he didn't appreciate true beauty when he saw it. This girl should be in the movies not on her back screwing a punter for fifty bucks. If it hadn't been for the acquaintance who had introduced her, he would have sworn she was a set up, particularly as she had still not turned any tricks.

"Who are you really?" he demanded.

Rosie panicked although managed to remain calm. Did he know the truth? Was that really why she was in there? If so, she was already dead.

"What do you mean? I'm Rosie," she smiled, straining every muscle in her face to make it look as natural as possible.

"You may well be Rosie, but you ain't like no prostitute I ever met. Who are you really?"

As Rosie contemplated what Darius did or didn't know, the TV showed a video of a young man's head thudding to the ground 3,000 miles away in England. Rosie's worries about what Darius knew evaporated as she watched the footage play again.

Darius watched Rosie's face change from a smiling beauty to a face of sheer horror. She was transfixed by something behind him. Darius' mind worked over-time. As he slowly turned to follow her gaze, he was relieved to see no masked gunmen or ghosts, the only two things he thought would cause Rosie's reaction. He realised it was the TV and watched as the video of the young man played again, the banner at the bottom of the screen telling him that the unknown man had been arrested that morning in the UK.

"What? Do you know this guy or something?" asked Darius irritated.

Rosie just kept staring at the TV, answering almost trancelike.

"No."

"So what the hell has got into you?" he asked. She was beginning to freak him out.

"I recognise him."

"Who is he?"

"I don't know."

"But you just said you recognised him?"

"I do."

"So you don't know him but you recognise him. What the fuck is that all about?"

"I don't know him because he's not supposed to exist," replied Rosie shaking herself from the shock. "I'm sorry but I need to make a call, can I use your telephone?" she leaned forward and began to turn the phone towards her.

Darius was still trying to work out what the hell was going on when he suddenly realised what Rosie was doing. He grabbed the phone and yanked it from her grasp. Darius had had enough. He grabbed Rosie's arm with his free hand and began to pull her towards him across the desk, raising the phone and swinging it back. It would do the job as well as any other blunt instrument.

Rosie struggled against his grip but Darius proved far too powerful for her. Lifting her out of her seat, she slowly slid across the wide desk towards him, her face flat against the surface. She couldn't see what Darius was doing but she could sense a movement to her right where the phone had been. She had no doubt what was coming next. Her cover was obviously blown. Rosie the prostitute, at that moment, ceased to exist.

Ashley Jones's hand swung back and grabbed the small black plastic box from her rear pocket. As the phone continued its arch higher and higher, building momentum for its downward thrust, Ashley's hand was already on its way back towards Darius. The black box pointing directly towards his chest. Darius' attention was focussed entirely on the phone and he failed to notice the very deliberate motions of the woman struggling beneath him. Content the phone had enough height for deadly impact, it was time.. Ashley, noticing the change in direction, wasted no time and pressed the button on the small box. Compressed Nitrogen forced two small probes to shoot out of the end of the box and imbed themselves in Darius' chest. He instantly let go of Ashley and desperately clawed at the two small probes. Before his hands could reach them, Ashley pressed a second button and watched as 50,000 volts of electricity overrode his central nervous system and sent his muscle tissue into uncontrollable contractions. After a few seconds his body slumped to the floor. Ashley placed the Taser electroshock gun on the desk and smiled as Darius' body twitched as the system continued to deliver its charge. She picked up the phone and dialled the number she had tried to call earlier.

"Hello, Parkside Police Station."

"Hi, I'm phoning about the young man on TV, how is he please?"

"Can I ask who's calling?"

"Just a family friend," replied Ashley, watching another re-run of the day's biggest news.

"I'm sorry but can you confirm his name to prove you're a friend," asked the officer 3,000 miles away.

Darius' body stopped twitching, the Taser's charge had run out.

"I'm sorry I can't talk now, I'll be there in a day or two. Can you just tell him I know who he is." Ashley dropped the receiver and ran out of the office, leaving Rosie the prostitute behind forever.

Chapter 4

The moment the caller had acknowledged knowing the suspect, the officer on the call had raised his hand and waved it around in the air frantically, only stopping when he received a tap on the shoulder from his supervisor confirming that the call was being recorded and a trace initiated.

"She's gone."

He removed his headset and turned to his supervisor disappointed not to have kept the caller on the line longer.

"Sorry."

The supervisor turned towards the desk at the back of the communications room. All calls to Parkside were being re-routed to the Cambridgeshire Police headquarters in Huntingdon where a specialist communications team was helping to track any potential leads as to the identity of their suspect. Being a Sunday, there was little chance of the DNA check being completed.

The officer operating the array of equipment at the desk to the rear of the room was motionless. His headphones remained in place as he listened intently to the line the call had come in on. Catching the supervisor's eye he pointed to the headphones. The line was not dead. As he listened, his fingers continued to tap at the keyboard in front of him, fine tuning the equipment in order to pick up even the faintest of voices at the other end.

Before the supervisor could place a headset on, the specialist jumped from his seat and threw his headphones to the ground holding his ears.

"Jesus!"

"What happened?" shouted the supervisor running to the specialist's side.

"I had the pick up set to max and I think she just kicked him in the balls. After she stopped talking, I heard a noise like the phone being dropped, something being scraped along a surface and then footsteps. I heard the woman say something quietly, it may have been "prick" and then an almighty thud and a rough sounding guy screamed "YOU FUCKING BITCH." I'll just rewind, hold on."

As the supervisor and the original officer donned their headsets, the specialist rewound the feed to the point where the woman had dropped the phone and checking they were ready, played the tape at a less deafening volume. The three listened as the woman took something from the desk and apparently kicked a man as she fled from the room before slamming the door behind her. They then listened as the man screamed in fury at the fleeing woman he called "Rosie" vowing to kill her in a variety of unpleasant ways.

"He doesn't seem to be moving," said the supervisor.

"Neither would you if you got kicked as hard as he was. I'm surprised he can even talk."

A shuffling noise silenced the group as they listened carefully to events unfold thousands of miles away. The man was obviously pulling himself towards the phone. The sound of a click followed by a short conversation suggested an intercom system was being used.

"Did you get the bitch?"

"Who?" asked another male voice.

"Rosie, she just kicked me in the nuts and ran out of here."

"Sorry, boss, she just left. She said you asked her to go see the doctor down at the clinic."

"Fuck, well get after her and don't come back 'til you get her or she's dead. You hear me?"

"Yes boss."

"Fucking soundproofing!" was the last the three heard as the man replaced the receiver of the phone.

"I'm not sure Rosie's going to be much use to the investigation, sounds like her days are numbered," offered the specialist.

"Doesn't sound good. The quicker we get the location of the call, the sooner we can help her. Any ideas?"

"Washington D.C., here's the address."

He handed a printout to the supervisor along with a copy of the recording.

The news of the breakthrough was immediately relayed to DCI Harris and DS Kelly along with the imminent threat to their potential witness.

DCI Harris looked at the address that had been passed to him. 'The Palace, Pennsylvania Avenue, Washington D.C.'

"That street sounds very familiar," mused Harris.

"Sherlock wouldn't have had a look in with you around," replied Kelly sarcastically. "It's only the most famous address in the world... Pennsylvania Avenue..." Kelly paused giving Harris a final chance to redeem himself but with only a blank expression, she gave up. "It's the same street The White House is on!"

"Oh," replied an embarrassed Harris, a feeling that was becoming all too familiar. Before he could impart any further evidence of his encyclopaedic knowledge, the door opened and the Chief Constable entered the office. Harris's heart almost stopped beating.

"Good morning Sir," said Kelly.

"Is it?" he responded. "Well?" he asked looking into Harris's eyes.

Harris explained himself and ran through his version of events. He stopped a number of times to elicit some response but each time he stopped, the Chief just nodded for him to continue.

"So it's all just a big misunderstanding?" asked the Chief Constable angrily.

"Actually yes. I genuinely believed he was making a break for it," said Harris.

"In front of fifty officers and the worldwide press?!" shouted the Chief.

"I know Sir but he head-butted me in the stomach and you know how it is, it was just automatic."

The Chief looked at the ageing detective. He did know 'how it was'. When he had joined the force at roughly the same time as Harris, police brutality towards criminals was not only tolerated but actively encouraged. Those days, however, were long gone and even looking at a criminal the wrong way could have you under investigation.

"We shouldn't forget you caught the bad guy," he pondered.

"Exactly. That guy is a scumbag rapist, it seems the press are forgetting that," added Harris a little more forcefully.

"So who is he?"

"Absolutely no idea. He came to, gave us his first name, Scott, and claims not to have a surname."

"What about the victim, how's she doing?"

"I'm not sure, she's disappeared."

"Disappeared? You have got to be fucking joking. She kicks off rumours of a Virginia Tech massacre and pulls a fucking Houdini?!" The Chief looked at Harris questioningly. "You sure you've got the right guy?"

"Absolutely. Everything but the injuries he inflicted on the previous victims match."

The Chief wasn't convinced. He had investigated enough cases to know something didn't feel right.

"It's him Sir, rest assured it's him and the DNA will prove it outright."

"How long?"

"The samples have just been sent and I've asked for a quick job, couple of days maybe."

"I'll call the boss at FSS and see if we can make it quicker than that."

The FSS was the Forensic Science Service, the custodians of the UK's National DNA Database.

"I'd appreciate that Sir," replied Harris.

"I'm not doing it for you, you pillock. The only thing that's going to take the heat off this case is to confirm the bastard is our serial rapist."

Kelly interrupted their conversation.

"I've just got off the phone from the Assistant Director in Charge of the FBI's D.C. office. The plot thickens."

"It seems The Palace is a very popular destination for some of Washington's more powerful individuals. As such, they have some extremely influential friends and there is no way the D.C. police will be allowed anywhere near to help us find this Rosie woman."

"So what is The Palace?" asked Harris. He didn't see Kelly's eyes raise to the heavens.

"I would guess a brothel," replied the Chief. "So, to summarise, we have a suspected rapist. Who, while being arrested, we abused on live TV. A serial rapist who no-one can identify. We have a first name, Scott, and have no idea whether it's real or not. The victim who didn't even give an accurate description of the suspect seems to have disappeared. And we get a call from a prostitute in Washington who appears to be the only person on the planet who knows who he is and who is now being chased across the city by a lawless pimp desperate to kill her. Does that sound about right?"

"Unfortunately yes," replied Kelly.

"We'll clear it all up when we get to talk to the bastard tomorrow Sir," encouraged Harris.

"I hope so for your sake, Harris, I hope so," said the Chief, alarm bells ringing in his head. None of it made any sense, none of it.

Chapter 5

The Chief Executive of the FSS did not normally check his phone messages on Sundays but after the debacle in Cambridge he had a funny feeling he may get a call from the Chief Constable. As predicted, the call came in just after lunch, requesting a fast-track procedure for checking the DNA of the suspect against the DNA left on the victims and against the database of known offenders. With a branch in Huntingdon, the CEO felt the least he could do was contact the Director responsible for the branch and ask if they could get someone in to start the testing. Unfortunately, the Director of the Huntingdon branch was a keen golfer and had teed off just after one. It was seven p.m. before he picked up the message and called in some favours.

The favour fell down the hierarchy to one of the most junior staffers, John Yates, who had only been with the FSS for eight months and when his supervisor called with a big favour, unlike the previous recipients, he had nobody to delegate it to. Not that he wanted to, the key words 'Chief Executive' and 'special favour' were all the ambitious young scientist required. Twenty minutes later, he had opened up the Huntingdon Office and collected the DNA sample from the Post Box and was already in the process of running the tests.

***

Danieliel Koning looked out across the skyline and felt as though he should pinch himself. His dream job. Chief Operations Officer. One of the corner offices in one of Manhattan's tallest buildings. Whoever said hard work didn't pay? Danieliel had put work before everything. Marriage had come late, only three years earlier, at 44 and that was only because his lack of relationships were calling his sexuality into question. Within a year he was the proud father of twins, one boy, one girl and only then did he find something that could compete with his love for the company. His children completed what he believed to be the perfect life. A beautiful wife, two lovely children, a lovely house in the suburbs and as of the next day, Monday, his new job. Life didn't get any better.

The previous incumbent, his old boss' last day had been Friday. Danieliel, keen to get off to a good start, had decided to come in on the Sunday to move into his new office and prepare a presentation for his new team. He was keen for the transition to be a smooth one. Their old boss had surprised everyone only a month earlier by announcing his retirement. A number of names were voiced as potential replacements and after a few sleepless nights, Danieliel got the good news. Some of his peers had been candidates and Danieliel was keen not only to impress them but to make them feel they were still valuable members of the team.

He spun his seat around and looked back at his new office. Two walls of floor-to-ceiling glass on the 92nd floor and over one thousand square feet of the most expensive real estate in the world. It had taken him less than fifteen minutes to pack up his old office, one floor down and about five seconds to realise just how much bigger his new office was. He was going to have to sit down with his assistant and organise some books, photos and ornaments to try and make the office a little less sparse. He hadn't realised just how much personal stuff his old boss must have had in there.

As he pulled his box across the desk and extracted the family photo that would take pride of place on his desk, the phone rang. His hand immediately moved towards it but stopped. He could tell from the flashing red light next to 'Ext 1' that it wasn't security letting him know they had moved his car into the car park. It wasn't his wife, she didn't know the number and would have called his cell phone. The rest of the building was empty so it wasn't even a transferred call. The dilemma was a tough one. The old COO had left on the Friday but his contract didn't kick in until the Monday. Was it his line to answer? He knew that after six rings the phone would kick to either Voicemail or Call Divert and it was already at ring number five.

"Hello?" he answered, bellowing authority. This was it, he was the new COO.

"We've got a problem, I've just got a DNA match flashed through to me."

"Sorry?" asked Danieliel, a corporate banker. He had no idea what the person was talking about.

"It's Clark here, we've scored a match on the DNA, 100% positive it's him, he does exist."

"Who is this?"

Danieliel's voice had lost the authoritative tone he had inherited from his old boss.

Clark was immediately on the back foot.

"Who the fuck is this?" he panicked, knowing he had said too much.

"Danieliel Koning, the new COO," imparted Danieliel angrily. "And who may I ask are you? Wait a minute I know you, Clark, Joseph Clark., I'm your new boss!"

"Mr Koning, please forget we had this conversation," suggested Clark slightly more forcefully than Danieliel liked.

Danieliel was not going to let it go that easily. It was important to get off on the right foot.

"I've always wondered what you did for us here, you've been a rather closely guarded secret, Clark."

Danieliel had asked several times who the mysterious Joseph Clark was. Each year he had been asked to sign off Clark's budget, a not insignificant sum of money, for which, the company, it appeared, received no return. His old boss had just brushed it aside as no concern of Danieliel's, intriguing him further. He hadn't even thought that his new role would allow him to uncover the mystery that was J. Clark, $2,000,000 on the budget spreadsheet.

"So what do you do?"

"I'm sorry Mr Koning but that's not for me to tell you."

"But I'm your boss," said Danieliel a little less masterfully than he would have wished.

"On paper only. Now please, for your own sake we didn't have this conversation." Clark hung up before Danieliel could respond.

Danieliel stared at the lifeless receiver. He then pulled a pad of paper from his box and tried desperately to remember exactly what Clark had said.

The phone was answered on the second ring. The recipient having recognised the number, was worried. It was Sunday and there was no reason for a call, particularly from him.

"It's me," said Clark.

Danieliel Koning's old boss tightened his grip on the mobile.

"What?" he asked gruffly.

"We found him, we've got a 100% DNA match, it came through about 15 minutes ago."

William Walker III almost dropped the phone as the words hit him. Speechless by the revelation it took some time to respond.

"Who knows?"

Clark did not want to admit to his earlier mistake.

"Just me and you."

"Containment?" asked Walker.

"Difficult, he's in England in a prison cell."

"What?"

"Did you watch the news today?"

"Of course."

"Well chances are you've seen him, it was his head that smashed into the ground in Cambridge."

"Jesus!" Walker's home phone rang and his wife called out to say it was for him and it was urgent.

"Hold on Clark," he said before picking up the phone on his desk.

"Hello?"

Walker's face reddened as Danieliel relayed the conversation he had just had with Clark.

"Danieliel, can you just hold a second please."

He muted the phone as he placed the cell phone to his ear.

"Clark, I thought you said it was just you and I that knew?" he asked menacingly.

Clark had known William Walker III for many years and realised he should have been more forceful with Danieliel Koning about forgetting the conversation. Not for himself but for

Danieliel's own sake. There were very few men in the world as ruthless as William Walker III.

"He doesn't have any idea what I was talking about," pleaded Clark.

"Quote "we've scored a match on the DNA, 100% positive it's him, he does exist"," answered Walker coolly.

"Point made, I'll deal with it immediately."

"Good, I thought my retirement may have been premature."

The chilling message was not missed on Clark.

"I need to make some calls, you know what to do." Walker hung up and demuted Danieliel.

"Sorry about that my wife wanted to know what I wanted for dinner. Will you be there much longer?"

"Couple of hours, maybe."

"OK, I'll call Clark and call you back."

Walker sat back in his seat and contemplated what the news meant. For twenty four years they had had the prospect of the boy's existence hanging over them. Some, after a few years, had suggested they should forget about it, he didn't exist. Walker had been a lone voice calling for vigilance but even he had begun to relax and drop his guard by retiring on his seventieth birthday, just a month before the deadline was up. He knew what had to be done and picked up the phone. He needed some very specialist help.

***

Danieliel had just put the finishing touches to his presentation and felt sure it hit exactly the right note. He printed off a copy to take home and as he waited for it to print wondered how much longer Mr Walker, William, would be before he phoned back. It had already been a couple of hours. However, a knock on the door removed him from those thoughts.

"Come in," he shouted, surprised when a non descript man aged forty-five to sixty walked towards him and was not a security guard.

"Mr Koning. Hi, my name is Joseph Clark."

The man crossed the office quickly and shook Danieliel's hand. Only after they shook did he realise he had failed to remove his gloves. He smiled apologetically as he removed them and sat down in the seat facing Danieliel's desk.

Danieliel didn't hide his surprise.

"Oh, I was expecting a call from Mr Walker."

"Yes, he sent me instead," explained Clark.

"So what do you do Mr Clark?" asked Danieliel.

"I resolve problems before they become problems."

"Sorry, but what the hell does that mean?"

Clark rose from his seat, walked around Danieliel's desk and looked down the 92 floors to the ground below.

"It means exactly what I said, I pre-empt issues and resolve them."

"What sort of issues do you pre-empt?"

Clark walked back towards his seat. As he passed Danieliel he withdrew a small pistol from his pocket and expertly placed a silencer on the barrel with the other. Danieliel could only see Clark's back and did not see what he was doing. As Clark turned around, the pistol pointed directly at Danieliel whose face drained.

"Problems like you Danieliel."

Danieliel stared speechless. His eyes eventually moved from the pistol to the family portrait.

Clark, watching Danieliel's pleading eyes, shook his head with genuine sorrow.

"I told you to forget our conversation but you just didn't listen."

Clark walked around the desk, pulling his gloves back on and instructing Danieliel to place his hands on the armrests of his seat. He removed two lengths of cord and lightly tied Danieliel's hands to the chair. The cord was similar to that used on dressing gowns and would leave no marks.

Danieliel relaxed slightly. He worked for one of the oldest and most respected banks in America. They weren't going to kill him, he was just being taught a lesson. They were just scaring him. If they were going to kill him, he'd be dead already. He had read enough novels and seen enough movies to know that.

Clark wheeled Danieliel away from his desk and placed him facing the window.

"Don't move or struggle and you may just make it out of here alive," said Clark as he headed back to Danieliel's computer.

Danieliel hearing those words became even more convinced this was just a scare tactic. He obviously had heard something he shouldn't have and they were making sure he'd remember to forget. A strange clicking noise caught his attention and as his head turned, Clark shouted a warning.

"Don't even think about looking over here."

Five minutes later, Clark returned to his side and announced cheerily "all done" and began to remove Danieliel's cords. Once he had removed them he checked for any tell tale marks or threads. Finding none, he grabbed a leg of the huge desk with one hand before raising the pistol and shooting the window three times, as the window exploded outwards, the wind rushed in before being sucked back out with even more force than it had rushed in. Clark held tightly to the leg of the desk and gave Danieliel's chair a helping nudge towards the gaping hole.

"Well you can't say I'm not a man of my word, you left here alive."

He gave the chair a final push sending Danieliel plunging a thousand feet to certain death. As the atmosphere stabilised, Clark quickly checked he had everything he needed. The three shell casings, Danieliel's presentation and the cords used to tie his hands.

Within ten seconds of Danieliel's exit, Clark was in the corridor making his way towards the fire exit. He was not looking forward to descending the 92 floors on foot, especially having just climbed them but it was the only way in and out of the building without anyone knowing he had been there. Investigators would quickly conclude suicide especially as Danieliel's perfect life had been altered in the last two hours. The perfect wife and two kids would be seen as a cover for Danieliel's real life as a closet homosexual. Clark had loaded a significant amount of gay porn onto his computer along with a few love letters from his gay lover who had just ended their secret relationship which had pushed Danieliel over the edge. Clark had replaced Danieliel's presentation with a suicide note claiming he could no longer go on being somebody he wasn't, particularly not without his one true love, Juan.

Chapter 6

London to Cambridge was only 60 miles, less than an hour in a fast car via the M11. The eight men wasted no time and clambered aboard the two supercharged Range Rovers. The blue lights mounted within the grills would ensure there would be no unnecessary delays. Their orders had come through the normal channels but unlike most of their previous work, this was domestic, something none of them had previously experienced. Their talents were almost exclusively reserved for the less salubrious parts of the world. They were guns for hire but only for a select few. When a conflict needed to be swung in a particular direction these men and their colleagues could make the difference. However this mission was much simpler, no kings were to be crowned just one small problem solved.

As they neared Junction 12 of the M11, they killed the blue flashing lights and blended in with the rest of the traffic, exiting the motorway and following the A603 towards the historic city centre. Taking Queen's Road, they followed the banks of the River Cam until they turned right onto Garret Lane, crossing the Cam into the heart of Cambridge University's Colleges. Pubs lined the street as they made their way slowly along it, looking for an ideal spot.

The German and Belgian drivers, like their passengers, were ex-military battle-hardened men from a diverse group of nationalities who had fought in just about every corner of the globe; not necessarily, however, on the side of their own countries. These men fought for money, their strongest allegiance. The leader was a British ex-colonel who had left the army disillusioned by a government which had sometimes commanded him to defend corrupt regimes whilst at other times to stand back and do nothing while innocent people were slaughtered and on some occasions, commanded him to help remove legitimate governments. He eventually realised that it was all about money and power; it was rarely about doing the right thing. He had heard rumours of an elite outfit of guns for hire that operated globally, men who were ready to move at a moment's notice. Men like him, well trained, experienced soldiers who no longer cared about politics and were willing to take risks for significant rewards. The Unit, as they were called, had men stationed throughout the world, men who could be called on twenty-four hours a day, three hundred and sixty five days a year who were ready to go within the hour. What none of them realised was that although guns were for hire to the highest bidder, they actually only ever had one client.

As a group, they exuded a power and authority which ensured that all but the bravest would turn and run - essential requirements in Third World war zones but not ideal for their current mission. The Colonel, however, had thought about this and had brought along a few props.

As the Range Rovers swept down the tight streets that characterised the historic areas of the city, the Colonel suddenly commanded his driver to stop. Both cars immediately came to a halt and following the Colonel's directions, reversed back to the small car park just behind them. The German driver stayed in the Range Rover. He had a slightly different task and with a nod from the Colonel, was on his way. Seventeen miles to the Northwest was the town of Huntingdon and home of the Huntingdon FSS branch.

The men assembled at the rear of the remaining Range Rover to receive their orders from the Colonel. As he outlined his plan in detail the men began to laugh. If nothing else, this was going to be fun. Happy that everybody knew what was required of them, the Colonel opened the rear of the Range Rover and removed the false floor. An array of weaponry was on offer, Heckler & Koch MP5's, an Accuracy International L115A1 sniper rifle, Sig Sauer P226 pistols, a pump action shotgun and various grenades, smoke, fragment and flash bangs. All in all it was enough to start a small war and in itself outgunned the predominantly unarmed Cambridgeshire constabulary. However, the Colonel bypassed all the weapons and withdrew a carrier bag, from which he proceeded to withdraw six shirts, one for each of the men. Another bag contained cans of beer. These were opened and after a number of large gulps each man tipped the remainder of the beer down the front of his new shirt. The Colonel happy with each man's appearance wished them luck before jumping back in the Range Rover and driving off.

The six men wasted no time and made their way back to the pubs they had just driven past. Normally the six would have paired off and slowly worked their way down the street, one pair either side with the final pair bringing up the rear. Everybody in their path would have been scanned and an analysis made of any potential threat. If any were detected, it would have been eliminated immediately with overwhelming force. However, on this occasion, all training had to be left firmly behind and a more undercover approach assumed, one that would allow six hard and war torn mercenaries to walk down a street in middle England and blend in without drawing attention to their violent histories. The group huddled together and became raucous, their normal deliberate and assured footing replaced by a stumbling, clumsy gait that had them clinging on to one another to stay upright. The new beer stained rugby shirts added to the look. They were well chosen and defined the men as just another group of rugby players who didn't know how to control their boozing after a Sunday kickabout. The rugby shirts were especially well chosen and would ensure the next part of the plan would kick in without much effort.

***

The German slowed down as he approached the roundabout. The navigation screen told him that the FSS offices were on the other side of the small woods that lined the roadside. The job was rushed and as such he had no idea what level of security protected the government building. He did however expect the car parks to be monitored by CCTV and therefore would approach the building on foot. Noticing a small parking area further up on the left, he drove past the entrance to a small industrial estate and parked. Opening the rear of the Range Rover, he extracted a number of weapons, night vision goggles and a black jumpsuit. Closing the boot, he turned and disappeared quickly into the treeline.

As he worked his way through the woods and towards the building, he could clearly see that there was only one car in the car park, just as the Colonel had predicted. Of course, being a

Sunday night at 10 p.m., it was not a particularly enlightened prediction but all the same it did make the job all the easier. The German checked for surveillance cameras and noted that the front of the building and the car parks were covered by CCTV. However, he could see a way to weave through those without being seen, at least until he reached the front door. After that, he was fairly certain he would be picked up but he was going to have to cover his tracks inside the building anyway.

***

John Yates, the young FSS scientist had spent the last three hours working through the DNA sample. Uploading it to the database had taken less than an hour. However the results were proving anything but normal. So far, the sample did not match that taken from any of the previous four victims. It seemed certain the suspect was not the serial rapist. As for the latest sample from the most recent victim, not only did it not match the suspect but it did not match the previous samples. Whoever had attacked the latest victim was not the serial rapist. It seemed the suspect was completely innocent, something even the young and naïve Yates knew was going to give the police a serious problem. It was bad enough beating up a suspect but an innocent suspect? Just as Yates reached for the phone to call his supervisor, his computer screen bleeped and a match flashed onto his screen. He replaced the receiver and checked the results.

Sample Match *************** eyes only Def. Min.   **Send**

He'd never seen anything like it, as far as he knew he had access to every name in the system. Yates knew a thing or two about computers and tried to circumvent the security. He hadn't wasted his Sunday evening to come up with a row of asterisks. After a number of dead ends, he eventually gave up. The area which had identified the match was deeply buried and not available to Yates. In fact, it wasn't shared with any other system. Of the three million samples stored, it seemed that around 50 samples were partitioned in a highly secure secret area. As he reached for the phone, the buzzer at the main door sounded. Thinking the only person likely to visit at that hour was his supervisor, to check up on him, he quickly deleted all tracks of his search for the secure area and hit the Send button, which alerted the Defence Minister of the match. He was surprised to see his screen instantly clear of any reference to the sample. Obviously, another security feature, out of sight out of mind.

The buzzer at the main door sounded again. John quickly double-checked he had cleared any sign of wrong doing and happy that everything looked OK, he ran to the front door. The main reception area was well lit and as John approached, he could see a man behind the door, most definitely not his supervisor. Skidding to a halt, his mind thought back to the DNA match and the reference to the Defence Minister. Instead of just opening the door, he walked across to the empty security desk and pressed intercom button.

"Can I help?" he asked nervously.

"Yes, open the door please," replied the German in perfect English.

"May I ask who you are?"

"Police taskforce." his said, sounding slightly irritated.

John wasn't sure but the words 'police' and 'taskforce' did seem to ring true. The man was in some sort of tactical outfit and certainly looked like and sounded like a policeman. John pressed the button and the door lock clicked open.

The German picked up his kit bag, opened the door and stepped into the reception area.

"Hi, I'm John" said John offering his hand to the German.

"Hi. Karl," responded the German shaking John's hand.

"I was just about to phone my supervisor, it seems you've got the wrong guy," said John offering an update.

"Oh, OK, can you show me please," asked Karl, directing John back into the building and away from the door.

"Of course, this way."

John led the way back to his workstation. On arrival at his desk, John began to explain how the six samples had been analysed. The four from the first four victims all matched but the last two didn't match any of the others. Meaning they definitely had arrested an innocent man. John left out any mention of the match and the link to the Defence Minister, it wasn't for him to tell non-FSS staff top secret results.

After John's in depth explanation, Karl asked, "So where are the samples, now?"

John pointed to the small fridge at the side of his desk.

"In there."

"OK, and the latest sample has been uploaded into the network?"

"Of course, that's how I checked it didn't match."

"Can you show me."

"Yes." John turned to his PC and showed Karl the readouts and the sampling that had been uploaded from the suspect.

Karl listened intently as John detailed exactly how the system worked. Comfortable he understood everything he needed to, Karl placed one foot behind John's chair and in one swift motion placed his hand on John's chest and pushed. John's chair moved back, caught Karl's foot and with nowhere else to go, tipped backwards. Karl pushed harder as the chair began to tip. John struggled as his body followed the chair and fell backwards. As the momentum built, John's neck hit the desk behind him and as Karl continued to push, John's struggling stopped as his spine snapped at the base of his skull. Karl stopped pushing and let the dead weight drop to the floor.

Karl took note of the point at which the chair had tipped and removing his knife carefully created a small rip in the carpet. Using another chair leg, he placed it in the small tear and pulled it backwards, the resultant ridge was exactly what he was after. Having staged the death scene, he moved towards the fridge. The DNA samples needed to be altered. Within ten minutes, he had taken the suspect's sample, replaced it with a small amount of the serial rapist's sample from one of the first four victims. Having sorted the physical evidence, he moved towards the computer and deleted any reference to the suspect's real sample, replacing it with a copy of the serial rapist's. He quickly checked for any evidence of his visit before heading down to the security office with a high power magnet to take care of any video evidence showing his arrival or soon to be departure.

Five minutes later, Karl was in the Range Rover and driving back to Cambridge having insured the suspect was now well and truly guilty of four rapes. The tragic accidental death of the young scientist would lead to a huge health and safety clampdown across the country, warning employers of the dangers of damaged carpeting.

***

The six mercenaries walked into the packed pub and found that their shirts did exactly what they had hoped. The pub instantly silenced.

"What the fuck…are you guys taking the piss?" came the shout from a large group of students proudly wearing their light blue and white Cambridge University Rugby tops.

"Fuck you, you fuckin' pussy," shouted one of the mercenaries, pushing the student in the chest.

The moment the six burly men wearing Oxford University Rugby tops walked into the pub, the landlord had dialled 999. He had run pubs long enough to know when shit was about to hit the fan.

Nobody was sure who threw the first punch but despite their size and number, the Cambridge students didn't stand a chance. The mercenaries waded through them like a men versus boys fight. They had a lifetime of experience in brawling and knew not only how to throw a punch to maximum effect but just as importantly how to take one.

Thankfully for the students, the police responded quickly to the call and arrived within five minutes. They were pleasantly surprised when the Oxford supporters accepted blame without protest and climbed peacefully into the police vans to be taken to the station and booked.

The Colonel watched from the shadows of a nearby doorway as his men were marched out of the pub and driven away by the police. The plan was working perfectly.

Chapter 7

Ashley knew they would go straight to the apartment she had rented under Rosie's name. She just prayed they wouldn't find the loose floorboard behind the toilet. When she first ran out of The Palace, her intention was to go directly to the apartment but on the way, she realised that that was the first place Darius and his guys would check. There was a chance she could beat them to it but she knew enough about Darius to know he had people everywhere. There was every chance one of his men was already there ransacking the place and waiting for her to show up.

She knew she should call in and get back-up but after seeing the news report in Darius' office there was only one thing on her mind. Getting to England. Calling in would mean spending the next week writing up reports and that could wait. She had a promise to keep, one that had been made when she was a little girl. But one that she always knew she would keep. However to do that she needed her passport.

The first thing she needed to do was change her clothes. Rosie the prostitute stood out in a crowd for all the wrong reasons. Ashley Jones, however, stood out in a crowd for all the right reasons. Spotting a Banana Republic store on M Street, she asked the cabbie to pull over and wait. Her ten minute stop was reminiscent of the Pretty Woman shopping scene, a sleazy prostitute transformed into an unrecognisable, elegantly beautiful woman. The cabbie had initially refused to allow Ashley back in the cab such was the transformation. Her long brown hair, previously flowing freely had been pulled tightly back in a ponytail, emphasising her striking bone structure. The mini skirt previously barely covering her underwear and leaving nothing to the imagination of her perfectly toned and sculptured legs was replaced by long elegant trousers. Her low cut cropped top that had broadcast to the world the tautness of her stomach and the lushness of her perfectly firm breasts was replaced by a simple but classic fitted black cashmere sweater.

Ashley knew there was nothing for it but to head over to the apartment. She needed her passport, it was the only way she would be able to fulfil her childhood promise. The cab turned left onto the Francis Scott Key Bridge and using the Jefferson Highway and Columbia Pike, covered the six miles into the heart of Arlington Virginia in a little over twenty minutes thanks to the relatively light Sunday morning traffic. Ashley asked the cab driver to pull up just around the corner from her apartment block. As she leaned over to pay the driver she took her time extracting the money and waited for the driver to scramble around for change, something she knew he'd take his time over, hoping she'd become impatient and insist he kept the change afterall. He did exactly as predicted and as she had hoped gave her plenty of time to carefully check that nobody was watching. The driver huffed and puffed as he checked pockets, ashtrays and finally his wallet for the $4.25 change. Realising the woman was adamant she wanted her change, he finally relented and handed it over offering as many quarters and dimes as he felt he could get away with. Looking at the handful of change Ashley smiled.

"Just keep it, thanks," she said as she opened the door and walked quickly into the coffee shop that overlooked her apartment block.

Taking a seat next to the window at the rear of the store, she had a perfect view of not only her apartment block but also everybody who came into the coffee shop. The apartment was located on the fifth floor and although she could see the window, she had no idea whether Darius' men were already in there. She didn't have to wonder for very long. Five minutes after taking her seat, a Black Chrysler 300M with its tell tale chrome wheels and blacked-out windows came screeching around the corner. Darius' men had arrived. Ashley watched as the three passengers rushed out of the car and ran into the building. She flicked open her mobile phone and dialled 911.

"Police!" she answered desperately in response to the operator's question.

Sunday morning was definitely working in her favour, the police operator was transferred instantly.

"Somebody's breaking my door down!" spurted Ashley through deep breaths of panic. Another customer looked across at her quizzically. She smiled and shook her head as if including him in the joke.

With the operator trying to calm her down Ashley managed to give her address before ending the call mid sentence. The tactic obviously worked and within two minutes Ashley heard the first Siren and within 30 seconds three police cruisers were screeching to a halt outside of the apartment block. Four officers in total ran into the building with their pistols drawn. Ashley watched as the Black Chrysler's driver slowly edge the car further down the street in an attempt to distance himself from the location but remain available to his colleagues should they manage to escape. None did. The police emerged a few minutes later with the three men in custody and loaded them into the back of the cruisers. They would be in for a very interesting afternoon trying to explain what they had done to the young woman who had made the call.

As events unfolded before her it became apparent that the police were taking Ashley's call very seriously. The next to arrive were two plain clothed detectives quickly followed by a Crime Scene Unit. The hunt for evidence as to her whereabouts was underway. However, the arrival of the detectives and Crime Scene Unit were too much for the Chrysler, which casually pulled away, no doubt alerting Darius to events. Ashley knew she didn't have long. Darius would arrange for another watcher, particularly as she had now cost him three men and a significant legal bill to ensure their release.

Recognising the opportunity, Ashley repeated her call to 911 and explained that she had called earlier and had managed to escape the burglars and fled to her mother's house. She gave an address in Chevy Chase on the other side of Washington. Ashley was using the state boundaries that existed around Washington to her advantage. The original operator was tracked down and after confirming Ashley was the same woman who had made the original call, the hunt for the missing woman was called off.

Ashley waited as one by one the police and crime scene investigators left the building and finally after twenty minutes the coast was clear. She winked across to her co-conspirator as she left a $5 tip and quickly made her way across the street to the apartment block. The elevator as ever was out of order and

Ashley climbed the darkened staircase cautiously. There was always the chance that one of Darius' men had sneaked in and was waiting in the shadows for Rosie. Fortunately, the staircase was clear and Ashley exited on the fifth floor to the devastation that was the aftermath of her calls to the police. Yellow 'Police line do not cross' tape covered the doorway to her apartment while a hasp and padlock, replacing the wrecked door lock offered some security. Fortunately, the hasp offered as little resistance as her lock had to Darius' men. One well placed kick splintered the rotten wood and the door sprung open.

Ashley panicked as the door swung free. The mess in the apartment was testament to the thoroughness of Darius' men. In a few minutes they had turned her living area upside down, carpets pulled back and floorboards ripped up. She took a deep breath and stepped inside. Her only hope was that the men had taken it one room at a time and not split their efforts. Three men, three rooms, living area with kitchenette, bedroom and bathroom. She walked towards the door that separated the living area and bedroom. She felt her heart pound in her chest as she pushed the door open. Her heart almost stopped, the bedroom was ransacked exactly like the living area. No wonder the men had been caught in the act, they probably hadn't even heard the police sirens over the noise of their destruction.

Ashley rushed through the bedroom and burst into the bathroom. It seemed the three had taken a room each, the bathroom was in as much disarray as the rest of the apartment. She made directly for the floorboard behind the toilet unit and stopped as she saw the hole where the floorboard had been. She stood motionless. Darius not only knew her real identity and who she worked for but more importantly, her chance to fulfil her childhood promise had just disappeared.

She sat on the side of the bath and contemplated what to do next. Everything pointed to calling in. Her supervisor would find out soon enough that her cover was blown. Procedure also dictated that she should alert the department immediately the moment her real identity were uncovered. But she had to get to England.

In desperation, she bent down to the hole in the floor and stuck her hand in. Her face lit up as her hand hit the small plastic pouch, perhaps Darius' man had been caught as he found it and left it in place for later. She pulled the pouch free and was relieved to see everything in place. Her passports, cash, i.d. and credit cards. Putting them aside, she placed her hand deeper into the hole and fumbling around, found the second pouch, heavier than the first. She pulled it out, opened the plastic and removed the carefully wrapped item. Unravelling the cloth, she revealed her Heckler & Koch MK23 pistol, the same pistol used by the US Special Forces.

Once the gun was loaded and the safety off, she relaxed. If anybody tried to come for her now, they were going to have a seriously bad day. She walked back into the living area and righting the chair by the phone she sat down. She had two calls to make and dialled the first number having memorised it from her earlier call.

"Good evening Parkside Police station, how can I help?"

"Can I speak to the detective in charge of the case regarding the man who was on TV?" asked Ashley.

"Can you hold the line please?" the operator fought to contain his excitement, it was the American woman again, he waved his hands in the air frantically.

"Of course."

"Thank you."

The operator muted the call and for good measure put his hand over the mouthpiece, "What shall I do? She wants to speak to Harris," he asked his supervisor.

"Put her through," he suggested shrugging his shoulders, they could still trace and record it from there, so he didn't see any harm.

Demuting the call the operator came back to Ashley.

"I'll just put you through," he said much to Ashley's amazement. He hadn't even asked her name nor why she wanted to talk to him.

After a strange buzzing tone in Ashley's ear, Harris answered his phone. "DCI Harris here."

"Good evening Detective Harris, I'm calling with regard to the man you arrested this morning."

Ever the professional, Harris wasted no time in showing his detective skills.

"Ah, you must be Rosie."

Everyone listening in the operation room's were aghast and could have strangled Harris with their bare hands.

Ashley nearly dropped the phone. She knew exactly what she had said earlier and she certainly hadn't given her name.

"Hello?" said Harris.

Ashley ignored him, trying to understand how they knew that name.

"Hello?" prompted Harris again.

"Yes, hmm, you surprised me mentioning that name. Would you mind explaining that please before we go any further?"

Harris was the one caught speechless. She was the only lead as to who the man was and he'd just put her on edge. Kelly appeared back from the loo and mouthed. "Who's that?"

He mouthed back "Rosie" instantly catching her full attention.

Harris putting his hand over the mouthpiece quickly explained what had happened. Kelly sighed deeply and took the phone from him, despite his protestations.

"Rosie, hi, I'm Detective Sergeant Kelly. Apologies for my colleague. When you dropped the phone earlier it remained off the hook and we heard the man shouting after you. Are you OK? Can we get the police to assist you?"

Ashley had listened quietly as Kelly explained what had happened. She also felt re-assured that Kelly seemed in control and quite frankly couldn't care less that they knew the name Rosie. If they were looking for Rosie they weren't looking for Ashley Jones.

"OK, I'll accept that. Now, the man you arrested, is he OK?"

"The man you're referring to, can you give me his name please?"

"I'm sorry I can't do that."

"Well I'm sorry but I can't discuss the case unless you can give me something to prove you know him."

"But I don't know his name."

Kelly was instantly deflated. It seemed Rosie was a dead lead, some nutter who liked the look of the suspect and had become infatuated.

"I don't understand, you said you knew who he was?" she said angrily.

"I do, I do, look it's complicated. I'm catching a flight as soon as I can get one. I should be there tomorrow morning. Will he still be there?"

"Yes."

"If by any chance you do let him go, please let him know I'm coming from America and it's imperative I speak to him."

"I really don't think there's any chance he won't be here," emphasised Kelly.

"OK, then I'll hopefully see you tomorrow."

"See you then," replied Kelly, surprised by how the call had gone.

Ashley hung up and dialled the next number.

"Thank you for calling British Airways…" Ashley listened to the recorded message and selected Option Two, Sales.

Chapter 8

After making his way back to the car, Clark called Walker.

"It's me. Issue resolved."

"Good, get back here, another issue has arisen," advised Walker matter of factly.

"Where are you, here or Southampton?"

"Here."

"I'll be there in ten minutes."

"And pack a bag, you're going on a trip."

Clark didn't need to go home for a bag, he always had a travel bag packed and ready in the car. His training wouldn't allow for anything less.

Ten minutes later, he pulled into the garage area of one of New York's finest apartment blocks. He parked in one of the spaces reserved for guests and made his way to the elevator. As he stepped in, the concierge's voice resonated from the speakers.

"Good afternoon, can I help you?"

"Yes I'm here for Mr William Walker III, can you send me up please?"

"Your name?"

"Joseph Clark."

The concierge called Mr Walker and confirmed Mr Clark was in fact expected. Receiving confirmation, the elevator started moving and covered the distance to the penthouse apartment, 77 stories in less than 60 seconds. As he exited the elevator, he never failed to be amazed by the view. The apartment had no solid walls, just floor-to-ceiling glass offering a 360 degree bird's eye view of New York on the edge of Central Park. However, for the best part of $40 million it was to be expected even if it was only Walker's pied-a-terre. His real home was out in the Hamptons, all 18 bedrooms and 20 acres.

Walker poured Clark a drink.

"I'm over here in the den," he shouted.

Clark nodded and tearing himself away from the view, he joined Walker, taking the seat opposite.

"I've been on the phone to one of my contacts in England. It seems we have a problem."

Walker paused to take a drink and Clark waited anxiously, desperate to know what the problem was. On the mention of England, he worried. He hated that fucking country, cameras everywhere you looked. If there was one country in the world not to whack someone, it was the U.K.

Walker continued.

"Somebody's recognised our boy."

"Fuck, who and where?"

"Well, they recognised him but don't know who he is."

"What the hell does that mean?"

"No idea but basically a woman has called them twice now saying she knows exactly who he is but it seems doesn't know his name."

"Shit!" the prospect of doing the one thing he didn't want to do seemed more likely.

"Yep, you need to go and take care of her straight away. My helicopter's on the roof, you should just make it if you leave now."

"What flight am I on?" Clark checked his watch.

"Sorry?" Walker looked at him confused. He had just explained that the helicopter was waiting for him. The quizzical look made him realise the confusion.

"No, no she's here, well not here, exactly, she's in Washington."

"Ah, OK." Clark breathed a huge sigh of relief.

"It seems she's a prostitute, her name's Rosie, here's her address but she's booked on the 21.55 BA flight to Heathrow so you need to get going."

With no intention of letting her catch the flight, Clark drained his glass, bid his goodbyes and climbed the stairs to the helipad just one floor above. The Sikorsky S-76D's rotors turned lazily. As Clark climbed in and settled into the large leather seat, the rotors picked up speed and by the time his seat belt was fastened, the wheels were lifting off the pad below. The helicopter turned as it rose to face South West, its nose dipping as the pilot increased the power and the race to Washington began. The two hundred mile trip would take just over an hour. Clark poured himself a drink and relaxed. Rosie's flight wasn't for another five hours. Plenty of time. He smiled.

Chapter 9

It took less than five minutes to transport the rugby thugs to Parkside Police Station. The desk sergeant took one look at them and sent them down to the holding area to be booked and processed. They already seemed to be sobering up and he called out to one of the young constables.

"Smith, come here a sec."

"Yes Sarge," he replied, checking over his shoulder that the group were behaving themselves.

"If they behave and you can get someone to vouch for them, don't keep them in."

"Are you sure?"

The sergeant watched as the group reached the end of the corridor and filed down the stairs in an orderly and controlled manner.

"Yeah, you know what these rugby guys are like, a few beers and their testosterone's all over the place. The minute they sober up they're fine."

"OK," replied Smith and hurried after the group.

The six mercenaries remained silent and followed the directions of the police officers to the letter. Each had his head bowed in shame, showing, as the Colonel had suggested, remorse for their reprehensible behaviour. As they reached the custody suite, they were shown to a line of chairs and told to sit down. The officers escorting them walked over to the custody sergeant.

The Belgian ex-paratrooper was the most senior of the mercenaries and had been given operational leadership of that phase of the mission. When the officers turned their backs, he signalled to his men, counting down silently with his fingers for all to see: three, two, one. They moved instantly. Any sign of remorse or drunkenness vanished. They all moved with an agility and swiftness which belied their bulk, like a pack of tigers striking at their prey.

Scott had woken up off and on throughout the day. Each time, however, seemed to be another check to see whether the headache and disorientation had gone. Just as he thought they may have become permanent fixtures, he awoke to find they had gone, not entirely but enough to actually wonder where he was.

He looked around at the four graffiti-covered concrete walls broken only by a single steel door with some type of metal porthole. The bed he lay on was nothing more than a raised section of concrete floor with a thin mattress. He sat up and found that the world hadn't quite stopped spinning. Leaning back against the wall, he steadied himself. His brain began to work more rationally disseminating and evaluating multiple points of evidence rather than just one at a time. He was in a prison cell.

Scott thought back to the night before. He had dropped off his bags and gone for something to eat. He hadn't eaten all day and was starving. He'd gone to the nearest pub and ordered some food and a pint and then, he racked his brain, nothing. He remembered walking over to a seat with his pint and nothing, absolutely nothing. It was as though his mind had stopped working from that point on.

He stood and walked to the door, stretching his back and shoulders as he walked. He needed to do his exercises but they could wait, he needed to know why he was there.

He banged on the solid metal door.

"Hello?" he shouted.

With no reply, he banged again.

"Hello?" he shouted much louder.

"What?" came an irritable response. Constable Bryant was on his way to the changing rooms after finishing his shift when he heard the shouting.

"Where am I?" he asked, only this time not shouting.

"Parkside Police Station."

Scott took the news in.

"Where's Parkside?" he asked.

"Cambridge. Are you the guy they brought in this morning?" asked the constable.

"Maybe, I've no idea where I am or why I'm here."

The constable checked the cell list and discovered Scott was 'the Ripper'.

"Don't give me that innocent crap, you're the fucking serial rapist," he shouted angrily.

Scott sat down as the revelation of why he was in prison sank in. He tried desperately to remember what had happened the previous night but nothing came to him. He then realised something important.

"Wait a minute, you said serial rapist, didn't you?"

"Yes, five defenceless young women, you sick fuck."

"From when to when?" asked Scott.

"Is this some sick shit, where you're getting off on me telling you what you've done?" asked Constable Bryant disgusted at Scott's tasteless questions.

"I'm not a rapist, I'm innocent. Just give me the dates!" demanded Scott.

"The last ten months," answered Bryant wanting to end the conversation.

Scott relaxed. He had only arrived in the UK 24 hours earlier and hadn't been there in the last year. More importantly, he could prove it.

With the issue resolved, Scott squatted on the floor. He had not done his exercises. His training had been drummed into him like a religion since childhood. Only with exercise and training could perfection be achieved and once achieved could only be maintained with exercise and training.

Scott worked his way through the daily ritual. Thirty minutes later, his body and mind were in perfect harmony once again. All of the effects of the previous night seemed to have dissipated. His uncle would have been happy. He always said the exercises cured everything. Scott had always thought it was just another excuse to make him do them.

A knock on the door was followed by an instruction to step back.

Scott obeyed and the door opened to reveal a young man about his age and size dressed in jeans and a T-shirt holding a tray of food.

"Your dinner!" he announced.

"You're the officer I spoke to earlier," said Scott as the constable laid the tray on the concrete table, nodding in response. "I didn't do it you know, I only came into the country yesterday."

"Look, I don't really give a shit. I'm trying to get out of here, I'm just doing the duty sergeant a favour because he's busy. Give your bullshit to someone else."

A loud thud from outside the door caught their attention.

"What was that?" asked Scott.

"No id…" Constable Bryant stopped mid sentence as another thud was followed by a muffled cry and then all that could be heard was the ear piercing sound of a fire alarm.

**

Smith had just reached the door of the custody area when the movement of the six men launching themselves at the officers caught his eye through the window. His four colleagues, taking the full brunt of the men's weight, buckled and fell. The custody sergeant, being on the other side of the desk, had some warning and tried to dive out of the way but two of the mercenaries had dived over the desk at him. One missed but the other caught him full on, the mercenary's shoulder crashing into his spine, snapping it cleanly and ensuring the rest of the sergeant's life would be spent in a wheelchair.

The sickening crack as the sergeant fell made up Smith's mind. There was no point entering the custody area. His colleagues were all down and none of them were moving. He was one against six and from the way they moved, he knew it was more like one against twenty. He didn't stand a chance. He threw the bolt on the door. He couldn't go in but they weren't going to get out.

The Belgian just made it to the door as Smith threw the bolt.

"Shit!!" he screamed kicking the door in frustration, the thud telling him what he already knew. The door was solid.

Smith flinched as the man kicked the door. With nothing more he could do, he backed away keeping an eye firmly on the door. As he reached the bottom of the staircase, he hit the alarm before rushing to alert the rest of the station.

The ear-piercing sound reverberated around the walls, making conversation almost impossible. The Belgian walked back to the desk and checked the policemen were secure. All four were tied. The desk sergeant on the other side of the desk remained unbound. He wasn't going anywhere fast. Grabbing the custody list from the desk, the Belgian scanned down the names and pointed to the three cells that had been occupied that day. One of them had to be their man.

"You three come with me, you two watch them," he motioned to his men.

"Our man is mid-twenties with dark hair and was arrested this morning, that's all we know. Anyone fitting that description, you know what to do," he shouted over the siren before opening the door that led to the cells.

"OK, cells 3, 7 and 10," he pointed as he shouted out the numbers.

The three mercenaries ran down the corridor, opening the designated cells, not even noticing that one was already open, nor caring that it had two occupants. The noise within the enclosed space was deafening. The siren blared, the men shouted orders, prisoners who were not let out screamed for their doors to be opened.

The four were lined up in the corridor as instructed, confused by the noise and their rugby-shirt wearing captors. None knew what to think and certainly had no idea what the hell was going on. The most confused of the bunch was Constable Bryant. He knew everyone who worked at Parkside and not one of those men was familiar to him. He stepped forward.

"What the fuck's going on?" he screamed.

His answer was a fist breaking three front teeth and sending him crashing to the floor. His hands grasping his mouth as blood spurted out.

"He fits the profile!" screamed the Belgian above the din around them and pointing at Scott. "And so does he! But they don't!"

Scott watched as the man with the clipboard pointed first at the punched man and then himself. Indicating that both he and the man on the ground 'fitted the profile', whatever that meant. The other two older men were quickly thrown back into their cells, leaving only himself and the wounded constable in the corridor with the three 'guards'.

"You know what to do," shouted the Belgian and turned back to the custody area. He had to work out how the hell they were going to get out, especially as they'd now have two bodies, not just one.

Scott watched as the men walked towards them. He still had no idea who the hell they were but knew they were not policemen but military of some sort. Their tattoos and general demeanour gave that much away. The siren and shouting of the other prisoners continued and added to the bizarreness of the situation.

"What's going on guys?" shouted Scott.

None of the three responded. One grabbed Scott and held him tightly as the other towered over Bryant, lifting his boot high over his head.

Scott had seen enough. There was now no doubt that these men were going to kill them both. The boot, if it came down, would split the constable's head in two. He twisted his hand and managed to grab the man's thumb. In one swift fluid motion he spun around, almost ripping the thumb cleanly from the man's hand, his right foot spinning up and around catching the boot man in the ribs. The noise of the ribs shattering was heard above the siren. Boot Man was propelled three feet backwards into the wall and slumped to the ground. As the kick landed, Scott's elbow was making contact with the head of the man whose thumb hung limply from its hand, the point of his elbow almost burying itself into the man's temple. Such was the force of the blow that the man's legs buckled and he fell to the ground motionless.

By the time the third man reacted, it was too late. Scott had spun around and unleashed another ferocious kick driving his weight up and through the man's stomach. The muscle tissue of his diaphragm all but exploded from the trauma. The man dropped to the ground struggling for breath. A trickle of blood at the corner of his mouth was a tell tale sign. His diaphragm was not all he had to worry about.

Bryant had watched the events unfold and even on seeing the three men on the ground, he could not believe what he had just witnessed. The guy had moved so fast it was like a blur.

"Shwat wash shat?" he asked through broken teeth.

"That was me pissed off," said Scott. "Wait here," he added before running down the corridor to the custody area.

"Shno fear," replied Bryant, moving back to lean against the wall.

As Scott reached the end of the corridor, the siren stopped. The sudden silence caught everyone off guard. Moans and groans previously masked by the siren could now be heard, none more so than those of the custody sergeant.

"Jesus, will somebody shut him up!" shouted the Belgian.

Scott listened as a dull thud was rewarded with silence. He poked his head around the door and counted three more men. Two were busy dismantling the door frame, the other had obviously just shut up whoever it was moaning and was walking back to help with the door.

The important thing Scott noted was that they weren't armed.

"Help!" shouted Scott, hiding in the cell corridor.

His plea was rewarded by the sound of running boots. Scott stepped out from the corridor and into the custody area, the two men running towards him dived at him. Scott dived also, up and over the men landing in a tight roll and springing to his feet.

The Belgian watched as he landed noiselessly. Before he knew it, the man had rolled right next to him and he kicked out with his steel toed boots.

Scott was already up and moving by the time the man's boot had reached where he had been. Scott kicked out at the man's standing foot, snapping it cleanly at the shin, and delivered a punch as he fell, instantly stopping the ear piercing scream.

Scott turned and walked back towards the two men he had left flying through the air. Both men eyed him cautiously. They had seen the devastation in the cell corridor. One stalked to the left while the other continued towards him.

Scott surprised them both when he rushed at them. Just as the first man swung for him, Scott dropped to his knees, his forward momentum sliding him under the punch and he delivered a crushing blow to the man's genitalia. With his colleague buckling in agony, the last man backed off. He had never seen anybody move as fast or hit as hard as this young man. He knew when he had more than met his match. It was also imperative that the Colonel knew what he was up against and he feared he was the only one of the six still capable of telling him.

Bryant stumbled out of the corridor to be met by the sight of Scott crushing the man's testicles with one punch and the final man throwing his hands in the air in surrender.

"Jeshus, who are you?" he asked, his mouth still aching from the earlier blow.

Scott, ignoring the question, moved towards the surrendering man, spun him around and pushed him face first onto the floor. With a knee in his back, he removed the man's shoe laces and tied his arms firmly behind his back.

***

Smith had run straight to the reception desk and explained to the Sergeant what had happened. It was then he realised that the fire alarm was probably not the best way to get people's attention. It was going to make communication a lot more difficult. With only five other officers on duty in the station, there was no way they could launch any sort of rescue bid. The sergeant radioed for all officers out on patrol to immediately return to base. He also called the Chief Constable.

By the time they had anything resembling enough force to tackle the six men, it was already too late. As they approached the door and looked through the glass, Bryant was checking on his colleagues while the rapist was kneeling on the back of one of the rugby guys tying him up.

***

The minute the fire alarm had sounded, the Colonel knew something had gone wrong. The lack of officers leaving the premises confirmed it. The fire brigade's arrival gave him some hope but they merely killed the sirens. The arrival shortly afterwards of what appeared to be every officer within a twenty mile radius confirmed the worst. He pulled out his phone and made a call. They needed to cover their tracks and minimise any potential threat to the unit and ultimately the client.

Scott turned as the door opened and the police swarmed in. Two armed officers ran straight towards him.

"Get down, face on the floor, arms and legs spread!!" screamed one of the officers.

Scott obeyed and was quickly handcuffed before being marched back to his cell. As they locked the door, he sat down and tried to make some sense of what had just happened. Whoever the men were, they had singled him out and the constable and clearly wanted them dead. Arrested as a serial killer and targeted by a death squad, it was becoming an intriguing day. What next, he thought to himself. Whatever it was, he planned to be ready. He closed his eyes. May as well be well rested, he thought before drifting off into a deep and peaceful sleep.

Chapter 10

Chief Constable John Forsyth walked through the doors of Parkside Police Station at 11.00 p.m. under a blaze of media. News of the attack inside the cells had been hard to contain, particularly following a fire alarm and the arrival of a number of ambulances. It seemed Cambridgeshire police were intent on being the main headline of the day.

The Chief was met by Harris and Kelly who themselves had just arrived. They had been called in due to their suspect's involvement in the evening's events.

As the doors closed behind him, the Chief didn't mince his words.

"I want to know exactly what the fuck happened here tonight."

"Everything's set up through here, Sir."

The desk sergeant stepped forward and led the Chief, Harris and Kelly through to the office. As they walked in, they saw a group of three men sitting in a huddle at the far end, two wearing police uniforms and the other holding his mouth and wearing a blood soaked T-shirt.

"This is Constable Bryant Sir, he witnessed everything," said the sergeant introducing Bryant to the Chief.

Harris, Kelly and the Chief listened carefully as the events were described, none dared stop the flow. The Chief's face reddened as Bryant described the point at which he was moments away from death as his executioner's boot hung treacherously over his head. When he went on to describe the actions of their suspect, first saving him and then single-handedly defeating their aggressors, all three looked at each other in disbelief. Surely some poetic licence or a knock to the head was distorting what actually happened. Bryant saw the look on their faces.

"I'm not kidding. The guy's like some sort of Bruce Lee or Jackie Chan."

"We believe you son, we believe you," offered Harris, his smile a little too obvious.

"Fine," said Bryant petulantly. "Let's see who's laughing when we go down to the cells."

Smith took over and described what he had done after witnessing the attack on his fellow officers, the Chief congratulating him on his quick thinking about locking the door.

"What's the latest on the custody sergeant and the other officers?" asked the Chief as Smith wrapped up his description.

"The custody sergeant, not good Sir. He's on life support and it's touch and go. The other officers will be fine, it's just concussion."

"I'll go to the hospital on my way home," said the Chief. "What about the perps, how are they?"

"Two dead, one critical, another two hospitalised and one down in the cells refusing to talk."

None of them could hide their shock at the devastation caused. Bryant smiled, triumphant in his vindication.

The Chief recognised an even greater disaster than the earlier one. Two, possibly three men were killed by a serial rapist in his custody. The fact that the men had crippled and attempted to kill one of his officers would be lost in the mire as the media focussed on the brutal deaths of the men at his prisoner's hands. He could see the same thought was hitting Kelly. He didn't even bother to look at Harris. That day was proof that the detective's retirement the following year was well overdue.

"Sir, following the events described by Constable Bryant, I have to seriously question whether we have the right man for the rapes," suggested Kelly.

"My thoughts exactly," replied the Chief, thankful that Kelly had made the comment first.

Harris shook his head in disbelief. He was certain the Chief had a hard-on for the ice queen and was now more convinced than ever. He would have to let the Chief know everyone was convinced she was a lesbian. In over two years not one cop had managed to crack her.

"Hello-o? He just killed two guys with his bare hands."

"Exactly," replied Kelly. She couldn't be bothered to explain the psychological profile of rapists and how the events in the cells matched no serial rapist in the history of policing. Before anyone else could explain, a knock on the door interrupted them.

"Come in!" shouted the Chief.

The door opened, a constable entered and walked toward the sergeant.

"Sir, a brief's just arrived to speak to his clients, the rugby guys."

"How the hell?" the sergeant looked around. No statement had been made, no names released nor had they allowed the prisoners access to a phone.

"What does he know?" asked Kelly calmly.

"He wants to speak to his six clients, immediately.'"

"Basically nothing, it must have been arranged either before or from outside," mused Kelly.

"But what will I tell him? He's very pushy. He's already taken a note of my number," asked the constable.

"Don't worry, son. Sergeant?" said the Chief, instructing the sergeant to take the constable's place.

"I should go too," suggested Kelly.

After a moment's hesitation, the Chief agreed.

"OK but Harris, you come with me. We'll see if we can get something from his client while you stall him up here."

It took the Chief and Harris less than two minutes to realise they were wasting their time. The prisoner was never going to talk, certainly not to them.

Kelly faired little better with the lawyer who had arrived to speak to his clients. On being informed that he only had four clients left and potentially only three, he wasn't fazed. His only concern was to see that his imprisoned client was OK. Those in the hospital could wait and those who had died were beyond help. When he retrieved his mobile from his pocket and threatened to phone his friend, the Lord Chancellor and then The Sun, Kelly relented and led him down to an interview room.

Five minutes later, the prisoner was led into the room to meet his lawyer. As the door closed, the Colonel, who had posed as the lawyer, smiled at his man.

"Jesus Colonel!" exclaimed the mercenary. "That guy kicked the shit out of us!"

The Colonel quizzed him for ten minutes, extracting every detail. Content he had the full story, he sat back and relaxed.

"But you don't know which was the guy we wanted?" he checked again.

"Well no, both were about the same age with dark hair."

The Colonel thought back at the video he had watched repeatedly of the man's head crashing to the ground.

"Was one better looking than the other?" he asked.

"Neither were my type, if you know what I mean, Sir," answered the man cautiously.

"I'm not checking if you're a fag you fucking idiot, was one better looking?"

"Well now that you mention it, the fighter was a bit of a pretty boy."

The Colonel now knew exactly which was which. He extracted a hip flask and took a swig of whisky after which he nonchalantly offered some to his man who initially refused but the Colonel insisted. The mercenary took a long swig and wiping his lips handed the flask back to the Colonel.

"Well, I'd best be off and check on the men in hospital and don't worry, we'll have you out of here by tomorrow at the latest, OK?"

"Sir, yes Sir," replied the mercenary.

As the Colonel left, he shook his man's hand for the last time. He hadn't lied about getting him out the next day. He would get out but it would be in a body bag. The hipflask was laced with poison and the mercenary would be dead by morning as would the three men still alive in hospital. Karl the German was already dealing with them. He had lost six men and all because somebody hadn't told him the truth about the target. He was obviously highly trained and someone was going to pay. First things first though, he needed more men. He made a call.

Chapter 11

Kelly caught her breath as she walked into the interview room. She remembered the suspect, despite his puking, being attractive but this guy was stunning. The pale white skin, had returned to its perfectly tanned lustre. His puke-filled hair was now dark and neat and his washed out face, dark and chiselled to perfection. The only downside she thought was his clothing but even then the white t-shirt he wore struggled to hide the perfect pecs and washboard stomach. The only thing standing between him and perfection was a small cluster of moles on his left temple forming what looked like a star. Even then, she thought, that's cute.

Pulling herself from her adolescent thoughts, Kelly took the seat next to Harris but couldn't help giving the suspect a very girly smile. The suspect smiled warmly in return and in that moment Kelly knew for definite they had the wrong man. It wasn't just that the smile could get any woman into bed. Rapists don't do it just for the sex, it's all about power and having to prove they have it. The smile reverberated through his eyes, captivating her. The deep dark brown eyes somehow telling her she was safe with him, no harm would come while he was watching over her. His eyes broke the momentary gaze and continued their surveillance, checking everything was OK. This man didn't need to prove anything to anybody and was most definitely not a rapist. Kelly was convinced.

Harris watched in amazement as Kelly smiled at the suspect. In the two years he had worked with her, he had never seen her smile like that. If only she wasn't a lesbian he thought, what a waste.

"DCI Harris and DS Kelly interviewing the suspect known as Scott at 11.25 p.m. on Sunday 5th October 2008. For the record, the suspect has refused legal representation. Can you please confirm this for the tape."

"Yes," replied Scott.

Harris took over,

"Can you please confirm your name in full for the record please,"

"Scott," replied Scott.

"Your full name please?" he repeated irritably. It had been a very long day and all thanks to the scumbag in front of him.

"My full name is Scott."

"What's your surname?"

"I don't have one."

"Don't be ridiculous, stop messing us about. Everybody's got a surname," shouted Harris. Kelly placed a hand on his arm to calm him down but he pushed it away.

"I must be unique then," smiled Scott.

Harris leaned menacingly across the small table.

"Do you know why you're here? For raping five women and now murdering two men!"

"Ridiculous,' said Scott calmly. 'I only arrived in the UK last night and those men were obviously trying to kill us or me in particular. So I think there's more to it, don't you? Should I contact a lawyer or are we going to do this civilly?" threatened Scott.

"Why do you need a lawyer to protect you if you're innocent?"

"Assholes," smiled Scott, "I need a lawyer to protect me from assholes!"

Harris lost his temper and threw a punch at Scott. Scott had anticipated it and casually moved his head to the side and watched as the punch sailed harmlessly past, infuriating Harris further. Kelly pressed the panic button and two policemen rushed into the room and headed towards Scott.

"Not him," she shouted. "Him!" pointing to Harris. "Get him out of here, right now and call the Chief down here immediately!"

Five minutes later and with calm restored, Scott sat facing Kelly and rather bizarrely the Chief Constable of the Cambridgeshire Constabulary.

"I'm sorry about my colleague, it's been a long day," said Kelly.

"That's OK," replied Scott.

"Now you mentioned you only arrived in the UK last night."

"Yes and it's been three years since I was here before that," explained Scott.

"OK, if that is the case it will certainly rule you out of four of the rapes. Can you just confirm where you were in the last ten months."

"I'm sorry but I can't tell you."

"What do you mean you can't tell us?"

"Exactly that. I can't tell you."

The Chief stepped in.

"Look son, we've past the time for games. Tell us where you've been in the last ten months, we'll check it out and if everything's OK, you'll be in a much better position."

"I'm sorry but I'm not being difficult and I'm not playing games. I genuinely can't tell you."

"Have you forgotten where you've been?"

"No."

"Can someone else tell us where you've been?"

"No."

Kelly thought of a way to get the information.

"What about your passport, we can track where it's been."

"Don't have one."

"But you said you entered the UK last night so you must have one?"

"I did and I don't."

The Chief sat back in frustration with the realistic possibility that Scott was an illegal immigrant claiming not to know where he was from and who by default would gain access to the UK. You can't deport someone unless you have somewhere to deport them to.

Kelly had the same thought but the accent was too good, definitely English. In fact almost perfect but for a slight twang of something she couldn't quite place.

"You're not going to get citizenship out of this, you know. We'll just lock you up and throw away the key until you tell us where you're from."

Scott placed his hands in the air next to his head, in a mock surrender.

"Look guys, I'm not an illegal immigrant. I'm not looking for citizenship. I'm not a rapist. It was kill or be killed and I wish I could but I can't tell you where I've been. I honestly am not trying to be difficult."

Kelly and the Chief looked at each another and both could see that they rather bizarrely believed him. However with no concrete proof, he was their only suspect.

Kelly moved her hand towards the tape recorder.

"Interview terminated 11.51 p.m. Sunday 5th October 2008." She pressed the Stop button.

Chapter 12

"I'll just give you a reference number. Have you got a pen?"

"Just a sec.," Ashley quickly searched through the mess on the floor and found the pen and pad that once sat next to the phone.

"The reference is Yankee, Bravo, 9, 3, Tango, X-ray. Do you want to read that back to me?"

"YB93TX," repeated Ashley.

"Correct. Now if you give that reference number to the ticket desk with your passport, they'll issue your tickets and boarding pass. Is there anything else I can help you with Miss Diaz, sorry Rosie?" The BA sales associate corrected herself. The customer had insisted she call her by her first name. She reprimanded herself. She hadn't made it to first class bookings by ignoring customer wishes.

"No, that's fine, thank you. Oh sorry just one thing. Is seat 4A available?"

"Just let me check." After the sound of the keyboard clacking, the agent came back. "Yes, would you like me to allocate it to you?"

"Yes please and thank you, you've been very helpful."

"Not at all Rosie, thank you for choosing British Airways. Goodbye."

Ashley said goodbye and hung up. She was not happy at having to use Rosie's identity to book the flight but thought it best. As the British authorities were expecting a Rosie, she better give them one. It was imperative nothing interfered with her meeting him.

She looked across the floor at the clothes strewn throughout the apartment. Rosie really did have some terrible clothes. It was only now that she didn't need to wear them that she could see just how bad they were. Ashley only ever travelled trans-Atlantic first class. It was the one luxury she insisted on no matter what. That trip alone would cost almost a quarter of her annual salary. Not that that was an issue. Ashley worked because she loved what she did, it most certainly was not for the money. Her trust fund generated in less than a month more than her annual salary. Her life had been one of luxury; the finest clothes, homes, education and holidays. Her parents were members of the American aristocracy; her father a career diplomat and mother a career socialite, a lady who lunched. Both from privileged and wealthy backgrounds, their invitation to dinner and parties with the rich and powerful meant that the world was Ashley's oyster, whatever career she chose, she could have. But it hadn't always been like that. Ashley could remember the times before America, before her adoption and her real parents. They were hard working salt of the earth types who loved their daughter above everything else.

Ashley tried not to think back to those days as it always upset her. Instead she remembered the day she announced she was quitting Harvard and joining the Navy. It never failed to bring a smile to her face. Her snob of a mother almost feinted, screaming in horror at the thought of her daughter becoming a...a soldier. Ashley had explained that she was joining the naval academy to train as an officer but that did little to re-assure her mother. To be fair to her father, he was just disappointed. He was not in the least embarrassed and if it weren't for her mother, he might even have admitted he was proud of her. Ashley brought herself back to the present, all that had been a long time ago.

She had a flight to catch and checked her watch. Not a chance she thought. Her home was forty miles away on the banks of the Chesapeake Bay, just South of the Naval Academy where she had graduated four years earlier. She desperately needed some clothes, all she had that wouldn't label her a prostitute were the ones she was in and they didn't exactly smack of first class. What she would have given for her own clothes, Chanel, Prada, D&G. All her lovely clothes just hanging in her wardrobe but she wouldn't make it. Oh well, she thought to herself, nothing else for it, a bit of shopping on the way to the airport.

***

From the moment he had left New York, Clark had not stopped talking on the phone. First he had called The Unit as he needed some assistance. Not a problem. Two men were at his disposal and would pick him up when he landed. Next was tracking down any info they had on the target, Rosie. Not a lot it seemed but they did know she had worked at The Palace which would be Clark's first stop when he arrived. Just before he landed, he received a call that changed his plan entirely. Walker had updated him on the disastrous operation in England. As he talked through the implications of this, he formulated an idea and Walker, on hearing it, agreed. He hung up and dialled The Unit. He needed a very particular operative asap.

As planned, the two Unit members had met him at the helipad and drove immediately to The Palace. Even though a native New Yorker, Clark had heard of The Palace but knew little of its owner Darius. However, the soldiers knew enough to paint the picture of a drug dealing pimp who'd done well. As they pulled up at the front door, Clark thought it must be the wrong building. It looked like just any other apartment block, but he was soon told that the first few floors were normal housing and the top few floors comprised The Palace. As Clark approached the lift, the two soldiers followed.

"Where are you going?" asked Clark.

"To watch your back," answered one of them.

"The day I need somebody to watch my back when dealing with a pimp, is the day I retire. Get back in the car," he ordered.

Clark was an average man. Everything about him was average, his height, weight, build, looks. If you had to give him a name you'd call him Mr Smith or as he frequently called himself Mr Johnson. Psychologically however he was anything but average. He was an exceptionally complex individual, with a high IQ and more than one clinical psychologist had advised his previous employers, the Central Intelligence Agency, that he needed help. However, little did the psychologists realise they were merely re-affirming the agency's belief that he was the perfect man for the job. Intelligent, detached and with little or no empathy. The next five years would be spent as one of the agency's most accomplished assassins. It was only after meeting William Walker III twenty five years earlier that Clark realised how lucrative his talents were.

Clark stepped out of the elevator into The Palace's reception area, it was like no whore house Clark had seen. He preferred his woman rough, they bitched less when he knocked them about and didn't need compensation for lost business. This place would cost him a fortune, after a session with him they wouldn't be able to work in there for a week. The reception area was immaculate and Clark wondered whether he was in the right place. It looked more like a high class lawyers' reception. However, as he approached the receptionist, she dispelled that thought, sitting in nothing more than her bra, panties and suspenders.

"Good evening Sir," she smiled perfectly.

"Hmm," Clark's mind was elsewhere, the thought of her screaming in pain tied to the bed was arousing him. He snapped himself out of it, promising himself he'd come back for a taste another time.

"Darius, please" he commanded.

"I'm sorry we don't have a Darius, Sir. I've got a Juan, a Richard and a Paul," she replied looking at the screen in front of her.

Clark's temper flared.

"I'm not some fucking bum boy, you fucking bitch!" More than ever he wanted her on the bed screaming in pain, he could teach this bitch a thing or two.

"I want to see your boss-man, Darius."

As he raised his voice two men appeared from behind the partition that separated the reception area from the rest of The Palace. Clark also sensed another two coming up behind him.

"Now, now Sir, calm down," suggested the man stepping between Clark and the receptionist. The other three moved in closely, surrounding Clark, leaving him little room for manoeuvre.

"I need to talk to Darius," Clark informed them confidently.

"A white boy with balls, eh? Well Darius ain't wanting to talk to you. So if you don't mind," the man pointed to the elevator as the man at his rear stepped aside.

Clark followed the pointed hand and looked towards the elevator but then slowly turned back to face the desk.

"You're failing to grasp the enormity of the issue," began Clark icily, his eyes suddenly darkening. "It makes no odds to me, I can speak to Darius now or in twenty minutes in the back of the ambulance rushing him to Intensive Care. It's your call."

Clark stared into the eyes of the man in front of him and could tell he had rattled him, nothing scared people more than looking into the eyes of a cold blooded killer. As he delivered his chilling message, his hands had very carefully removed the two Walther P99 silenced pistols from their holsters, with his hands crossed across his stomach the heads of the two men at his sides would be all but removed within the next second. The other two heavies and the receptionist would be shot once each through the forehead. Clark had already planned each shot, taking into account any reactionary movements. For example the receptionist would be shot last and he would shoot 18 inches diagonally down to the left of where her head now was as she would duck down to the right. Clark had killed enough people to know exactly how people reacted in any given situation.

Darius had watched on the CCTV as the man had entered and then been surrounded by his men. He had also noticed the man's hands move, something he knew his men hadn't.

The buzzer on the reception desk buzzed and cut through the deadly atmosphere. The receptionist tentatively moved her hand towards it, pressing it down.

"Send the man up please," boomed Darius.

The three men surrounding Clark stepped back instantly, surprised to see the guns that had not been there previously pointing at them.

"You wouldn't mind leaving these here would you please?" asked the man at reception nervously. He had never met anyone like Clark before.

"Not at all," replied Clark, he had another gun in an ankle holster and several throwing knives in his belt.

Clark was escorted into Darius' office by the receptionist, still promising himself a return visit as she walked back out of the office, her thong leaving nothing to the imagination.

"Yes, very nice but I'm afraid not for sale," said Darius, as he followed Clark's gaze.

"Everything's for sale," replied Clark licking his lips at the thought of the girls blood mixing with her sweat and rolling down into the small of the back. Screaming for him to stop.

"There is some truth in that," agreed Darius. "Now how can I help you?"

"I need some information about one of your girls," asked Clark.

"Can I ask why?"

"No."

"Well I'm sorry I can't help you." Darius rose to his full size towering over Clark, signalling an end to their conversation.

Clark did not want to resort to violence to obtain his information, it was not always reliable. "Wait, I believe this girl may no longer work for you, her name's Rosie."

"That fucking bitch," spat Darius. "All I know is she isn't who I thought she was."

Clark's ears perked up at that piece of information. "What do you mean?"

"She was supposed to be a prostitute but if that girl's spread her legs for a few bucks, I'm a fucking Benedictine monk."

"So who do you think she is?"

"Don't know. Maybe some sort of journalist looking for a story or something. The bitch zapped me with a fucking Taser and legged it this morning."

"Shit, do you know where she went? Like a home address or something? Phone number, anything that can help me track her down?"

"We tried her home address, fucking bitch got three of my men locked up. Other than that all I've got is a cell number."

Clark couldn't believe his luck. "Perfect."

Darius opened his drawer and retrieved the number from his phone book, writing it down on a sheet of paper before handing it over. "So who are you? Some kind of government dude or something?"

"No," replied Clark simply, as he stood and left Darius' office, he had what he needed.

"What you going to do to her?" shouted Darius after him.

"Exactly what you'd want me to do to her. Fuck her and then kill her."

Darius smiled for the first time that day.

As he made his way to the car, he made a call, barking instructions before reading out Rosie's number. As he hung up, another call came through. He answered and smiled. The operative he had requested was on the way. They would arrive by helicopter at about eight.

***

Tyson's Galleria was only a five minute diversion on the way to Dulles International and would be perfect. Nieman Marcus would resolve her wardrobe crisis. Of course it would take longer than five minutes but Ashley had plenty of time. It was at least two to three hours before she needed to be at the airport, only another twenty minutes from the Galleria.

As the cab pulled into the mall, Ashley's face drained, it was Sunday and at 5.50 p.m. she had less than ten minutes to get into the store, pick her clothes, pay and leave. It was never going to happen. The second the cab stopped she bolted into the store. Being a regular may just save her. The security guard tried to stop her entering the store but she wasn't having any of it, shouting "I'll just be a second, it's an emergency!" She quickly made her way to the ladies' designer-wear section and was met with a huge smile by Doug, the very heterosexual manager of the department. Ashley almost kissed him. She had hoped he'd be on duty but managed to stop herself when the leery eyes quickly covered every inch of her body. No attempt was made to hide his mental undressing of her right there in front of him. Ashley had always found him repulsive but as repulsive as he was, he was the best judge of style in the Washington area. It seemed all the other women agreed that his drooling over them was a small price to pay for the perfect outfit. He'd been there for years despite numerous complaints.

"I need a complete wardrobe before I board a flight tonight!" she gasped, staring into his eyes as deeply as her stomach would allow.

Working on commission and faced with one of the stores biggest spenders, it was not a difficult decision.

"Lock in," he announced to his assistant rubbing his hands in anticipation.

***

Clark directed the driver to Reagan International. They needed a van. At the second counter, he got what he wanted, a Ford Freestar minivan, blacked out windows and a sliding side door. It had been over forty minutes since he'd called in with Rosie's number and he would have hoped to have heard back by now. He was beginning to worry; the last thing he wanted was to have to intercept Rosie at Dulles airport.

"Where to?" asked the driver as he turned the key in the ignition.

"Head towards Dulles but don't rush," replied Clark willing his phone to ring.

Five minutes later his wish came true. His phone rang.

"Clark," he answered.

"Hi, I've got the location for you, I'm sending it to your PDA now."

"Excellent." Clark hung up the phone and removed his PDA from his belt. A message pinged into his inbox and as he clicked the link, the screen changed to a map of the area. A red dot designated the location of the target. Clark zoomed in on the location and checked his watch.

"Tyson's Galleria and quick, it must be shutting soon," he barked.

He looked at his watch again, it was 7.02 p.m. and it was Sunday. He was no great shopper but he knew shops didn't stay open after 7 on a Sunday.

***

As Doug rang the purchases through the till, he passed them to Ashley who was carefully packing them in her new Gucci roll-on. One outfit however was kept aside, that was for the airplane. She couldn't possibly do first class in BR she thought. As Doug ran her credit card through the machine she disappeared into a changing room and donned the new outfit, jeans boots and the most fantastic jacket. Doug really was a star she thought, it all fitted perfectly. As she stepped out of the changing room, she casually glanced at the time.

"Oh my God! It's 8 o'clock! I need to get to the airport."

She grabbed her bag and began to run for the exit.

"Wait a minute, I need to let you out," shouted Doug running after her.

He ran with her to the main doors where thank God she could see her taxi still waiting for her. She was sure he'd have gone but obviously he was a trusting type. As they walked to the taxi, Doug suddenly threw his hand to his mouth.

"Oh my God I've left your credit card," he began to turn his head. "Back th…"

Before he could finish his sentence, his head simply ceased to exist. A second shot thumped through the taxi's windscreen before lodging itself in the cabby's forehead. Ashley didn't even have a chance to scream before the impact on her neck stopped her.

***

"There she is!" shouted Clark.

The van's side door slid back as the marksman took aim with his H&K PSG1A1 sniper rifle, the newest in the line and still the most expensive factory rifle available. One thing that never failed to amaze Unit members were the weapons they had access to. It was almost as though they were a testing ground for new weapons. Almost daily, new toys would be delivered and it seemed nothing was out of their reach.

The driver kept the speed steady, knowing exactly how his colleague worked. They had been a team since the day they joined the army, twenty years earlier. One was the spotter and the other the shooter and they still held the Green Beret record for recorded kills.

As they drew closer, Clark withdrew his gun and took aim at Rosie. As the sniper dealt with the collateral, Clark took care of Rosie.

"Leave them, just take her!" he shouted as they screeched to a stop next to the taxi.

With Rosie dumped in the boot, Clark ordered the driver to get them to the helipad. Ten minutes later and with one additional passenger, the minivan was speeding towards Dulles International Airport. It was going to be close.

It had been a long day for purser Brian O'Toole. He was supposed to have another day off but had received a call two hours earlier. The other purser had phoned in sick and he was on standby. At least Flight BA0292 Washington Dulles to London Heathrow was a night flight and was usually fairly mundane. Also, he was in first class so it should be nice and quiet. He may even get a couple of hours sleep if he were lucky.

By the time he made it onto the plane, pre-boarding had already begun and so far, it was looking good. He looked at the passenger list and couldn't believe his luck. Only one first-class passenger was booked on the plane. With only five minutes left before take-off, Brian was already selecting the seat he would sleep in. It seemed that his one passenger wasn't going to make it. As the captain introduced himself over the PA, the phone rang in the first class cabin. Brian answered.

"Hi, just to let you know, a last minute booking, First Class, on his way to you now."

Brian hung up the phone just as the passenger walked towards him. Ever the professional, he walked towards the man and offered to hang up his coat.

"Thank you."

"Not at all, sorry, but do you have your boarding card?"

"Of course," replied the passenger handing over his card.

"Ah, Mr Clark, seat 1A, just this way Sir."

As Brian showed Clark to his seat, a noise behind them made them turn. Both smiled as the new passenger entered the First Class cabin. Brian immediately made his way towards the new arrival and offered to take her coat which she graciously accepted as she handed over her boarding card.

"Miss Diaz, seat 4A." Brian pointed to the seat to her left.

"Please, call me Rosie."

Part Two

Chapter 13

Walker replaced the handset slowly before switching off the small desk light, throwing the penthouse into complete darkness. He leaned back in his seat and looked out across the emptiness of Central Park to the dozing city that never sleeps. Twenty five years ago, Walker had sold his soul to five men; it had been a very lucrative agreement. He sat in a $40 million dollar apartment, his house in the Hamptons was worth at least that again and he had holiday homes in the Caribbean and the South of France. He also had a private jet and more money than he could spend in many lifetimes. However, Walker was now wondering whether it was all worth it.

The call had not gone well. The anger in the men's voices was evident even before they discovered the reason for the call. Two had been roused from their beds with the promise that if the emergency didn't warrant their involvement, heads would roll. The emergency did warrant their involvement but the revelation of what had happened and the threat to the five men meant tempers flared. Initially their wrath fell on Walker but he had managed to push some of it back when he reminded them that he was the one who had cautioned vigilance all those years ago. Their anger needed to be vented and the next obvious recipient was The Unit and their botched operation. The Colonel bore the full brunt and his penalty was quickly agreed. Permanent retirement. Walker was to see to it immediately after "pulling his finger out of his ass and fixing the fucking issue". The undertone was clear, one more failure and the Colonel would not be taking Walker's fall.

With that, the men had ended the call. Walker knew the five men would be panicking. They had everything to lose. And when you had everything, everything was a lot to lose.

Chapter 14

Scott woke up to a plate of eggs and bacon pushed through a slot at the base of the door. He checked around the room and quickly concluded it had not been a dream.

"What time is it?" he shouted.

"Seven a.m.," came the terse response.

In two hours he was supposed to be at a meeting with his tutor to talk about his aims and ambitions for his Economics degree. Just as well it was going to be delayed. He had no idea what his aims and ambitions were. Up until two weeks ago, he didn't even know he'd be going to university, never mind Cambridge. It had been a very weird few weeks and had all started with the strange letter he received three weeks earlier. A meeting was scheduled which he was invited to attend; a meeting which according to the letter would have a significant impact on his future. The meeting was set to take place in law offices in Singapore.

Scott, never one to miss an opportunity, requested leave from his employers, something he had never previously done and it was therefore accepted without question. He had then travelled to Singapore and arrived at the designated offices for the meeting which was nothing like what he had expected. It was over almost before it had started. Basically, his mother, a woman who had died before he had known her, had little to leave him except the one thing she treasured above all else. Education. It seemed his mother was a Cambridge graduate and had had some influence at the University, so much so, that she had somehow and completely anonymously managed to secure the placing of her child (sex yet to be determined) two months into her pregnancy. The lawyer had gone on to explain that the rather strange arrangement had been organised in haste and no further explanation given. Except that almost 25 years from the date of the letter, a place was reserved for her child on the Economics course at Trinity College, Cambridge, along with accommodation.

All costs would be borne by her estate and a small sum of money left over would provide a basic allowance. Scott was overcome with emotion. He had never known his mother and she had only ever been described to him as beautiful, wonderful and generous. He had never even seen a photo. He had no idea who his father was, whether he was alive or dead. Nobody knew, his mother having taken that knowledge to her grave, three months after his birth.

His employers had not been overly happy at his change of plans. However they had accepted that it was a once in a lifetime opportunity and within an hour of his notification, they offered him a significant bursary to stay within their employ while he studied, guaranteeing him a substantial increase on completion of his course. They were extremely keen to retain his talents. Never considering anything else, Scott accepted the offer gratefully.

***

It was 7.35 a.m. when the shit started to hit the fan and as far as Harris and Kelly were concerned, it never really stopped.

The door burst open and the custody sergeant rushed into the room, his face filled with dread.

"Jesus, what's happened?" asked Kelly having just walked into the office herself. Harris was sitting sipping a coffee looking as bemused as ever.

The sergeant caught his breath before he could respond. It had been a long night and a distressing one. He had replaced his friend and colleague from the previous night who remained critical in Intensive Care.

"The prisoner, one of the rugby guys, he's dead!"

"What do you mean he's dead?" asked Harris.

"Not breathing dead."

"But how?" asked Kelly, worried he had been murdered.

"No idea, we pushed his food under the door, went back a half hour later to pick it up and found him dead. Stone cold, must have died during the night," he gasped.

"But he was completely fine last night," objected Kelly.

"Well who knows, sometimes your time's just up," said Harris imparting his wisdom to the group.

Kelly looked at him quizzically. She knew sometimes people just dropped dead but it was incredibly rare and was another bizarre twist to their already baffling case.

"You'd better let the Chief know," she said to Harris.

"You call him, he's got a soft spot for you," he said smiling.

Kelly instantly blushed, the over lingering looks of the pervy old Chief had not gone unnoticed.

Before she had a chance to pick up the receiver, it rang. With her hand already on it, she answered before the end of the first ring.

"Hi, I've got the FSS on Line One for you."

"Thanks." And before she pressed the flashing red light to take the call, she whispered to Harris.

"FSS!" and then hit the loudspeaker. The sergeant, realising he was finished with, left the office and closed the door behind him.

"Hi, Detective Sergeant Kelly here," she announced after hitting the flashing button.

"Morning detective, I'm Brian Musgrave a supervisor here at FSS Huntingdon. I've got a couple of things here. Probably most importantly for you, we have a match between your suspect and the serial rapist. However, not with the latest victim."

Kelly and Harris digested the information which didn't really make sense. They'd only caught him because of the last victim. If anything matched it should have been that.

"Are you sure?"

"Until we run the tests again, yes. Unfortunately I can't verify it with the tester…"

"Why not?" Harris butted in.

"Actually that's the other reason for my call, it seems there's been a terrible accident."

Harris and Kelly could do nothing but stare at the phone in disbelief.

"John Yates one of my team seems to have fallen over in his chair and broken his neck. He's dead."

"Don't touch anything, that area is a crime scene," said Kelly quickly. That was one too many coincidences.

"But you can see the tear in the carpet where his chair must have caught…"

"Brian trust me, everything to do with this case is not as it seems."

Another phone ringing interrupted them. Harris stood and walked across to the other desk and picked it up.

Kelly took the phone off speaker and picked up the receiver and proceeded to tell Brian exactly what to do. As she ended the call, she looked across at Harris who seemed to be just holding the phone in mid air and staring blankly at her.

"What?" she asked

"That was the hospital, all three of the rugby men died during the night!"

"But only one was critical, the other two had fractured limbs."

"I know but all three died."

"Holy shit!"

"And then some!!" added Harris.

After a moment or two of silence.

"What next?" asked Kelly. "What next?"

As the time neared 8.00 a.m., their fellow detectives began to arrive. Jokes about the previous day's dropping quickly died down as they were brought up to speed as to the turn of events. The arrival of the Detective Superintendent who headed the department silenced the room. His absence on the previous day had been noted, particularly following the Chief's involvement. If Detective Superintendent Keith Addison had not been basking in the Mediterranean sunshine with his latest conquest, he may have been slightly more prepared for what was about to hit him. Unfortunately, his flight from Malaga had not landed until 2.00 a.m. whereupon he'd gone straight home and crashed out. He hadn't seen the news, read a paper or even listened to the radio in the previous twenty four hours. He had also 'accidentally' left his cell phone in the office on the Friday, so that his wife couldn't catch him out on his 'weekend with the boys'.

Kelly and Harris briefed him and brought him up to speed.

"Fuck! How many dead, did you say?"

"Seven and the custody sergeant is critical - less than a fifty/fifty chance," replied Harris.

"Fuck!"

A knock on the door announced the entry of Detective Constable Ben Merrick.

"Sir, sorry to interrupt but I've got a Detective Inspector Newell on the phone from Newcastle. He urgently wants to talk to the officer in charge of the rape case."

"Put him through," replied Addison.

"Line 3, Sir," he said before leaving the room.

As they waited for Line 3 to start flashing, all wondered what next. As it started to flash, Kelly pressed the button, instantly connecting them to DI Newell on speakerphone.

"Hi, is that DCI Harris?" asked Newel.

"Yes, you're on speaker with Detective Superintendent Addison and Detective Sergeant Kelly."

"Good morning," replied Newell.

"How can we help?" asked Addison.

"If you'll bear with me here, Sir. About two years ago, I was investigating a serial rapist who had raped six women in less than a year. Anyway one night we get a break, he's just raped a girl and she escaped and managed to give us a good enough description in order to track him down. We went in and caught him comatose in his bed, caught him bang to rights exactly where she said. He comes round and protests his innocence, doesn't know how he got into the room etc… you know, the usual. Anyway the last victim disappears, we don't know where she's gone, presume a break down or that she was a student who went home without giving us her address. He's fingered as the serial but his DNA doesn't match, which felt right as he just didn't match the profile. But the CPS in their infinite wisdom reckon he must have planted the false DNA and that we should go for prosecution anyway. They use the victim's running away as her being too scared to go to trial and before you know it, the guy's sent down for 15 years."

"Oh my God!" said Kelly.

"What?" asked Newell.

"You've not had any rapes like it in the last year have you?"

"Nope, not a one, which was beginning to make me think we did get the right guy."

"But what you describe is exactly what's happened here. Can you send us everything you've got?" said Kelly.

"Will do. Can you let me know what happens, I've got a young guy up here stewing in prison for what this pair have done."

"Definitely," replied Addison ending the call.

Silence filled the room as each worked out what the implications of the call were. It was Kelly who broke the silence first.

"The only issue we have is the DNA match. Other than that, it's completely the same."

"I'm willing to bet a few bob the young scientist didn't fall. This whole thing stinks!" said Addison.

Noticing they were off their call, DC Merrick stuck his head in again.

"Sir, the Chief wants you all in his office asap and he emphasised ASAP."

Chapter 15

The long wheel base Jaguar Sovereign swept along Whitehall, its four police outriders ensuring a quick and smooth passage through the Monday morning rush hour traffic. A right turn into Horse Guards Parade announced to anyone watching that the UK's Secretary Of State for Defence had arrived at his office.

Receiving a nod from his bodyguard, George Cunningham stepped out of the back of the limousine and walked the few steps into the Ministry of Defence for only the second time in his life. His rise to stardom within his political party was nothing short of meteoric. MP at 25, Parliamentary Private Secretary to the Chancellor at 26, Minister of State for Policing, Security and Community Safety at the Home Office at 28 and four days earlier appointed into his new role at the Ministry of Defence at the tender age of 30. There was no doubt in anybody's mind that George Cunningham would one day govern the country and the current Prime Minister was merely keeping George's seat warm.

At 8.31 a.m., George sat at his desk and turned on his computer. His e-mail inbox showed 257 unread messages. He knew that a lot would be well wishers, wishing him well in his new job. He was amazed they even had his email, it had only been set up on Friday night but the brown nosers were a very resourceful bunch and had obviously pulled out all the stops to ensure their congratulations were the first to arrive. He scrolled through the list, firstly by name. He recognised most of them and was unsurprised to see the usual suspects. He'd let his secretary send a simple thank you on his behalf. Leaving the names, he clicked on 'subject' and the list immediately rearranged itself. Again, he was unsurprised as most of the 257 mails fell into either C or W, his well wishers wishing him 'Congratulations' or 'Well Done'. After moving the well wishers into another folder, the number of e-mails totalled a rather more acceptable 22 unread.

The first few turned out to be nothing more than department circulars that had been sent to all staff. One was from the Prime Minister, a copy of some e-mails sent to his predecessor that he had promised to forward on to him. Already knowing their content, he moved on.

Ten minutes and another 15 e-mails later, George came across his final e-mail, subject heading URGENT – DEF MIN ONLY. He chastised himself for not noticing 'Urgent', otherwise he would have opened this one first. He clicked on the mail and was instantly confused.

From: FSS
TO: DEF MIN
Subject: URGENT – DEF MIN ONLY

FYEO

A member of K Squad has been identified in relation to a sample being analysed in Huntingdon, the reference code for the case is 47362192. No identification can be released nor that a match occurred unless approved by Secretary of State for Defence.

Message ends.

George read the computer generated mail again and wondered what the hell it meant. He had no idea what the K Squad was nor why only he could authorise the notification that a match had been found. He pressed the buzzer on his desk.

"Yes Mr Cunningham," chirped his secretary.

"Please call me George," he repeated again for what seemed the 20th time. "Can you get me Tony please, asap."

Five minutes later Tony Wilson, the Minister of State for the Armed Forces entered his office.

"Hi, Tony," greeted George.

"Hi George, what's up?" he asked cheerily.

"The K Squad," replied George.

"The what? Never heard of it."

George watched Tony closely and having known him for a few years knew he wasn't lying. If Tony didn't know it meant no one in the building would know. His predecessor had been clear when he left, whatever you do keep Tony on your team, he knows this place inside out, there's no one and nothing he doesn't know. It seemed that had been an over statement, in less than two working days he'd already caught him out. There was only one other person to call, his predecessor, the newly appointed Home Secretary.

"Hi James, how's the new job?" asked George, having called the Home Secretary's mobile number.

"Nightmare, place is a fucking disaster, you?"

"Nothing to do."

Both men laughed at the compliment.

"Thanks for that, just need to work my magic here. Anyway how can I help?"

"We secure on these phones?"

"Of course."

"What's the K Squad?"

"I'll call you right back," replied James in a distinctly more serious tone.

George replaced the receiver and awaited the call back. After fifteen minutes, he began to wonder what he hell was going on and was lifting the phone to call James back when there was a knock on the door and the Home Secretary walked in.

George's look of confusion was answered by James.

"We've got a meeting with the P.M. in twenty minutes. I'm not authorised to tell you what you want to know but he is. Grab your jacket, we'll take my car."

Chapter 16

Harris, Addison and Kelly entered the Chief Constable's office just after 9.00 a.m. and took a seat as instructed.

"So where are we?" asked the Chief.

Kelly and Harris turned to Chief Superintendent Addison who took the lead and sitting forwards, began to update the Chief.

"Well, Sir…"

The Chief, however, had other ideas and looked across at Kelly.

"Perhaps it's better coming from someone involved in the case, Detective Sergeant Kelly?"

"Ummm yes Sir. Of course Sir," she said looking at Addison who sat back in his chair and subtly nodded for her to carry on.

For the next ten minutes Kelly outlined what they had discovered. The FSS match, the supposed accidental death of the scientist, the death of all the rugby fans and finally the call from Newcastle.

"Views?"

Addison, not one to be put off by the earlier rebuke, jumped in.

"We're pretty certain we've got the wrong man. The only thing that really doesn't add up is the DNA match, particularly as the one he should have matched is the only one he didn't."

"DCI Harris?" asked the Chief.

"I'm less convinced than my colleagues of the suspect's innocence Sir."

The chief's eyebrows raised slightly as he turned away from Harris and faced Kelly.

"Kelly?"

"I believe we definitely have the wrong man Sir," replied Kelly with conviction.

"It certainly seems that way but why the hell do we now have seven dead bodies with a central link that seems to be our suspect?" asked the chief, as he summed up.

"That's the bit that's got us baffled, Sir" replied Addison. "I've sent someone out to check the FSS death which we assume is foul play and I've asked the coroner for causes of death on the rugby players asap."

"We've also been trying to contact the lawyer who visited last night but so far have been unable to trace the firm he allegedly represented," added Kelly.

Before the Chief could respond, his phone rang. He lifted the receiver.

"Hello?"

"Please hold for the Prime Minister," came the clipped voice.

**

After visiting the hospital and dealing with his team members, Karl had driven one of the Range Rovers back to London. He had arranged to meet the Colonel the following morning at nine and approached his flat with trepidation. Karl still couldn't believe that almost his whole team had been wiped out, three of them at his own hands, an action that would haunt him for a very long time.

As he neared the exclusive block of flats in the heart of London's Mayfair, he checked that nobody was watching before mounting the steps and pressing the Colonel's buzzer,

"Hello?" came the voice from the speaker.

"Hi, it's Karl."

"You're early," responded a surprised Colonel, releasing the door catch.

Karl pushed the door open and quickly mounted the four floors. Finding the Colonel's door wide open. He walked in. The Colonel shouted from the kitchen.

"Tea or Coffee?"

"Neither, thanks," Karl answered as he walked through to the kitchen.

The Colonel was pouring the boiling water into his cup when the bullet ripped a hole through the back of his skull and destroyed any possibility of an open casket funeral. Karl quickly left the flat, removing the silencer and pocketing his prized 9mm Korth semi-automatic.

Karl checked his watch, 9.03 a.m. just under an hour to get to Heathrow to meet the flight from Washington as instructed.

***

"You're on speaker phone with myself, the Home secretary and the Defence Secretary," informed the Prime Minister.

"Good morning," replied the Chief, wildly indicating for his guests to leave his office immediately. As the door closed behind them, the Chief continued.

"How can I help you Sir?"

"I'm calling on a matter of national security. I'm afraid I can't go into the detail but it seems your suspect is not who you think he is and I assure you has nothing to do with the rapes."

"We had pretty much come to that conclusion but his DNA matches the first four samples."

"When did those rapes occur?" asked the Home Secretary.

"Over the last ten months."

"It wasn't him, he wasn't in the country," he replied firmly.

"He told us that but wouldn't tell us where he was."

"He can't but I'll vouch for him as an alibi," offered the Home Secretary.

"As will I," added the Prime Minister.

"I'm sure that gives you sufficient comfort to eliminate him from your enquiries," said George, the Defence Secretary.

"Yes of course but we've got the incident last night. I can't just let him go. Somebody may be trying to kill him."

"That's our concern and that's why we want him in a car and on his way to us as a matter of urgency. We'll be waiting for him at the Defence Ministry," instructed the Home Secretary, the Chiefs ultimate boss.

"Yes Sir," replied the Chief, confused but delighted to get the suspect the hell out of his station and constabulary.

As the call ended, he called DCI Harris and DS Kelly to his office and informed them of their trip to London.

Chapter 17

BA0292 touched down at exactly 9.47 a.m., thirteen minutes ahead of schedule. Clark had spent most of the flight sleeping. His companion, supplied by The Unit, had turned out be particularly untalkative. All he had managed to ascertain was that she was a freelancer who had carried out some assignments for The Unit before. When he had tried to find out her name she had simply said that Rosie was fine.

As the cabin doors opened, Clark switched on his cell phone to check his messages. Within seconds, the familiar ringtone told him he had voicemail. He dialled his service and listened as Walker informed him that a car would be waiting for them at the airport. Clark and Rosie, despite being the first passengers off the plane with no luggage, didn't surface from the airport for another hour. Immigration control first thing on a Monday morning was not a pleasant experience. Every minute of queuing and delay enhancing Clark's hatred for the 'fucking Brits'.

Clark spotted the Range Rover and directed Rosie to the waiting car. After brief introductions, Clark instructed Karl to get them to Cambridge as fast as he could. Safe in the car, he made a call that would make their day a little easier.

"It's me. Anything?" he asked.

"Not a thing. We've not been able to find out how she knows him," replied the Unit's sniper in Washington.

"Shit, keep trying, check every lead you can. I need to know how she knew him."

Clark snapped his phone shut in frustration. If they just knew how the real Rosie knew him, they could get the fake Rosie past the police and in to see him. From the telephone transcripts it was clear Scott had no idea who she was anyway.

"No luck?" asked Rosie.

"Unfortunately not."

"There's still time. It'll take us a couple of hours to get to Cambridge in this traffic."

"No it won't," interrupted Karl hitting the blue lights and turning them into an emergency vehicle. "It'll be just over an hour."

***

Ashley's hand immediately shot to the pain in her neck as she came round. She could feel a small lump and knew it was going to be a bitch of a bruise. The dart had thumped into her with a tremendous force. Looking around the small darkened room, she knew she was in a basement, the coldness of the stone leaving little doubt. A small blanket on the floor offered little protection from the cold and the hardness. A small staircase led up into the building but the manacle around her ankle ensured she wouldn't be going anywhere near them. The only thing she was sure of was that it was still dark outside. A small window set high in the wall provided that information.

The noise of a door unlocking drew her attention to the staircase. The footsteps became visible as a man quickly made his way towards her.

"I see you woke up!" he said as he approached.

Ashley remained silent and refused to allow the man eye contact as he stared at her.

"Don't worry you'll tell us what we want to know. We can either get it the easy way…," he smiled. "Or we can get it the fun way." His eyes dropped and lingered on her body.

"So let's try the easy way first. How do you know the man in England, Rosie?"

Ashley's face tried desperately to remain dead pan while her mind raced. This was nothing to do with the Darius operation but they were calling her Rosie. So who the hell were these guys and what did they want to know about the man in England?

"I don't know what you're talking about," she replied fearfully. From the way the man was holding himself it was obvious he did not see Ashley as a threat.

"I quote," the man said taking a piece of paper from his pocket. "'Can you just tell him I know who he is'. Well?"

"Well what?" Jesus they had a transcript of her call. Who the hell were they?

"Who the fuck is he and how do you know him?"

"But I don't know him."

"You said you did."

"I said I know who he is. I didn't say I knew him."

"So who is he?"

"A guy I recognised."

"From where?"

"I've never seen him before!"

"But you said you knew him?" he said angrily

"Yes, I did."

"So you admit you knew him."

"No I said I knew him."

"FUCK!!" raged the man kicking the chair that sat next to him.

Ashley had watched the man's temper grow and felt sure he would lash out soon. As he turned slightly to kick out at the chair, she pushed forward with all her strength and outstretched her free leg. As she connected with the man's standing knee, her leg was completely straight. The noise was sickening as the man's knee, bearing his full weight, literally snapped, sending him crashing to the floor emitting an almighty scream of pain, unlike anything Ashley had ever heard before. As he hit the floor, his mind was only on one thing, stopping the unbelievable pain, he didn't even notice Ashley's leg before it was too late, the ankle crashed down on his larynx smashing amongst other things his voice box, instantly silencing his scream. As he gasped uselessly for air, Ashley was already searching through his pockets for the key to her manacle. Within seconds, she had not only secured the key but also the man's SIG-Sauer P226 pistol.

The door flew open and thundering footsteps announced the arrival of the man's colleague. Obviously, he had also expected little threat from Ashley as he crashed down the stairs to see what had caused the screams.

"We're not supposed to kill her yet!" he shouted.

The scene that met him at the bottom of the stairs was certainly not what he had expected. His friend and companion of over twenty years lay flat on his back, his body spasming in the final throws of death as it desperately tried to get oxygen. The girl who he thought was being tortured was in a classic shooter's crouch with a pistol pointed directly at his head.

"Fuck!!"

"Yep," said Ashley ominously. "Now who the fuck are you and what do you want?" she demanded.

The sniper watched the final jerk of his best friend and caught Ashley's eye. While her eyes were caught in his gaze he moved his hand towards his holstered gun. Being a trained sniper, he spent hours a day on the gun range perfecting his talent. A talent he believed should cover every weapon. As such, his proficiency with a pistol was second to none and that included the speed at which he could draw and hit a target. He often thought that had he been born in the days of the wild west, he would most definitely have been the 'fastest gun in the west'.

Ashley watched the man as he first looked at his colleague and then stared intently at her, his eyes were almost mesmerising, dark and lifeless. She had seen them before, many times in fact; you could always spot the snipers. The eyes always gave them away. As this flashed through her mind her body instantly reacted, snipers equalled death. Ashley subconsciously depressed the trigger, sending a bullet into the man's right eye. A second shot rang out, the man's already dead brain not able to stop the signal sent only a nano second earlier to pull the trigger of his own pistol. Fortunately by the time the bullet left the pistol his hand had dropped sending the bullet harmlessly towards the floor.

Ashley fell back and saw the man fall to the ground, her heart beating at the sight of the pistol in the sniper's hand. It hadn't been there when he entered the basement. Had she not shot him when she had, she would be dead. The speed with which he brought the gun to bear was unbelievable. She had not taken her eyes off of the man other than for the spilt second she had looked into his eyes.

Shaking herself into action, she listened out for more voices or foot steps. Hearing none, she slowly made her way to the top of the stairs and into the body of the house. A quick look around revealed no further threats and after ascertaining she was, to all intents and purposes, in the middle of nowhere, she relaxed. If anyone else was to arrive she'd hear them coming.

A more thorough look around revealed no clue whatsoever as to whom she was dealing with. A rental receipt was made out to 'Cash', no name. The bodies in the basement revealed nothing about the two men other than they were almost certainly ex-military. Ashley slumped down in the chair in the lounge and tried to work out what she should do next. If what was happening had to do with her call to England, whoever she was up against was an extremely well connected and resourceful group. They had to be. Otherwise, she had no idea how they could know what she had said on the phone nor would there be two dead ex-soldiers in the basement. Knowing that whatever she was up against was going to be more than she could handle on her own, she picked up the phone. It was time to call in.

Chapter 18

Scott insisted they drive via his accommodation block before going to London. He wanted his own clothes. As Kelly waited in the car, Harris escorted Scott into the Wolfson building, the accommodation block for Trinity College and directed him towards the crime scene. The yellow 'police line, do not cross' tape covered the doorway. Harris moved towards the tape and began to take it down.

"What are you doing?" asked Scott.

"Going to your room!" replied a confused Harris.

"But that's not my room, it's the one three doors down." Scott pointed further down the corridor.

They walked down the corridor and minus his key, Scott shoulder-charged the door to gain entry. Harris noted the small room was almost identical to the crime scene, it too was clinically clean and devoid of any personal belongings except for a small case sitting in the centre of the room.

"I hadn't unpacked. In fact, I had only just arrived, when I went to grab something to eat at the pub," said Scott in response to Harris' confused look.

Harris didn't respond. He just walked back out into the hallway and tried to understand why the rapist had set Scott up in a room three doors away from his own. It just didn't seem to make sense but for the first time since he arrested him, he actually believed Scott was innocent.

Scott appeared back in the hallway two minutes later. The white t-shirt and blue jogging trousers supplied by the police had been replaced by a pair of jeans and clean white t-shirt. Scott nodded to Harris indicating he was ready to go. Two minutes later and an approving nod from Kelly, they were on their way to London.

***

Walker was awakened by his phone ringing,

"What?" he barked. It was 5.22 a.m. and he had only just managed to fall asleep.

"Hi, is this a bad time? It's Nugent from The Unit command centre."

"No, No, please it's fine, what's up?" Walker chastised himself for the barking.

"You're on my call list for any updates on a package in England."

"Yes?" prompted Walker eager to hear the news.

"A call was placed a short while ago that suggested the package was to be moved. A satellite was immediately routed to the area and we're currently tracking the package in transit to London."

"Excellent, I have a man on site, I'll let him know." Walker smiled, he knew he could trust Clark to make sure the problem was taken care of.

"That won't be necessary, a team has been authorised and is already en route," replied Nugent firmly.

Walker was taken somewhat off guard. He alone controlled The Unit's resources. "But who authorised that?"

"I'm not at liberty to say but if I were you, I'd make sure your man is kept well clear. This has don't fuck with it written all over it," warned Nugent.

Walker knew of only five people who he would not be at liberty to know had authorised the action. Two of them he knew wouldn't know how to contact The Unit. That left three and if one of them was getting involved personally, Walker's days were numbered.

"Thank you Nugent, I appreciate the heads-up," offered a very nervous Walker hanging up the phone.

Walker got up and packed an overnight bag. He had to get out the house. If he was right, the conference call had not ended when he hung up. Another decision had been made. William Walker III was to be punished for the Colonel's failure. The men would not have known that there was a note on the system to update him with any info on the package.

Walker knew he couldn't run. The Unit had access to every police, military and intelligence system in the world. They'd track him to the ends of the earth with ease and he'd be dead within the week. The only option was to bargain his way out of the hole. He considered waking his wife, they'd most definitely take her out when they visited. She'd be his sacrifice, his punishment for the mistake. He was fed up with her anyway, they'd be doing him a favour. He stepped into her bedroom, they hadn't shared a bed for over 15 years and said goodbye to her sleeping figure. Grabbing his bag he ran down to the front door and jumped into the nearest car, speeding away, wondering how long it would be before the assassins arrived.

Once out of danger, he phoned Nugent back.

"Hi, it's Walker. I need the tracking code for the package."

"I'm sending it to you now," replied Nugent.

Walker immediately forwarded the code to Clark and called him, explaining what he wanted him to do.

Clark looked down at the screen as Walker spoke, the aerial view of the car speeding through the English countryside seemed almost surreal. Clark hit a button and a map was overlaid onto the video picture telling him exactly where the car was. His PDA, fitted with GPS, then calculated exactly how far away the package was. As Walker finished speaking Clark's mouth dropped open.

"You want me to do what?!"

Chapter 19

Scott rested his head on the door pillar and tried to get some sleep. It was an hour to London and if he slept it would save the continuous questions from Kelly. He was sure she meant well but God, she went on a bit. Where was he from? Who was he? Why did the Prime Minister want to see him? Did he have any family?

Until he knew what the hell was going on, Scott was saying nothing. He had been trying to work things out but nothing made sense. Framing him as a rapist and then trying to kill him in the cells didn't link up. They could have just killed him instead of drugging him. The only conclusion was that they were separate; being framed for the rape was just a coincidence which alerted whoever wanted him dead as to where he was. But who wanted him dead? Who even knew who he was to go to the trouble of trying to kill him? And even then if they knew who he was, they would not have sent unarmed men to kill him. Even that didn't make sense.

Either he'd been set up and there was a leak or it was something else entirely. Whatever it was, he couldn't do anything about it for the next hour and with Kelly quiet at last he began to doze.

"What the fuck was that?" shouted Harris, swerving the car onto the hard shoulder of the motorway.

Scott awoke the moment his body slid across the seat into Kelly's; his eyes alert and trying to see what the problem was. It was his ears however that picked up the threat; the whump of the helicopters rotor blades evident through the roof of the car.

"A helicopter just appeared from nowhere and flew straight at us," explained Kelly, looking out of the window to try and see where it had gone.

"It missed us by fucking inches," screamed Harris from the driver's seat, having pulled them back onto the main carriageway. He too was desperately searching the sky for the chopper.

Scott looked out the back window and spotted the little chopper. It had swooped over their heads and was now doing a tight turn to come back at them. Scott recognised it instantly, a small chopper with two M134 Gatling guns and two sets of rocket pods. It was the very agile and extremely deadly AH-6J attack helicopter, a favourite of the US Army special forces and affectionately, if it was on your side, referred to as 'little bird'.

The first pass had obviously been a confirmation fly-by. Scott knew the second pass would not be so friendly. The Gatling guns were already spinning, a pre-cursor to their unleashing a deadly rain of 7.62mm projectiles at over 6,000 rounds per minute that would tear through the car like a hot knife through butter.

"Oh shit!" exclaimed Scott. "They're behind us, we need to get off this road NOW!"

"It's five miles to the next exit!" replied Harris his voice breaking. He could see the small chopper in the side mirrors.

"Sod the exit just get off the road!" shouted Scott.

At that moment all conversation ended. The roar of the miniguns exploded into their ears as the chopper swooped towards them, the car behind them disappeared in a shroud of small explosions as the bullets tore through it before continuing on their relentless march towards them, gaining ground with every bullet.

"Put your foot down!" screamed Kelly watching the road behind them being ripped apart.

"It's on the floor, already!" shouted Harris fully aware of the bullets tearing towards them.

The car lurched as the first 7.62mm projectile destroyed the rear bumper, the next less than one hundredth of a second later disposed of the registration plate.

"We're dead," screamed Kelly as the rear window exploded.

***

Clark could only think that Walker was going mad but having worked for the man for twenty five years, he knew one certainty, with Walker nothing was ever as it seemed.

"Can you stop here please Karl," said Clark.

"What, on the hard shoulder?" asked a rather mystified Karl.

"Please."

As the car slowed and pulled to a stop, Clark stretched his seat belt as far as it would go. He then quickly placed it over Karl's head and before Karl knew what was happening, he was fighting for his life.

"Rosie, do you mind?" asked a huffing Clark, the younger and stronger Karl was proving a reluctant corpse.

Rosie not knowing why Clark was doing what he was doing but knowing he was paying for her services, reached forward and delivered a sharp and deadly karate style blow to Karl's throat. His fight ended as his body slumped forward.

Clark knew they wouldn't have long, stopping on the hard shoulder would mean a police response. He climbed into the front of the car and pushed the dead weight into the passenger seat before quickly pulling away. They had stopped for less than two minutes and thanks to the blacked out windows in the car, had elicited no response from passing traffic.

"What's happening?" asked Rosie as they pulled away.

"Slight change of plan. Will that be a problem?" asked Clark staring into her eyes.

"As long as I get paid, I don't care. I'm freelance," she replied coldly.

"Excellent. Can you climb in the back and see what sort of equipment we have?"

As Rosie climbed into the boot area, Karl's phone buzzed, Clark didn't hesitate to answer it.

"Hello," he said gruffly.

"Base here. We have a problem your passengers are no longer welcome. I repeat your passengers are no longer welcome."

"Understood," replied Clark.

Clark hung up the phone, his temper flaring. Walker was right, they were marked men. Both he and Walker had devoted their lives only to be written off without a thought or a thank you. The fuckers would pay.

"Few MP5's and Sig Sauers and a sniper rifle," shouted Rosie from the boot.

Clark didn't respond, he just pushed his foot to the floor and watched as the time to the target reduced. With only two minutes to go, he spotted the helicopter. The small gunship sped menacingly ahead disappearing quickly out of view. He pressed his foot down harder but with nowhere to go, nothing changed. He wasn't going to make it. He was still over two miles away although they were closing at the equivalent of over 240 mph, less than 30 seconds away. But Clark knew a gunship wouldn't take that long, it would be over almost before it started.

Clark watched the screen and without warning slammed on the brakes and screamed at Rosie.

"Sniper rifle!"

As the car skidded to a stop, Rosie struggled to pull the rifle out of its holder. Clark was at the boot of the Range Rover almost instantly, grabbing the half prepared rifle from Rosie's hands. He slammed in the magazine and ran up the small incline onto the bridge that he had spotted on the map. As he reached the railing, he could already hear the clack clack clack of the minigun. Hoping he wasn't too late he put the rifle to his shoulder and looked through the scope, magnifying his view ten fold. They were still nearly half a mile away as he took aim and pressed down on the trigger.

Chapter 20

Within thirty minutes, the house was unrecognisable. Helicopters littered the front yard while highly armed personnel patrolled and scoured every inch of the property. A clean up crew had already been and gone, assuring no investigation would be necessary into the killing of the sniper and his spotter. As far as anyone was concerned they had simply ceased to exist.

Ashley's call to her boss had ensured a rapid and overwhelming response. The Defence Intelligence Agency did not take kindly to its agents being kidnapped. Ashley's direct boss was the head of the Strategic Support Branch, a highly secretive and clandestine branch within the already mysterious DIA. Its remit was wide ranging, protecting the national security of the USA with negligible limitations unlike the Central Intelligence Agency which, after years of scandal, had severe restrictions over what it could and could not do. The SSB also had the ability to operate domestically and internationally and was America's front line defence. As such, it had within its employ some of the hardest, brightest and most ruthless individuals operating beyond the bounds of any legal or governmental control. Whatever needed to be done, the SSB would deliver. Its position within the defence community ensured that it had unrestricted access to its sister defence agency, the all seeing, all hearing NSA and first option on any military staff. In other words, only the best of the best were ever offered positions within the SSB.

Ashley's entry to the Naval Academy had immediately caught the attention of the DIA's recruiters. It wasn't that often a high flying Harvard student quit their course to join the services. Her achievements throughout her time at the Academy ensured the attention turned to action and on the day of her graduation, Ensign Ashley Jones received a request to join the Superintendent of the Naval Academy for coffee. On arrival at his office, Ashley was shown in only to find that the Vice Admiral was not present, but replaced by a man dressed in a civilian suit introducing himself as Brigadier General Robert T. Jackson, (retired) Head of the SSB. He had explained their role and how he felt she could fit in. Without a moment's hesitation, Ensign Ashley Jones accepted the job and unknown to her, jumped two pay grades instantly and left the room a full lieutenant.

News of the new appointee spread like wildfire throughout the SSB. There was no one who didn't know the wealth of her parents, her high school, university and Academy scores nor her spending habits or looks. Entry to the SSB straight from Academy was unheard of. All of the current staff had had to earn their right to be there and as such, Ashley's appointment had not been well received, particularly as daddy had probably called in a few favours for his little darling. Only one thing stopped them trying to get rid of her from day one, the kitty for the first to bed her was touching a $1,000.

Jackson knew his department inside out and knew how the men felt and what their objective was. He could have warned Ashley but felt it would do her no favours. She was entering a world where if you didn't stand up and be counted, you'd die. Ashley had felt the tension the second she had walked into the SSB area of Bolling Air Force Base, the home of the DIA. Eyes lingered heavily while smiles were few and far between. It was obvious that she was not a welcome addition to the team.

Ashley had always been a popular girl. Despite her wealth and looks, she was an extremely likeable person. Her warmness and sincerity were genuine. In less than two days, she had broken down the hardness of her new colleagues and within a week, the kitty for the first shag had been quietly redistributed. The only thing that was certain from that point on was that if anyone fucked with Ashley, they fucked with the whole of the SSB.

Ashley's call to the SSB operations desk had resulted in the calling out of two fast response teams, each comprising of six ex-special forces operatives, highly skilled in counter terrorist and hostage rescue situations. Within ten minutes, two H-76 Eagles, the military variants of the Sikorsky S-76 with their response teams were airborne and on their way to secure Ashley's location.

Jackson arrived forty minutes after Ashley's call and found her sitting in the lounge.

Ashley immediately stood to attention and saluted Jackson as he entered the room.

"Sir," she said as she snapped her hand to her temple.

"Jones, seems you've caused a bit of a stir?" replied Jackson returning her salute.

"Sir, yes Sir."

"So, what the hell does Darius think he's doing?" asked Jackson taking the seat next to Ashley and instructing her to sit back down.

Ashley immediately felt guilty, she had not reported her leaving The Palace and subsequent plans to visit London.

"Well actually I don't believe this has anything to do with Darius or his operation."

Jackson looked at her quizzically, mentor to protégé and immediately understood something else was going on.

"I think you better explain," he said quietly, dismissing with a wave Ashley's guardian angels from the room.

Ashley explained how she had been called to Darius' office and assumed her cover was blown. However, it appeared that all Darius knew was that she wasn't a prostitute and it seemed he had no idea the DIA were onto his arms dealings. She explained how, as he tried to kill her, she had recognised a young man on the TV in England who was being arrested and with whom she had lost contact. After escaping from Darius, she had made contact with the police station to find out how he was. She explained that they would not give her information over the phone and as a result, had decided to make a quick trip to England to check on him. She apologised but explained that it really was a family emergency and had every intention of calling him as soon as she had landed.

"So who is he?"

"Just a family friend."

"Must be a very good friend," mused Jackson, looking directly at Ashley.

"Yes," she replied nervously hoping he didn't pry any further. The less he asked, the less she'd have to lie. She couldn't tell him the truth, at least not until she knew for certain.

"So how did you end up here?"

Ashley explained the killings at the mall, her abduction and the questioning that related to her friend and their use of her cover name Rosie.

"Any idea who your friend may have upset?"

"No," lied Ashley. She didn't even know him but she couldn't tell Jackson that.

"Any idea how they tracked you to the mall?"

"Absolutely none, nobody knew I was going there and I definitely wasn't followed."

"And you say they knew exactly what you said on the phone call to England?"

"Yes, word for word, like they had a transcript of the call."

"And the bums you killed, you reckon they were ex-military?"

"Definitely."

"If I didn't know better this has our name written all over it, or another agency's. Where did you say the arrest was?"

"Cambridge."

"OK, give me a minute," replied Jackson, dialling a number on his phone. "Jackson here, get me the duty officer."

"Good morning General Jackson, Dave Thomas here, duty officer."

"Hi Dave, I need you to check for any activities we've tracked or been involved with in the last 24 hours in or around Cambridge, England."

"Just SSB or DIA overall?"

"Sorry Dave, anybody, any agency."

"Will do. Will I call you back on this number?"

Jackson was somewhat taken aback. He had been told that his mobile was highly secure, untraceable and his number was most definitely not available. Apart from to the NSA, obviously.

"Yes, thanks."

Five minutes later, a rather flustered Dave Thomas called back.

"General, I've never experienced anything like it…"

"Why, what's going on?"

"Sorry, I'm watching a live feed from just South of Cambridge…Jesus!"

"Dave?"

"Somebody outside of the Agency has control of one of our satellites and is tracking a car."

"How the hell can they do that?"

"I've no idea but whoever is in that car is toast. There's a helicopter shooting the shit out of it as we speak. It's unbelievable!"

"What? right now? You're watching the feed real time?"

"Yes, whoa, the car just swerved and shot off the road into a field."

"Jesus, have you alerted the local police?"

"Yes, but wait a minute the helicopter's stopped shooting. In fact, it's just stopped."

"What do you mean it's just stopped?"

"Just that, the car swerved into the field and the helicopter just stopped and appears to have landed."

"What? And who's controlling the satellite?"

"God knows, it's our satellite, under our control, but somebody is overriding our authority and is controlling it."

"Who has that authority?"

"It doesn't exist, nobody has authority over us."

"Jesus man, will you just speak plain fucking English!"

"We have a security breach, someone's using our system without our authority."

"What else have they got?"

"They have transcripts of a few telephone conversations, two of which are between Washington and Cambridge and one between the British Prime Minister and the same place in Cambridge."

"Holy shit, how?"

"I've got no idea but if it wasn't for your call, we'd never have found out. Their link is so buried it would never have shown up unless we went looking."

"Have you called the Director?"

"I'm just about to."

"OK, call me back if you find out what's happening."

"Will do."

Jackson composed his thoughts as the repercussions of his conversation played out in his mind. He'd been in the game long enough to know that anybody who could access the NSA was a powerful adversary and anyone who could do it without being detected even more so. One thing was for sure, if they were in the NSA's system they were definitely able to get into the DIA's and his. He turned to Ashley.

"You've been through a very traumatic experience. I want you to take some leave."

"But…"

"What you do on your leave is up to you but if you were to find your way to England and find out what the fuck is going on, I'd be very interested to hear from you." Jackson watched Ashley to make sure she was reading between the lines.

Ashley began to nod her head understanding. "Of course Sir."

"Now if there's anything I can do to help, please let me know and for God's sake be careful."

"Yes Sir, of course Sir."

Jackson looked at his watch, "Now if I'm not mistaken there's a United flight from Dulles just before ten a.m. which would give you time to get home, get your stuff and get the hell out of here."

Ashley stood to attention, saluted and quickly left to secure a ride to her house. She had a plane to catch.

Just as she left, Jackson's phone buzzed.

"Jackson here."

"General Jackson, I've just spoken with the Director and he is extremely concerned about the National Security surrounding our previous conversation. Have you spoken to anyone else about my call Sir?"

"No, of course not," lied Jackson.

"Thank God, I just got my ass chewed off for not speaking to him first. He wants to meet us both asap, he's on his way in and has arranged for you to be picked up. He wants you personally to take control of the investigation."

"OK, I'll wait here until the car arrives."

"It's a chopper Sir, not a car."

"OK. Oh and Dave, what happened with the satellite feed, the chopper and the car?"

"Sorry Sir, there's somebody at the door, I'll tell you when you get here, goodbye," rushed Dave as he hung up the phone, leaving Jackson wondering what on earth was going on. However, it seemed he didn't have long to wait, thumping rotors announced the arrival of another helicopter. Jackson walked outside and watched as the white unmarked Bell 430 landed in the middle of the lawn. He walked over to the pilot and checking it was from the NSA Director, climbed in. Thirty seconds later, they were airborne and on their way to Fort Meade, Maryland.

Much to his staff's surprise, fifteen minutes after Jackson had left, a car arrived for him, sent by the Director of the NSA. All they could offer was an apology to the driver informing him that he had already left by chopper and no-one knew where he was going. Only Dave Thomas knew the truth. The NSA Director had sent the chopper but then he wouldn't be telling anybody. Dave and his deputy, the only two other people aware of The Unit's infiltration of the NSA's system, were already dead. The official version would record a car crash. However, if the real autopsy report had not been doctored, the police would have been searching for a gunman. Both had died from a gunshot wound to the head.

The Bell 430 flew directly towards Fort Meade but as it continued past the huge complex, Jackson became concerned. The fact that the NSA Director, Lieutenant General Kenneth Coleman had not called himself had been praying on his mind. He had a very good working relationship with Coleman and would have expected a call inviting him over personally.

"Where are we going?" asked Jackson as they continued East at full speed.

The co-pilot turned round in his seat.

"Don't worry, it won't be much longer Sir," he smiled.

"Why on earth should I be worried?" asked Jackson, finding the use of the word strange.

The co-pilot, unsure how to reply, pulled out a small calibre pistol and shot Jackson between the eyes. The shock on Jackson's face froze in time as the small bullet ricocheted throughout his skull killing him instantly. Five minutes later, out over the Chesapeake Bay, Brigadier General Robert T. Jackson (retired) was buried at sea, his body dropping over one hundred feet to its watery grave.

Chapter 21

As the first bullet hit the boot, Scott dived over the seat and yanked the steering wheel to the left as Kelly's screams over their impending doom rang in his ears. The suddenness and fierceness of Scott's turn resulted in the car shuddering as it veered wildly to the left struggling to maintain its grip on the road surface. If it were not for the enhanced suspension of the high-speed BMW pursuit car, they would have flipped over but fortunately, the two right hand wheels managed to maintain their grip and the car slewed 90 degrees before hurtling across the hard shoulder and out into the neighbouring field, landing with a thump five feet below road level.

The manoeuvre did not phase the helicopter pilot. The AH-6J was one of the most agile helicopters in the world and as the car began to turn, he simply followed the car round, keeping the machine guns trained on the car, the bullets continuing on their relentless path into the body of the car.

***

Clark followed the track of his bullet as it flew though the air dropping over two feet in the ½ mile distance that it had to travel. Even before the bullet hit, Clark was up and moving, racing back to his car. He wanted to be back in London before anyone knew what had happened.

***

The pilot of the chopper had his finger firmly pressed against the trigger, guiding the little chopper towards the target. The first he knew anything was wrong was when the rotors suddenly stopped turning; the momentary pause before they tipped forward was almost surreal.. With the front top heavy both pilots looked at each other in horror, they were one hundred feet from the ground and with a couple of tons of weight behind them, they didn't stand a chance, if they were extremely lucky they wouldn't feel anything. The helicopter plummeted down piling the pilots into the ground. The death screams of the pilots suggested they had definitely not been lucky.

***

Scott was the first out of the car quickly helping Kelly and Harris out before rushing to the first car that was shot. Its smouldering wreckage, however, told him nobody had survived. He moved to the downed helicopter. The large bullet hole in the engine housing told Scott all he needed to know, Somebody was on his side. Whoever had taken the shot was an expert and had known exactly where to shoot. He looked around but knew the shooter would be long gone.

A very shaky Kelly appeared at his side and took in the scene.

"It seems somebody may be on your side afterall," she said looking over her shoulder towards the same bridge Scott was looking at.

"Hmmm," replied Scott. The more that happened, the stranger things got.

Sirens began to sound all around them as police cars, ambulances and fire engines appeared from every angle. Scott suddenly realised that Harris was not with them and remembered Harris' head had thumped into the steering wheel as the car landed in the field.

"Where's Harris?" he asked looking back at the car.

"He was just behind me," replied Kelly searching the area between them and the car.

Scott ran back to the car and found Harris slumped to his right propped against the side of the car, a pool of sick by his side.

"Shit, quick get a paramedic over here right away, he's badly concussed," screamed Scott to Kelly.

Five minutes later, Harris was strapped to a board and being choppered to the nearest hospital. Scott and Kelly spent the next twenty minutes explaining what had happened and were only allowed to continue on their journey to London after the intervention of the Chief Constable. A helicopter arrived shortly afterwards to ensure they arrived at the Ministry of Defence with as little risk to the public as possible.

Chapter 22

Kenneth Coleman closed the door to his office and walked slowly to his desk. He knew the weight of the three deaths would haunt him for a very long time, particularly Jackson's. He was a good man, although that was his ultimate weakness. He was just too good and he would never have understood. It was Coleman's call. He could have brought Jackson in and tried to get him on side but it would just have delayed the inevitable.

He sat down at his desk just as his direct line began to ring. He subconsciously looked around the room wondering if he was being watched. Did they know he had just sat down?

"Hello?" he answered tentatively.

"Hi, is it done?"

"Yes."

"And Walker?"

"We'll find him," replied Coleman firmly.

"You'd better!" retorted the caller ominously. "The fucker just screwed up our plans in England. Our problem has not been resolved."

As the phone went dead, Coleman sat back in his chair. He had a funny feeling things were going to get a lot worse before they got better. He desperately wished they hadn't reeled him in but they had and it now it was too late. His salary would never have paid for the life his position should have afforded him. Had he not worked for the government, he would have been earning ten times what he was. It was only thanks to them that his kids had the education and lifestyle he had dreamed of giving them. But today, the price was high, perhaps too high. Jackson was a good man, just like he had been.

Coleman knew in himself he was still a good man. He reached into this top drawer and without thinking anymore about what he was doing, he removed his silver plated Colt 1911A1 pistol and in one swift movement removed the top of his own skull.

Chapter 23

Henry Freeman's office covered the entire top floor of one of Manhattan's most illustrious skyscrapers. The impressiveness of the office was matched only by its occupant, Henry Freeman who was a man literally on top of the world. He was the Chief Executive Officer of the North American division of the world's largest and most powerful corporation, Transcon. Corp. There was hardly a household brand left that had not been swallowed up by the leviathan, from soft drinks to the armament market, Transcon Corp companies were market leaders. If they were in a market they topped it. If they weren't in it, it was because there quite simply wasn't enough profit to be made. However, very few even knew the name, its existence was shrouded in secrecy.

Even the world's most advanced computers would struggle to work their way through the maze of trust funds and dummy companies that led back to Transcon. That, however, had not stopped the conspiracy theorists coming up with a number of theories surrounding the corporate mystery. The most popular suggestion was that it was in fact just a front for the US government. Less popular was that the UK was re-building its once great empire and the more extreme, was that the company was under the control of the children of Hitler's breeding programme, set up to create the perfect Aryan race, using the missing Nazi funds to build the Fourth Reich.

The board table in Henry's office was bigger than most New York apartments. Over fifty chairs lined its perimeter of the table and they were filled with the Managing Directors or CEO's of America's larger companies, most of which were owned outright or at the very least under majority control by Transcon. The monthly board meeting was an extremely secret affair with the majority of attendees arriving by helicopter to avoid any potential recognition. A number of Transcon companies were public rivals and the connection to one owner would significantly impact their brand and ultimately their sales.

Henry sat at the head of the table and made decisions that would impact the majority of the population, decisions that made the ones taken by the country's politicians almost insignificant but then Henry pretty much decided what government policy was anyway. Henry may be unknown in the public world but in the political world, Henry Freeman and Transcon were king makers. If you wanted to rule, Transcon had to want you to rule. Their control over the media was absolute. Opinion was made and swayed where they wanted. Wars started and ended on their say. Their ethos was simple, if it was good for business, it was good for Transcon.

Henry Freeman was a tall handsome man who cut an imposing figure. His fifty four years as a member of the world's elite had been easy on his appearance and he could pass for a man ten years younger. His arrogant and assured manner commanded instant attention and his words followed to the letter. Henry had the power to captivate and terrify those he dealt with and nobody ever doubted they were dealing with a powerful and ruthless man.

As the conversation reverberated around the room, Henry cleared his throat, silencing the attendees and bringing the meeting to order. These men had no illusion that they served at Henry's discretion and their total loyalty and obedience had been bought and paid for many times over.

Just as Henry was about to start, the door to the boardroom opened and a young and extremely attractive blond woman scurried towards Henry.

"Mr Freeman," interrupted his secretary. "I'm so sorry to interrupt but I have an urgent call for Mr Ernst."

Henry looked to his right hand man and most trusted aide, Max Ernst. Ernst immediately stood up, snapped his heels to attention and dipping his head slightly, led the secretary from the room. Ernst's strong Germanic features, short cropped blond hair, piercing blue eyes and tall muscular physique were an intimidating sight. Everyone who met him assumed he was German. His looks were identical to a stereotypical Gestapo officer as portrayed in the movies. However, Ernst was in fact

Russian and a former member of the KGB's Alpha Group, the elite special forces unit and was in fact not unlike his stereotypical doppelganger in that he was indeed a cold blooded killer.

Ernst's talents had first come to Freeman's attention over twenty years earlier when Freeman needed a business rival to disappear. The former Alpha Group member had turned freelance assassin and was hired by Freeman through William Walker. Ernst had exceeded all expectations and had not only eliminated the rival but unveiled a plot to destroy Transcon. Ernst had acted on his own initiative, wiped out the threat and had been by Freeman's side ever since. Ernst had an IQ in the genius level and unknown to all around him, was one of Freeman's closest advisers as well as his bodyguard.

The secretary led Ernst as to her desk.

"It's a Mr Hunter on the phone Sir. He says it's urgent."

"Transfer it to my office, please," instructed Ernst as he walked across the large reception area to his office, strategically located next to the elevator and staircase - the only access points to the top floor. Nobody entered the office of Henry Freeman without Ernst knowing.

"What's up?" said Ernst as he picked up the call.

Mike Hunter was the head of The Unit, a former deputy director of the CIA, a veteran of some of the CIA's more infamous operations during the Vietnam and Central American scandals. He had been recruited by Transcon through Walker to set up and run their paramilitary organisation.

"Coleman just blew his own brains out!"

"Fuck!"

"It get's worse. We missed Walker. We arrived at 6.30 and he was already gone but we didn't know that until they had already taken out his wife."

"Fuck!"

Ernst slammed his fist on the desk. Freeman had made it clear that Walker had to go. Walker had been Freeman's closest advisor for over thirty years. His position as COO of Transcon's corporate banking division was merely a cover for his real role, protecting Transcon and its owners. Walker had been banker, lawyer and confidant to all five of Transcon's owners. His retirement the previous week had not been well received and the subsequent disaster at the weekend highlighted Walker's failure to resolve an issue that had weighed heavily on all of the owners' minds for many years. Ernst knew little of the detail but had managed to conclude that Walker seemed to know something that threatened the very existence of Transcon.

For that reason, the permanent retirement of Walker had been ordered and Ernst was given the responsibility for making it happen. Following Walker's retirement, The Unit was under Ernst's responsibility and so far, Mike Hunter was seriously failing to impress his new boss.

"I'm afraid there's more. We also missed the target in England," added Hunter nervously. The tension on the phone was palpable. Had Hunter had more notice, he would have retired before Walker. He did not relish the idea of reporting to Ernst. Mike Hunter was not a man who scared easily, having served in some of the world's most bloody war zones. But every time he met Ernst, he felt as though he was one step away from the showers with no water.

"Are you deliberately trying to fuck me off?" snapped Ernst. Freeman had made it clear that whatever happened the man in England had to die and quickly. Every breath he took was a breath too many. Ernst had asked why but Freeman had told him all he needed to know was, the man had to die as an absolute priority, nothing had a greater priority. Whatever Ernst needed, he could have.

"Of course, not!" replied a defensive Hunter.

Ernst tried his best to remain calm.

"What happened?" he asked through gritted teeth.

Hunter explained what they knew. They believed that Walker had been tipped off and may have re-directed Clark's efforts. He also explained that Clark had a freelancer with him, that The Unit had arranged to replace the mysterious Rosie. Which led to his final bombshell, Rosie's escape.

Ernst was speechless. Killing somebody wasn't that fucking difficult. As he let Hunter sweat, he started scratching 1's onto his pad, diagonally crossing out each fifth one.

"Let me get this right. In the space of twenty four hours and in the pursuit of killing just one man, we have lost, by my count..," Ernst paused as he tallied up the total. "At least 12 of our own people and that doesn't account for any collateral casualties."

"I appreciate that when you put it like that, it doesn't sound particularly impressive," agreed Hunter.

"NOT PARTICULARLY IMPRESSIVE!?" screamed Ernst his temper fracturing. "TOTALLY FUCKING HOPELESS IS WHAT IT IS!"

Realising he was screaming, he lowered his voice. "Twenty four hours, you've got twenty four hours to redeem yourself," he said ominously.

Hunter had no illusion as to what the penalty would be. The instructions to retire Walker had shocked him as he had always thought Walker was untouchable.

"Hmm, we may have a problem. Without the NSA, it may prove slightly more difficult."

"Don't worry the deputy is also our man. He'll get the top job."

Hunter hesitated, not wanting to push his luck too far but felt he had to ask.

"We don't have any contacts in the DIA, do we?"

"Why?" asked Ernst.

"We think they may be involved somehow."

Just when Ernst thought it couldn't get any worse, it had. He struggled to control his temper.

"Perhaps you better start at the beginning and tell me everything you know because I'm getting a bit FUCKED OFF trying to work out what the FUCK is going on here between your tid bits of information."

Hunter, like a chastised school child, started from the beginning and told him everything he knew up to the point of this most recent call.

Ernst didn't hesitate when Hunter stopped.

"I'll call you back, after I've spoken to our man."

Ernst quickly dialled a number.

"Good afternoon, Department of Defence, Secretary Nielsen's' office," answered the receptionist.

"I need to speak to the Secretary immediately, please" said Ernst.

Chapter 24

The Boeing 787-800 was on its final approach into Chicago's O'Hare International and was causing quite a fuss. One of Boeing's first production models, that would be the aircraft's first landing in Chicago and the first sighting of one of the most advanced airliners to take to the skies. However, the aircraft anoraks were firmly outnumbered as even the world's newest aircraft couldn't upstage its passenger, Republican presidential candidate Dan Baker, whose polling figures were recording a large lead and there were still four weeks until the election.

Dan's rise to stardom in the republican party was nothing short of miraculous. He had been elected to the House of Representatives at the age of 26, to the senate at 30 and had become Governor of Florida at 42. Although Republican, his landslide margins could only be explained by vast numbers of democrats voting for him. The Yale graduate had it all, movie star looks, super rich, charm and an air of authority that could not be taught nor bought. He was tough on crime but understood and fought against the causes of crime, believed in the right to bear arms but wanted greater controls to combat criminals not week-end shooters. He was tough on welfare but wanted to help the truly needy and wanted to minimise taxes and maximise services by driving efficiencies.

The democrats had come to the conclusion long ago that Dan Baker was unbeatable. His debating skills were unequalled, his finances limitless and following an attempt to smear him, they had suffered a backlash that had resulted in a ten point swing for Baker. The media loved him, the viewers adored him and his constituents worshipped him. In fact Dan's second term as Governor had been unopposed. The Democrats had run the numbers and seen sense.

The Governor of Florida had led the polls since he had announced his intention to run eighteen months earlier. He had been the republican's first and only choice to replace the current two-term incumbent. The republicans were a dead cert to win eight years earlier and with the perfect president in waiting, the party chair had advised Dan to wait and perhaps try for Governor first. Yes, of course he could have been president but did he really want to retire at fifty when he could wait and ensure the party had control for at least 12 years? Nobody ever doubted Dan was destined for the White House. The incumbent had polled strongly after his first term and with Dan in the wings, the decision had been what was best for the party. Dan was always considered a guaranteed two termer and if the incumbent could win, the party would hold the presidency for at least another 12 years. Dan was again put on the back burner.

The 787 taxied to the waiting ladder and stopped. The door opened and the soon-to-be president elect appeared at the top of the stairs. His perfect smile greeted the onlookers and was met by a resounding cheer followed by a chant, 'BAKER! BAKER!' Flashlights lit up the dull October morning as Dan Baker descended the steps and ignoring the Secret Service agents, walked towards the crowd and 'pressed the flesh' with his potential voters. Everybody was greeted with the same respect and interest and despite having heard the same thoughts and feelings countless times over, Dan smiled and accepted them as though they were the best ideas he had ever heard.

A crying baby was thrust into his arms and he held it like his own, looking into its face and smiling. The baby's eyes lit up and the crying turned to laughter. A picture that would cover the front pages of every newspaper across America and beyond. Handing the now happy baby back with a smile, he bid his farewells and God Blesses to the crowd, thanking them from the bottom of his heart for their support before being interrupted by an aide with a cell phone.

"It's Mr Freeman, he says it's urgent!"

"OK," replied Dan, taking the phone.

A final wave was met by a cheer more normally heard by movie and rock stars.

As he stepped into the chopper, the rear doors closed, the Sikorsky S76D lifted off and the small flotilla of helicopters turned and dipping their noses sped off as one. Where his opponents used cars and an ageing airliner, Dan Baker travelled by helicopter and used his own personal airliner to fight his campaign. Money was an irrelevance and for every dollar spent by the democrats Dan spent five. His television ads ran almost non stop, covering every major channel during prime time shows. If somebody didn't know Dan Baker was running for president, they had to be deaf, blind and living in isolation with no electricity. His brand recognition was second only to Coca-Cola.

As Dan turned from the window and put the phone to his ear, the smile faded.

"What's up?" he asked.

Henry Freeman brought Dan up to speed with the day's events which, as expected, were not well received.

"Do I need to remind you in simple words what's at stake here?"

"No, I'm perfectly aware of what's at stake Dan."

"Good, then take your finger out your ass and fucking kill these fuckers!" Dan snapped the phone off and threw it against the cabin wall.

Dan Baker, the carefully constructed political façade, had disappeared revealing the real Dan Baker and unknown to all but very few, a twenty percent owner of Transcon and a ruthless son of a bitch who, in four weeks, would win the presidential election and show his true colours. The ultra popular liberal republican was somewhat less liberal than he had portrayed. In fact, he was about as right wing as they came.

Chapter 25

The helicopter swooped low over Buckingham Palace. Kelly's face was pressed firmly to the side of the glass as she strained to see as much as possible.

"Don't you want to see?" asked Kelly, noting Scott's lack of interest.

"Seen it all before," replied Scott nonchalantly.

"What, you've seen this before?" she pointed to the Palace below.

"Yes."

"Even the gardens?"

"Yes."

"I don't see how. You can't see these from the ground. There's a huge wall all around them."

"I just have, OK?"

"When?"

"I can't tell you that."

"Why?"

"I'm sorry I can't tell you."

Kelly considered Scott's answers and turning away from the window looked at him,

"Have you met the Queen?" she asked, incredulous.

"I'm sorry I can't tell you that," replied Scott breaking into a smile.

The helicopter swept over the front of the palace before swooping down the Mall, and across St. James Park before setting down on Horse Guards Parade, less than 500 meters from the palace.

A car sat waiting for them as they exited the helicopter. Scott, however, dismissed the car and walked through Horse Guards and out the other side of the building onto Whitehall. Ignoring Kelly's continual objections, he crossed the street and led Kelly to the front door of the Ministry of Defence.

Kelly stopped as she read the plaque by the door.

"Just who the fuck are you?" she asked becoming increasingly frustrated at being kept in the dark.

"Scott," replied Scott laughing as he opened the door and stepped aside for Kelly to enter the building ahead of him.

"Thank you," said Kelly surprised by his gentlemanly manners. Her police colleagues usually barged in front of her and left the door to slam in her face. Equal opportunities in the police meant exactly that.

Scott strode across the large reception area and was provided with an escort to take them to the Defence Minister immediately. A short trip in the elevator deposited them on the top floor and before Kelly knew what was happening, she had been left in the foyer while Scott entered the office.

"Good morning, Prime Minister," said Scott, walking towards and shaking the hand of one of the two gentlemen seated by a very grand and somewhat out of place fire-place.

"Good morning Scott. This is George Cunningham who, as of Friday, is our new Defence Minister."

George took Scott's hand and shook it although the quizzical look revealed the Prime Minister had not yet revealed who Scott was.

The Prime Minister, Adam Smith, had been in power for over seven years and was still as popular as the day he had been elected, which in Britain was no mean feat. He was a personable and likeable man with razor sharp wit and intelligence and whose ancestry could be traced back to the famous economist of the same name.

After hearing of the second attack, the Prime Minister didn't waste any time.

"Any idea who's trying to kill you?"

"Absolutely none, Sir."

George interrupted. "I'm sorry but is there any chance of knowing what's going on?"

Scott looked at the Prime Minister to take the lead.

"George, Scott here works for us and when I say us I quite literally mean you and me. Although he's taking some time out to go to Uni."

"What does he do?"

"Hmm, how can I put it…" the Prime Minister pondered his words. "He takes care of difficult situations."

"Like what?"

"Well let's say we get word of a bad egg, one that we know did something which is most definitely not in the interests of our country but we don't have any jurisdiction or in fact hard evidence that we can take to court."

George started to nod, beginning to understand what the Prime Minister was getting at.

"Well Scott here and a few others like him make these problems disappear."

"I thought the SAS did that sort of thing?" asked a confused George.

"Bit too public," replied the PM.

"So what unit are you attached to?" asked George looking at Scott.

"K Squad," replied Scott.

"And they're attached to?"

"Nobody."

"You're not quite getting it George," interrupted the PM, "K Squad is ultra secret. The only people who know it exists are Prime Ministers, Defence Ministers and members of the squad."

"What about the Joint Intelligence Committee, surely they know?" asked George referring to the group that had complete oversight of all of the UK's intelligence community, ensuring that all of her majesty's assets were being used in a co-ordinated effort in the defence of the nation.

"Nope, me and you. That's it. Oh and the Queen."

"The Queen?"

"It was her ancestors who set up the squad."

"How long ago?"

"Some time during the Empire, nobody's entirely sure."

George was becoming more and more bewildered at how a personal squad of assassins could be hidden for so long and why on earth they were still necessary.

"But why?"

"I explained that already," replied the PM, becoming tired of the questioning.

Scott stepped in.

"Maybe I can explain. I deal with the untouchables, the people who stand behind corrupt governments who stick two fingers up at the international community and say I'll do what I want, you can't get to me. I'm talking about terrorists, drug lords, arms dealers, human traffickers. The scum of the earth, basically, whose every breath means misery for others."

George still wasn't convinced.

His morals were struggling to understand the justification for the ultimate penalty.

"But we abolished the death penalty," stated George turning to the PM.

"Yes but these people won't ever see the inside of prison. There's no other way to protect our citizens. K Squad has many restrictions, one of which is that they cannot carry out operations within any of the sixteen countries where the Queen is the head of state. Otherwise the person could be tried and brought to justice."

"So who decides what they do?"

"Me and you but we must agree before a sanction, that's what we call them, can be issued. The sanction is then issued and one of the five members will be given the task."

"Five?" George was surprised at the low number of squad members.

"Yes, it's a very tight outfit and that's one of the reasons that what has happened to Scott is so worrying. If somebody is targeting K Squad, one of our greatest secrets may have been exposed."

The PM looked at Scott.

"I don't think so, no other squad member has been targeted as far as I am aware."

"But how do you recruit squad members, I mean where do you find them?" asked George

"Interesting question, let's just say Scott is rather unique but I'll let him explain." The PM nodded at Scott.

"Squad members can be recruited from any sector of Her Majesty's Services. I for example was a member of the Special Boat Service before being selected."

"And that makes you unique?" asked George.

"I think the PM was referring to my background prior to joining the forces. I was an orphan and raised on a remote island in the South China Sea. The majority of K Squad members come from one of Her Majesty's Special Forces."

"So you're not even British?"

"I believe my mother was. I have no idea whether my father was," replied a slightly irritated Scott.

"Scott's allegiance, I can assure you, is in not in question. This young man has done more for this country than we could ever have hoped," interrupted the PM.

"Sorry, I didn't mean it negatively, I was just surprised as to how somebody raised on a remote island came to be where he is now," recovered George.

"It's simple. I wanted to see the world. I visited the main island of Borneo when I was sixteen and met Royal Marines stationed at the UK's Jungle Warfare Training School in Brunei. I immediately wanted to join but two things stood in my way. I was only sixteen, you need to be seventeen for the Royal Marines and I had no papers to prove who I was."

"So how did you get in?"

"Persistence I suppose. I followed them back to their barracks and discovered the base was run by the Gurkhas. I insisted on meeting with the CO of the base and told him I wasn't going to move until they allowed me to join. Fortunately after a couple of days at the base gates, they humoured me and allowed me to join them in some exercises where I proved my worth and soon after, I was allowed to enlist in the Gurkhas where you could enlist at sixteen. From there, I joined the Marines, the SBS and was enlisted in the K Squad."

"You were a Gurkha?" exclaimed George.

"Only for about eighteen months."

"I've never heard anything like it, I didn't think anyone but a Gurkha could join them other than officers of course."

"I don't believe they can," replied the PM, "but then Scott here wasn't your normal recruit. He missed out a fairly major part of his story. Didn't you?"

"I wouldn't say major part. I believe the PM is referring to some training I received from the islanders who raised me."

"Some training!" laughed the PM. "By the age of sixteen, Scott here was already a highly trained fighter. The islanders had trained him in martial arts from the moment he could walk. I read the report filed by the Gurkha CO after he had seen Scott on a few exercises. Exceptional talent, unlike anything he had ever seen. He instantly enlisted him despite the lack of papers and ethnicity. Too good to lose he had stated in his justification. Scott probably doesn't know this but his enlistment was originally rejected. His first few months of pay came straight out of his CO's pocket. It was only after the Regimental Commander visited and witnessed the young Scott in action that the CO was reimbursed and Scott's enlistment backdated."

"You're right, I never knew that," said Scott quietly.

"From then on, Scott excelled in everything he did, Royal Marine Officer training, the hardest there is. He was fast tracked. The thirty-two week programme cut down to 12 for him. After a year, he was promoted to Lieutenant. From there, he went through Special Forces selection and broke half the records, joined the SBS and soon after was selected to join K Squad."

"Quite a history!" exclaimed George, turning to Scott.

Scott merely shrugged his shoulders, uncomfortable with the attention.

"And you guys have no issue with the killings?" asked George.

"As long as they're a threat to the sovereignty of the country and a threat to others lives, no."

"Our agreement and the conditions of operation are prerequisites. No sanctions can ever be issued that do not meet these criteria. Those two conditions are controlled by us and one by the K Squad just before a kill" added the PM.

"What if I don't believe I can give the order for a sanction?"

"I'll accept your resignation and have you out of here in the next two minutes," said the PM with a completely straight face. "We are constantly at war and these guys," pointing to Scott. "Keep it as far away from our front door as they can. We hit first and we hit hard."

"Fair enough," replied George. "I'm in."

***

Kelly sat in the outer office waiting for Scott, wishing she knew what was being said. She had found out after the door shut that the PM was also in there. The plot was thickening. Her thoughts, however, were interrupted by her cell phone ringing.

"DS Kelly," she answered.

"Hi, Operations Room here, I have a Rosie on the phone asking for you."

"Put her through please."

"Hello?"

"Hi Rosie, it's Detective Sergeant Kelly here."

"Hi, I just called to tell you I was on my way but they said you're not here, you're in London."

"Yes sorry, it's a long story, I can't really talk now but if you give me your number I'll call you back shortly, is that OK?"

"Of course, my number is 07673245480."

The number should have alarmed Kelly but with everything going on she missed why an American having just landed would already have a British cell phone number.

However, Clark hadn't missed the error and almost punched fake Rosie as she began to recite the recently purchased pay-as-you-go number.

***

"I honestly don't think there's a link between the rapes and the attempts to kill me. Why get me thrown in jail when you want me dead, it just doesn't make sense."

George and the PM also struggled to understand the rationale. Scott was right which of course left the dilemma that he was being targeted because he had been recognised.

"Maybe somebody recognised you from the TV footage and knew who you were."

Scott suddenly remembered the mysterious Rosie.

"Actually somebody did. An American girl called Rosie but I don't know who she is or how she fits in."

"Maybe you killed someone she knew and is getting her revenge?"

Scott looked at George deadpan. "If I kill somebody the only person who knows it is dead."

George looked into Scott's eyes and could see he was not in the least bit exaggerating.

"Perhaps we should ask Kelly?" suggested Scott. "She spoke to Rosie."

"Get her in, but before she comes in, no mention of the K Squad." The PM checked for agreement and receiving two nods asked for Kelly to be sent in.

Kelly entered the room and after getting over her initial nervousness quickly updated the three on Rosie. With little new information, the PM quickly concluded that no-one had any idea what was going on and until they did, lives were at risk. As long as Scott was around, people were likely to get killed in the crossfire.

"Scott, you're not going to like this but I'm afraid the best thing we can do is get you out the country until we find out what's going on. Too much is at stake if you have been recognised."

Scott had arrived at the same conclusion. Staying there meant innocent people could die.

"I agree Sir. Perhaps I should head home until you give me the all clear or let me know if I can help."

The PM, understanding Scott's offer perfectly, nodded subtly. If they found out who was behind it and they were not on sovereign territory, Scott wanted the sanction.

Scott checked his watch, it was 11.45 a.m.

"Sir. I'm rather keen to get going. You couldn't help get me on the Qantas flight leaving at 12.20 could you? It just catches my connection in Hong Kong."

"No problem," he replied picking up the phone. As he replaced the receiver, the PM had a thought.

"DS Kelly, perhaps you should accompany Scott. He may have information that he doesn't even know is relevant."

Scott looked at the PM as though he couldn't be serious.

"I agree," said George. "DS Kelly, is that OK with you?"

"Yes, of course," she stammered. She had never been to Hong Kong and had to admit that the thought of the mysterious and very attractive Scott disappearing from her life had surprisingly disappointed her. "If it's OK with Scott that is."

"Scott will do as he's told," said the PM, picking up the phone and instructing a change to two seats in first class.

As they made to leave, the PM had some final words.

"And Kelly, not a word to anybody about where you're going, not even your boss."

Twenty five minutes later, Scott and Kelly stepped on board Qantas Flight 30 direct to Hong Kong. Scott was under one of his many assumed names. Although he had a number of identities and covers, he surprisingly had no passport in his own name. Kelly on the other hand carried a letter from the PM which he assured her would more than cover for her lack of passport.

Chapter 26

Kelly had been in such a rush that she had forgotten to call Rosie who sat with Clark in the Range Rover willing the phone to ring. With every second that passed, Clark felt sure Rosie had blown it. Just as he was concluding he'd have to dispense with her services, her phone rang,

"Hello," she answered.

"Hi Rosie, it's DS Kelly."

"Hi there, I was beginning to think you'd forgotten about me."

"Sorry got caught up, anyway I have Scott here with me and he's wondering how you know him?"

Rosie froze, not knowing what to say. Clark, listening in, also had no idea what to say and with no idea what else to do, reached over and switched the mobile phone off.

"What the hell are you doing?" protested Rosie.

"Not fucking up. Hold on," Clark dialled a number and after only two rings it answered.

"Hello," responded Walker tentatively.

"It's me," reassured Clark.

"What's wrong?"

"We've got a line to the target but we need to know how the girl is supposed to know him so we can reel him in."

Walker thought for a second, conscious he did not want to be on the phone long, even though it was a pay as-you-go phone he'd never used before.

"Tell her to say she knows who his father was but won't discuss anymore until they meet face to face."

"Will he buy it?"

"Yes."

Both hung up, having been careful not to mention any key words.

Clark relayed the detail to Rosie before switching her phone back on.

It rang less than two minutes later.

"Sorry, I ran out of juice," explained Rosie.

"No problem wasn't sure if it was me or you," said Kelly, still excited that she was sitting on the phone in a First Class seat on her way to Hong Kong.

"I'll just pass you to Scott, hold on."

"Hi Rosie," said Scott cheerily.

"Hi Scott."

"So Rosie, how do you know who I am?"

"I don't know you as such but I know who your father was."

The silence that followed had Rosie wondering whether the line had been cut off.

"You know who my father was?" repeated Scott slowly.

"Yes, but I'm not saying any more over the phone. We need to meet."

"But I'm on a plane, I've already left the country."

"That's OK, tell me where you're going and I'll meet you there," suggested Rosie.

Without referring to Kelly, Scott gave her the details. The mention of his father was too much for rational consideration.

"We'll be in Kota Kinabalu tomorrow morning at 11.05 a.m., arriving Dragonair from Hong Kong."

"I'll see you there," promised Rosie before ending the call.

Clark was ecstatic. The gamble had paid off. Now all they had to do was get to Kota Kinabalu, wherever the hell that was before 11.00 the following morning. He picked up his PDA and checked the flight schedule software and discovered two things - it was a fucking long way away and he had no chance by commercial airline of beating Scott to it.

His next call was to an air charter brokerage firm he had an account with.

"I need to get to Kota Kinabalu asap from London."

"No problem Sir, just let me check…"

After a few minutes of clicking at her keyboard the operator returned.

"It's very short notice Sir but we can do something."

Clark recognised the international code for it's a fuck you price.

"We can get you a Gulfstream G550, a very luxurious and comfortable jet that will get you there in thirteen and a half hours. Now would you like the quote to include a return leg?"

Clark just wished she'd get to the punchline.

"Is there much of a difference?"

"Actually no it's pretty much the same price."

"I'm sorry but I am in a hurry here, can you just give me the fucking price?"

The operator dropped the polite tone.

"$320,000, Sir."

"Holy shit, I don't want to buy the fucking thing."

"Sir do you want the plane or not?"

Clark had no option.

"I want it."

Clark proceeded to give the woman his account details, an account held by a small private company registered on Grand Cayman, one of the world's more famous tax hideaways. Known only to himself, the million dollar fund instantly dropped by a third.

Clark would be in the air within the next sixty minutes and taking the time difference into account, should be landing thirty minutes before Scott.

Chapter 27

Walker perked up as Clark relayed what was happening. It was time to get his life back. He knew it was pointless phoning Freeman. He did what he was told. He needed to speak to Dan Baker. He was the only one with the influence to change the others' minds and he was fairly sure that Dan was the one who would have wanted him dead in the first place. If he could turn Dan, the others would follow.

Walker purchased a new Pay-As-You-Go phone and inserting the phone charger into the cigarette lighter socket, dialled Baker's number.

Dan was in the middle of a breakfast meeting with Chicago's more influential business owners when his cell phone rang. Not recognising the number, he almost didn't answer but very few people actually had his number, so he answered.

"It's Walker," said Walker confidently. He wasn't going to let Dan intimidate him.

"Hi William, what can I do for you?" asked Dan cheerily with no hint of any animosity. He motioned to his guests that he had to take the call, stood up and walked out of the room.

"Cut the act Dan. I've got you're man."

Finding a quiet corner.

"Listen you fucking cock sucker, do not fuck with me."

"Why? What you going to do? Kill my wife? Oh sorry, you've already done that!"

"Don't give me that shit. If you'd wanted her alive you'd have taken her with you. We've done you a favour."

Walker should have known better, Dan's mind worked very like his own.

"Do you want him or not?"

"Of course," replied Dan trying to remain calm.

"Call off your dogs and I'll make him disappear. I am not a threat to you. I fucked up, you killed my wife. I've paid for my error," reasoned Walker.

Dan considered Walker's proposal.

"Well, whether you've been punished or rewarded is debatable. But I'll call you back with an answer."

"I'll call you back. This phone's going in the bin. You've got 30 minutes."

Walker opened the car window and tossed the phone in the nearest bin and put his foot down. He wanted to be as far away from it as possible.

Dan dialled Ernst.

"Max Ernst here."

"Any news?" barked Dan.

"I'm sorry Mr Baker, nothing yet but we'll find them. We know Walker is still in the New York area but as for the target, we're still looking."

"Fuck. I need a conference call, I'll hold."

Ernst knew that meant get the other four on the phone immediately.

He quickly opened up a secure line and started dialling.

"Mr Freeman, Mr Baker wishes a conference call immediately."

Freeman dismissed everyone from his office and waited.

Ernst dialled a number in London,

"Mr Russell, Mr Baker wishes a conference immediately."

Charles Russell was CEO of Transcon EMEA, covering Europe, the Middle East and Africa. Charles dismissed his lunch guests and waited.

Ernst dialled a number in Geneva.

"Mr DuPont, Mr Baker wishes a conference immediately."

Andrew DuPont was the Chief Financial Officer of Transcon Global and the CEO of Transcon Banking and had within his control more monies than any other individual ever born.

Andrew left the conference room where he had been holding court and went back to his office to wait.

Ernst's final call was to Hong Kong.

"Mr Astor, Mr Baker wishes a conference immediately,"

Peter Astor was CEO of Asia, Australasia and South America. However, with the explosion in the Eastern economies, particularly China and India, the South American division was about to merge with the North American one, which would create Transcon Americas under Henry's control.

Peter moved from his lounge to his study and waited.

Ernst with all five now holding pressed a button and instantly connected the five most powerful men in the world. Five men who had known each other since University. Five men who had taken an oath to do whatever it took to rule the world. Five men who had killed to get what they wanted. Five men who would do anything to protect their world.

Thirty minutes later, Walker called Dan back.

"If you get it done with no more issues, you have a deal," said Dan.

"Thank you," replied a relieved Walker.

Chapter 28

United Airlines 922 powered down the 11,500 foot runway of Dulles International Airport. Ashley Jones had not stopped since leaving the scene of her kidnapping earlier in the morning. A race back to her house had been followed by a mad dash back to the airport to catch her flight at 9.31 a.m. As she took seat 2A, at the rear of the First Class section, she kicked herself for all the things she hadn't done. She hadn't cancelled her BA tickets nor checked in with her boss before leaving in case there had been any new developments. Although she re-assured herself that he would have called her had there been any.

She also realised that she had told the policewoman she would already be there. Damn, she thought. Ashley didn't mind spending $11,000 on her tickets for First Class but she did mind the exorbitant cost of using the sky phones, ten bucks a minute was just wrong. She knew herself it was ridiculous but principles were principles. She reluctantly lifted the phone and placed the call.

"Parkside Police Station."

"Can I speak to Detective Sergeant Kelly, please?"

"I'm sorry she's not available just now, would you like to leave a message?"

"Yes please, Can you tell her Rosie said she'll arrive tonight and see her tomorrow. Goodbye."

Ashley's abrupt end to the call caught the operator off guard. The mention of the name Rosie would set off a number of procedures but due to her hanging up, would fail. All he could do was dial Kelly's number and reaching her voicemail, leave the message.

Twenty eight seconds thought Ashley checking her watch. $10 per minute and $10 connection, $20, she'd check her statement. It wouldn't be the first time they'd tried to stiff her for more money. With nothing left to do, she reclined in the large armchair and tried to sleep.

***

Kelly finished her champagne and looked across to see if Scott was still catatonic. He had not spoken to her since the call with Rosie had ended half an hour earlier. They had been allocated seats 4D and 4G, side by side, and thanks to the space in First Class they were offered some privacy from the other passengers.

"Are you sure you're OK?" asked Kelly.

Scott simply nodded, his thoughts firmly on what Rosie had said. She knew who his dad was, past tense. The dad he never knew would remain so. Scott had always harboured the dream that one day his father would find his long lost son.

A hand appeared on his thigh, startling him. He looked up to see a concerned Kelly looking straight at him.

"What?" he asked.

"You can tell me what's wrong, it won't go any further," she said reassuringly.

"I don't even know who you are," he said despondently, "I only know you as DS Kelly, I don't even know your first name."

"And I don't know your surname."

"I've told you before I don't have one. And don't you have a first name?"

"Jane."

Scott smiled for the first time since the call.

"Jane?" he looked into her eyes.

"It suits you, you look like a Jane."

Kelly let the silence fall easily between them. She could see Scott was struggling to decide whether he could trust her and she felt he should make his mind up himself.

After what seemed an eternity, Scott looked at her and said, "OK."

"OK, what?" asked Kelly.

"I'll tell you about me but it's reciprocal, you tell me about you."

"Deal."

"OK, you first," said Scott smiling.

Jane smiled and rose to his challenge without complaint. "My name's Jane Kelly, my dad was a policeman and his father before him was a policeman. My mother was a housewife. I have no hobbies or interests, boyfriends, husbands or lovers. I live for my work. It consumes me."

"Is that it? Your life in a nutshell?"

"All twenty eight years," replied Kelly with a sigh.

"What a waste," said Scott quietly.

Kelly took offence at her life being referred to in that way and turned away.

"No, the husbands, boyfriends or lovers, you're a very attractive woman, Miss Jane Kelly."

The redness came quickly as Kelly blushed at the compliment.

"Thank you," she replied bashfully. "So come on then, what about you?"

"Not quite as simple. My mother and I were shipwrecked just off the coast of the island of Borneo. I don't know why we were the only survivors but can only assume it may have been that my mother could swim. Amazingly, most of the seafarers in that part of the world can't. Anyway, I'm told we spent days at sea before finally washing ashore on a small remote island. The islanders were wonderful and immediately took us under their wing. My mother was very weak and didn't recover. She died a few weeks later. I was only three months old. The islanders had offered many times to take my mother to the mainland for help but she had begged them not to, only saying that her life and mine were in danger. She begged them to raise me as their own and made them promise her that they would. Not thinking she would die, the elder of the island agreed, thinking it would calm her down and let her rest. The next day she died, it was almost as though his promise allowed her to die in peace. The elder, having made the promise, could and would not renege on it. I was taken into his house and raised as one of his own and am in his eyes his son. The only details my mother left were the name of a lawyer in Singapore. Papa, my adoptive father, contacted the lawyer but he simply took contact details for Papa and informed him the only thing he had was a letter that I would receive at a later date. He knew however it did not contain any detail as to who my mother was nor who my father was."

"God, I'm so sorry."

"That's OK."

"But Rosie knows who your father is?"

"Was."

"Oh."

"But the islanders are wonderful and treat me as their own," said Scott more cheerfully.

"So what's the link to the Prime Minister?"

"That's something we can't discuss but let's just say I sort of work for him."

"Oh, OK," replied Kelly struggling to hide her disappointment.

"Time for sleep, I think," replied Scott reclining his seat into a fully flat bed, the discussion having reached a natural end.

Kelly wasn't ready for sleep, her mind still racing as to who the mysterious Scott really was. With no one else to talk to, she picked up the sky phone and dialled her messaging service. She had three messages. One told her Harris was OK, nothing more than a slight concussion, her second was her mum asking when she'd be home for dinner and the third was the message Rosie had left via the police station which told her nothing more than she already knew which was strange.

Hong Kong was a blur. As the doors opened, Scott and Kelly had to sprint to catch their connection, jumping on board the Dragonair flight with only seconds to spare. Scott was becoming increasingly nervous as he took his seat. In three hours, he would find out who his father was.

Chapter 29

As flight UA922 taxied to the jetway at Terminal Three, Ashley switched her phone on. The familiar welcome tone from Nokia was followed by the tell tale messaging sound. She quickly opened the text and found she had three voice messages. The gaze from the stewardess warned her to not even try using the phone before the door was opened but Ashley couldn't care less. Her DIA badge sat ready to ward off even the most scary of the stuck up waitresses. As she dialled the number and put the phone to her ear the stewardess immediately rose and walked towards her. Ashley let her get all the way next to her before flashing the badge and mouthing 'back off'.

As she listened, the first message caught her attention. One of her colleagues had called just after her flight had left to ask if she had any idea where Jackson could be. He hadn't been seen since he had climbed aboard a mysterious helicopter just after he had spoken to Ashley. Ashley knew this was major. Jackson was head of the SSB, the most clandestine unit of all the US's intelligence operations. His location was tracked at all times. If he had been kidnapped and was being tortured, the lives of hundreds of agents were at risk. Alarm bells would be ringing across the intelligence community as they tried to understand which operations could be compromised and decisions made as to which of those should potentially be cancelled.

The next call she hoped would tell her he was OK and it had all been a huge misunderstanding. Unfortunately, it was not. The next call was actually concern over where she was. She had not responded to the earlier contact and she was now considered missing. Could she please call as soon as she received the message as a matter of urgency. Oh shit, Ashley thought. That call had been over four hours earlier. Before calling in, she checked the third message, hoping Jackson had been found.

It wasn't, the third message was the most shocking of all. It was one of her colleagues calling to let her know that Jackson's body had been found. One bullet had killed him instantly and the time of death suggested it was not long after his disappearance. Concern over operational integrity had been reduced but not discarded. However, Ashley's disappearance was raising eyebrows and lots of questions were raining down from on high. The message went on to say that even the Secretary of Defence had been asking questions. The final comment from her colleague was that there was some very strange shit going on and wherever Ashley was, she should watch her back.

Ashley walked off the plane in a daze. The news of her boss' death was hitting her hard. She didn't even notice the two men standing at the end of the jetway, at least not until they each grabbed one of her arms.

"What the hell are you doing?" protested Ashley loudly struggling against the men's grip. They were taking no risks and were most definitely going to leave bruises behind as they refused to let go.

"Don't do that Miss Jones, there's no need to make a scene."

"Make a scene! Let go of me right now!"

"We're FBI officers," the man on her right flashed his credentials. "Please don't struggle."

Ashley relaxed and as she did their vice like grips relaxed also. Although only enough to minimise bruising.

"Do you know who I work for?" she asked.

"Yes we do and our orders are to get you back to the US asap."

"On whose orders?"

"A warrant has been issued for your arrest, your flight details were picked up and we were sent over from the embassy to escort you home."

Ashley stopped walking and pulled away from both men,

"Arrested for what?"

"Murder."

"Of who?" she asked in disbelief.

"Brigadier General Robert Jackson."

Ashley just looked stunned and refused to move. A third man joined the group and motioned for them to enter a doorway near the jetway, a set of stairs led to the tarmac below.

Ashley pulled back harder,

"I'm not going anywhere. We're not in America, you can't just pull me off a plane and detain me in a foreign country."

The third man stepped towards Ashley and made a point of invading her personal space, spittle from his mouth sprayed onto her face as he spoke.

"You forget we're not anywhere, we're airside in an international airport terminal. You will be refused access to the UK as you are currently wanted for murder. Now you can come with us quietly or not, it doesn't bother us."

Ashley knew resistance was futile. If a warrant had been issued for her arrest and a flag attached to her passport, she would be refused access and deported anyway. At least this way she could clear things up quickly, prove her innocence and help catch Jackson's killer.

"OK."

Ashley was led down the stairs and bundled into a van before being driven to a waiting jet. The small jet's engines were already turning as they boarded and five minutes after they had buckled their seat belts, the wheels were being retracted as the Cessna Citation X made its way back to the US. It was the fastest private jet on the market and would cover the distance in less than six hours. They would land, thanks to the time difference, only an hour after they had left.

***

"Where is she?" asked the agent standing at the immigration desk. "The flight landed over 40 minutes ago."

"She should definitely have been here by now," agreed his colleague checking his watch.

The agent walked over to the MI5 liaison officer who had secured their access to the immigration hall. MI5 was the name commonly used for the Security Service, the UK's domestic intelligence service.

"It seems she's a no show."

"Can't be, she was definitely on the plane," replied the MI5 officer.

"Look for yourself. The hall's nearly empty and there's no one else coming out."

Nodding, the MI5 officer picked up the phone and talked for several minutes before replacing the receiver.

"It seems there's been some confusion. The air marshal on the plane has just filed a report about a young lady being arrested as she stepped off the plane. He had gone over to check the disturbance but backed off when the men identified themselves as FBI agents from the embassy and arrested her for murder…"

"Shit!" interrupted the American agent as he set off running to grab his colleague.

"What?" shouted the MI5 agent after him.

"They weren't the FBI…we're the only two FBI agents at the Embassy!"

"Oh shit!" mumbled the MI5 agent.

***

Clark checked the time, it was exactly 5.00 p.m. in New York. He dialled a prearranged number but was met by a busy tone. He tried again and the phone rang once.

"Hi, it's me," answered Walker standing in the middle of New York's Union Station at a public pay phone.

"You OK?" asked Clark.

"Yes," replied Walker. "Everything's fine. If we kill him, we're in the clear."

"Thank God."

"Thank Dan Baker," explained Walker.

"I've been thinking, what if he asks Rosie how she knows him before we get a chance to kill him?" asked Clark.

"Hmm, good point. Put Rosie on the phone."

Clark pulled Rosie's headphones from her ears and ignoring her moans at interrupting her movie, handed her the phone.

Clark could only watch as Rosie nodded almost constantly as Walker spoke to her.

"OK, will do," she said as she handed the phone back to Clark.

"Hi," said Clark.

"She knows enough to keep his attention until you get out of the airport."

"So are you going to tell me?"

"No because the moment you kill him, you need to kill her. The information I gave her would sign your death warrant."

Clark looked across as Rosie laughed and giggled at whatever inane rubbish she was watching. It was the only time she had shown any emotion since they had met. He had never met a more emotionless person but then professional assassins were a strange breed.

"OK," replied Clark. Usually, killing an attractive woman would have caused him some anxiety but Rosie's attractiveness was somehow dulled by her chosen profession.

**

Ernst received the breakthrough almost immediately. Walker was proving very lax following his deal with Baker, mentioning a number of keywords in his conversation with Clark.

The NSA housed more supercomputers and mathematicians than any other organisation in the world. The computers monitored every airwave and electronic communication device known to man while the mathematicians ensured that no encryption device remained unbroken so they knew exactly what was being said. Phones could be tracked by the SIM card alone, meaning the phone didn't even need to be switched on to be tracked. Crimes were being solved simply because mobile phones were at the scene of the crime. Their owners traced and arrested. Ernst's call to the Deputy Director of NSA (and soon to be Director) had ensured the priority for key words had been changed. Al Qaeda was no longer top of the list. William Walker, Joseph Clark and Rosie Diaz were now the number one words on the NSA's watch list. Any communication anywhere in the world with any of those names would automatically be grabbed and analysed.

At 5.05 p.m., the call placed from Gulfstream G550 jet registration G-FRDS had been analysed and placed as a high alert. The flight plan for the aircraft had already been tracked and the LLC company who had chartered it, traced back to Joseph Clark. By 5.07 p.m., the Deputy Director of the NSA had sent an email containing an audio copy of the call and the subsequent flight info to Ernst.

Ernst listened to the call and instantly wished he hadn't. The reference to death warrant for what Walker had said to Rosie registered immediately. Although how a Scottish guy who had died twenty odd years earlier threatened Transcon, he had no idea. However, to be safe, he called the deputy director and suggested that they both stay quiet about the audio and merely say they had tracked the plane. He agreed without hesitation, even though he hadn't listened to the audio. After the day's events, listening and having the ability to listen, were just as lethal.

At 5.09 p.m., just as Ashley was being escorted onto the Citation jet, Ernst walked into Freeman's office and dismissed everyone in the room with a wave of his hand.

Freeman waited until the door closed before speaking. For Ernst to do what he had just done, something big must have happened.

"Well?"

"I've got them and know where they're going."

"Where?"

"Kota Kinabalu."

"Where the fuck is Kota Kina… what?"

"Just off the island of Borneo."

At the mention of Borneo, Freeman went white and fell back into his seat.

"What?" asked Ernst concerned at Freeman's reaction.

"It really is him. I kept thinking it's been some horrible mistake and that it wasn't him." Freeman stopped talking.

"But?" prompted Ernst, intrigued by what he was hearing.

"Their boat was sunk off the coast of Borneo."

"There's something else. The Secretary of Defence just called. Rosie Diaz doesn't exist."

Freeman, recovering from one bombshell, could hardly believe the second.

"What?"

"Rosie Diaz was an alias being used by a Defence Intelligence Agent called Ashley Jones. We've just picked her up and are flying her back here."

"Why's the DIA involved in this?"

"That's the thing, they're not. They have no idea what she's doing. Officially, she was working on a case involving arms deals by some two bit pimp in Washington."

"Get Baker on the phone," instructed Freeman as he divulged the latest information.

Two minutes later Baker was fully up to speed.

"OK, first we need to know everything about this DIA agent. Where she was born, who her parents are, everything. Second, we need to know what this DIA agent knows and whether anyone else knows it. We could torture her but we'd never know it was the truth. She needs to meet our target."

"But Clark's going to kill our guy," interrupted Freeman.

"So stop him," explained Baker irritated by the stupidity of the question.

Ernst nodded to Freeman, he'd take care of that.

"So how do we get them to meet?" asked Freeman.

"I don't know, just do it but when we've got our information make sure that everybody who knows anything dies. In four weeks I am going to be president and nothing is going to stop me." Baker hung up.

Freeman looked at Ernst who was already picking up the phone.

***

The Unit's Citation X had just cleared UK airspace when they received a change of plan. The captain immediately swung the plane around 180 degrees and powered the engines to full speed. They didn't need to worry about conserving fuel anymore as they'd have to refuel anyway.

Ashley watched her captors carefully as the plane swung around, none offering any reason for the sudden change.

"Where are we going?"

"Change of plan, nothing to worry about," replied the man spraying spittle as he spoke.

"But we're not going to America?"

"No. You've been cleared of the murder."

Although innocent, Ashley was still relieved to hear she was no longer a suspect. It was devastating enough to have lost her mentor, never mind being blamed for his murder. At least now she could get to back to Cambridge.

"So where are we going?"

"Kota Kinabalu."

"Where the fuck is that!? Take me back to London immediately!" she demanded.

"I'm sorry my orders are to take you directly to Kota Kinabalu."

"Why the hell are you taking me there?" demanded Ashley.

"To meet the man you're looking for."

Ashley was surprised by the response. Only Jackson knew where she was going and that she was trying to meet someone. Nobody else other than the policewoman in Cambridge knew that; but she only knew her as Rosie.

"How do you know who I was meeting?"

"I don't. The orders came from way above my pay grade and told me to get you there asap. They've even arranged in-flight refuelling to get us there quickly."

"In-flight fuelling! How long will it take to get there?"

"The pilot reckons about ten and a half hours. We'll land just after 4.00 p.m. local time."

Ashley knew something was very wrong. The only way people knew where she was going was because Jackson told them and he had been kidnapped immediately after their conversation. Alternatively, they had been listening to her calls. However, surrounded by four heavies on a small private jet, she could do little but go along with whatever was happening.

She had known from the moment her arms had been grabbed that these guys weren't the FBI. FBI agents were all college graduates, impossibly polite and followed procedures to the letter. The three goons who had picked her up were not part of that club. She had guessed CIA at the time, certainly ex-military and assumed they had been called in due to Jackson's knowledge of American intelligence operations to ensure all leads were hunted down as potential threats. However, none of this related to her activities, although she was beginning to have her doubts. Something at the back of her mind was telling her that Jackson wouldn't be dead if she hadn't recognised a young man from a long and distant past.

Chapter 30

Chagos Archipelago was one of the most remote places on the planet. Its location, in the middle of the Indian Ocean over 1000 miles South of India's most southern point, ensured it would remain so. No commercial aircraft or ship ever came within hundreds of miles of it and to all intents and purposes, the small group of islands simply didn't exist to the majority of the world's population. However, that did not stop it becoming one of the most valuable and important assets of the US military. Diego Garcia had proven its worth many times over during the ongoing war on terror. Its location offered an excellent platform for the US military's strategic bombers.

The island lay within the authority of the British Overseas Territories and had been leased to the US in 1970 until at least 2036. With one of the longest runways in the world, its capabilities were unrivalled when combined with its absolute seclusion. It even provided an alternative landing site for the space shuttle.

The B-1R rolled onto the largest lump of concrete in the Indian Ocean. It was the latest development of the B-1 Lancer supersonic strategic bomber and unlike its predecessor, it only required two crew. The two pilots had had little notice of the last minute training exercise. However, this was not unheard of during the testing stages of prototype aircraft and neither thought anything of it as they powered up the four Pratt & Whitney F119 engines, each capable of over 35,000 lbs of thrust. The new engines allowed them to push through the sound barrier without the use of afterburners. This new development was called supercruise and allowed the B-1R to travel at super sonic speeds for significantly longer. It also meant that their maximum speed had almost doubled to MACH 2.2. As the engines powered the aircraft down the runway, the final orders were still being received. Their target was 3,000 miles away and thanks to a supercruise of MACH 1.5, would be reached in just over 2 hours.

With only ten minutes to their target, the final mission directions came through. A target designation was received automatically by the offensive weapons system and in conversation with the aircraft's autopilot, the two systems agreed on a slight deviation in their heading to maximise potential success. The pilots, oblivious to the target designation, could only watch as the systems took control.

Five minutes after their change of course, a slight tremor in the airframe alerted the pilots to a weapon being launched. The AIM-120D quickly accelerated and before they could see the intended target for the dummy weapon, the auto pilot had already commenced their turn for home.

The AIM-120D, or 'slammer' as it was referred to by pilots, fundamentally changed the role of the supersonic strategic bomber. With a 112 mile intercept capability, the air to air slammer made the B-1R the largest fighter bomber in the US Air Force. Although still not capable of dog fighting its way out of trouble, the MACH 2.2 capability more than made up for that deficiency as did the long range capability of the slammer.

As the aircraft settled into its homeward journey, the offensive weapon system alerted them to a successful mission with a 'target destroyed' message. Both congratulated themselves although they did wonder why; other than powering the engines for take off and ensuring a safe landing, neither had done very much.

***

A hundred miles away, a Gulfstream G550 registration G-FRDS had ceased to exist. The impact of the MACH 4 missile would have sufficed without the 30lb high explosive. It had been about to commence its descent to Kota Kinabalu and was still some way out over the South China Sea when it literally vaporised. Small sections of wreckage plummeted 35,000 feet spreading themselves across miles of empty ocean, ensuring nobody would ever know the cause of its destruction.

Ernst had certainly ensured that Clark wouldn't kill their man. Ernst had also left a message for DS Kelly. Asking his secretary to pose as Rosie, she had explained that she was unavoidably detained and would not arrive until 4.00 p.m..

Ernst, for the first time that day, actually felt as though he was in control of the situation.

Chapter 31

Scott and Kelly stepped off the Dragonair Airbus A320 and walked down the steps towards the arrivals gate at Kota Kinabalu International Airport. Scott's emotions had run wild for the previous few hours. Apprehension, grief and excitement were competing with each other. However, none of them could beat the nerves which had taken hold. Kelly had tried to calm him down but realised that whatever she said would not help. Switching her phone on, a familiar chirp alerted her to two new voice mails.

Listening to the first, she wasn't sure how to break the news. Scott was going to have to wait another few hours. The second was even less welcome. Her Chief Constable had heard of her foreign junket and had secured her a seat on the next flight back to the UK in less than an hour. He felt sure that a day in Scott's company was sufficient to glean any potential leads.

Scott could sense something was wrong as he watched Kelly's expression as she listened.

"Bad news I'm afraid." Scott's heart fell. "Rosie's delayed until 4.00p.m.," continued Kelly.

"Oh, OK. Well, we'll just hang about here until then," replied Scott, hugely relieved.

"There's more, it seems my Chief isn't happy with my globe trotting and wants me back. I'm booked on the 3.45 p.m. to Kuala Lumpur and then onto England."

Scott was surprised at how genuinely disappointed he felt at Kelly's imminent departure, particularly before Rosie's arrival.

"Do you have to go before Rosie arrives?" asked Scott.

Kelly blushed at the thought of Scott being disappointed in her leaving so soon. She couldn't believe the effect he was having on her. Kelly considered the justification for ignoring her Chief's instructions and reasoned that Rosie was in fact a potential suspect. In fact, it would be remiss of her to leave without checking she was not involved in the attempts against

Scott's life. She knew it was weak but what the hell. She smiled at Scott and dialled Parkside to speak to the Chief.

"Parkside Police station."

"Hi, it's DS Kelly. I need to speak to the Chief Constable please?"

The line went quiet for a second. The officer who had answered the call was obviously considering the request.

"Are you sure, I mean is it really urgent DS Kelly?"

"Yes, it's very urgent," she winked at Scott.

After what seemed an eternity, the officer came back on the line.

"I'm just going to put you through, please hold."

"Kelly, this had better be fucking good," exclaimed a weary sounding Chief.

Hearing the sleepy voice of the Chief suddenly reminded Kelly about the time difference. She held the phone away from her face and mouthed 'oh fuck' before answering.

"Of course Sir," she sounded as confident as she could as she quickly worked out it was only 3.30 a.m. in England.

"Rosie's been delayed and I don't believe I should leave before I check out who she is."

"That's it? That's the reason you called me at this godforsaken hour? Kelly do whatever the fuck you think is best. Just let me sleep." The Chief hung up.

Kelly cursed herself for being so stupid. She was sure the Chief had been impressed with her and all that had just been blown in one stupid call. If only she had waited until later.

Scott was looking at her questioningly wondering what had happened. She looked so glum.

"I can stay."

"What, is my company that bad?" Scott looked at her, wounded.

"No, God not at all, it's just I forgot about the time difference."

"Oh shit, sorry, I should have realised. I'm so sorry," said Scott.

"That's OK, he'll get over it," she hoped. "But at least I get to meet the mysterious Rosie!"

"True, now what to do for 4 hours?" beamed Scott.

Kelly could think of lots of things she would like to do with Scott, none of them however would have been in the least bit professional. She had also come to the stark realisation that Scott did not see her in remotely the same way.

"Coffee?" she suggested, hoping he'd surprise her and say 'no, let's get a room and get naked.'

"As long as it's decaf," he replied. Scott's thoughts were firmly fixed on the meeting he was going to have in four hours.

"Which way?" asked Kelly, hiding her disappointment.

Before Scott could respond, a tannoy announcement caught their attention.

"Could any visitors waiting on a Miss Rosie Diaz due to arrive at 11 a.m., please come to the airport manager's office please."

Scott didn't hesitate and grabbed the nearest airport employee demanding the directions to the office. After sprinting through the terminal, Scott crashed through the manager's door.

"I'm waiting for Rosie," explained Scott to the terrified manager whose door had almost come off its hinges.

The manager just thrust a phone towards Scott.

"Hello?"

"Rosie's dead!" said Walker by way of introduction.

Chapter 32

Walker tried the number again.

"I'm sorry, but the number you are calling is unavailable."

He had been trying to get hold of Clark for more than 30 minutes and just kept getting the same annoying woman with her posh English accent. He tried again.

"I'm sorry…" he hung up, something was wrong. He could sense it. Just like he had that morning when he left the house in time to avoid the assassin sent to kill him. Clark was gone and if Clark was gone, the deal was off and he was a dead man.

He nervously looked around the bar he had taken refuge in. Monday night was football night and large groups had gathered around each of the three screens. Walker didn't know much about football but had lived in New York long enough to realise that the "Go Giants" chant meant the New York Giants were playing. The payphone was located next to the toilets through a door at the end of the bar. A glass panel in the door meant that Walker could see right through the bar and back to the entrance. Unfortunately, when the door opened, the noise was deafening but the game was too close to allow for toilet breaks and he'd only been disturbed once since he'd arrived.

With no sign of any tails, he dialled international directory enquiries and got the number he needed. He paused before dialling to consider what to say. He knew his life was on the line and this was his last chance to save it.

"Do you speak English?" asked Walker as the phone was answered.

"Yes of course, how can I help you?"

"I need to speak to the airport manager urgently."

Walker had used his most commanding authoritative tone in the hope of cutting through any of the usual 'can I help, I'm sorry he's not available' bullshit. It worked.

"I'll just put you straight through."

Twenty seconds later, the manager came on the line. Walker kept his eye firmly on the bar's entrance, nobody had entered.

"This is the manager, how can I help?"

"I believe there's been a terrible accident and I need to speak to visitors waiting for a plane to arrive," said Walker who had changed his tone to one of despair.

The manager instantly knew what he was referring to. He had just had a call from his air traffic controllers about the Gulfstream jet that had failed to arrive and was not responding to any call signs.

"Of course Sir, what are their names?"

Walker explained he didn't know and waited impatiently as the tannoy message was delivered. His eyes were firmly fixed on the front door of the bar as he waited. Nobody entered.

***

"I've got a hit," shouted one of the operators.

"Where?"

"New York, Upper West side, 108th and Amsterdam."

Mike Hunter, the head of The Unit had taken over control of the operation personally. Ernst's threat to redeem himself within 24 hours still rang in his ears. He had taken a risk by narrowing the parameters that the NSA systems would use to alert them. Previously, thousands of calls had been pouring into them and by the time they got a hit, Walker had already gone. He had guessed that Walker would try to call Clark again on the plane. Fortunately, that had paid off. Walker had been careless and obviously didn't realise that just dialling the number alerted them. He had been there for twenty minutes when the systems hit the jackpot and found a phone dialling the watery wreck ten thousand miles away, less than three miles from where Hunter was standing. With two teams standing by, Hunter took no risks and sent both teams to the bar.

Ten minutes later, the first team pulled up outside the bar and radioed back to Hunter.

***

"Rosie's dead!" repeated Walker.

"I thought she was just delayed until four?" replied a disbelieving and very upset Scott.

Walker was taken aback by Scott's response. They had managed to contact him and changed the time. They must have got hold of the real Rosie; that would explain the change in plan.

"No, she's dead. I'm very sorry to break the news but her plane crashed." Walker kept a close eye on the front door as he quickly worked out what to do.

"But she was going…"

"To tell you who your father was," interrupted Walker. He knew he had been on the phone too long but he needed to get Scott away from The Unit's trap and under his control. He realised there was no going back. Baker wanted him dead, no matter what happened. Baker obviously blamed Walker for fucking up and not making sure she and her baby died all those years ago. Walker realised his only hope was to help Scott. Only Scott could stop Transcon, he just didn't know it.

"Yes," replied Scott wistfully.

Walker heard a door opening and quickly looked towards the entrance. It was shut. He then remembered the doors to the toilet were behind him. It must have been somebody coming out of there. Had his mind not been trying to work out where to try and meet Scott, he may have wondered why somebody came out of a toilet that nobody had gone into.

"I know who your father was also," offered Walker.

"Who?" asked Scott eagerly.

Walker felt the cold steel press against the back of his head, just before he felt nothing.

The man with the silenced pistol replaced the receiver and calmly left the way he had come in, through the ladies' toilets. He closed the window quietly behind him and was miles away before the body of William Walker III was discovered. His faceless head causing more than a few beers to be expelled violently by the unsuspecting football supporters.

***

Scott stood in the manager's office holding the dead phone. He had heard the spit of the pistol and the subsequent wet splat and realised that another lead to his father was gone. Whatever was going on had nothing to do with Scott's work and everything to do with his past. A past that he had no knowledge of, nor links to.

"So what are we going to do?" asked Kelly breaking the silence.

"We're going to start taking control," replied Scott firmly. Without asking the manager, he placed a call. He needed to get hold of a few things.

Chapter 33

Kelly had protested from the moment Scott had told her she was leaving. She had to stay. If, as he believed, there were two Rosies, she should be there. After all, Rosie had spoken to her. She also was not entirely convinced of Scott's conclusion that the strange message telling her that Rosie was still on the way meant there were two Rosies. She wanted to wait around until four to find out. Scott, however, was having none of it. Enough innocent people had died. Kelly was leaving on the 3.45 p.m. flight as originally planned. His previous friendly and affable persona had been replaced by a serious don't mess with me approach.

Scott waited until Kelly's flight's door had shut and pulled away from the gate before quickly making his way to the VIP area of the airport. The only flight due to land at 4.00 p.m. was a small private jet, origin unknown.

***

Ten hours and two inflight fuellings later, the specially converted Cessna Citation X touched down at Kota Kinabalu. Following instructions from the control tower, it moved towards the VIP area and was instructed to wait for immigration officials who would clear them for entry as soon as possible, obviating the need to enter the terminal.

Within seconds of coming to a stop and powering down their engines, a small white minibus approached the jet, stopping near the steps that were in the process of being lowered. Two customs officials dressed immaculately in pristine white uniforms exited the van and boarded the plane.

***

Ashley watched as the two young men approached the aircraft. They looked almost identical in their white uniforms. In fact, Ashley realised they were identical. Completely identical. How sweet she thought, twins taking the same job and working together. The sight of them put a smile on her face for the first time in hours. The journey had been tortuous. None of the men had spoken, no food or drink had been offered. All had sat in almost complete silence. Ashley had tried to make conversation to try and work out who they were but it seemed none wanted to give anything away as her attempts were met by simple grunts or shakes of the head.

The two young officials boarded and Ashley was surprised at how thoroughly their eyes scanned the plane, darting from one occupant to the next with remarkable speed. Ashley was in no doubt that these guys were extremely capable immigration officials and only wished the same vigilance were practised in American ports of entry.

"Four male passengers, one female and two aircrew?" checked the first immigration officer with the captain. His English was perfect, another surprise for Ashley.

"Yes, that's correct," replied the captain taking a form from one of the officials.

"Passports?"

As she heard the request for passports, Ashley saw her chance. She also noticed the other immigration official seemed to be taking a great interest in her, his eyes constantly swinging back to her. She was used to being looked at, it was something she had grown used to. But for some reason she did not get the feeling he wanted her in that way.

"Ahem, I've got a problem."

All eyes spun towards Ashley as she spoke. The spitter looked at her as if he'd quite happily slit her throat if she didn't stop talking.

"I've not got my passport," she continued.

"I think I've got it here," said spitter as he looked at a pile of papers in front of him.

As he did so, the man sitting next to Ashley placed his arm behind her and grabbed her shoulder and, out of sight of the officials, began to squeeze tightly. The message was clear, shut up or else.

The immigration officer immediately noticed the look of pain on the young woman and made an instant decision.

"I'm afraid you'll have to come with me Madam," he instructed.

"She's not going anywhere," instructed the spitter menacingly, pulling a gun from under his paperwork and aiming it at the twins.

His men instantly followed and before the two officials could move, they were staring down the barrels of four guns.

The twins, much to Ashley's surprise, seemed unfazed by what had happened and was stunned to hear the first's reaction.

"Well, I'm sorry gentlemen but I'm going to have to refuse your entry on this occasion," he said before turning towards the door.

The distraction was all his twin required. Four spits emitted from the pistol that had appeared in his hand as his brother turned away. Each spit from the silenced FN 5.7 resulted in a red mist from each of the four men's heads. The speed with which it had happened was beyond comprehension as was the accuracy of the four shots. All having hit perfectly between the men's eyes. Ashley had seen some impressive shooting in her time but that was in a different league.

The captain had thrown his arms in the air, the second he realised what was happening and just in time to stop a bullet being fired into his skull.

"Rosie?" asked the first twin, who had somehow fired the fourth shot straight through her captor's eyebrow from his hip. Unbelievable.

"Umm…yes," replied Ashley not thinking it was the time to enter into name semantics.

"Would you like to come with us, please. Scott is waiting for you."

Both had replaced their pistols and one was offering his hand towards her.

"But that was incredible," she said taking the hand offered to her.

"Bit sloppy actually I'm better with a rifle, Kirk's the pistol man," explained the twin who had taken out three men with perfect head shots before they had even reacted.

Ashley could only shake her head in disbelief as they led her from the plane and down into the waiting minibus. Before she had a chance to ask where they were going, the minibus slowed down and the man she didn't think she'd ever meet, jumped in the open side door of the minibus.

Chapter 34

Todd Nielsen stepped out of his front door as the Lincoln Town Car came to a halt at the bottom of the grand staircase that swept up towards him. He quickly climbed into the back of the car and relaxed as they wound their way down the long gravel driveway. Todd could never stop himself looking back at the sprawling estate, set in the heart of the Bradley Farms district, the address of Washington's rich and famous. He knew that buying the estate had raised more than a few eyebrows and questions as to how he could afford the $14 million price tag.

Todd Nielsen had not led the privileged life of his neighbours. In fact, his life had been far from privileged; a childhood in the slums of Detroit, a slut of a mother and drunk of a father. His role models were few and far between. However, all that had changed on his seventeenth birthday. Todd, despite his teachers' protestations and numerous offers of scholarships, had joined the army. His intellect allowed him to rise through the ranks quickly and before long, a posting to the Pentagon found him working for the Defense Appropriations Committee as an adviser to its members. It was there that Todd had met the man who would transform his life. Dan Baker, the young ultra rich senator from Florida had somehow managed to gain a spot on the most powerful of all appropriations committees, defense. Being of a similar age, the two quickly became friends and Todd Nielsen discovered a new world. The world of the rich. Travel was by private jet, helicopter or limousine. Food at the most exclusive restaurants. Drinks in the most exclusive clubs. Women, the most beautiful and refined who literally threw themselves at the wealth. Todd had found his true calling, money.

Dan took Todd under his wing and in return for swaying more than a few votes towards Transcon Corporation companies, Todd's career took off. Promotions came thick and fast, offers from private sector organisations arrived almost daily but behind the scenes, Dan was always directing and two years earlier had secured Todd the ultimate role, the US Secretary of Defense. Transcon in the meantime had become the single largest supplier to the US armed services. Todd didn't for a minute doubt to whom his ultimate loyalty lay, he just looked forward to the day when that man was in The White House. His dilemma would then be resolved.

No sooner had they sped through the automatic cast iron gates than his phone had rung. The screen said 'Private Caller'.

"Hello?" he answered, checking his watch. It was only 6.45 a.m.

"It's Ernst, we have a problem."

Before saying another word, Todd pressed the button to raise the screen between himself and the driver.

"What now?"

"We've lost the target."

"What do you mean you've lost the target?" spat out Todd. "I put my ass on the line giving you the information I gave you yesterday, never mind losing a few of my staff."

"The captain of our plane called. Two immigration officials boarded and blew our operatives away and then took the girl."

"Was our target with them?"

"No, they were identical twins and he isn't a twin."

"What did the captain do?" asked Todd.

"He turned his plane around and got the fuck out of there, dumping the bodies over the sea."

"Shit, have you spoken to Dan?"

"No, I'm hoping you can help us get a lead on them before I call him."

"You have access to everything I have. Is there nothing from NSA?"

"Nothing. But there is one thing."

"What?" blurted Todd.

"The trip to meet the Prime Minister. We went over the tapes, it seems he was meeting someone we know."

"Who?" interrupted Todd impatiently.

"George Cunningham, your new counterpart in the UK."

Todd smiled. "I'll give him a call, right away!"

Chapter 35

As Scott boarded the minibus, the first thing that struck him was that the woman was like no Rosie he had ever met. She was stunning. His eyes were transfixed on the young woman and for the first time in his life, he was lost for words. The twins, however, had different concerns. They were in the process of speeding away from killing four men on the runway of an international airport, dressed in stolen uniforms and driving a stolen van. Something they felt sure would not be rewarded. .

As they streaked across the concourse, they could see the real immigration officer on his way to the Citation X. Kirk put his foot down harder on the accelerator. Kyle, his twin brother kept staring back towards the small jet and much to his relief watched the doors being shut and the plane start to move. The immigration officer came to a stop where the plane had sat only seconds earlier. It seemed the pilot was as keen to avoid the issue of the killings as the twins were.

Ashley was still trying to work out what the hell was happening as the minibus came to a screeching stop next to a helicopter. Without any preamble, Ashley was herded onto the helicopter and within two minutes, the Malaysian Army was short of one Augusta Westland A109 light observation helicopter.

With the twins taking the controls, Scott and Ashley sat in the back of the helicopter and finally had the chance to talk.

"So who are those guys?" asked Ashley pointing forward.

"Colleagues of mine, Kirk and Kyle," answered Scott awkwardly. He didn't really know what to say. She knew who he was, he just didn't know how to ask.

"My name's not really Rosie, you know, it's Ashley," blurted out Ashley, feeling the need to dispel the myth that was Rosie.

Scott looked at Ashley and smiled. He liked the name Ashley.

"Anyway, I'm sure you want to know more about you than about me," she added, blushing. She couldn't believe how nervous he made her feel. The likeness with his father was uncanny. She couldn't remember much about him other than his strong handsome features and even then Scott seemed to have accentuated those features.

"No, that can wait. Tell me about you just now. I'd rather wait until we get home before you tell me," replied Scott. He was relaxing in her company and wanted it to remain that way. He loved listening to her talk, and watching her. She really was quite beautiful.

Ashley nodded and started with her full name, although quickly pointed out that only Ashley was real. Her surname was her adopted one but she would explain that later. She told him about her life and couldn't believe how easy and natural it was to tell him things she had never told anyone before; how she really felt about her parents, how much of a snobby bitch her mother was and the weed that was her father. She told him about how she enjoyed telling them she was quitting Harvard to go join the navy and how she loved her job although was sufficiently vague for Scott not to know what she really did.

"So that's me. Ashley Jones at your service," she finished and catching Scott's eye, quickly turned away and blushed again.

An awkward silence fell between them as neither knew what to say. The feelings they felt looking into each other's eyes were not something relative strangers normally discussed. Fortunately for them both, a gesticulating arm in front caught their attention.

Following the direction of the arm they looked down to two small islands surrounded by the crystal clear azure waters of the South China Sea. One island was nothing more than a sand bank, its only vegetation, a small grouping of trees. The other island was much larger although still small in real terms. Its green lush centre framed by pristine white sands. Ashley immediately fell in love.

"I'm afraid there's nowhere large enough to land, we'll have to hover over the water and you'll have to jump in," instructed Kyle.

Ashley looked at Scott and before she could ask, Scott explained.

"They're not coming with us, they need to get the helicopter back and they've got a job to go to."

"Oh, OK," replied Ashley, wondering how low they could hover over the water and whether shark documentaries were filmed near there.

"Don't worry," said Scott putting his hand on her knee. "There are no sharks or anything."

Had her expression been that obvious?

"Well none that I can see!" he added looking down at the waters and laughing.

Ashley pushed his hand away from her knee and looked down apprehensively. The helicopter inched closer and closer to the sea and island as Kirk carefully manoeuvred as close as he dared. Finally, he gave the instruction for them to go.

Scott opened the door and stepped down onto the skid rail, he then turned and offered his hand to Ashley who took it and slid across the seats and joined Scott on the skid rails. The crystal waters were only inches below them and as she jumped, she pinched her nose. Scott burst out laughing as he watched Ashley land in two feet of water with her nose held tight and eyes firmly closed. The water barely reached knee level, despite them being 30 yards from the shoreline.

A slap landed on Scott's upper shoulder. "Thanks," she said before storming off towards the shore.

"Sorry I should have told you it was really shallow," apologised Scott.

The twins, Kirk and Kyle were already out of sight by the time Ashley and Scott reached the beach and the waiting islanders who were looking at the pair with some confusion.

"What are you doing back? And who's this?" asked the elder of the group pointing towards Ashley.

"It's a long story Papa," replied Scott, helping a stunned Ashley from the water.

***

Kirk and Kyle spun the helicopter around and sped off. They really needed to get the chopper back before it was missed. From the day they were born, the two had never been separated nor stopped competing with each another. The two had joined the army on their seventeenth birthday and their instructors had literally sat back and let them train each other. No other recruits could come close to the time and effort the twins put into their training in a bid to outdo each other. Active duty saw no change as they each battled to outdo the other. Commendations racked up as the two proved themselves to be fearless warriors. A stint in the paras was followed by the SAS before the inevitable offer to join K Squad was issued. They readily accepted, on one condition. The two had to remain together, no separate missions. With some reluctance, the condition was met. However, not once in the previous three years was it ever regretted, the two made a formidable team.

Chapter 36

The deputy head of the Strategic Services Branch, Colonel Frank Renton, closed the door behind him as he entered the conference room. The room full of SSB department heads was already in silence, a sombre mood had descended upon the whole department following the murder of General Robert Jackson. The conference room sat in the heart of the DIA's ultra secretive headquarters located within Bolling Air Force Base in the Southwest corner of Washington D.C. Before he had a chance to speak, the door opened and Vice Admiral Jim Banks entered the room. The individual department heads stood up in unison to salute the DIA Director.

"Please sit," he instructed. "I just wanted to pass on my condolences to you all and to assure you that we are doing everything in our power to bring the killers to justice."

A murmur of appreciation reverberated around the room as the Vice Admiral took a seat.

Frank Renton stood and addressed the group, a group which included some of America's hardest and most dangerous individuals; a group which any sane person would do everything in their power not to upset. The SSB solved America's problems before they arose. They worked with whoever helped them secure the national security of the United States and destroyed anyone who threatened it. Snatching, torture and execution were everyday occurrences for the US's most secret intelligence force. As congress restricted the CIA's activities, the president relaxed the controls on the SSB. America was at war and the SSB was on the frontline.

"Firstly, I'd like to thank Admiral Banks for joining us this morning, it is very much appreciated." Frank looked at Admiral Banks and nodded. "Now, down to business. What do we have?" he turned to the ten department heads and waited for their updates to flow but they all just looked at one another.

"Anything?" asked Frank after a few seconds' silence.

"I'm afraid, all we know is that he boarded a non descript helicopter after we resolved the kidnapping of Agent Jones," offered the Head of Covert Ops. "The trail dies there."

"We have no obvious link to any case," offered the Intel Head.

"What about Agent Jones' kidnapping, any link?"

"That's the strange thing, we've lost contact with her, she's disappeared."

Before Frank could respond, a knock at the door interrupted the meeting. The door opened and Admiral Banks was summoned from the room. Just as the meeting was about to recommence, shouting from the outer office interrupted proceedings again. Although nobody could make out what was being said, it seemed Vice Admiral Banks was extremely fucked off about something. A slamming door was quickly followed by a knock on the conference door. The door opened and a Brigadier General in full US Army uniform entered the conference. A few groans could be heard around the room, instantly drawing a cold stare from the new entrant.

"Good morning gentleman. To those of you who don't already know me, I am Brigadier General Joshua Brooks, formerly Deputy commanding general of the US Army intelligence and Security Command and now Head of SSB."

Frank was stunned, Admiral Banks had all but told him the job was his. Obviously the shouting had been the Admiral being informed from someone higher up the chain that Brooks was the new boss. Brooks was infamous within the intelligence community, a stickler for procedure. Nothing happened unless the requisite forms were completed and approved. His appointment into the SSB was beyond bizarre; it was absolutely nonsensical. This was the one area in the whole of government where documents had to get lost. Deniability was an absolute necessity.

Not waiting for the none existent welcomes, Brooks continued. "I understand feelings will be running high over the death of General Jackson. However, let me assure you that we cannot let his death detract from our duties. We have to maintain the security of our nation."

Unperturbed by the continuing silence, he continued.

"On that note however, I wish to put out as an absolute priority the warrant for the arrest of Agent Ashley Jones."

He smiled inwardly as the room ignited.

"What the hell for?" shouted Frank above the protestations, silencing his colleagues.

"It would seem Miss Jones fled the country shortly after the killing of General Jackson and managed to slip through Heathrow undetected. Nobody has any idea where she has gone. However it seems that shortly after deserting her assignment, a large sum of money was deposited into her bank account, with a similar sum deposited shortly after General Jackson's body was found. She is now our number one suspect in General Jackson's murder," explained Brooks.

Silence reigned as the men digested the information, particularly the reference to large sums of money, a damning piece of evidence that would be difficult to refute. All knew she had expensive taste but not all knew about her extensive trust fund and they struggled to doubt the evidence that had just been disclosed.

"I think that will do. Back to work men and finding Agent Jones," ordered Brooks before turning and leaving the conference room. He walked down the corridor and barked at his new secretary to clear General Jackson's personal belongings from his office immediately. He'd return in ten minutes and would expect them all gone. Between the sniffs into her already drenched handkerchief, the secretary nodded her understanding and with tears dripping from her eyes, she went about emptying the belongings of a boss she loved dearly into a brown cardboard box.

Brooks stepped into an empty office and dialled a number.

"Secretary Nielsen's office," answered the woman.

"Can I speak to him please, it's Brigadier General Joshua Brooks."

Before he finished speaking, the secretary put him through.

"Josh, how's it going?"

"Great thanks, how's Banks?" asked Brooks.

"He'll calm down sometime in the next decade but don't worry about him, how'd it go?" asked Nielsen brushing aside the screaming match Banks, the DIA Director, had had with him over Nielsen moving Brooks into his command structure without his knowledge.

"Did he offer to resign?"

"Yes but I refused. Look, I know you want his job but just bide your time. It'll be soon, I promise."

"OK, OK, anyway it worked a treat. The money deposits got them suspicious."

"Excellent but I can't emphasise enough that we need to find her asap and I do mean yesterday asap."

"Got you, one thing though. If anybody goes snooping, what about the transfers? Will they hold up?"

"Of course, the money's there and some genius has played about with the timings, backdating the payments to fit the timeline. Also, the money comes from a source that if they look hard will lead back to a small but extreme fundamentalist terrorist group. Sorry, got to go, my other phone's ringing."

Brooks was left holding the phone as Nielsen ended the call abruptly. He walked back to his new office and found it devoid of personal belongings as instructed. His next job would be to sack the secretary, he'd bring his old one over from INSCOM. She knew just how he liked things. It was all about order, everything had its place.

***

Nielsen answered the other call.

"Nielsen."

"Hi. How'd it go?" asked Ernst.

"Let me assure you within five minutes every member of the intelligence community of the United States and her allies will be finding Ashley Jones as a top priority. The SSB will call in every favour they have to track down the mercenary bitch who killed their boss." As Nielsen spoke, he noticed a message pop on his screen. George Cunningham was holding for him. "Can you just wait a minute Max, I have George Cunningham holding for me."

"Of course." Ernst had just had his first piece of good news for hours and was happy to savour the moment.

Two minutes later, Nielsen came back on the line and explained what Cunningham had told him.

"Excellent, did he say what he wants?"

"Just what was discussed at the last Bilderberger, whatever that was."

Max Ernst smiled. If what Cunningham had just given them was right, the least they could do would be to ensure George Cunningham MP would become Prime Minister at the next election.

The Bilderberger was a conference held every year attended by the most influential men on the planet. The topics of discussion were a closely guarded secret but what was not was the abundance of future world leaders whose attendance at the conference preceded their rise to power. The Bilderbergers made and broke political careers and Transcon shareholders wielded more power than any when it came down to final selection. Although more than a few Bilderbergers would have revolted at the idea of a Transcon shareholder running for President had they known of Dan Baker's real source of money. Transcon, according to more than a few, were becoming just a little too powerful.

"Are our friends down at Diego Garcia still looking for some targets to practice on?" asked Ernst already knowing the answer.

Chapter 37

The introductions and explanations took up the rest of the afternoon and by the time Scott had a chance to talk to Ashley, it was time for dinner. Papa, understanding how important the occasion was, had arranged for Scott and Ashley to dine alone in private and had organised everything for them. Ashley had been swept away to a neighbour's home while Scott had joined Papa to prepare for a dinner that would change his life. Scott spent one minute in the shower and much to his surprise most of his time trying to decide what to wear. Jeans didn't seem right but neither did trousers. Bermuda shorts and a crisp linen shirt won in the end.

Ashley had a much easier decision. With no luggage, she was at the mercy of the islanders and spent most of her time in the shower, scrubbing away any remnants of the four men's brains. Stepping out of the shower, she found a floral skirt and small white blouse laid out for her, she quickly dried herself and put on the simple clothes. Checking herself in the mirror, she couldn't help but wish her suitcase had made it with her. However as she entered the room, a hush descended. The simplicity of the dress highlighted Ashley's natural beauty and the women were already certain she was the one for Scott. Although she tried to convince them otherwise and that she didn't even know him, she couldn't help but think the idea was not exactly repulsive. After all, he was absolutely gorgeous and had a body to die for.

***

The B-1R rolled down the runway and loped into the sky, both pilots commenting on how the plane felt notably heavier than it had earlier, something they would have to file in their mission report. Neither could believe that they were back in the air so soon after their previous mission. However, having flown so little over the last few months, the experimental plane had been temperamental at the beginning of its flight testing. So they were more than happy to get to play with the new aircraft again. Their mission brief was already in the system and the computers quickly calculated their optimal route and with over 3,500 miles to target, it automatically requested a tanker to top them up for their return. The plane banked hard and accelerated to its cruising speed of over 1.5 MACH. Time to target flashed up, 3 hours 42 minutes.

***

The sight of the small table sitting on the deserted beach as the moonlight streaked across the water's surface took Ashley's breath away. Two burning torches sat either side of the table and completed the picture postcard scene.

"It's lovely," said Ashley as Scott offered her a seat.

Scott couldn't help thinking the same of Ashley but thought it best to keep it to himself.

"Thank you. I've always thought this a very special spot," replied Scott as he pushed Ashley's seat in behind her.

"It's like we're the only two people left in the world," said Ashley as she looked out across the empty sea.

Scott nodded as he looked at Ashley, his eyes falling as the torch light shone through the thin blouse and clearly outlined her perfect braless breasts beneath the cloth. Ashley turned back towards Scott and caught a bashful Scott's lowered gaze.

Used to being watched, Ashley was surprised when the thought of Scott's gaze sent a tingle though her body.

"Well, perhaps we better get started," suggested Ashley taking a sip of wine.

Scott remembering the point of the meal agreed with an enthusiastic nod.

***

The B-1R, much to the pilot's surprise, began to reduce its height and slow down as it closed in on the target area. Both checked the computers to try and ascertain what the target was, both had expected an air to air trial similar to the earlier one. However, the drop in height suggested there must have been a target down below, an uninhabited island or a drone ship. Neither however could see anything below other than an island off in the distance but lights were clearly visible so it couldn't be that.

***

"I was born in a small village in Scotland, my parents were the housekeeper and gamekeeper on a large estate owned by a brilliant young businessman. I was only four when they died."

"I'm sorry to hear that," interrupted Scott.

"I'll come to that," said Ashley dismissively, before continuing.

"Although I don't remember much, I do remember how wonderful they were. I was very loved and it seemed their lives revolved around me. Even the businessman doted on me and called me his special little girl. I think it was about a week before my parents died that I met you."

Scott almost choked on his wine at Ashley's mention of their childhood meeting.

"We've met before?" he spluttered.

"You were only a baby. The businessman had visited unexpectedly with a woman and you were with them. I don't know who she was but I know everything seemed very tense. The businessman was shouting and screaming at my parents, something he had never done before and even told them they were fired. I'll never forget it because my mother cried all night when we got home. The next morning, the businessman apologised but things were never the same. You had disappeared and the businessman left, never to return. One week later, a car crash claimed the lives of my parents. I was saved and adopted by the Jones's. I kept thinking the businessman would come and rescue me, his special little girl, but he never did."

Scott just stared helplessly at Ashley, as confused as he had ever been. Minutes passed before he spoke,

"So who am I?" asked Scott.

"You were the little baby boy who visited the businessman."

"But how do you know that?"

"Your birthmark, the small cluster of moles that look like a star, I remember it vividly."

"But I'm sure lots of people have something similar."

"Yes but they all don't look exactly like their father."

"Who?"

"The businessman. You are the spitting image of him, only perhaps slightly more handsome. But he was definitely your father."

"So who was he and who was my mother?" asked a frustrated Scott.

"No idea," replied Ashley shrugging her shoulders.

"I've tried to track him down but nobody seems to remember him, it's almost like his very existence has been wiped from the face of the earth. The estate was destroyed in a fire shortly after my parents died and the locals don't remember much and no records exist to show who owned it. It's all very bizarre."

"Maybe you just dreamt it," ventured Scott quietly.

"I don't think so," replied Ashley pulling the small heart shaped locket from her neck, presenting it to Scott. "Because he made me promise to give you this if I ever saw you again."

Scott held the locket carefully in his hands and slowly opened it. His heart sank as the locket revealed nothing more than two empty spaces where photos should have been.

"It's always been like that," explained Ashley quickly. "But he told me it contained much more than you could see with your eyes."

"What does that mean?" asked Scott carefully checking every square inch of the locket.

"I had no idea until one day, during a science lesson, when we were using a microscope I thought perhaps..." Ashley took the locket back from Scott, turned it over and pointed to the hallmark stamp. "This wasn't what it seemed. I magnified it 100 times and discovered the name of a bank and a list of numbers."

"So what was there?" asked Scott eagerly.

"No idea, I've tried a few times but hit a brick wall each time. They won't discuss the account with anyone but the account holder."

"Who's that?"

"They won't tell me but I guess you or your father!"

"So that's it, the only link to my past is an empty locket," Scott stood and taking the locket from Ashley walked to the sea's edge. For a second he contemplated just throwing the locket as far out to sea as he could but before he could do anything, Ashley was beside him and holding his arm. He turned and looking deep into her eyes held her like he had never held anyone before. The intimacy of their embrace was overwhelming, a tear ran down Scott's cheek as he nestled his head against Ashley's.

The tear rolled and dropped onto Ashley's shoulder. She turned her head as he turned to her and their mouths met. Before either could control the moment, their mouths parted and both eagerly accepted each other. Tongues entwined and made it clear both wanted more. Hands strayed and within minutes both lay naked in the sands, the water lapping at their bodies.

Scott's hand ran down the length of Ashley's body, his fingers brushing the baby soft skin, firm succulent breasts and erect nipples. A tremor passed through Ashley's body as the anticipation of what was to come rushed through her body. The fingers carried on down and brushed over her flat toned stomach and down towards her neatly trimmed bikini line. Scott lightly brushed past before quickly moving down her thigh. The disappointment of his deviation evident in her deep moan as they kissed. Noting the urgency, he retraced his route and found her ready and waiting, her legs parting slightly as his hand moved towards her. The wetness of the salt water did not mask her own wetness. Her hand felt for him and urged him towards her parting legs.

He thrust into her, her head sweeping backwards as she caught her breath, her hands clawing at his back as she struggled to contain the tremors surging through every nerve ending in her body. Ashley had had sex before but nothing like this. She almost always felt awkward and clumsy but not here, on a beach with almost a complete stranger, it felt like the most natural thing she had ever done.

Scott's taught muscular body thrust and thrust but the gentleness of the strokes seemed in contrast to the force being used, almost similar to the waves that seemed to lap against them despite the obvious power of the sea. With every stroke, they moved closer and closer to the inevitable explosion. Scott, sensing the final countdown, pulled Ashley closer. A powerful woman, she had never felt more vulnerable nor more secure in her life, nor had she ever fallen so quickly for a man. As her orgasm came, her body spasmed as the shockwaves of pleasure rocked her and continued as Scott exploded inside her, sending another wave rocketing through her.

Scott lay looking into her eyes as they stayed anchored together, neither wanting to break the moment. Neither wanting to broach how it happened and certainly not wanting to admit it was a mistake. Neither believed it was but it would take one of them to say it wasn't and neither was brave enough.

***

Both pilots looked on in horror as the plane suddenly jerked upwards. The only visual target in front of them was the inhabited island and whatever bomb had just been ejected by the weapons system was huge. The plane had lightened dramatically since its drop and before they could see what had happened the bomber turned sharply and accelerated back to Mach 1.5.

The bomb was actually two bombs, two MOAB's which was an acronym for Massive Ordnance Air Bomb or more colloquially the Mother Of All Bombs, each weighing a massive 21,700 lbs. and delivering the equivalent of 11 tons of TNT each. The blast was further enhanced by its detonation 30 feet above the ground, clearing a huge swathe of ground. Those not incinerated by the blast were as likely to be suffocated by the vacuum-like aftermath as the oxygen was literally sucked from the air.

Twenty seven seconds after their release, the two bombs exploded over the island one to the north and one to the south. The flash of the explosion lit up the sky for miles around, although the blast effects were felt only locally. The over ground explosion ensured that only those who witnessed the flash would ever know an explosion had taken place. As with its predecessor, the daisy cutter, designed to clear ground for helicopter landing sites, the MOAB left no crater or obvious sign of detonation and more importantly no tremors would travel through the earths crust alerting scientists across the world.

The two pilots could only assume a terrible mistake had been made, both had tried to stop the release but the system did not allow manual override. It seemed the future of warfare protected against human error not system error. They radioed in their concerns and were told not to worry, they must have been mistaken. The island was most definitely uninhabited and were reminded of their mission brief, no radio contact no matter what. With fuel running low and over a thousand miles to land, they started to slow in anticipation of their imminent inflight refuelling. A refuelling that had been cancelled when they called in their concerns, no tanker would meet them and one of the USAF's newest and most expensive planes would crash helplessly into the ocean miles from anywhere. Even if the pilots ejected, they were outside helicopter range and hundreds of miles from any shipping lanes. The sharks would have them long before the first airplane could pinpoint their location.

***

At twelve twenty three a.m. local time, the islanders lives ended, their bodies incinerated in the 2700°C heat of the blast. Nobody suffered. One second they were laughing and joking, the next they simply didn't exist. Their flesh and bones disappeared into the wave of superheated air, scattering their ashes across the island.

Part Three

Chapter 38

Ernst clicked on the link in the email and waited as his screen changed to an almost totally black screen. Only small orange pixels stopped him thinking his computer had inadvertently shut down. He checked his watch. According to the mail, something should happen at around 11.23 a.m. local time, in only a few seconds. The KH-13 satellite was the latest increment in the keyhole programme under the control of the NRO, National Reconnaissance Office and to all intents and purposes did not exist.

Its relentless eye watched everything, through any weather, day or night and was able to read the tiniest of details down to the serial numbers on dollar bills, it missed nothing. Its orbit had been diverted earlier in the day using its inbuilt rocket boosters, at exactly 11.20 p.m., the island had come into view and would remain so for the next ten minutes. Only people receiving the email would have access to the pictures. Even the NRO were blacked out from their own satellite feed. Unknown to them, the power failure message was one issued by the NSA agents who had taken control of the feed on behalf of Ernst.

Ernst stared at the screen while keeping an eye on the clock, it was now 11.24, nothing had happened, the picture had not changed. After another ten seconds he was contemplating making a call when his screen almost blinded him, the intensity of the flash had not lessened on its 9000 mile journey through cyberspace. By the time Ernst had recovered, he was sure the flash had broken his screen as the previous darkness had returned minus the orange pixels.

He picked up the phone.

"What happened?" he demanded.

"Total and complete devastation. We've just run a heartbeat check, everything on that island is dead," replied Hunter proudly from the Unit's headquarters.

"What the hell is a heartbeat check?" asked Ernst, more confused.

"The satellite can pick up rhythms. We just checked the island and not one rhythm matching a heart rate has been found."

"But there's no fire?" questioned Ernst looking at his screen

"The bomb effectively blows itself out, the flash draws in oxygen and once burnt leaves an inert mix of air that quite literally extinguishes the fire."

"So he's dead."

"Everything on that island is dead! And I mean everything," replied Hunter emphatically.

Chapter 39

Both stared in disbelief across the sea at the darkness of the island. Silence had descended but neither knew, as their ears were still pounding from the shockwave, what had hit the smaller island over a mile away. Ashley grabbed Scott's arm and pulled him towards the small boat that had transported them from the main island to their seclusion and safety on the smaller island. Both were still naked, their clothes strewn across the island from the blast. Scott knew nobody had survived. He had seen enough death to know what the body could take. The heat and blast had reached them over a mile away, even half submerged in the water. As they lay in their post coital clutch, they had felt the searing heat and the power of the blast. Scott was not in any rush to get back to the main island. He knew nothing awaited him there. His current life like his past was now history.

"We need to check," explained Ashley. She too knew it was pointless but they had to check anyway.

"I know," nodded Scott. "We need to check," he added robotically.

Ashley grabbed whatever clothes she could find and handed Scott his shorts. Placing her dress over her head, she climbed into the boat. Scott rowed with purpose, the anger rising with every stroke, the power of the strokes building, pushing them closer and closer to the main island. Within ten minutes of the explosion and three minutes after the satellite had dipped behind the horizon, Scott and Ashley landed on the deathly quiet beach.

The devastation was complete, the palm trees had been reduced to smoking stumps. The earth was scorched and the inhabitants of the island had simply vanished. Only the charred remains of their huts gave any indication of life on the island.

Scott dropped to his knees and struggled to gasp for air, the enormity of the situation finally hitting him. Ashley tried to comfort him but nothing she could say or do would help with the despair that Scott felt. Everybody he had ever loved had perished and he knew it was his fault. Something about his past was making somebody do anything in their power to kill him. If he hadn't come home, his Papa, his cousins, his friends would still be alive.

Scott stood and turned back towards the small boat, grabbing Ashley's hand as he walked and directing her into the forward seat. Scott sat in the middle seat and began to row, the island staying in his view as he rowed towards the mainland.

Ashley realised Scott wanted silence but wondered where they were going. It had taken over an hour by helicopter to get to the island. They must have been at least a hundred miles from the mainland.

"Where are we going?" she asked softly.

Scott didn't miss a stroke as he responded.

"War!"

Chapter 40

Ernst switched his screen off and for the first time in two days relaxed. The nightmare was over. Whatever the target had on Transcon was gone, vapourised in a cloud of superheated flames. After a few seconds, he picked himself up and walked across to Freeman's office, ignoring the secretary's protestations that he was on the phone to the President of Russia. He barged in. Freeman, holding a phone to his ear, struggled to hide his contempt as Ernst strode towards him.

"What the hell are you doing Max?" he asked covering the mouthpiece.

Ernst ignored the question and cut off the caller, leaving Freeman holding a dead phone.

"He's dead!"

Freeman who was struggling to contain his temper, instantly smiled.

"Excellent, have you called anyone else yet?"

"Nope, I thought you'd want to let them know."

"Thanks, oh and can you phone Yuri back to apologise. I got cut off, I'll call him later," asked Freeman as Ernst left the room.

"Will do."

As the door closed, Freeman picked up the phone and dialled *1234. The combination dialled his four other partners, connecting him securely to their personal mobiles wherever they were. Even the NSA with all their supercomputers couldn't listen in.

"Good day gentlemen," announced Freeman breezily to the group.

"Hold on!" responded Baker gruffly.

Everyone remained quiet as they waited for Baker.

"Sorry, just had to ditch my Secret Service detail."

"Well, I'm pleased to announce that our problem is resolved, all trace of our little problem has completely disappeared."

"Excellent," responded Baker.

"Exactly how did he disappear?" asked a wary Charles Russell in London.

"I believe we blew him up on an island somewhere near Malaysia," replied a triumphant Freeman.

"Oh fuck," replied Charles. "That was us! George Cunningham's just been on the phone ranting about some fucking island that just blew up. He started screaming we had screwed him one time too many."

"What exactly did he mean, screwed one time too many?" asked Baker, the chill in his voice changing the tone of the conversation.

"I'm not sure, Dan. That's all he said," replied Charles tentatively, knowing it would not satisfy him.

"Well I suggest you get on the phone and find out exactly what the fuck he meant and remind him who's boss."

"Will do."

"NOW!" screamed Dan.

Dan had always been the boss, the other four had realised almost from the day they met that they would follow him wherever he went. Dan was destined for greatness; his looks, charm, authority and ambition would take him wherever he wanted to go and for Dan that was The White House. He was going to be the President of the United States of America, no matter what it took. First he needed money, nobody got anywhere in politics without money and for Dan that meant having more money than everyone else that stood against him.

Everything he had ever planned had the goal of Dan Baker being inaugurated as president. First, he needed partners that would help him achieve that and that's where Henry, Charles, Andrew and Peter came in. They were the brightest of the intake into Yale along with Dan and would help him build his fortune, not that they had any say in the matter. Dan's family had all been Bonesman, members of the ultra secret Skull and Bones Society and he arranged for the four to be tapped and become one of fifteen new members. Over the following couple of months, Dan cultivated friendships with his four selected partners and even formed a secret sub society, the Acton Group, with only five members.

The Acton Group met in complete secrecy and over the next four years, Dan groomed his partners into hatching a plan to take the business world by storm. All had initially balked at the idea but over time, Dan broke down their sensitivities, helping them to understand that they could have anything they wanted, it just depended on what they were willing to do to get it. Dan had chosen well and before long, was organising the breaking of legs to ensure Charles won a cross country race or a car crash to ensure Andrew retained his debating crown. None even raised an eyebrow. Success and power as Dan had taught his partners was a very powerful drug; once you'd had it, you'd do anything to keep it.

Dan had known he was different from an early age. Things just didn't affect him the way it did others. Guilt, remorse, empathy were feelings he just couldn't comprehend. However, he quickly realised that whether he felt them or not, he had to at least act them. People reacted strangely when you didn't. It was at the age of twelve that Dan finally realised what was wrong within when he read an article that used the mnemonic CORRUPT to help describe the criteria of a sociopath.

C - cannot follow law
O - obligations ignored
R - remorseless
R - reckless
U - underhanded
P - planning deficit
T – temper

Ever since, Dan's favourite saying had been one by an English historian, Lord Acton, after whom he had named his secretive group. He had famously stated that, power tends to corrupt; absolute power corrupts absolutely.

"In one month, I'm going to be President of the United States and nobody is going to stop me. Do we all understand?" continued Dan to the small group.

To a chorus of yeses, he continued.

"Firstly, whatever happens, I don't like the pompous tit in the UK and if what George is crying about is true, perhaps we should just get rid of him."

"Who, George?" asked Freeman surprised. George had been groomed for some time to be the next British PM.

"NO! For fuck's sake, do I have to spell everything out? The Prime Minister!"

"Oh, sorry," replied Freeman.

"Is that a good idea? I mean a head of state, surely that's…"

"Peter, stop being a fucking pussy," interrupted Dan. "We're almost at the finish line and you're worrying about some pompous English twat."

Charles re-entered the conversation.

"George apologised profusely when I called him just now. He's just upset because after he found out where the island was, we blew the fucking thing up!"

"Shit," replied Henry understanding what a difficult a position the UK's Defence Secretary was in.

"It's not all bad though, only one other person knows where it was."

"Who?" asked Dan.

"The PM. Seems George is an ambitious little shit and is asking if we can help."

"Perfect," replied Dan. "Henry, George, you know what to do."

Chapter 41

"Will somebody please tell me, what the fuck is going on?" exclaimed the president, slapping his latest briefing paper down onto the coffee table.

He was joined in the oval office by Gerald Walters his National Security Advisor and Stephen Hughes his Director of National Intelligence, two of his closest and most trusted aides.

Receiving nothing more than shrugs, he continued.

"Let me get this right. In the space of twenty four hours, the head of the NSA blows his brains out. An entire NSA shift die in a car crash; the head of the SSB gets murdered and we lose a B1 Bomber and you're telling me they're unfucking related??!!"

"Yes Sir, we can't find any link," replied Hughes shifting nervously in his seat.

Sam Mitchum's second term as president had been disappointing. The economy was floundering, Iraq was an unmitigated disaster and just about every American ally had deserted them. A proud man, Mitchum struggled to comprehend just how different things could have been. His first term had been triumphant, his second however would be his legacy. One thing he was certain of was that he was not going out on a scandal but that was exactly what this whole FUBAR, using one of his old Marine terms, reeked of.

"Can't find a fucking link??!!" screamed the president, his face flushed with anger.

"Well there is one other thing," offered Walters who had been Mitchum's NSA throughout his presidency.

"What?" demanded the president impatiently.

"The appointment of Joshua Brooks as head of the SSB is just bizarre." Walters looked at Hughes as he spoke.

Hughes was responsible for all of America's Intelligence Services and was often referred to as the intelligence Czar. A recent creation, the role had already proved its worth, resulting in a co-ordination and team mentality unseen in the previously competitive community.

"You're joking!" exclaimed Hughes almost falling off his chair.

"You didn't know?" asked Walters, genuinely surprised.

"First I've heard of it. What the fuck is that anally retentive prick doing in there?!"

Walters studied Hughes. He had planned the meeting carefully with the president. Both knew something was going on but they just didn't know who they could trust.

Walters nodded almost imperceptibly to the president.

"OK Stephen, I'm sorry but you're here under false pretences. We weren't sure if we could trust you."

Hughes jumped out of his seat, the indignation clear in his face .

"Sit down! Now is not the time for theatrics. I'm sorry, get over it and let's move on."

The president waited for Hughes to calm down before continuing.

"Something is rotten in the state of Denmark."

Chapter 42

Scott rowed through the night never once breaking his rhythm. The small row boat powering through the water. Ashley slept on and off through the night. Every time she woke up, she pleaded with Scott to let her row. However, he just shook his head defiantly. Ashley tried to talk to him but every time she tried she was met with a wall of silence. Not since his declaration of war, had Scott uttered a word. Even when Ashley sighted land for the first time, Scott remained silent. Much to Ashley's amazement, he stepped up the pace and accelerated towards the mainland.

Ashley just watched in awe as after eight straight hours of rowing, Scott still managed to sprint to the finish. She watched fascinated as each muscle in Scott's back tightened and relaxed as he powered through each stroke. She had seen muscular men in her time, the freaks on Mr Universe, the sprinters with their huge leg muscles and the long distance runners with their leanness. It seemed to her Scott somehow managed to be an amalgam of them all, his musculature although not bulky was exceptionally defined. His stamina was unparalleled and his power seemed endless as they neared the marina.

As their boat drew alongside a seemingly deserted yacht, Scott jumped up and onto its deck, holding the boat for Ashley to join him. As Scott pulled her aboard, she could see a large multi-layered red roofed building off to her left, a seventies style tower block to her right and a smaller building straight ahead and could just make out the sign, Sutera Marina.

"Where the hell are we going?" whispered Ashley.

"We need to find some clothes," replied Scott kicking the door to the main cabin open.

The small lock broke and the doors flew open to reveal a tight staircase that led down to a galley. Scott left Ashley standing on the deck as he headed down into the bowels of the boat.

"Come on!" he beckoned as he walked through the galley towards the bedroom area.

Ashley feeling somewhat exposed on the deck of the boat they had just broken into, did not need to be asked twice and quickly descended into the galley of what appeared to be an exceedingly luxurious yacht.

Scott waved Ashley on to follow him and before long, they were selecting clothes from various wardrobes that adorned the master suite of the yacht.

"Perhaps we should shower before we get dressed."

Ashley had noticed her reflection in the mirror, the remnants of the island covered her body, the black ash covering her from top to toe. Scott looked in the mirror and his mind was cast back to the explosion. Ashley rushed to his side and took him in her arms and for the first time since the explosion Scott cried. Ashley felt every sob as his body rose and fell in her arms. The tears dropped onto her shoulder as his emotions finally came crashing down. Ashley guided Scott back onto the bed and lay with him silently. Within minutes the exhaustion took its course and both fell sound asleep.

Scott woke up four hours later, still entwined in Ashley's arms. Disentangling himself, he quickly showered and dressed and checking Ashley was still sleeping, quietly made his way onto the deck. Closing the door behind him, Scott jumped down into the row boat and rowed across to the jetty. Tying the small boat to the jetty Scott made his way into the Marina building and walked directly towards the men's locker room where he singled out locker number 231. The combination padlock opened to the code 1281 and revealed Scott's secret stash, one of many Scott had secured throughout the world. Scott was not one of the world's most accomplished assassins for no reason. He had back-up plans for his back-up plans. He pocketed the $3,000 cash, passport and credit card in the name of David Thomas, a Canadian citizen before placing the Fabrique National Five-Seven pistol into his belt at the base of his back and exiting the locker room.

***

"Scott!" called Ashley from the shower as she heard something knock against the hull. "Scott?...Scott are you there?"

Ashley began to panic. She had woken up and stepped straight into the shower. Seeing Scott's wet towel, she had assumed he had just had one. She now wished she had looked for him before showering but had wanted to be clean and rid of the ash which had set him off just a few hours earlier. The sound of the bedroom door opening and closing brought her back to her senses. Scott wouldn't leave her, they had a connection. Something very special had passed between them. She opened the door of the ensuite and found herself staring into the face of three complete strangers.

"Whoa, Christmas has come early boys!" proclaimed the largest of the three men leering at her naked and dripping body. The three were dressed identically, deck shoes, Bermuda shorts and polo shirts. The large one was huge and like no sailor Ashley had ever seen before, whereas the other two were exactly like every sailor she had ever met, preppy.

Ashley quickly stepped back and tried to shut the door but the men stepped forward and stopped her, pushing the door open and exposing her even further. She tried to cover her nakedness but one of the men grabbed her towel, while another took her dressing gown from the hook, relieving her of any possible coverings.

"You can't hide that mighty fine body from us," said the one grabbing the towel.

Ashley covered herself as best she could with her hands.

"Get the fuck out of here, NOW!" she screamed.

The largest man stepped forward and made to cover her mouth.

Ashley stepped back before suddenly rocking forward, bringing her knee crashing towards his groin. Although big and cumbersome he saw it coming and moved surprisingly quickly.

"Feisty little bitch, excellent!" he smiled as she connected harmlessly with his thigh.

Ashley could almost taste the alcohol on his breath and realised she was in real trouble.

"Who wants to go first?" asked the man holding the towel.

"ME!" came a sinister voice from behind.

For the first time since seeing the naked Ashley, the three men took their eyes off of her and turned to see who had barged in on their fun.

Scott stood calmly watching the three as they turned towards him. The two smaller men stepped aside letting their brute of a friend square up to the much smaller Scott. Scott tossed a towel to Ashley who quickly covered herself.

"Did anybody touch you?" asked Scott icily, his eyes darting between the men.

"No," replied Ashley, stepping round the back of the men and out of the ensuite.

"OK, why don't you wait for me in the galley?" instructed Scott.

Ashley looked at him and could see by the look in his eyes that Scott had no intention of debating the point.

"What you going to do asshole?" the brute poked Scott hard in the chest, making him take one step back.

Scott checked Ashley had left the room before withdrawing the FN 5.7 pistol from the small of his back. The brute immediately stepped back and raised his hands in surrender.

Scott raised the pistol and pointing it skywards let the men see him placing it safely on the sideboard at the back of the bedroom. He then turned and walked back towards the three who suddenly began to realise they may be in trouble.

"We were just having some fun man, you know how it is. I mean you saw her, fit yeah and afterall you have broken into our boat," blabbered the man still holding Ashley's dressing gown.

As Scott looked at the dressing gown, the brute made his move, throwing a wild punch at Scott's head. Scott ducked and threw a punch so quickly, the brutes two friends didn't know why he suddenly bent over. Scott finished him with a knee to the face that shattered his nose and cheek bone. However that was nothing compared to the damage Scott had caused to the man's libido. When he regained consciousness he would discover he had all but been castrated, his testes destroyed by Scott's lightening fast but crushing punch.

Dressing Gown and Towel hadn't even moved such was the speed and ferocity with which their friend had been dispatched. One second he had thrown a punch and the next he lay crumpled on the floor with Scott standing menacingly over him.

Both stepped back.

"But she told you we didn't touch her," protested Towel.

Scott looked down at the brute. "And that's the only reason he's still breathing!"

Dressing Gown and Towel glanced at each other before launching their combined assault, both diving towards Scott at the same time from different angles. If they could get him on the floor they thought they could take him.

The moment the two had started their move, Scott's mind had already calculated what needed to be done. Signals had been sent to individual nerve endings and Scott was also on the move. Fighting was as natural as breathing to Scott. He didn't think about merely hitting his opponent, his moves calculated the exact point of impact and power required to deliver the desired result. He had already decided the three men's behaviour towards Ashley was deserving of a permanent reminder. The brute had almost touched Ashley and had been by far the most intimidating. As such, his fate was the worst. Dressing Gown would have a limp, his left kneecap, his favoured side, would be smashed while Towel would lose the use of his right arm, never again would he humiliate a woman by stealing her towel.

Scott spun to his left the instant the men commenced their rush towards him. Then spinning to the right, he came towards Dressing Gown first. He ducked and delivered a crushing straight legged kick just as Dressing Gown's full weight rested on his left leg. The momentum of Dressing Gown's weight continued forward while his kneecap was forced backwards. The crack was audible as the kneecap had no option but to give way as Dressing Gown crashed towards the floor, his mouth twisted in agony. As the knee snapped, Scott was already spinning over the top of Dressing Gown. He crashed his elbow into the back of Dressing Gown's neck as he spun over the top of him towards Towel. The blow instantly rendered him unconscious. The screaming could take place once Scott was gone.

Towel only registered what had happened to his friend when Scott was already on top of him. Towel desperately tried to shift his momentum but it was too late. Scott sprung off of Dressing Gown's back and grabbing Towel's arm, wrenched it up and behind his back. Using Towel's own momentum, he spun him round and sent him crashing to the floor. His right arm took the full brunt of the fall, his elbow and hand twisted to ensure maximum damage. Before the pain of Towel's smashed elbow even registered, Scott stamped down on his shoulder, instantly killing the pain and every nerve ending, tendon and ligament that would have given Towel any chance of using his arm again. A quick flick of the same foot caught Towel on the side of the head, rendering him unconscious along with his two friends.

Scott didn't look back as he picked up his pistol and calmly exited the bedroom.

The second Ashley heard the first crash, she knew she should not have left Scott alone. She couldn't believe she had left him to tackle three men. She quickly grabbed a dressing gown and headed back to the bedroom to help him.

Scott, however, beat her to it, exiting before she had the chance to help.

"What happened?" she asked anxiously.

"I taught them a lesson they won't forget."

Scott steered Ashley back towards the galley. Ashley pulled away and looked at the devastation Scott had left behind, the three men lay motionless, the largest had blood still pouring from his nose. Another was twisted awkwardly while the third one's leg seemed impossibly contorted.

"Jesus Christ, you've killed them!" exclaimed Ashley.

"No they're fine, just getting a little shut eye after a tough lesson in how not to fuck with my woman."

Although feeling the punishment didn't quite match the crime, Ashley couldn't help but feel a little surprised at how good being referred to as Scott's woman made her feel.

Scott took Ashley by the arm and led her into another bedroom where she could finish her shower and get dressed.

"I got this for you, I hope it fits." Scott held out a dress he had managed to buy from the Marina store.

Ashley quickly threw the dress on and although not one of her usual designer brands was impressed at how well Scott had chosen, both in style and size.

"Perfect," she announced as she buttoned the last of the buttons.

Exactly thought Scott, remembering some of last nights more pleasant memories. Ashley really was a very beautiful woman. However, it was not long before the less welcome memories of the previous night blighted his thoughts.

"We need to get going and not only because of our friends next door," suggested Scott, trying to remain focussed.

"Where to? Switzerland?" ventured Ashley as she quickly towel dried her hair.

"Yep, the bank in Geneva, then London."

"London?"

Scott suddenly realised that Ashley knew very little about who he really was, despite their intimacy. They had never had a real chance to talk about who they were now, they had only discussed who they had been.

"I'll explain on the plane."

Chapter 43

"Stephen, this is Dwight Jennings." The president introduced the man whom he had summoned to the oval office. "Dwight is with the FBI and is the Special Agent in Charge of the Washington office."

"Good evening Dwight." Stephen Hughes shook his hand.

"Good evening Mr Hughes," replied Dwight.

"Stephen, please," instructed Hughes.

"Please, everybody sit." The president motioned towards two sofas.

All four men sat, Hughes and Walters on one sofa, Dwight on the other and the president on a chair at the head of the two sofas.

"Stephen," began the president. "We have reason to believe that a conspiracy is underway which is a direct and realistic threat to the national security of our and many other nations."

Stephen Hughes couldn't help but notice that all three men were studying his reaction very carefully. His reaction, in fact, was one of total shock and seemed to pacify his audience.

"Yes, Mr Hughes," continued Dwight. "A conspiracy that we have been tracking for over two years now."

"Two years!" exclaimed Stephen still reeling from the news.

"To say this conspiracy runs deep is an understatement," emphasised Dwight.

"But Mr President why am I not aware of this? Two Years?" replied Stephen, the indignation clear in his voice. As head of the US intelligence network, it seemed ridiculous that he was not leading the investigation.

"We don't know who we can trust," said the president but realising his mistake corrected himself. "Of course I trust you implicitly but your organisations, I'm afraid, are rotten to the core. I couldn't risk involving you earlier."

"So why now?"

"Because all of a sudden, they're getting bolder. It's like they think they're untouchable. Killing General Jackson was the last straw."

"They killed Jackson?!"

Dwight stepped in. "We believe so, two men we were tracking lost us when they jumped aboard a chopper. Our agents couldn't follow but the timings and chopper description are consistent with the kidnapping and murder of General Jackson."

"Holy shit! Who are they?"

"Mercenaries, who appear to have free access to any and all of our top secret facilities and information."

"So who's behind it all?"

Gerald Walters spoke for the first time. "We have absolutely no idea. Every time we get a lead we hit a brick wall, another nameless account funding the operation."

"Perhaps we should start at the beginning," suggested Stephen, having regained some of his composure.

"Always a good place," agreed the president.

Chapter 44

As far as the eye could see, a line of ships waited patiently to fill their holds with any number of combinations of fuel. The Punto Fijo oil refinery was one of the world's largest and sat in the idyllic surroundings of the Caribbean sea on the Paraguana Peninsula on the northern tip of Venezuela.

Eduardo Ramirez looked out across the horizon and smiled as each of the waiting ships bore his ER shipping insignia in their characteristic yellow and red. It was a sight to behold and one Eduardo Ramirez enjoyed every single day. From the first day he had set foot on the peninsula, over forty years earlier, to discuss potential shipping contracts, he had known he was going to stay. As the contracts grew so did Eduardo's hunger to own more and more of the peninsula. Where as the west end of the peninsula was dominated by the refineries, the north was almost entirely dominated by the Ramirez estate.

His empire had grown and was now one of the largest privately owned tonnages in the world. Eduardo's favourite statistic was that every day, one in every two people touched something that had been shipped on one of his boats. Whether it was grain in Africa, petrol in America or plastic in Asia, there was a one in two chance that his ships had carried it. Obviously, with this statistic flowed fabulous wealth, ensuring the Ramirez estate was one of the most opulent and extravagant estates of the world.

It was also one of the most secure. Eduardo Ramirez lived in almost complete seclusion. Despite his massive shipping fleet, Eduardo Ramirez was synonymous with a different type of trafficking. Believed to be the world over as one of the world's leading drug lords, his home in Paraguana was a veritable fortress,. The 16,000 acres were surrounded by over 15 miles of razor topped wall and patrolled at all times by at least a hundred heavily armed and highly capable guards.

Eduardo sat down on his lounger and closed his eyes, relaxing as he soaked in the warmth of the afternoon sunshine.

"Mr Ramirez, I have a Mr Baker for you Sir. He says it's urgent." The perfectly tailored butler rushed to Eduardo's side, holding a cordless phone.

Eduardo smiled. He had been expecting the call. Despite the fact that the had not spoken in over twenty years, he had a funny feeling Dan would call him.

"Hi Dan, how's it going?" said Eduardo cheerily.

"How's it fucking going? How's it fucking going? Fine until I heard you were crashing my party. What the fuck are you playing at Eduardo?"

"Now, now. Is that any way to treat an old friend?"

"Friends my ass."

"OK, old business colleague?"

"Stop fucking about Eduardo, what the fuck do you want?"

"I just wanted to see how you were doing. I mean, it's not everyday a protégé becomes president."

"You're throwing some very dangerous words around Eduardo!" replied Dan, changing his tone to a more chilling one.

"I don't like your tone Dan, I suggest you remember with whom you are speaking," replied Eduardo, matching Dan's chilling tone.

"Don't fuck with me Eduardo, just stay away. You coming here will do none of us any good."

Before he could respond, Dan hung up, leaving an enraged Eduardo Ramirez holding a dead phone.

***

The American Airlines flight from Boston touched down only two minutes late and quickly disgorged its 126 passengers into the main terminal at Queen Beatrix International Airport on the island of Aruba. Dressed almost entirely in Hawaiian shorts and shirts, the plane load of tourists rushed through the terminal and presented themselves to immigration and passport control. Armed predominantly with nothing more official than their drivers' licences the stream of Americans passed through unchallenged and swiftly left the building in search of buses and taxis to take them on to their hotels and apartments for their week long holiday on the island paradise.

One passenger however had planned a much shorter stay. She made sure she was almost exactly in the middle of the crowd as the eager tourists pushed past the immigration officials. As she flashed her Connecticut drivers' licence she smiled warmly to the Aruban official who unlike his American counterparts, had a permanent smile fixed on his face.

"Bon Bini, Miss," he looked at her licence. "Long."

"Hi."

"I hope you enjoy your stay," he said as he passed her licence back to her.

"Thank you."

She took her licence and placing it back in her wallet, walked through the baggage hall carefully scrutinising everyone and comfortable she was receiving no undue attention, exited the terminal.

The first thing she noted as she stepped out of the terminal was the wind. It blew relentlessly and reminded her of the Mistral in Marseille. This worried her. She grabbed the first taxi she could find and asked the driver to take her to the Riu Palace. Fifteen minutes later, the taxi drew up at the front door of the hotel. She paid the driver, tipping him just enough so he wouldn't remember her as being either tight or generous and walked into the lobby of the hotel, through the reception area out into the pool area and across the back of the complex into the next door Radisson. A booking for Miss Long was found on the system and she was informed a package was waiting for her in her room.

With a room in the main tower, she moved across the foyer to the elevators and climbed to the fourth floor. Her room was the third down on the left and as she opened the door, she was met by a breathtaking view of an almost perfect picture postcard scene of the Caribbean. With little time to enjoy it, she moved across to the baggage waiting for her and checked everything she needed was there and most importantly, that none of it had been tampered with before repacking its contents into one large dive bag.

The only thing left to do was to change her clothes. Walking across the beach in a long dress with a dive bag would not exactly look the part. She changed into her bikini and instantly lost 10 pounds and 10 years. Her previous outfit had been chosen carefully to help blend in with the crowd. Something she could not achieve in a bikini, no matter how unattractive the swimsuit was. Her physique was exceptional.

Breaking down the cardboard packaging, she picked it up and deposited it at the maid's station at the end of the corridor. She then returned to her room and wiped it down thoroughly, ensuring no traces of her visit remained. With one last check that she had everything, she hoisted the dive bag onto her shoulder and made her way back down to the hotel lobby.

The change in her appearance was certainly noted. Every hot blooded male became aware of her and was keen to offer her some assistance with her bag. Each offer was refused politely but firmly to ensure her swift transit through the hotel and out onto the beach. The weight of the bag would have certainly raised a few questions, particularly how a petite girl could carry a bag that size so easily on her shoulder. Once on the beach, she paused briefly to soak in the stunning view, powdery white sand gently lapped by crystal clear waters and in the foreground, a pier stretching out across the water. It was her first trip to Aruba, a favourite amongst honeymooners and from first impressions, she could certainly understand why. She thought it might well be worth another visit, under more leisurely circumstances.

She spotted the speedboat bobbing gently against the pier, positioned exactly as her instructions had detailed, opposite the donut shop on the pier. On reading the instructions, she had been sure there had been a mistake but there it was, the donut shop halfway up the pier. What she hadn't known was that the pier had a number of retail units running down the centre of it with a walkway on the outside. With another three offers of help between the beach and the pier, she couldn't get there quick enough. Her business was about keeping a low profile. The swimsuit was a mistake she would not make again.

She boarded the Sessa Key Largo 25 boat, its rear end dominated by two large 150 hp engines. Without hesitation, she removed the key from under the seat, turned the ignition and unhitching the ropes powered the boat away from the pier. Once clear, she pushed the throttles forward and set a course due South. In twenty minutes she would be on station. She opened her duffel bag and began to lay our her equipment, the small radar dish and screen first, followed by her Walther WA 2000 sniper rifle.

Chapter 45

Scott knew where he wanted to get to. The only problems were how to get there without a passport for Ashley and without announcing his miraculous rebirth. Trying to get a replacement passport for Ashley raised two issues. One, it would announce her miraculous rebirth and two, the US embassy in Malaysia was in Kuala Lumpur, over 1000 miles away across the South China Sea. His only option was to purchase a forged passport. However that was fraught with danger as nine times out of ten the forgeries were picked up almost immediately. Only passports recently separated from their owners, who had yet to report them missing were of any use and Scott knew no one he trusted enough to guarantee him that..

"Can you just pull over next to that café please," asked Scott pointing towards a small beachside café.

As the taxi slowed down, Ashley looked at him quizzically. They were miles from the airport.

"I'll tell you in a minute!" Scott said sensing the enquiring eyes on his back.

As the taxi pulled away, Scott spotted exactly what he was after. Depositing Ashley at a nearby table, Scott ordered her a coffee and changed some cash for coins. He then went to use a payphone next to the toilet area.

Ashley could only sit and wonder what was going on. Scott had hardly spoken to her since they had left the marina and she was still trying to work out what had happened there. Ashley was no wimp but couldn't help feeling vulnerable after the humiliating and frightening experience. Had it not been for Scott's intervention, she knew she would have been in trouble. The three drunk sailors had only one thing on their mind and Ashley had no doubt she would not have been able to fight them off. She looked at Scott and instantly felt safe. His eyes were fixed on her, protectively watching over her. She could see him speaking into the phone but the mouthpiece covered his mouth allowing her only to make out a couple of words. She was sure he had said 'sure travesty', just before hanging up.

Scott replaced the handset and smiled for the first time since the explosion. He finally felt as though he was taking control. His grief had overwhelmed him, choking his thought processes but thanks to the three drunks, he had been shaken out of his darkness.

He had been raised as an islander where death was not mourned, it was celebrated. True warriors, the islanders believed death was merely another step towards immortality. Scott realised that in the eyes of the islanders he had been selfish and worrying about his loss, rather than celebrating their gain. However, despite their casual acceptance of death, the islanders also firmly believed in an eye for eye. Their lives may be celebrated but if their wrongful deaths were not avenged, Scott knew they would never rest.

"Come on, we need to get going!" instructed Scott as he neared the table.

"But my coffee, it's not even arrived yet," protested Ashley.

"No time, we've got a boat to catch."

"A what? I thought we were going to Geneva?"

"We are. We just need to make a little detour."

Chapter 46

It had been an extremely shocking meeting for Stephen Hughes. The depth of the investigation was only exceeded by the depth of the conspiracy. From what Agent Jennings had described, the men in the meeting were quite possibly the only people not in on it. Government employees, elected officials, congressman and senators all seemed to be on the take somehow, although none of it traceable. Select steering committees, the real power in Washington's democracy, who controlled trillions of dollars in the US economy were all in on it. Advisors, advising the president on policy and strategy were in on it.

Stephen had argued that they had always known that business unduly influenced politicians and government. That, however, was not disputed. The problem was that this went much further and deeper and somehow seemed more concerted and connected. When big business bought its decisions, it was usually an oil company wanting preferential duties, or the tobacco industry wanting to quell class action law suits. It was never an all encompassing control and certainly never reached beyond legislation or procurement.

Stephen had sat and listened to Jennings describe the level of infiltration within the military and intelligence communities. It seemed nowhere was sacred, at every level and at every juncture, the conspiracy was there. Law enforcement, the judiciary, the list went on and on. Names of people under the direction of outside influence rolled off Jenning's tongue; name after name of people Stephen Hughes thought to be of impeccable character and totally trustworthy. Cabinet members who it seemed had another paymaster. By the time Jennings finished, Stephen was surprised there was a government in power at all. It seemed anyone with any influence was batting for another team.

"So what are you going to do?" asked Stephen still reeling from the revelations.

Jennings turned to the president, who took his cue.

"Absolutely nothing. We have not one shred of proof that would stick in court, not that we can trust the courts. Nor do we know who's even behind it."

"Holy shit," Stephen's mind was racing as he struggled to comprehend the implications of what was being said.

"You realise you can't discuss any of what you have heard here tonight?" instructed Walters.

"Of course," responded Stephen dismissively, his mind still working through the revelations.

"All that I ask is that you watch your back and if you see anything you think can help us, please contact Dwight immediately," asked the president, while Dwight handed over his business card.

They all stood up, shook hands and slowly drifted out of the room. As they moved into the empty reception area, Stephen Hughes checked his watch and offered his apologies, he had a dinner date and was running very late. As his back disappeared out of sight, the president, Walters and Jennings walked back into the office.

"Did he bite?" asked the president.

"Absolutely, the greedy little shit could hardly contain himself," replied Walters who had always warned the president about Hughes.

"Is everything in place?" asked the president, still struggling to believe one of his closest friends was involved.

"Yes Sir. If he so much as sneezes, we'll know where, how hard and who to," replied Jennings.

Chapter 47

The endless line of limousines outside the Chicago Hilton and Towers had not stopped all day. The private dinner hosted by Dan Baker was by no means an intimate event. The audience with the next president had cost its 1,000 guests over $25 million dollars between them. Dan had only organised the dinner following concerns over constant questioning of his funding. Suggestions of funding by the Saudi Royal family had recently surfaced on more than a few internet sites and had kicked off a debate that needed taming or else would cost Dan a few points on election day.

Dan had finally relented and allowed his team to organise one big fund raising event but made it clear that everybody paid the same, no matter what. The last thing Dan wanted was owing anybody anything when he got the job. He wasn't going to be like previous incumbents and spend the first few days in office paying off old debts and thanking backers with legislation that would repay them ten fold for backing him. With Transcon behind him Dan had all the money he would ever need.

Of course, his refusal to accept donations for favours was causing more than a little unrest in the business community. Having a president in place who didn't need their backing was something of a novelty. As such, the uptake for the fundraising dinner was unprecedented. The $25,000 tickets sold out in minutes. Resales of the tickets on ebay had caused widespread controversy with one ticket being sold for $1 million dollars. It seemed the business community had found their equivalent to Woodstock and would do anything to get hold of a the ticket.

Eduardo Ramirez was one such ticket holder and was still enraged from his earlier call. Nobody spoke to Eduardo the way Dan Baker had spoken to him. Nobody. Initially, he had purchased the ticket as a joke, a little reminder to Dan that Eduardo was one of his backers. Many years earlier, he had lent the young Baker a large sum of money with the promise of a significant return. That return had indeed been significant. However, had it not been for the original loan, Dan Baker would not be where he was today. Eduardo liked having powerful friends and there would be none more so than an indebted American president. It had been over twenty years since he had last spoken to Dan. Their business deal had been carried out in complete secrecy and to this day Eduardo still did not know how Dan had managed to achieve the ten fold increase so quickly.

Eduardo picked up the phone and dialled a number.

"Get my plane ready," he barked before hanging up. The joke was about to become a reality, Dan would learn not to underestimate Eduardo.

"We're going to Chicago!" he shouted over to his bodyguard who sat motionless under a nearby shade. "Get the helicopter ready!"

Ten minutes later, Eduardo and his ever present team of bodyguards, were boarding Eduardo's Sikorsky S76 helicopter for the short flight to the airport where Eduardo's Boeing Business Jet 3 sat waiting.

**

Fifteen miles south of Aruba, she pulled the throttles back and switched the small radar dish on. Its antenna began to rotate and the screen came to life. The small green line sweeping around an empty sky. Everything was ready. The sea was a little choppier than she would have liked but the wind not as bad as she had first thought it would be when she stepped out of the airport. All she needed now was the target.

The job had been uncharacteristically rushed. Normally she had days or even weeks to plan a hit. This time, she had only hours. Seven hours ago, she had been waiting in Boston for a flight to Europe when the job came through. Could she make it to Aruba in five hours? Yes she responded and was told to get there asap. Everything would be in place, a long term issue needed to be resolved and an opportunity had arisen that was unlikely to be repeated.

**

Eduardo increased the power and lifted off. He loved flying and was in the process of completing his airline training which would let him fly his airplane but for now he had to make do with the helicopter. He spun the nose around and pointing due north dipped the nose and increased the power. Queen Beatrix International Airport, home to his Boeing Business Jet, lay just 20 miles to the North.

***

The first blip on the screen announced the target was approaching, 5 miles to the South. In less than two minutes, he would be in range. She lifted the Walther WA2000 rifle which against her petite frame looked even more ridiculous than normal. It's bull pup design giving an uncharacteristic stocky look to the rifle. As the scope came to her eye, her body relaxed, her breathing controlled. Her mind began to think of nothing other than a perfect shot. The motion of the boat became rhythmic and entered into the factors that her mind calculated and re-calculated.

Within a minute, the target started to come into sight of the scope but was still well out of reach. As each second passed, the detail became greater and greater until still over half a mile away, she had the perfect shot. The pilot of the helicopter became clearly visible. Her breathing stopped and as the boat reached the pinnacle of its sway, she depressed the trigger. The 7.62 mm round exploded from the barrel and flew through the air, dipping slightly as it arched towards its target. The front screen of the helicopter stood no chance as the bullet tore through it like tissue and continued relentlessly towards its target. A fraction of a second after the window had exploded, the pilot's head bore the full brunt of the metal bullet's fury. His head had gone.

With perfect impact and a confirmed kill, she fired one more round. This one fired slightly lower and to the right, the huge bullet tore through the petrol tank and the resulting explosion ensured nothing but small pieces of debris would be left of the aircraft and its occupants.

By the time the explosion ripped through the helicopter, the engines of the Sessa were already at full power. Twenty minutes later, she was docking the speedboat in Oranjestad, the main town on Aruba and disembarking with one small bag, ˜essed in jeans and a t-shirt. A ten minute cab ride deposited her at the front door of the airport and thirty minutes later, she was handing over her boarding card and passport for her flight to Amsterdam with KLM.

"I hope you enjoyed your stay," the stewardess checked the boarding card and passport, "Miss Martinez."

"Couldn't have wished for better, thank you."

Miss Long's driving licence had disappeared to the bottom of the Caribbean sea along with her rifle and radar system. Miss Martinez would last until Amsterdam where she would disappear never to be seen again. She was not one of the world's most prolific assassins for no reason.

As she waited patiently for take off, a slight tremor in her bag announced the arrival of a new message. Retrieving her small blackberry-like device, she noted with some surprise her new target referred to simply as PM, London.

Chapter 48

Scott's little detour involved a taxi, a bus, two ferries and a taxi and was nothing short of a major diversion. Their ultimate destination was Bandar Seri Begawan, the capital of Brunei which Ashley now knew was just South of Sabah and five hours away if you didn't have a passport or forty minutes by plane if you did. Ashley had tried to understand what difference a lack of passport made in Brunei but Scott was staying tight-lipped offering nothing more than a 'you'll see' response which, after a number of hours, had infuriated her so much that she didn't even care any more what they were doing.

As the taxi pulled to a stop at the airport, Ashley couldn't help but wonder what they were going to do. She still didn't have a passport and they needed to get to Geneva, preferably unannounced.

"I just need to make a quick call," announced Scott as he stepped out of the cab.

Ashley followed Scott as he made his way to the nearest call box. Two minutes later, he was leading her down a corridor and through a door marked 'no entry', another 'no entry' door and before long they were both stood at the foot of steps leading to an aircraft.

Scott, without hesitation, began to climb and was welcomed warmly by a man dressed in a captain's uniform. Ashley followed and shook the captain's hand as he offered it to her and as she stepped beyond the captain, an equally impeccably dressed stewardess guided her into the body of the aircraft. The captain shut the door behind them.

Ashley stared in disbelief as she realised they were the only two passengers on the huge and it seemed very private Boeing 747 VIP, one of the newest products available from Boeing. The 747 VIP was based on the latest configuration of the Jumbo 747-800 Intercontinental and was the ultimate private jet, the perfect accoutrement for one of the world's richest men, the ultra rich Sultan of Brunei.

After showing Scott and Ashley to their seats and offering them a drink, the stewardess disappeared.

"OK, what the fuck is going on?" asked Ashley, a cocktail glass in hand.

"Let's just say the Sultan owes me a favour." Scott took a sip of his cocktail and smiled as the plane began to power down the runway. "Next stop, Geneva," he said raising his glass to Ashley.

Ashley however didn't move. "Enough now, just please tell me what's going on," pleaded Ashley, suddenly realising what 'sure travesty' meant. She had misheard what he had said, it had obviously been 'your majesty'.

"OK, OK." Scott downed his cocktail in one and turned to face Ashley.

"I'm an assassin for the British government," he said completely straight faced.

Ashley looked deep into his eyes and waited for him to crack but after a few seconds gave up.

"Fuck off, just tell me what's going on, enough of the games."

Before Scott could respond, the captain knocked on the wall as he approached, announcing his presence.

"Sir, I hope you don't mind my intrusion," said the captain to Scott.

"Not at all," Scott turned towards the captain and smiled.

"I just wanted to offer my sincere gratitude for what you have done for my country and our highnesses, the Sultan and Crown Prince," he said bowing deeply.

Scott blushed and before he could speak, the captain continued. "May I also apologise for offering my gratitude as my highness asked that I do not say anything to you but as I was the pilot of the plane hijacked that night, I am also greatly indebted to you."

Ashley didn't know who to look at, the captain or Scott.

"Please, it was nothing, I'm just happy nobody was hurt," replied Scott bashfully.

"You are too kind, what you did that night required true courage and I thank you from the bottom of my heart." The captain bowed again and left.

Ashley just stared at Scott in search of an explanation.

Scott turned and looked out of the window.

"As I said, I'm an assassin for the British government. I solve problems that nobody ever wants to admit happen. I am the ultimate deniability. I don't exist within any organisation, I'm not an intelligence officer, I'm not a double 'O' agent. I'm an assassin. I only go in when all other options have been exhausted and even then only when it's not appropriate for official involvement."

Scott turned back towards Ashley and noticed the doubt had gone and for the next few hours he told Ashley everything he could think of about his life. She too opened up and by the time they were nearing the outskirts of Geneva, both had opened themselves to each other like they had to no one ever before.

Although having talked for hours, their intimacy the previous night had not entered the conversation and without either saying it, they knew it had been a mistake. Not that they regretted it, far from it, it was just both knew they had to be on top of their game and any relationship would have to wait. Sex was off the menu at least until some serious revenge had been dished.

It was only as they were on the final approach to landing that Ashley remembered the words of the captain.

"So what exactly did you do to warrant this favour?" she asked waving her arms around the cabin.

"Oh nothing much, just rescued the Sultan's eldest son from some crazed hijackers that were threatening to kill him."

"Nothing much?! Why you?" asked a very impressed Ashley.

"The hijackers took refuge in North Korea, no official forces could go in. Myself, Kirk and Kyle went in as mercenaries by HALO (High Altitude Low Opening parachute jump). We killed the hijackers and flew the plane out without the Koreans ever knowing we were there."

"Holy shit!"

"Not really, just a bunch of two-bit amateurs trying to make a quick buck."

Ashley had a feeling Scott was underplaying his part ever so slightly.

Both were surprised when the call from the captain announced their imminent arrival in Geneva. The control tower noting the royal call sign had cleared the plane for landing and cleared its route to the VIP reception centre.

Within minutes, the plane had powered down and the front door opened to allow Ashley and Scott to leave the plane. Thanks to a call ahead from the Sultan, passport control was unmanned and after a cursory welcome from the manager of the VIP reception area, they exited the building and were met by a chauffeur-driven Rolls Royce.

"It seems the Sultan is very appreciative of your nothingness!" exclaimed Ashley as she climbed into the back of the luxuriously appointed car.

"Hmm," said Scott refusing to rise to the bait.

The chauffeur turned as he closed the door and said. "The Sultan has reserved a suite for you at the Rocco Forte Le Richemond. I hope this will be OK."

Scott turned to Ashley who, checking the time, nodded her agreement. It was at least eight hours before the bank would open.

Chapter 49

Dan kicked off his shoes and collapsed onto the huge sofa that dominated the lounge of the Conrad Hilton Suite. The dinner had been a great success. His speech went down a storm with both the guests and more importantly the press. Initial polling showed an increase of two points and that was only on the back of the initial television reports. After the morning papers, that would rise further.

"Can I get you anything before I head off?" asked John Harding, Dan's campaign manager.

"No thanks, I'm just going to watch the news and hit the sack."

"OK, well I'll see you in the morning."

As he headed towards the door and to his own room, he stopped. "Oh I almost forgot, Max Ernst has been calling, he said it was urgent."

Dan pulled his phone from his pocket and hit the speed dial button for Max. It was answered before the end of the first ring.

"Hello?" said Max.

"Hi, it's Dan, what's up?"

"Are you alone?"

"Yes…"

"I'll be there in one minute," said Max breathlessly.

"But I'm in Chicago."

"I know, I'm on the floor below you but nobody knows I'm here. I'm coming right up." Max hung up.

Dan was left wondering what the hell was going on. Max was unflappable and from the day he had met him, Dan knew he was a man that would prove invaluable to him. His position as right hand man to Henry Freeman had been carefully and skilfully engineered. Max Ernst was Dan Baker's eyes and ears not only in Transcon but also amongst the shareholders. Henry Freeman trusted him implicitly, unfortunately the trust was not reciprocated. Max knew who was boss and his allegiance had (and always would) lie with Dan Baker.

Dan opened the door and was brushed aside by the over eager Max.

"Jesus, what's the rush?" exclaimed Dan, closing the door.

"Nobody can see me here," Max scanned the room for anyone else before continuing. "They're on to us!"

Dan stood back and watched as the man he had come to consider a rock, crumble before him.

"Just hold on, what the hell are you talking about? And who exactly are they?"

Max poured himself a scotch from the bar. "Hughes called me this afternoon, said he had come into some very interesting information and wanted to up his fee."

"Hughes?"

"You know Stephen Hughes, the Director of National Intelligence."

"Oh yes, weasely little fucker," nodded Dan.

"Anyway, it seems the President and National Security Adviser got him in a room with an FBI guy and told him about a huge conspiracy."

"Really, what conspiracy?" teased Dan.

"Ours!" blurted an exasperated Max.

"They're fishing, they've got fuck all," declared Dan waving it away with a sweep of his hand. "Mind you, what did you say to him?"

"Nothing that could come back to me. Also, he called the mobile registered in the name and address of a woman in Brooklyn."

"Good," Dan paused, thinking. "Where is he now?"

"At home with a big fucking smile on his face, thinking he's just upped his take from us," replied Max.

"Fine, cut him off, tell him his services are no longer required. That'll wipe the smile right off his face. After I take office, make it permanent. Until then, he doesn't know enough to hurt us. It may mean some tough questions for Transcon but just put the lawyers on it and they'll kill it off until I take office at least. Nobody blackmails us."

Max calmed down. Dan, as ever, was right.

The phone began to ring in the suite. Dan looked at it. He had left strict instructions not to be disturbed. It continued to ring. Dan reluctantly picked it up.

"What?" he snapped.

"I'm very sorry to disturb you Sir but the caller is insistent that the call is a life or death emergency and will not stop calling."

"Who is it?" asked Dan his interest piqued.

"A Mr Eduardo Ramirez, Sir."

Chapter 50

It was 2 a.m. before they finally checked in and reached the suite which was more spectacular than they had imagined. Located on the top floor, the Royal Suite seemed endless with three bedrooms and a grand lounge, surrounded on every side by large terraces. Despite their no sex pledge, they jumped into the same bed and with more than a little restraint managed to get through the night with little more than an occasional fumble. Meaning both were fresh and ready to leave at 8.50 a.m..

The hotel's store had worked its magic and the chauffeur almost failed to recognise the two of them as they walked towards the Rolls Royce, a mark of his professionalism. As the two walked by, the turned as many female heads as male heads. They made an extremely attractive couple and people were certain they had just seen two movie stars but couldn't quite place them.

"Where to Sir?" asked the chauffeur.

"Banque Privée Edmond de Rothschild, 18 rue de Hesse, please."

Without another word the chauffeur pulled away and five minutes later, they were deposited in front of a grand building in the heart of Geneva's business district.

As the car drew to a stop, the enormity of the situation hit Scott for the first time. He was about to find out about his father, the locket in his hand held the key to whatever it was his father wanted to ensure he and only he would ever see. As the chauffeur held the door open, Scott paused. Ashley sensed the trepidation and took hold of his hand, squeezing it gently. Scott squeezed gently back and smiling at Ashley stepped out of the car. The doors opened at precisely 9.00 a.m. and Scott and Ashley walked past the elegantly dressed doorman into the opulence of the main lobby. A smartly dressed young clerk appeared from thin air.

"Sir und Frau des guten morgens," he offered with a smile.

"Good morning," replied Ashley.

"Ah, good morning," he responded in accentless English. "How can I help?"

"We need to discuss an account," said Scott stepping forward.

"But of course, please come with me." The clerk led them to an ante-room off the lobby and offered them a seat on one of two sofas in the small room. He left without another word.

Scott was not in the mood for sitting around and as the clerk left the room, he stood up and began to pace nervously. On his seventh circuit, the door opened and an exceptionally well dressed man in his late forties entered the room. Everything down to the shine of his shoes was impeccable. His hair greying but perfectly coiffed, his suit obviously the finest Saville Row had to offer, his watch discretely Swiss and pen, of course Mont Blanc.

"Good morning, my name is Herr Krauss and I am one of the managers here at Rothschild."

Scott walked towards Herr Krauss and offered him his hand.

"Hi. I'm Scott and this is Ashley."

Herr Krauss shook Scott's and then Ashley's hand.

Good morning "Ashley…" he said as he shook her hand.

"Jones," replied Ashley.

"Ah I think we have spoken previously Miss Jones, have we not?"

Ashley blushed slightly as she had to admit she did not remember Herr Krauss. However, there was every possibility she had spoken to him. She had tried many times to access the account and in fact had received more than one warning that her interest in an account not in her name was unwelcome and most definitely not legal.

Herr Krauss, however, was ever the professional and noting Ashley's slight embarrassment quickly changed the subject. "I'm sorry Scott I did not catch your surname?"

"It's just Scott," replied Scott matter of factly, as though it were perfectly normal.

Again, Herr Krauss ever the professional let the matter pass.

"Do you have any details for the account in question?"

Scott handed over the locket along with a copy of the details they had written on a separate sheet of paper.

Herr Krauss immediately recognised the number. His mind worked with account numbers in the same way that other people's worked with faces. Once he saw a number once, he never forgot it. He most definitely had spoken to Ashley previously. He also remembered the account had a number of conditions to be met but only as each were met would the next become apparent.

"If you'll just excuse me for a moment," he said as he exited the room.

Two minutes later, the door opened and the clerk walked into the room. Scott's heart immediately sank. After all that, it seemed the account was a dead end.

"If you'll just follow me please," he asked holding the door for Scott and Ashley.

Ashley could see the disappointment in Scott's face and put her arm around him as they walked back into the lobby. However, instead of taking them to the front door, the clerk directed them to a nearby elevator. Showing them in, he selected the top floor and the lift slowly ascended five floors. The opulence of the lobby was nothing compared to the grandeur of the executive suite. The plush carpets and exquisitely panelled walls were adorned with what were obviously priceless works of art. The corridor itself would have put most art galleries to shame. The clerk directed them towards the end of the corridor and after a cursory knock on the door, opened the door onto a luxuriously appointed corner office. Herr Krauss sat behind his desk and waved them onwards towards two chairs sitting in front of his desk.

"Please, sit down. Tea or coffee?" he offered.

"Coffee please," replied Ashley.

"Just water for me thanks," said Scott.

"Apologies for the cloak and dagger downstairs but Miss Jones was recognised as a previous visitor. However, your accompanying her did peak our interest. I am not a manager but am in fact the Banks Senior Director of Private Banking. The account Miss Jones has previously tried to access is one of our most secure and as such any reference to it causes some concern."

"I apologise for any concern I may have caused but the contents of this account are very important to both of us and will perhaps explain the death of our parents," explained Ashley.

"I'm sorry to hear of your loss, but I'm afraid you'll have to wait just a little longer," replied Herr Krauss rising from his seat and taking his embroidered handkerchief from his jacket pocket, walked towards Scott. Dipping the end of the handkerchief in a glass of water that sat on the edge of his desk, he asked, "May I?" as he placed the end of the handkerchief on Scott's temple and his cluster of moles.

Scott shrugged at the strangeness of the request and sat perfectly still as Herr Krauss rubbed his moles with the handkerchief. Content that they were in fact real he said. "Thank you. Now if you don't mind waiting, my predecessor Herr Meyer is on his way and will be here shortly."

"Why?" asked Ashley confused as to why Herr Krauss could not deal with the matter.

"A stipulation of the account I'm afraid. Herr Meyer knew the account holder personally."

"But what if he were dead?" asked Scott suddenly aware that his fate may rest in the hands of an elderly banker.

"That eventuality is covered but as Herr Meyer is fighting fit and enjoying his retirement to the full, there is no requirement to go down that route," explained Krauss.

The phone rang on his desk and rather than answer it in front of them he excused himself and left the room to take the call elsewhere.

"I don't like it!" whispered Scott. 'We've effectively announced that we're alive and now we're having to wait for a retired banker to come in from wherever he is. I think it's a set up."

Ashley kicked herself for not having thought the same. She had blindly accepted everything Herr Krauss had said. The reputation of Swiss bankers had certainly worked its magic on her.

Scott stood up and walked across to the window.

"I think we should get out of here, we can follow Herr Krauss home after work and interrogate him to find out who he's working for."

Looking down on the lanes of traffic, Scott noticed a car erratically swerving from lane to lane, its final manoeuvre of skidding to a stop in front of the bank's front doors making Scott's decision for him.

He stormed across the room, grabbed Ashley's hand and dragging her out of her seat said, "Let's go!"

Chapter 51

"Eduardo, my friend, I'm so grateful you didn't come to my dinner," said Dan as he took the call.

"Wrong Eduardo, I'm afraid. This is Eduardo Jnr. Well I was!" spat Eduardo Ramirez's son.

Dan was taken aback. He assumed Eduardo was calling back after their earlier call.

"I'm sorry what do you mean - was?"

"You know exactly what I mean, you fuck!"

"I'm sorry I have no idea what you mean. I spoke to your father a few hours ago," replied an indignant Dan.

"So you're trying to tell me after you threaten him to stay away, it's just fucking coincidence his helicopter crashes and he dies?"

"Holy shit, I'm sorry I had no idea. I promise you this was nothing to do with me."

"Save it for the dumb fucks that believe a word you say, you fuck. You're a dead man, you hear me, a fucking dead man!!" Eduardo slammed the phone down.

Max watched and waited as Dan replaced the handset.

"Eduardo Ramirez is dead," explained Dan.

"Who?"

"A man I knew once. Anyway, it seems his son thinks I did it."

"Did you?"

"No, absolutely not."

"He'll calm down. I'm sure he'll be fine," reassured Max.

"No, you don't know young Eduardo, he's crazy. His father was the only person who could keep him in check. He wants me dead and won't rest until it's done."

"Do you want me to deal with it?"

"Please, but be careful. Don't underestimate Ramirez. Also he may have papers that could damage me. His father was a sneaky bastard."

"I'll handle it personally."

"Thanks."

Chapter 52

"Where are you going?" protested Herr Krauss as Scott and Ashley stormed out of his office.

"Do you have a back door to this place?" asked Scott brushing past the banker roughly.

"But Herr Mayer has just arrived. He got here as fast as he could," pleaded Krauss.

Scott paused. He hadn't waited to see who exited the car, an error in normal circumstances he would never have made. The thoughts of his father, concern for Ashley's safety and avenging the islanders were all clouding his judgement. He had been trained to detach himself from emotions and act on instinct. However it was only now that he realised how badly they could affect his judgement.

"OK, we'll stay but if Herr Meyer isn't in the office within two minutes we're leaving." Even if it weren't Herr Meyer in the car, Scott could handle a car load of guys.

Ninety seconds later, a tanned and fit seventy year old bounded into the room, dressed as impeccably as Herr Krauss. Herr Meyer may have been retired but he would never lose the banker look.

As he caught sight of the two clients, he immediately stopped and gawped at Scott, in a very unbankerly fashion. His mouth literally dropped as he caught sight of Scott's face.

"Oh my God, you are the image of your father!" he exclaimed.

Scott was instantly captivated and walked across to Herr Meyer and taking him by the hand sat him down on the sofa.

"Herr Krauss, please bring the paperwork." Meyer said quietly unable to take his eyes off Scott's face.

"You knew my father?" asked Scott, desperately wanting to confirm that he had just heard correctly.

"A wonderful man," replied Meyer. "A truly wonderful man."

Herr Krauss returned quickly with the paperwork for the account and placed it in front of Herr Meyer.

"Now please, if you don't mind, can you both wait outside while I discuss this young man's account." Meyer looked at Krauss and Ashley, confirming he meant them.

"I'd rather Ashley stayed," insisted Scott.

"Impossible. I will only discuss the account with the account holder," replied Meyer adamantly.

Ashley rose from her seat and winked at Scott before following Krauss from the room.

As the door closed and Meyer was happy they were alone, he turned to Scott.

"What do you know about your father?" he asked.

"Absolutely nothing, I don't even know his name," said Scott.

"Well I can certainly tell you that…And a lot more."

Chapter 53

The flight from New York landed twenty minutes early and ensured Mike Hunter would make his early morning meeting with Charles Russell with time to spare. The head of the Unit had decided to take personal charge of the operation; it wasn't every day they were given the task of assassinating one of the world's foremost leaders. His car was waiting exactly where it was supposed to be and within forty minutes, he was leaving the greyness of London's mayhem for the greenery and tranquillity of London's largest royal park.

Regent's Park was an oasis of calm in an otherwise bustling city and covered over 480 acres, it was one of eight royal parks in the greater London area and was the largest within central London. Originally, fifty six villas were planned to be built within the royal grounds but only eight ever were, making them some of the most sought after real estate in the world. One villa, Winfield House, home to the American Ambassador had the largest private gardens outside of Buckingham Palace. Another was home to Charles Russell, the head of Transcon EMEA and had recently been valued in the $150 – 200 million bracket.

As the car drew up to the grand mansion, Hunter struggled to believe that they were in the middle of a park in the centre of one of the busiest cities in the world. Had he fallen asleep during the trip and woken at the front door, he would have sworn they were deep in the English countryside visiting some grand stately home. Before he had a chance to open the door, a butler had opened it for him and taken his small bag for him.

Refusing to let his bag out of his sight, Hunter quickly followed the butler and was led through the grand hallway into an adjoining library which Hunter reckoned was bigger than his whole apartment. Safely reunited with his bag, Hunter relaxed and took a seat on the sofa in front of the roaring fire, set in the largest fireplace Hunter had ever seen.

Charles Russell entered the room dressed from head to toe in tweed, looking every bit the English country gent. His accent, however, put to rest to any doubt.

"Good morning, Mike," was delivered in a thick Texan accent.

"Good morning Mr Russell," replied Hunter somewhat nervously. Despite working for Transcon for many years, Mike Hunter had very little interaction with the bosses. Most of his contact was through Walker who had guarded the secrecy of the Transcon bosses with religious fervour. It was only recently that Hunter had actually put two and two together and with Walker's retirement and Max Ernst's involvement, all had become clear.

"Please call me Charles. Now, how are we progressing?" asked Charles taking the seat facing Hunter.

"Very well, I have already contacted a number of freelancers who are, as we speak arriving in London. After our meeting, I will be giving them their final instructions and I believe by this time tomorrow, the country should be mourning the tragic loss of its Prime Minister."

"Excellent. Any tie back to us?"

"Absolutely not, Sir. All are freelancers who work for the highest bidder. No member of our staff will be involved. My meeting will be by telephone only, using voice distorters and secure lines. The freelancers will probably assume Al Qaeda is stepping up the war on the West."

"Well good luck and let's hope by tomorrow we've got a new Prime Minister." Charles stood up, as good a signal to Hunter as any that their meeting was over.

"We will," assured Hunter as he stood up and walked out of the room, the doors to the library opening for him as though by magic. The butler stood waiting and escorted him back to his waiting car.

The butler, having insisted on carrying Hunter's bag again, handed it back as he sat in the car and bid him 'a good day' in a clipped English accent. As the car sped away, Hunter looked round once again at the bizarre country scene which less than a minute later was lost in the greyness of London's busy Marylebone Road.

"Let's go past Downing street," suggested Hunter to his driver who accepted the instruction with a nod.

Eight minutes later, Hunter was driving down Whitehall and looked casually at the gates and police guard that separated Downing street from the rest of the world.

***

London's Luton airport was the second smallest of the five that served the city and lay 35 miles to the North of London. With over 99% of its flights servicing European destinations, primarily by budget and charters airlines, Luton was never seen as a major security threat. Its ownership by the local council further enhanced this and the distinct difference between the three major BAA operated airports was tangible.

The timings of the six arrivals had been planned to avoid any potential conflict with the Moroccan arrivals, the only flights that caused more eyebrows to be raised by Passport Control, Immigration and Customs than any other. As such, the six individuals arriving from Malaga, Paris, Dortmund, Geneva, Berlin and Amsterdam slipped into the country without anyone knowing that six of the most sought after and highly skilled assassins had converged on one city. Had they been detected, alarm bells would have rung across every one of the UK's security agencies and the country put on high alert for possible terrorist activities.

The last to arrive was the Amsterdam flight and fresh from her activities in Aruba, the previously named Miss Martinez was greeted by the UK official as Miss Green. Her UK passport did the trick ensuring only a cursory glance to confirm a photo match.

Her task, unlike the other five arrivals was to go straight to Downing Street and await further instructions. Of course straight to Downing Street did involve one stop at a safe house to secure the necessary equipment for the task. She boarded the bus that would transfer her to the nearby train terminal at Parkway where she could catch a train to London King's Cross. She would then catch the London Underground. Commonly known as the tube, it is the oldest and still one of the largest underground networks in the world consisting of 253 miles of track and 275 stations. Despite the city's congestion, nowhere was really more than thirty minutes away if it was served by the tube.

By the time she reached King's Cross tube station, the morning rush hour had subsided and she boarded a 'Circle Line via Paddington' train and got off at Bayswater station. A short walk from there was a row of tall Victorian houses, one of which was her London safe house. Entry through the first door was simple and required nothing more complicated than the key secured behind a loose piece of door frame. However the second door was a different matter and required a 12 pin keycode that if entered incorrectly would lock out the code for twelve hours. Although it appeared to be made of wood, the door and frame were made entirely from steel and covered with a wooden facing. It was, to all intents and purposes, a vault.

Once inside, she secured the various tools of her trade and was back out and lost in the bustle of London's West End within five minutes. She had a rough idea where to position herself but after an hour of surveillance, she settled for the one location that would give her an unrestricted view of Number 10. The only problem would be getting there without being noticed or discovered. Although not easy, she was in position within the hour and had a perfect view of everything to the rear of the building, the business end of Number 10.

Chapter 54

The massive aircraft approached the runway in complete darkness. Only at the last second were the runway lights illuminated as the C-5M Super Galaxy touched down. Ernst had spared no expense in fulfilling his promise to Dan Baker to take care of Eduardo Ramirez. The largest air lifter in the US military, each aircraft cost a massive $180 million and as long as Ernst got it back in one piece, the cost would be reduced to a mere one million for the 24 hour loan. If anything did happen, The Unit would not only have to fund a replacement but somehow prevent the general who had leant it to them from going to prison.

The rear end was already opening as the C5 came to a halt at the end of the runway and the roar of five powerful diesel engines kicking to life could be heard from the hold. With the aircraft stationary, the plane began to lower, its ramps extending and the five Strykers moved out onto the now darkened runway. As the drivers pulled the vehicles to a stop, the heavily armed members of the unit began to file into the vehicles, each dressed from head to toe in black. It was only thanks to their night vision equipment that they knew everyone was aboard and accounted for. Ernst gave the instruction and the five vehicles sped off into the darkness, no lights would be used on the forty mile journey.

As the vehicles disappeared, the ten guards left behind took up defensive positions around the aircraft. Their orders clear. Anybody who saw the C5 was to be killed on sight. The first of two fuel trucks arrived, driven by the advance party. They had landed just before the airport closed for the night in a small Gulfstream jet and had quickly secured control. It was they who had ensured the runway lights were on for the landing and it was they who would ensure the C5's gargantuan fuel tanks were full and ready for departure when Ernst returned in less than 2 hours.

The Paraguanan Peninsula on the Northern tip of Venezuela was deserted at the best of times but at 3 a.m. it was devoid of any life whatsoever. The Strykers were the army's newest troop carriers and the eight-wheeled 18 tonne vehicle came in a number of variations. For this trip, Ernst had selected two M1128 MGS's with their 105 mm cannon and three M1126 ICV's with their 50mm machine guns. With a further nine heavily armed ex-special forces Unit members in each, the firepower available to Ernst was enough to ensure an overwhelming advantage against Ramirez's guards. However, Ernst was leaving nothing to chance. In addition to his overwhelming force, he also had visual superiority. A KH-13 satellite was stationed over the Ramirez compound and would stream the exact location of every one of his guards in real time to small computer screens located in eye pieces worn by each of the Unit members. The small eye piece was attached to each of the soldier's helmets and could be lowered and retracted as required. Each unit sent a signal to the satellite ensuring its own image stood out from the crowd in bright blue, other units showed up as green and thermal sources with no unit glowed red. The image cast onto the screen therefore highlighted for each of Ernst's soldiers exactly where they were, where their colleagues were and most importantly where Ramirez's guards were and quite literally allowed them to see round corners and through walls.

At 3.50 a.m., the first of the MGS Strykers drew to a stop just out of sight of the main gates. Another two ICV's stopped closely behind. The other MGS had taken a slightly different route and was drawing to a halt near a service entrance accompanied by the final ICV. Ernst in the lead MGS, surveyed the satellite image displayed on the MGS targeting system. He designated the targets and sent the details to the second MGS. Each had three targets. As Ernst checked everyone was ready, he signalled to open fire. The first round from his MGS was a fragmentation round, its target one of two barracks housing a number of guards, all of whom could be seen from the image on his screen lying in horizontal lines on bunks. The other MGS had a similar target and within a second, two flashes on the screen confirmed direct hits.

The second round from Ernst's MGS took out the guard tower over-looking the main gate. The second round from the other MGS was a high explosive round taking out the generator and plunging the compound into darkness. Red dots were running wildly all over the screen. Chaos had descended on the Ramirez estate. The final MGS round obliterated the main gate and sent the ICV's off and running with their 50mm machine gun cutting down anyone in their way. The other MGS destroyed the Service gate and the final ICV sped on up into the compound. The two MGS's following quickly behind targeting and firing at anything in their way.

With half his guards wiped out in an instant, the fight was already over. The second rate druglord guards stood no chance against the 21st century all seeing elite soldiers. As the ICVs drew to a stop at the main house, 75% of Ramirez's guards were already down. The MGS's delivered a few well placed rounds that reduced the numbers further and within five minutes of the first shot, Ramirez and only ten of his men were left standing.

Ernst had been clear that Ramirez was to be captured alive and therefore the final assault on the house would be on foot. The doors of the Strykers swung open and Ernst and 44 of the Unit's best men began to sweep through the massive villa. Every room was systematically cleared and checked. The KH-13 vigilantly scanned every inch for any thermal signal and sending the data down to each of the soldiers ensured the job was as simple as shooting a line of sitting ducks. The only check before killing was that the face did not match Ramirez.

Ernst stood and watched as his men swept through the first floor with ease. Five more down. The second floor, three more down. As he made his way up the staircase, it was obvious that the last room on the third floor held Ramirez and two other bodies, either his guards or his family. Whatever, the mission was almost complete.

Ernst moved to the door and standing to the right of the door behind the wall stretched over and knocked on the door, quickly pulling his arm back. As predicted, the door erupted into shards of splinters as a volley of bullets crashed into it from inside.

Waiting for the gunfire to stop, Ernst shouted.

"Ramirez, you're surrounded. If you want to live, throw down your weapon and come out."

The offer was met with silence. Ernst checked his watch, he wanted to be out of there in the next ten minutes. It was imperative they took off before daylight. He counted to thirty and with no response, cocked his MP5-10, spun and dived through the door. Firing two bullets as he entered the room, sending Ramirez's bodyguard and a woman straight to hell. Before Ramirez could respond, Ernst was already aiming a bullet straight at his head.

The soldiers around him looked at each other in surprise, none knew Ernst could even shoot, never mind pull off some crazy manoeuvre that none of them could replicate. Ramirez dropped his gun and raised his hands.

"Who the fuck are you?" he screamed looking at the woman's lifeless body.

"I'm what happens when you fuck with the wrong person," replied Ernst.

"Mother fucker, Baker," spat Ramirez.

"That's Mr President to you," smiled Ernst.

"Not yet," smiled Ramirez knowingly.

Ernst instantly thought back to Baker's warning of the father being a sneaky bastard and that there may be documentation that could damage him.

"What the fuck does that mean?" Ernst slapped Ramirez hard across the face as he asked the question.

"It means exactly that," Ramirez spat a mouthful of blood defiantly at Ernst's feet. "And you never know maybe he won't win." He smiled into Ernst's face blood trickling down his chin.

Ernst suddenly realised exactly what he meant. When he had threatened to kill Baker, he wasn't meaning it literally, he was going to kill his chances of becoming president.

"Where are they?" asked Ernst sinisterly.

"Where are what?" asked Ramirez.

"The documents?"

"Ah you know about the documents," smiled Ramirez.

It took all Ernst's strength not to smash the butt of his gun into Ramirez's smiling face.

"Yes," he replied through gritted teeth.

"They're safe but if anything happens to me they won't be if you know what I mean."

"I'll warn you once and only once. I don't bargain. Where are the documents?" Ernst raised the gun to Ramirez's knee.

"I told you…"

Ernst pulled the trigger and Ramirez's kneecap exploded into a cloud of blood, tissue and bone. As Ramirez screamed Ernst moved across to the other knee.

"Where?" he asked coldly.

Ramirez struggled to focus as the pain swept through him.

"I tooolldd youu..," he stammered.

Ernst's pulled the trigger and the other kneecap exploded.

Ramirez passed out from the pain but was brought round by a slap from Ernst who made sure Ramirez saw the gun now pointing at his crotch.

"Kneecaps can be replaced, cocks and balls can't!" explained Ernst. "Where?" he asked again.

Ramirez was struggling to remain conscious. His body in shock from the trauma wanted to shut down and heal but Ernst was keeping the mind alert enough to realise further trauma was likely if the right response was not given. But he also knew the right response was the truth and the truth was they were too late the documents had already been sent to America. Nothing they could do could stop them. Ramirez didn't know where they were or who they were going to.

"You're too late they're…they're gone," he mumbled.

Ernst pulled the gun away, grabbed Ramirez and shook him awake. "What do you mean too late?" he asked.

"I've already sent them…" Ramirez began to drift off.

Ernst slapped him and instructed one of his soldiers to give him a glass of water from the nearby desk. Throwing the water in his face brought Ramirez round again.

"Sent them where?" asked Ernst desperately.

"To America!" explained Ramirez wincing as a surge of pain ran through his non existent kneecap.

"Who to?"

"I don't know!"

"Don't fuck with me now, who the fuck did you send them to?!" shouted Ernst, panic rising.

"My nephew took them…and is going to give them…to whoever he thinks…will stop Baker." The moans of pain were breaking up his speech and driving Ernst insane.

"What's your nephew's name?"

"Eduardo."

Ernst looked at him in disbelief. "You've got to be fucking kidding me, another Eduardo fucking Ramirez!"

"No!"

"So what then?" prompted Ernst irritated.

Ramirez realised he was saying too much and decided enough was enough, he was going to die anyway and hopefully he'd take them down with him.

"Fuck you and Baker, you're going to kill me anyway," he said defiantly.

Ernst checked his watch, one minute to go. He raised the gun and shot Ramirez in the groin and then the stomach. Both bullets were lethal but not immediately. Eduardo Ramirez was going to die a slow and very painful death.

"Your call. I can end it quickly, what's his name? I'll get it anyway!" Ernst offered the doubled over Ramirez.

"Fuck you!" he coughed, spraying blood over Ernst's feet.

"No Eduardo, it's you that's fucked."

Ernst turned and with the wave of his hand signalled their job was done.

As the ICV's began to make their way from the compound, the two MGS's opened fire with a number of incendiary shells. Nothing would be left of the Ramirez house by the time the sun rose.

Within an hour, the vehicles were back on board the C5 and the massive airframe was using every inch of the runway to get back into the air.

Ernst was already at a workstation barking out orders. The hunt was on. Eduardo, nephew of the recently deceased Eduardo Ramirez, was now the most wanted man in America.

Chapter 55

The old banker hadn't stopped talking for twenty minutes and with every word, Scott became more and more entranced. His memory for detail was amazing and it seemed every detail could be recalled and replayed for any given moment.

The first revelation for Scott was discovering his name, Kennedy. His father was James Kennedy and from what the banker understood was born and raised near Glasgow in the west of Scotland. Herr Meyer had first met him when Scott's father had turned 21 and following a number of business successes had paid himself a substantial bonus and on the advice of a business colleague had contacted Herr Meyer at Rothschild to open an account. Over the next ten years the two had got to know each other and as far as someone can be friends with a Swiss banker, they had become friends.

James had started his business at the age of sixteen and it became evident his talent for business was unrivalled, buyout after buyout resulted in one of Scotland's largest corporations by the age of 21, Britain's by the age of 27 and just before he died, was making major progress in America and Asia. However, before his death, Herr Meyer had little contact with James who had met a woman and become almost a recluse. In his last few months, he had hardly been seen and after the birth of Scott he had all but disappeared. The first Herr Meyer had known of his death was when a client had called and told him about the tragic car crash.

Scott asked a lot of questions about the car crash. Where, when, who else was involved, how it had happened. Herr Meyer knew little other than what the papers had reported. However, soon after the crash, a letter had arrived which had been sent by James before the crash. In it were instructions for access to his account by his son, details of the birth mark and a letter to be placed in the vault to be opened only by Scott if and when he came to claim his inheritance. The letter was business like and very different from the notes that Meyer was used to receiving from James. Meyer couldn't emphasise enough how his father appeared to have died with the weight of the world on his shoulders.

Scott then asked about his mother but Herr Meyer knew very little. After James had met her, he had never visited the bank again. Herr Meyer explained that his father had told him that he had met a very beautiful woman and was ecstatic about becoming a father but they spoke little after that.

"I'm sorry, I don't have any more I can tell you but he was a truly wonderful man. You can be proud of him. I have met very few great men in my years and your father was one of those few."

"What became of the company?" asked Scott.

"Disappeared. Overnight it just ceased to exist."

Scott's look of confusion at the answer prompted a greater response.

Herr Meyer elaborated.

"That's the biggest mystery to me. How does a successful company suddenly split and become a number of different organisations overnight? I'm not a corporate banker Scott but something very strange happened to your father's company. Perhaps your father's letter will explain more."

Herr Meyer stood and gestured for Scott to follow him. Rather than walk towards the door, he walked towards a wall of books and pulling on one particular book, the bookcase opened revealing a small elevator. Guiding Scott in, Herr Meyer pressed a button and two minutes later, the elevator opened into the bank's vault area. An armed guard waited at the first set of gates and on seeing Herr Meyer smiled and welcomed him warmly.

Once through the gates, a key code allowed them through into the main vault. A wall of small doors surrounded them on three sides and as they stepped inside, Herr Meyer passed a key to Scott before removing another from his pocket. He approached one of the doors.

"Please put your key in the left hand hole," he instructed before placing his in the right.

"Now if you can just turn it clockwise 90 degrees on my count 3, 2, 1."

Both turned and the lock turned easily despite not having been used for nearly twenty-five years.

"Impressive," remarked Scott,

"Swiss engineering, some of these vaults have not been opened since the day the bank opened nearly 200 years ago and I guarantee that every lock works as well now as it did then," he winked. "Although most have been replaced over the years."

"Now I will leave. There is a private room just to the left outside the vault. Please take as long as you like. All day if you wish. Just ring the buzzer when you're finished and I'll come and get you. In the meantime, if you don't mind, I am going to entertain that rather lovely young lady of yours."

Scott nodded his approval without his eyes moving from the box. As Meyer left the vault, Scott reached forward and grabbed the handle on the end of the box and pulled it clear. 2 feet long, 8 inches high and 1 foot wide, the box was made of metal but seemed much lighter than he would have expected. He walked out of the vault and entered the private room where a desk and chair sat waiting. He placed the metal box carefully down on the highly polished desk and took a seat.

He lifted the lid with trepidation. His father's things would be inside. A man about whom he could only dream of. He had no image to call on, no personality to remember. A man who Scott felt had deserted him, a man who was nothing more than a stranger.

The first thing he saw was the letter, 'Scott' was written across the envelope with the words from 'your father' beneath it. The words set him off, tears streamed down his face. He removed the envelope and before he had a chance to open it, spotted the photo beneath, a man and woman cradling a baby. A man who, as all who had met him had commented, bore an uncanny resemblance to Scott. The picture was of his mother, father and himself as a baby. His mother was truly beautiful just as the islanders had described. Scott held the photo and cried like he had never cried before, staring into the faces of the two people he wanted more than anything in the world to have met.

Placing the photo in his pocket, he pushed the letter to one side and checked what else lay inside. The deeds to a plot of land somewhere in Scotland, the details of two bank accounts, one was opened very shortly before Scott's birth, the other he could only assume from the date was the one opened on his father's 21st birthday. The final item detailed the holdings of one JK International registered in Scotland in 1967. Scott, like Meyer, was no corporate expert but the document detailed a huge list of company names and dates of incorporation for each and the shareholding, each listing James Kennedy as the only shareholder.

Scott turned back to the envelope and breaking the seal, withdrew the handwritten pages.

Dear son,

If you are reading this letter my greatest fear has come true.

The first few words of the letter ensured any sentiment could wait. His father was telling him what had happened. As he raced through the letter, his anger rose. With every new sentence, the hatred within him grew more intense. Even before he had finished reading, he had already buzzed the buzzer. As he read the words.

'Yours always, Dad'

Scott screamed. "MOTHER FUCKERS!!!"

Part Four

Chapter 56

It was his first trip to the US and the first job his uncle had ever entrusted him with on his own. Seventeen year old Francisco Ignacious Eduardo Ramirez, Eduardo to his family, was the illegitimate son of Maria Ramirez, sister of the recently killed Eduardo Ramirez and was not sure what to do next. He had tried when he landed in Miami to call home but the line was dead. He had tried again from the airport and even tried his mother's mobile but it too was dead. The guard house line was dead also and Francisco thought the lines must have a fault, they couldn't all be out at once.

That left him with one major dilemma. His uncle had merely instructed him to take the boat to Aruba and get the first flight with a connection to Washington. Once there, he'd tell him what to do. All Francisco knew was that the papers were dynamite in the right hands and deadly in others.

He hailed a taxi. The Ramirez shipping business had an office in Columbia Heights. From there, he could at least find somewhere to stay and wait for his uncle to let him know what was happening. For years one of the roughest neighbourhoods in Washington, the area had seen a sharp rise in house prices due to the ever widening gentrification of the Washington area. However, it was still home to a large Hispanic population and was the base for all Ramirez business in the DC, Maryland and Virginia areas. It had also returned a significant profit over the last couple of years following the sale of a number of slum buildings Ramirez had acquired over the years.

***

The search had returned nothing. Every flight to and from Venezuela had been checked for any individual with the first name Eduardo. They had also searched for any children Eduardo Ramirez's sister had had but came back with nothing to suggest she had ever had a child. Ernst, on hearing the news had racked his brain for any other clue. He was certain Ramirez had referred to him as his nephew and scoffed at the suggestion he was called Ramirez. Why had he scoffed? Ernst looked again at the notes in front of him. Maria Ramirez was listed as single, never married. A good catholic family. Of course, the nephew was a bastard born out of wedlock and as such would have been all but a pariah but his name would be Ramirez.

He immediately widened the net but again nothing came back. No Ramirez had flown in in the last 24 hours from Venezuela. It was only thanks to the map on the wall that he widened the net to include Aruba. He hadn't noticed how close the small island was to the Paraguana peninsula but did know it had a huge number of flights daily to the US. Within minutes, the first hit came back. Francisco Ramirez had boarded a flight from Aruba to Miami with a connection to Washington Dulles and had landed just three hours earlier. CCTV footage was instantly requested and received and within ten minutes, the photo of Francisco Ramirez was being sent to every agency that Transcon had any sway over which meant just about every law enforcement officer in the greater Washington metropolitan area was now looking for the young Ramirez.

***

The taxi drew to halt outside of a run down bar on the corner of Irving and 14th. Francisco was sure the bar used to fit with the surroundings but not anymore. Columbia Heights was definitely up and coming and the bar was very much out of tune with its deli and swanky coffee shop neighbours. Keen to prove his business acumen, Francisco started to consider a proposal for his uncle. They did not need the bar in that particular location and judging from the money being spent in the area, the property value must have sky rocketed. He would advise his uncle to sell the bar and relocate to a cheaper neighbourhood. As he walked towards the door, he was formulating the words to use. It was important that he came across properly. So, busy considering his proposal, he failed to notice the bouncer that was following his move towards the bar's door.

"Where the fuck do you think you're going?"

"For a drink!" replied Francisco sarcastically. Francisco had been drinking in bars since his 16th birthday, having always looked old for his age and with the legal drinking age of 18 in Venezuela, he had never once encountered a problem. He pushed on the door.

"ID," demanded the bouncer placing his hand across Francisco's chest.

"Take your fucking hands off me," demanded Francisco staring the much larger man deep in the eye. Francisco couldn't believe how much of a cliché the bouncer was. Tattoos covered both arms and were on show by virtue of a white vest top. The man looked like every two bit Hispanic punk Francisco had had to endure on TV.

The bouncer did not take well to being eyed by a little punk and firmly pushed Francisco back onto the street.

"Fuck off, and don't come back."

He turned his back and opened the door to enter the bar himself, in a you don't worry me attitude. Francisco had had the benefit of an excellent education and, had it not been for his insistence on joining the family business, would have been destined for university. However, academic studies were not the only education he had received. His uncle had made sure he knew how to fight. Not any type of fighting but dirty street fighting where the only rule was to make sure you won no matter what.

Francisco turned around and storming back towards the bouncer kicked, him with all his might between the legs. The bouncer didn't see it coming and the first he knew of the attack was the intense pain in his groin. Looking down, the top of Francisco's designer shoe was firmly lodged between his legs and was still pushing up. The bouncer crumpled to the ground in agony.

Francisco stepped over the bouncer and walked into the bar where the barman was reaching for what seemed to be a baseball bat.

Francisco had had enough, it had already been a long day and he wasn't in the mood for any more bullshit.

He pointed to the barman and shouted. "Enough, my name is Francisco Ramirez, my uncle is Eduardo Ramirez!"

The barman immediately let go of the bat, the mere mention of the Ramirez name enough to convince him Francisco was to be obeyed.

However, before calm was restored and the barman and bouncer had a chance to apologise, four men rushed from the back of the bar area. One Francisco recognised as Victor 'Vic' Garcia, the boss in Washington. He had been to Paraguana many times.

"Francisco, thank the lord you are OK," he screamed as he hugged the somewhat bewildered Francisco, tears streaming from his eyes.

Without a word, Francisco was swept through to the back area.

"What the fuck is going on Vic?" protested Francisco as the door was closed behind him.

"I spoke with your uncle," the tears continued to stream down his face. "He's dead, had just enough time to call and tell me you were coming. Everybody's dead at Paraguana."

Francisco's legs gave way and he slumped into a chair which had just been placed behind him.

"He said you had papers that would nail the fucker who killed him and asked that whatever you do you make sure you get him."

"So boss, who is this fucker?" asked Vic, looking towards Francisco Ignacious Eduardo Ramirez, the new head of the Ramirez organisation.

***

"Mr Ernst?" the trepidation in the caller's voice had Ernst on edge instantly. It was the sort of trepidation that was always accompanied by bad news. The Unit Operation centre number showed on his caller id screen which meant the bad news was going to be dreadful.

"Yes?" he barked.

"We've picked up a call that was made from Paraguana to Washington early this morning,"

"So?"

"I think you'll find it interesting. I'll play it for you," the noise of clicking a keyboard echoed down the line.

"Vi…icc?"

"Hello? Who is this?"

"It's Eduar…cough…do"

"Jesus boss are you OK?"

"I'm dead...some fuckers...just shot us up, everyone's dead...Everyone........... Francisco is coming to you...he has papers that'll nail the fucker...Look after him for me!"

"Of course boss."

Three distinct booms could then be heard before the line went dead.

The caller from the operations centre came back on the line. "That's it Sir. Not sure what the booms were but the line just went dead after that. The call was made at..."

"That's OK," Ernst knew exactly when the call had been made and couldn't believe how stupid he had been. His anger had got the better of him and had allowed him to leave Eduardo alive and near a fucking phone. It was only thanks to the incendiary shells that Eduardo hadn't given detailed descriptions of his killers. "Do we have the address in Washington?"

"No, it was a cell phone but we have a location, the phone hasn't moved, it's in a bar in Columbia Heights."

"Hit it and hit it hard!" Ernst almost screamed down the phone.

Chapter 57

The anger was etched on Scott's face as he entered Krauss's office.

"Would you mind giving us a minute please," asked Scott of Krauss and Meyer.

Ashley had been sitting on a sofa in the corner of the room, a pot of coffee steaming in front of her but was now standing, anticipation etched on her face. The contents of the box could explain almost as much to her as to Scott.

As Krauss and Meyer left the room, Ashley rushed to Scott and seeing the pain in his eyes hugged him. They both stood motionless for a few seconds before Scott broke away, wiping his eyes he took a seat and asked Ashley to sit with him.

"My father and your parents all died in the same crash." exclaimed Scott. "And from what my father says in his letter, they were probably murdered."

Ashley's face went white as Scott broke the news. Scott let the news sink in before continuing.

"It seems people within his organisation turned against him, just as he was completing a major deal. The deal was make or break and required every piece of spare cash the company had. Just as the deal was about to go through, a large hole was found in the company accounts which meant not only could the deal not go through but the company would fail to meet its requirements and would default on a number of payments. The company would be bankrupt and overnight thousands would lose their jobs. My father knew it was not the case but his accounts department and the bank agreed if he didn't find $50 million to complete the deal, the company would have to close."

"A person he refers to as 'a dear friend' suggested they may know where to get the money quickly and it seems the deal went through. However, the whole thing was a scam, the loan agreement changed and was not the one my father signed. Even his lawyers betrayed him, switching the copies. Suddenly, a new clause was included that handed over power to the loan company in the event of my father's death."

"Oh my God," Ashley's hands covered her mouth as the horror of the story unfolded. "Your father was murdered just to get his company!"

Scott nodded. "It seems so. But that's not all, there is one condition that remains. Should any direct descendant of James Kennedy fail to lay claim to the estate before their twenty fifth birthday, all power, assets and control will revert permanently to the loan company."

Ashley's mouth dropped, she knew Scott's twenty fifth birthday was less than a month away.

"Mother Fuckers!" exclaimed Ashley as the anger began to take hold.

"My thoughts exactly," replied Scott angrily.

"So how do we find them?" asked Ashley eagerly.

"I've got a few leads, the lawyer in London, the name of the loan company registered in England and the Swiss bank they used in the deal, based in Zurich," said Scott.

Ashley knew what was coming next. Her lack of passport was going to ground her in Switzerland while Scott flew off to London.

Scott could already see the disappointment in her eyes. She was an intelligence agent without a passport. She knew she was getting the waste of time trip to Zurich. Swiss banks didn't divulge information, period. But they had to try.

"I'll do Zurich," offered Ashley before Scott had to ask.

"Are you sure?" asked Scott, playing along.

A sarcastic smile suggested they could stop playing and move on.

"OK, but take this," Scott handed Ashley the FN 5.7 he'd picked up at the Marina back in Kota Kinabalu. It was amazing how lax entrance checks could be when an exceedingly rich royal paved the way.

Once the pistol was safely out of sight, Scott opened the door for the bankers.

"Please come in gentleman," he offered, stepping aside.

Scott had considered whether he could trust the bankers but on hearing his own thoughts had chastised himself. These men had kept his father's secret safe for twenty-five years and their knowledge of Swiss banking could unlock an important key.

"Gentleman," he addressed the bankers gravely as they sat. "My father did not die in an accident but was in fact murdered to cover up the theft of his company!"

Much to Scott's surprise neither banker blinked, it was as though Scott had just told them the weather forecast for the next day.

Herr Meyer cleared his throat.

"I can see you are surprised by our reaction but unfortunately I always held the death of your father and the disappearance of his company with the utmost suspicion and did in fact contact the authorities, anonymously of course, to inform them of my suspicions."

"What happened?" asked Ashley.

"Nothing. I chased it up a few months later and no record could be found of my previous call. They put me through to a senior officer whose voice I immediately recognised as being the officer I had spoken to months before. He was more interested in who I was than the details of a potential murder. I hung up and it was then that I realised that whatever happened to your father, those involved had very powerful help."

"Why didn't you tell me this earlier?" asked Scott.

"I didn't know what your father left for you. I didn't want to spoil what may have been a wonderful moment for you. I'm sorry I would have told you as soon as you came back but you ordered us out of the room."

Scott could see Herr Meyer was being sincere not only in his answer but also in his concern for what had happened to his father.

"I'm sorry Herr Meyer and on behalf of my family I thank you for at least caring enough to try," replied Scott warmly. "You may be able to help us however. We have the name of the bank that transferred funds to my father business, it's in Zurich. UBZ."

Herr Meyer and Krauss exchanged knowing glances, Herr Krauss answered.

"Hmm, a rather unsavoury member of the Swiss banking fraternity I'm afraid. We have few dealings with them but I can perhaps arrange a meeting with their Chairman. However, I'm afraid they are known for their dealings with the world's less savoury individuals and as such hide much more than is appropriate behind our banking laws."

"Herr Krauss as a current banking board member is being kind. They are a bunch of crooks," interrupted Herr Meyer, unable to hide his disgust.

"So are we wasting our time?" asked Scott.

"No, not at all. If a woman," Herr Meyer turned to face Ashley. "Of such exceptional beauty as yours Madame, cannot get information out of him, nobody can." He turned back towards Scott and smiled mischievously. Obviously the Chairman of UBZ had a weakness for women.

***

"Dernier appel pour monsieur David Thomas, vol Air France pour London City. Dernier appel, merci," boomed the public tannoy system.

Scott heard the final call for him as he rushed through the baggage check. The flight was ready to go and with no baggage in the hold, they would not wait long for him. It was touch and go whether he'd make the 13.40 flight but the next flight at 14.00 was into Heathrow whose security checks he'd rather avoid. The next flight to Luton was in another 3 hours and that was too late for a couple of the leads he wanted to chase down. He wanted to be finished in London that night and back in Geneva with Ashley first thing the following morning.

With seconds to spare, he made the flight and with 90 minutes to kill before landing, retrieved the letter again from his inside pocket. Scott laid the papers in front of him and worked through each page methodically just to be sure there was nothing he had missed. However, other than the three leads and the reference to 'a dear friend', nothing more than the despair in his father's voice could be gleaned. With each reading, Scott became more frustrated and felt more useless. He knew of course that he couldn't change the past but it didn't stop him wishing he could.

As the plane began to dive for the airport runway, Scott put the letter away and looked out over the London skyline dominated by Canary Wharf. One thing he was sure of was that there were some people down there who were going to wish they had never fucked with his father.

Chapter 58

The assassins had ensured that no tails had followed them to their designated meeting point and only after a thorough check that this was the case, were they given their final destination. By 5 p.m. the last assassin had been checked through the staging location as per Mike Hunter's instructions and had arrived at the safe house in Pimlico, central London, a stone's throw from Downing Street. As each had arrived, the rather uncomfortable realisation that the operation involved a number of their counterparts hit home. However, with a payday of $2.5 million each, the protestations were short lived.

A presentation over an encrypted video conference was then set up and the plan laid out in detail to them by one of The Unit's top planners who had, in a previous life, been responsible for stopping exactly what he was in the process of explaining. The identity of the assassins and the planner were protected as each sat in a darkened room. However, as the presentation progressed, a number of suggestions from the highly skilled killers resulted in a few small changes. It seemed the assassins were more capable than the planner had given them credit for. However with none having less than 15 years experience with some of the world's toughest regimes, these individuals were second to none. The initial plan had suggested a four minute assault. The assassins were confident three would be more than enough.

As the conference call ended, the assassins made their way down to the basement and selected the weapons they would need to carry out the mission. The array of weapons had been carefully selected to ensure that each of the assassin's preferred weapons were available to them. The selection covered just about every manufacturer of weapons and assault equipment and left nothing to chance. From knives, to night vision goggles, to anti tank and stinger missiles, every eventuality had been considered.

Hunter had sat behind the camera during the video conference and watched as the planner had taken the group through the plan in intricate detail. As the system closed down, he stood up and approached the planner.

"Well?" he asked.

"I'm glad they're working for us," replied the planner. "They know their stuff. I'd say by midnight we'll be looking for a new PM."

"Excellent. Well, I'm off. There's every chance this country will get shut down and as much as I love you Brits, a couple of days here would drive me nuts."

With that, he shook the planner's hand and was gone. A booking on the 19.25 BA flight from Heathrow to JFK would have him home just as the news of the tragic terrorist attack in the UK was breaking.

***

The Blackberry device buzzing in her pocket elicited little reaction. She was in the zone monitoring the comings and goings. So far, nothing out of the ordinary. Her hand slipped down and retrieved the device and pressed the button on the side to retrieve the new message.

11 p.m. was all it said.

Chapter 59

The Hummers came from the South and East and arrived at exactly the same time. Two stopped on 14th Street and two stopped on Irving St. Each held four men and within seconds, four had secured the fire exit while the others made their way into the bar, guns drawn. The patrons of the bar were not unaccustomed to the sight of authorities with guns and took little notice as the men swept through the bar. The barman put up the weakest protest but with twelve large armed men bearing down on him, he knew he was wasting his breath.

After a complete search returned nothing more than the phone that had been used earlier, the commander of the Unit stormed across the bar to the barman and grabbing him roughly, slammed his upper torso on top of the bar.

"Where the fuck is he?" he asked pushing the gun to the barman's throat.

The barman had been in Washington for more than twenty years and had had more than a few scrapes with the DC police.

"You, you can't do this! I've done nothing wrong! Let me go! I'll have my lawyer sue the ass off you!"

The unit commander laughed as he realised the barman thought they were cops.

"I'm not a cop you dumb fuck. Tell me what I want know or I'll blow your fucking brains all over that mirror," he said menacingly. Noting a movement in the mirror, he watched and noticed one of the patrons shifting nervously. They knew something, he thought.

The barman knew nothing, the boss had gone out. It wasn't his job to keep tabs on him.

"I don't know," he answered.

The Unit commander caught his eye and shook his head very slightly, just enough for the barman to know that was not the right answer. He pulled the trigger and sent most of the barman's head into the mirror.

"The guy in the blue baseball cap, bring him here," instructed the commander as though he had eyes in the back of his head.

Two of his men spotted the cap and immediately grabbed its wearer, thrusting him through the now quivering patrons and depositing him on the bar unceremoniously in front of the commander.

"Where is he?" he asked, the tone suggesting only one answer was acceptable.

"Metro, ten minutes ago," he replied, the fear in his face told the commander that he was telling the truth.

The commander tapped him lightly on the face. "Well done, good answer."

He turned to his men. "Right, let's go."

Within ten seconds, they were gone. Had it not been for the headless corpse of the barman, most would have struggled to believe the last minute had actually been real.

Even though a violent murder had been committed in front of a bar full of people, it took over an hour for the DC Police to respond. When they did, it was a significantly more senior officer than would normally work the streets and after a half-hearted interview of the patrons, logging details of the licence plates and description of the killer and his eleven accomplices, he left and filed the tragic gang shooting by hooded thugs. Case closed. His retirement fund had just swelled by a cool $50,000 and all he had to do was ensure the streets around 14th and Irving were a no go for an hour or so and cover the killing of some two bit spic who was probably an illegal anyway.

The commander saw the two Metro station entrances as he walked out of the bar and ordered eight of his men into the stations before calling in to the operations centre.

"Hi, they're in the Metro," he told the operations supervisor who immediately and with the help of the NSA took control of the CCTV network that covered the Metro and tying it up with his facial recognition software, waited for a hit. It was pointless looking themselves, the computers could see and check every face in micro seconds. If Ramirez were still in the Metro they'd get a hit as soon as he left the train and stepped onto a platform.

***

As Francisco had opened the envelope containing the documents, Vic had caught sight of the name and immediately gripped Francisco by the scruff of the neck, grabbed a gun and fled. Vic had sent his three bodyguards into the street first and only when they said it was clear, did he follow with Francisco, shielding his new boss as best he could. They abandoned the car and Vic instructed his guards to go down into the metro, again waiting for the all clear. He then followed with a now totally bewildered Francisco who had barely recognised the name he had read although it had sounded familiar. Dan Baker meant little to a young man from Paraguana but to a crime boss in Washington it meant that unless some miracle struck, it was not a matter of if they were killed but when. The documents in Francisco's hands were as good as a death warrant certified by the President of the United States himself. Vic knew allegiances were already swinging towards the new president and realised that whoever they approached would gain instant power by turning them over to Baker. They would not be able to trust anyone, save for one man, the current President. But what chance would a bunch of Venezuelan crime bosses have of seeing him? That left only one option, to disappear and that's exactly what Vic Garcia planned to do.

Less than a minute before The Unit had taken control of the CCTV system on the Metro, Vic, Francisco and their henchmen had exited the station in Anacostia, the crime capital of Washington D.C.. Almost exclusively black and Hispanic, the area had once been a buzzing middle-class suburb. However, the development of I-295, blocking access to the waterfront in the 50's and the building of a number of public housing apartment complexes, drove the middle classes out and plunged the area into decades of neglect. Vic Garcia, born and raised in Anacostia, knew the area better than anyone. If there were one place in the world he knew they could hide from the government, it was in the deprivation of Anacostia. White men stood out a mile and white government types even more than that. With his network of pimps, prostitutes, dealers and landlords on the look out, he'd always be one step ahead.

Francisco couldn't believe what he was seeing. He was supposed to be in America, the richest and most powerful country in the world but he'd struggle to find worse looking areas in Caracas. A gunshot rang out in the distance as they walked into a building with more windows boarded than not. As they entered the stairwell, the smell of stale urine and faeces hit Francisco like a hammer in the stomach causing him to wretch. Stepping over a down and out and a dead rat, they made it to the third floor and entered what a real estate agent would struggle to describe as a grotty two bed sparsely furnished dump. Francisco looked at Vic who smiled back.

"What the fuck is this?" asked Francisco, as a cockroach scuttled across the kitchen surface.

"Safe," replied Vic losing the smile. "At least for a few days, then we'll move."

***

The Metro system had 86 stations along its 106 miles of track and within half an hour it became obvious that Ramirez was not in any of them. A quick review of earlier recordings also failed to show any results for the young Venezuelan. With the realisation that it seemed they had lost him, it was left to the supervisor at The Unit's operation centre to report back to Max Ernst.

"Wait!" shouted his colleague as he was about to dial. "I've got something. Look here!" he added, pointing to his screen.

At the bottom of the screen four men could be seen shrouding a younger man. All wore baseball caps and from the angle of their heads were obviously avoiding the CCTV cameras. Facial recognition software could do many things but without a view of the face to compare against its target it was useless.

"I'll bet that's him, the timing is bang on," stated the operator confidently.

The supervisor agreed and reading the station name, called Ernst to update him. Ramirez was in Anacostia.

Chapter 60

As the plane taxied to the arrival gate, Scott pressed the power button on the phone and realised how fundamentally his life had changed. Only four days ago, the thought of letting somebody know that he had arrived safely was as alien a concept as he could have conceived. Scott worked alone and the only person who knew whether he was alive, dead or exactly where he was, was himself. Now he was sending a text to Ashley telling her he had arrived safely and in so doing telling her exactly where he was. After committing that cardinal sin, he exited the plane and after a short wait at the immigration desk while the immigration officer checked his Canadian passport, he was out of the terminal and boarding the DLR to Canning Town and London's Underground network.

An underground network that carried almost a billion passengers every year, between its 275 stations which meant, that, on average, during every hour of its operation over 150,000 people were being ferried within its confines. However, with over 8,300 cameras scanning every face that entered and exited, Scott was not taking any chances and had a baseball cap sitting firmly over his head with as wide a peak as possible. There was also no better way to travel around London.

After one stop, he changed from the Jubilee Line to the Hammersmith and City Line heading West and exited at the Barbican, in the heart of London's financial district, most commonly referred to as the City. Home to the FTSE, the Bank of England and numerous members of the banking elite, the area was also a mecca for some of the world's most prestigious corporate law firms. One of which was the particularly prestigious, Foxon Gerard and Smythe, of whom one of their most illustrious partners was John Butler-Jones, the former lawyer of Mr James Kennedy Esq. (deceased).

As Scott approached the building, a twinge of nervousness ran through his body. This man was partly responsible for the death of his father and Ashley's parents, as an absolute minimum. Scott dealt with these kind of men all the time but he didn't need to talk to them first.

The receptionist smiled warmly as Scott walked towards her. Even in a bizarre outfit of suit plus baseball cap, he cut a dashing figure. Catching his reflection in the mirror, he quickly removed the cap and received an approving wink from the receptionist, much better.

"Hi." Scott flashed his best smile and donned an American accent with just enough drawl to suggest Southern state and certainly explain away the baseball cap faux pas.

As she smiled back, Scott could see her pupils grow in size, a good sign. He leaned forward conspiratorially.

"I hope you can help?"

"Of course," she replied eagerly nodding her head.

"I've really messed up, I've got this really important document to deliver to Mr John Butler-Jones."

"I'm really sorry but he's not in today, he's working from home."

Scott had to stop himself from smiling, the news couldn't have been better and thinking quickly.

"Yes I know that and that's where I've to take these very important papers but somebody's just pinched my blackberry which had his address on it."

"That's no problem," she replied smiling, "I'll just get his secretary," she added picking up her phone.

Scott placed his hand tenderly on the back of the receptionist's. "No, please don't. My boss will find out and kill me for losing the blackberry. You see it's my third in three months and if I lose another one, he'll fire me." Scott leaned in closer almost whispering, "Is there any way you could just give me the address. That way, no one needs to know I lost the blackberry which I'll replace before they know it's gone."

The receptionist was about to say that she wouldn't know the address but it was obvious from the pile of packages behind her desk that she dealt with the couriers and mail for the company.

"Please," pleaded Scott. "Nobody will ever know."

The receptionist looked around to check nobody was watching. "Oh all right, but just this once and you didn't get it from me, OK?" She quickly scribbled down the address and handed it to Scott. "Before you get it, name and law firm, please," she demanded.

Scott was used to giving false names and never stumbled for a second. He normally used the names of lesser known Prime Ministers of the UK but when he met particularly stupid ones, he used well known ones. Although very deserving of a Winston Churchill, Scott thought it more appropriate to flatter her.

"Andrew Law, Clifford Chance," naming one of the least known PM's who, due to ill health, had served only 7 months in office and paired this with the largest law firm in the world. She'd have to search for some time to check he wasn't genuine. He hadn't mentioned which office he worked out of.

As she handed him the slip of paper, he added. "And you are?"

"It's on the back…with my phone number," she blushed.

Scott read the name, Julie Hughes. "Well, it's been lovely to meet you Julie and I can't tell you how much this means to me," replied Scott waving the slip of paper. Turning and walking towards the door, he heard Julie call out. "Call me!"

"Definitely," replied Scott without turning around.

Once out onto the street, Scott checked the address. Gerrards Cross, Buckinghamshire. Not somewhere Scott immediately recognised but he knew enough to know that it wouldn't be too far from London as Buckinghamshire was well within its commuter belt. That, however, could wait. Next stop was Companies House. Closing at five, he had just over two hours to try and trace the loan company. Back on the tube and ten minutes later, he was exiting Tottenham Court Road tube station and after a short walk, had located Companies House and was speaking to a research assistant.

Two hours later, the loan company information had not given him any more leads.

A nearby internet café gave Scott all the information he needed on Gerrards Cross. A very affluent commuter town just 20 minutes from Marylebone Station. Scott typed the postcode into a mapping website and printed off the exact location of the house in relation to the train station. Five minutes later, he was back in the underground and after a quick journey to Marylebone Station, he was on the 17.33 overground train to Gerrards Cross.

With twenty minutes to spare, he pulled out his phone and called Ashley.

***

Ashley's journey, despite being significantly shorter, had taken almost twice as long, although she was the first to admit the scenery was spectacular and the time flew by. The train had left Geneva at precisely 12.45 and thanks to the efficiency of the Swiss railway had pulled to a stop at exactly 15.28 as published in the timetable. Her meeting with the Chairman had been scheduled for 17.45 and had allowed her some time to enjoy the vast array of stores before arriving at Union Bank of Zurich's only branch, at 17.40. She was getting used to Swiss time keeping.

Although just as grand in appearance as Rothschild's in Geneva, Ashley could not fail to sense the overwhelming lack of class in comparison to the Geneva bank. Everything seemed rushed and hassled whereas Rothschild had been quiet, relaxed and undeniably efficient. UBZ felt like a bank under pressure, which it was.

At 17.46 and 32 seconds, a flushed and harassed looking lady came bustling towards Ashley and introduced herself as the Chairman's secretary.

As instructed, Ashley followed the secretary, struggling to keep up without breaking into a run and was led up to the first floor and towards an open door at the end of the corridor. She was shown through the door and saw a gentleman, in his sixties, sitting by his desk refusing to lift his head from the book that lay in front of him.

"Miss Jones," announced the secretary who received nothing more than a gruff 'Ja' and a wave of dismissal from the man. Herr Meyer knowing Ashley's real name had refused to accept any other name to secure the meeting.

The secretary pointed to a chair by the conference table for Ashley and hastily left the office, closing the door quietly behind her. The man behind the desk who Ashley could only assume was the chairman had still not looked up.

After waiting thirty seconds in complete silence, Ashley thought bugger this and cleared her throat. "Ahem."

The Chairman looked up angrily but catching sight of Ashley immediately stood up and smiled the dirtiest smile Ashley had ever seen. She could almost feel his eyes peeling off every item of her clothing as he stalked towards her. She smiled as best she could under the circumstances. As he approached, he reached out for her hand which rather than shaking he bent down and kissed.

"Miss Jones, so lovely to meet you," he slimed.

"Thank you for seeing me at such short notice," she said.

"Anything for my good friend Herr Krauss," replied the Chairman.

Ashley had to cough to stop herself laughing at the suggestion Herr Krauss would even stay in the same room as this letch, let alone call him a friend.

"Would you like coffee or perhaps tea, water or?" looking at his watch. "Perhaps something a little stronger?" he laughed suggestively.

"Water would be fine, thank you."

Buzzing his secretary, the chairman demanded a water and an afternoon tea. Ashley couldn't help thinking afternoon tea was some poorly hidden code for something alcoholic.

"So how can I help you, Miss Jones?" asked the Chairman, failing to raise his eyes higher than Ashley's cleavage.

Ashley knew that the disgusting male who made her stomach churn was one of the only men in the world who could help her find the killers and as such she leaned forward. Her blouse moved further away from her skin revealing more cleavage and the majority of her lacy and extremely see-through bra.

A bead of sweat almost immediately appeared on the chairman's brow as he struggled to remain calm and not look too obvious in his attempt to catch a glimpse of the stunning Miss Jones nipple which he could just make out and no more. He moved slightly in his seat to secure a less obstructed view.

"I need some information about a transaction your bank made."

"I'm sorry but unless you are involved in the transaction that will not be possible."

Ashley sat upright as the disappointment of the answer registered and the Chairman's wonderful view disappeared.

The secretary knocked gently on the door and deposited the drinks without a word, before excusing herself for the evening; it was 6.00 and closing time.

Ashley's heart sank, closing time would mean an end to her opportunity of getting the information.

"We're not quite finished here, tell the night guard that I'm still in my office," the chairman winked at Ashley immediately reawakening her spirits. The old dog thought he had a chance!

As the door closed, Ashley leant forward again ensuring her blouse fell open.

"I wouldn't ask if it wasn't life or death and it was twenty-five years ago."

The Chairman, now mesmerised by the glimpses of Ashley's breasts, desperately wanted her to stay exactly where she was.

He leaned forward conspiratorially, catching a glimpse of the other nipple.

"Well, that is an awfully long time go," he suggested. "Perhaps if you give me the details of the transaction I can check to see if client confidentiality would be breached. I mean, they might not even be clients any more."

Ashley inched further forward. "That would be wonderful," she said handing him the transaction date and the account which had sent the funds.

"Now, don't move," said the chairman, meaning exactly what he said, praying the view would be just as good on his return.

He made his way from the conference table back to his desk and entered the transaction details into an old looking system. Ashley looked on quizzically as the chairman waited for the information to appear on the screen.

"It's pre 95, have to use the old system to get the details," he explained.

The chairman took the details from one screen and entered them into a newer system that looked more like a traditional PC. After a few seconds, he began to read the details on the screen in front of him and smiled back at Ashley.

Ashley's hopes rose as the old letch looked particularly happy with himself. However, as he walked back towards her, the excitement of the find had obviously aroused him a little too much and it seemed he had no intention of hiding his new found enthusiasm. Ashley averted her eyes and hoped he'd sit rather than stand in front of her.

Thankfully he did sit and Ashley was once again able to look the chairman in the face.

"It seems we're in luck. The account holder who transferred the funds is no longer with us. In fact I was only informed this morning of his sad demise. An excellent customer for many, many years," he shook his head as he spoke.

"I'm sorry to hear that," replied Ashley, crestfallen at another lead dwindling away.

"Now, exactly how much does this information mean to you?" asked the chairman, the twinkle in his eye telling Ashley exactly how much it would cost.

Although the lead was dead, there was still a chance that it would lead them onto something else. She needed the information.

"What do you have in mind?" her voice had taken on a more husky, sexy tone as she reeled the chairman in.

"How about dinner?"

"I'm not hungry, well not for food anyway," suggested Ashley, leaning forward. She had undone another button in her blouse and it flapped open enough to allow the chairman a very enjoyable eyeful.

As Ashley predicted the previously forward letch was flustered and was not used to having his wish handed to him on a plate. He would normally have had to ply his women with alcohol to get anywhere near them and never anyone in Ashley's league.

The Chairman's mind had moved from his business head to his leisure head and when Ashley suggested a couple of minutes to get herself ready, he almost jumped out of his seat and rushed from the office, taking note of the time. In 120 seconds he'd be back in there and Ashley would be ready for him.

As he closed the door, Ashley buttoned up her blouse, walked over to his computer screen and noted the name and address of the client on the screen. In his eagerness to please, the chairman had failed to clear his screen. Ashley had noticed this in the reflection in the window. All she needed was 10 seconds alone in the room and she'd have everything she needed.

With the name and address memorised, Ashley walked across the office and opened the door to a chairman who was wetting himself with anticipation. When he saw the blouse firmly buttoned to the neck and the look of disgust on Ashley's face, he realised he'd been played, well and truly played.

"Prick teasing bitch," he spat out as she walked down the corridor and out of his life.

Ashley was just leaving the building as her phone rang. It was 18.35 in Switzerland, 17.35 in London.

"How's it going?" asked Scott.

"Eduardo Ramirez, Paraguana, Falcon, Venezuela," replied Ashley as she stepped past the night guard on her way through the front door of UBZ.

"Who?"

"A guy called Eduardo Ramirez but he died yesterday!"

"Yesterday? Shit!" exclaimed Scott frustrated at another dead lead before considering the coincidence and adding.

"How did he die?"

"Don't know yet but I think I need to speak to my old colleagues," Ashley made subtle reference to the DIA. They had discussed her contacting them ad nauseum but Scott felt the chances of her being tracked far outweighed the help they could offer with what they had so far.

"I don't know, whoever has been tracking us has access to government agencies and resources and they killed your boss!"

"We don't know that for certain," protested Ashley, although the chances of it not being related she knew were minuscule.

Scott remained silent, not justifying her response with a reaction.

Ashley took the hint.

"OK, OK but if we don't get any further by tomorrow, I'm calling them," she concluded firmly.

Scott smiled as she made her stand.

"OK, let's see how we get on today, I've still got two people to visit."

"Two?" replied Ashley surprised.

"Yep, my father's old lawyer and one other."

"But I thought you didn't get anything at Companies House?"

"I didn't."

"So who then?"

"There are only two people in the world with the power to destroy my island who knew where it was and that I was there!" replied Scott. "And I'm going to pay a surprise visit to the one I think I can trust tonight!"

Chapter 61

The helicopter set down on the Spirit of Washington heliport in the South East of Washington and deposited its one passenger before immediately departing. Max Ernst strode off the helipad and into the waiting limo which contained the Unit Commander responsible for tracking Eduardo Ramirez

"Met Police HQ," instructed Ernst to the driver before raising the sound proof partition.

"OK, where are we?"

On hearing the update of Ramirez fleeing to the Anacostia area of D.C., Ernst had immediately called a chopper to take him to Washington. Baker had entrusted him personally with resolving the Ramirez issue and so far he had failed. With Ramirez disappearing into the most neglected and crime ridden area of the capital, it seemed the hunt was getting harder rather than easier. Four hours had passed since their last sighting of Ramirez and Ernst was beginning to panic. The information he had was dynamite in the wrong hands although there were very few of them left. There was always the chance Ramirez may hit lucky and approach somebody not within Transcon's control.

"Nothing. They've just disappeared. They walked out of that station and vanished."

The answer was exactly what Ernst had feared. They were going to find very few if any allies in that area of Washington.

"I've put requests out for every black and hispanic Unit member to be sent to Washington with immediate effect," added the commander.

Ernst was impressed the man had realised that his predominantly white team were going to achieve nothing more than drive Ramirez even deeper into the deprivation of Anacostia.

"Excellent, how many and how long?"

"I'm afraid only about twenty," replied the commander slightly embarrassed, it seemed the Unit had not embraced the age of diversity.

"What about freelancers?"

"If you OK the expenditure, I should be able to treble that easily."

"Do it," replied Ernst without hesitation.

As the commander got on the phone to instruct the trawl for black and hispanic freelancers, Ernst called Baker. It was not a call he was looking forward to but it had to be done.

Ernst quickly brought Baker, who was uncharacteristically quiet, up to speed.

"I'll only say this once," replied Baker slowly. "In three weeks, I will win the election to become the next President of the United States of America. I don't care what needs to be done to ensure that happens. Do you hear me, I don't care what you have to do. Just kill that little fucker and do it quickly." Baker hung up.

For twenty-five years his plan had been perfect. With less than four weeks to completion, it was all of sudden one disaster after another. The bastard child, Ramirez, Hughes…fuck, he had forgotten all about Hughes. The stupid little fuck had called his office earlier in the day. He should have told Ernst but he had enough to do. Ramirez was the real threat. Hughes was just a nuisance, he could wait.

***

Stephen Hughes was in trouble, the Director of National Intelligence had one major flaw, gambling. Not just a few thousand dollar problem but a few hundred thousand dollar problem. A problem that he felt sure would be fixed with his next sure thing. Unfortunately, that sure thing always turned out to be not quite so sure after all. With debts well beyond his government salary, the additional monies paid to him by Transcon for his 'consultation' services were not just a luxury but an absolute necessity.

Following his call to Ernst the previous day, he had expected a call informing him of his new payment details. However, it never came and the number he used was now unobtainable. He had tried Transcon all day but the answer was always the same. 'I'm afraid Mr Ernst isn't available.' He had even tried to speak to Henry Freeman, the boss but he too was unavailable and it was clear from the reaction that his call was not welcome.

The final blow was dealt when one of Washington's less than illustrious citizens called him to find out where the fuck his money was. Hughes apologised profusely and immediately checked with his off-shore private bank as to why the man's payment had not been sent. The answer was simple, he had no funds to pay him. The payment he had received from Transcon, via an anonymous subsidiary only two days earlier that would cover his debt payments for the month, had been withdrawn the night before. How they had managed to do it he didn't know but he was in no position to complain. The payments were highly irregular and any complaint would raise more questions for the Director of National Intelligence than answers. Questions that would more than likely see him imprisoned.

Hughes was a desperate man, the gambling bosses had already threatened him with serious bodily harm. He could claim death threats had been made against him and obtain extra security but as had been pointed out, that didn't save his sweet little mother or ensure his darling daughter or wonderful wife didn't meet with some horrific tragedy. Hughes was fucked. He could either spill the beans to the president about the conspiracy and Transcon's involvement and risk jail or try to find another source of income. Jail was not something Hughes could contemplate and therefore his focus was entirely on who could benefit from his information. Of course, foreign intelligence services would pay him vast sums of money but Hughes was many things but he was not a traitor. Transcon, as far as he was concerned, was an American corporation and as such everything they did benefited the American economy. Ergo, he was not a traitor. Plus they still executed traitors.

After many hours of panicked thought, Hughes finally had a brainwave. The illustrious governor of Florida, the next US president was an exceptionally wealthy individual who, with his help, could be fully up to speed on all issues long before he took office. It was a brainwave that completely by chance would finally tie Dan Baker to Transcon and cost Stephen Hughes his life.

Chapter 62

The train pulled into Gerrards Cross just after 18.00 and by 18.15 Scott had found Butler-Jones' house. Tucked away towards the back of the small town, it really was quite spectacular. An Edwardian mansion house covering two floors and set in over two acres of land. A quick recce of the grounds uncovered minimal security, motion sensor spotlights and infra red cameras mounted on each corner of the house. Although it looked impressive, to a professional like Scott, it was a dream come true. There were more blind spots in the system than good spots and the homeowner would assume he was safe because the lights would come on should anybody come close. Scott picked a spot in the woods just out of sight of the house and waited for darkness to fall. The sun had just set but the twilight would last for at least another thirty minutes.

By 19.00, darkness had fallen and Scott was on the move. More slippery than an eel, he was up and over the wall of the garden grounds without the faintest noise. The route to the small door he had decided was his best access point had him weaving in and out of the motion sensors until he found himself next to the door at the rear of the house. He gently turned the handle and was not particularly surprised when it opened. Gerrards Cross looked like the type of place where people were a lax when it came to locking their back doors.

Scott slipped into what appeared to be a boot room, Wellington boots lined the floor while Barbours and other waterproofs hung from pegs that covered the wall. A door across the small room stood ajar and through the gap, Scott could see a large kitchen which seemed empty although he could hear voices coming from deeper in the house. Pushing open the boot room door very gently, Scott entered the kitchen and listened to where the voices were concentrated. They appeared to be coming from the room to the right at the bottom of the corridor which Scott guessed would be the family room. Scott could see through the small gap in the kitchen door that an identically sized room lay across the hallway on the other side. Scott assumed this would be the formal lounge. Three more doors led off the hallway and it was one of these that Scott wanted. Scott pulled the kitchen door and stopped the instant it was about to creak. He quickly grabbed some kitchen oil and rubbed it into the hinge. His patch job complete, he continued and once the door was open wide enough, he quickly and silently entered the hallway.

Scott looked at the first door and noted the slight difference in the design of the door and size of the frame. It was an addition and more than likely a toilet added after the house was built. Of the two doors that remained, one was much closer to the kitchen and assuming the dining room would be nearer the kitchen, Scott plumped for the third door as the room he wanted. However, it was directly opposite the family room from where the voices continued to emanate and where the door was wide open.

In one swift and fluid motion, Scott crossed the hallway and entered and closed the third door and found himself standing in John Butler-Jones private study. If anyone had seen him they had made no noise and after waiting a few seconds, Scott walked across to Butler-Jones' desk. As he sat in the seat, his blood began to boil. The photos on his desk of a happy family hit Scott hard, a daughter in a graduation gown and a teenage boy holding a set of keys next to a new car. They reminded Scott of all the things he had dreamt of throughout his life had he grown up in a normal family. It was not that he didn't love the islanders nor the path he had taken but being an assassin was a particularly lonely job and in fact perfect for an orphan but at the same time not many kids dreamt of being an international assassin.

Scott retrieved the slip of paper the receptionist had given him. He stood up, walked back towards the door and began to input the phone number she had written underneath Butler-Jones' address. He had checked that the 01753 at the start of the number was for Gerrards Cross and assumed it was the office number for Butler-Jones. He hit the green dial button and after a few seconds, the phone on the desk began to ring, as did a bell in the hallway. Obviously, Butler-Jones didn't want to miss a call. Perhaps his father's murderers kept him busy thought Scott as he waited for the murdering deceitful and betraying bastard to come into the study.

Scott heard the footsteps pounding towards the door before it swung towards him, blocking Butler-Jones view of Scott as he entered the study. Scott pushed the door closed, as though it had swung back on itself and moved silently behind Butler-Jones and waited for him to lift the receiver.

"John Butler-Jones," he answered.

Scott pressed the red button and ended the call, before placing his hand firmly over Butler-Jones' mouth and pressing one of his fingers firmly into his ribs.

"Don't say a fucking word or I'll kill your family too," threatened Scott.

Scott felt Butler-Jones try to nod but Scott's grip was so firm he couldn't move.

Scott released Butler-Jones' head and spun him round to face him. The man was greying, in his late fifties, almost as tall as Scott and obviously kept himself fit.

Butler-Jones' eyes widened as the image of a man he knew twenty-five years earlier flashed in front of him but before he could react, a fist struck him square in the jaw, sending him crashing over his desk and into the arms of his chair. A crack from his side and the instant pain signalled that at least one rib had cracked thanks to the awkward landing.

Butler-Jones ignored the pain and desperately struggled to right himself and check that the ghost he had just seen was in fact as real as his punch. He had not been mistaken. The face of James Kennedy, a face that had haunted him for twenty-five years was alive and standing in his study looking even younger and fitter than he had twenty-five years earlier.

"Are you OK, dear?" a female voice shouted from the hallway.

Scott looked at Butler-Jones and indicated a slashing motion across his throat.

"Yes, I'm fine, just knocked the chair over," he shouted back, wincing as each inflation of his lung pressed against his broken rib.

"Are you sure?" she asked the door handle began to move.

"I'm on the phone!" he replied angrily. The door handle stopped turning and the foot steps retreated.

"But you died twenty-five years ago, it can't be," struggled Butler-Jones.

"Not me, my father!" explained Scott, his voice full of hatred, staring down at the injured Butler-Jones with fire burning in his eyes.

"My God, I never knew!"

"Would you still have betrayed him, had you known he was a father!"

Butler-Jones looked at Scott with deep confusion, "Betrayed him?"

"You switched the loan agreements, which was as good as a death warrant!"

"What agreement?"

"The loan for $50 million!"

"I'm sorry but I have absolutely no idea what you're talking about," replied Butler-Jones pulling himself to his feet, his hand firmly pressed to his rib cage in a vain attempt to stop any movement.

"But my father left me a letter and told me he was betrayed by his lawyer and then named you as his lawyer."

"I was your father's lawyer but I'm not a commercial lawyer. I was his personal lawyer, I looked after his estate."

Scott pulled the letter from his pocket and re-read it, his father did mention being betrayed by his lawyers and then named only one lawyer. The natural assumption had to be that his father meant John Butler-Jones had betrayed him, it had to be. Otherwise Scott had just assaulted a friend of his father's who could help him.

"Prove it!" demanded Scott.

"Umm…OK…umm…" Butler-Jones tried to think how best to prove it. "OK, look at the letter on my desk," he blurted.

Scott turned to the desk and seeing the letter began to read,

Madam,

I refer to our recent discussion with regard to your estate...

Scott read through the detail wondering exactly how this confirmed the man's status. However the sign off at the end caught his attention

I have the honour to be, Madam, Your Majesty's humble and obedient servant.

Scott moved to the top of the letter and on the letter head noted John Butler-Jones name and the name of the company under which the tag line private client specialist was clearly noted. Not only was he a private client specialist, he was the Queen's private client specialist.

He read the letter again, there was a distinction between lawyers and his lawyer.

"Your father had a team of in-house lawyers to deal with business transactions," explained Butler-Jones. I only dealt with private matters, tax issues, personal properties, his will and any other personal matters that he wished to keep separate from the business."

Scott slumped into the nearest chair and buried his head in his hands.

"I'm so sorry for hitting you," he said. "I thought you had helped them set my father up."

Butler-Jones still holding his side shuffled across to Scott and placed his arm on his shoulder.

"At least you let me explain myself. If I were you and had thought a man had betrayed my father, I'm not sure what I would do, I'd probably have killed me."

Scott looked up and into Butler-Jones eyes, his guilt plain to see.

"Let's just say if I hadn't needed information, you'd already be dead," explained Scott matter of factly. "Sorry!" he offered sincerely.

Butler-Jones sat next to Scott. "That's OK, I understand."

An awkward silence fell between them as both struggled to come to terms with the news that one was nearly killed and the other almost killed the wrong man.

Butler-Jones broke the silence. "So how can I help?"

Scott thought for a second. "How well did you know my father?"

"Until tonight, I thought we were good friends," replied Butler-Jones.

"Tonight?"

"You. I never knew your father had a son, he never told me about you. I didn't even know he had a woman."

"So he kept her a secret?"

"Maybe not, we only met a couple of times a year to go through any issues and usually caught up with everything then. It had been quite a while since our last meeting when he died. He kept cancelling our meetings and then…the car crash…"

"I believe I was a few days old when he died," explained Scott. The timescales would fit, it could have been almost a year since Butler-Jones had seen his father before the crash.

"Wait a minute," Butler-Jone's mind began to race. "Does that mean you're not twenty five yet? I mean your father died on the 6th November."

"I'll be twenty five on November 2nd."

Butler-Jones jumped from his seat and ignoring the searing pain in his side, rushed across to the filing cabinet and after raking through the bottom drawer produced a copy of a legal contract which he read feverishly, coming to a stop mid-way through the fourth page.

"I never understood the point of this until now."

Butler-Jones pressed the paper into Scott's hands and pointed at the clause which his father had detailed in his letter.

Any reservations about the trustworthiness of Butler–Jones disappeared that instant. The man was a friend, not an enemy.

"Yes, my father explains it in his letter."

"But don't you see, we just need to go to court to prove you're his heir and the company is yours."

"What company? It's disappeared, all gone from what we can gather. It was swallowed up by a multitude of different companies. Anyway I'm not interested in the company. I just want to find the fuckers who set up the loan company, killed my father and who then broke up the company and sold it for what I assume was a huge profit."

Butler-Jones shook his head wildly. "No, no, no!!" he shouted.

"Look, let me tell you what happened when your father died. I was his personal solicitor and his appointed executor. But almost as your father drew his last breath, this contract was presented to the courts and your father's known assets were handed over to the loan company. His last will and testament was ignored as it predated the contract and as such I was excluded from the hearings. Don't get me wrong, I kicked up one hell of a stink but after a while even my Senior Partner told me to calm down or he'd be forced to let me go. I was becoming an embarrassment to the firm. It was also obvious I was dealing with some very powerful men, everywhere I went doors were slammed shut. The press refused to run the story despite it being sensational. Anyway after a few months, I realised I wasn't doing myself, my family or in fact any living soul any good. So I went into the office one morning, apologised to my senior partner for my behaviour and went back to doing what I do."

Scott shrugged his shoulders.

"But I didn't entirely drop it, you see. I didn't know about the scam and the betrayal but I did know what had happened was definitely not like anything your father would ever have agreed to. It's been a bit of a secret hobby ever since, keeping track of what's happened to your father's company. I've tracked every transaction, traced back every shell company and trust fund they've tried to hide behind to one company."

"It's still one company?"

"Yep, although it's grown quite a bit but everything was founded entirely on your father's business. Everything it is today, is grown from what your father started. Which means every single bit of it belongs to you!" he stated tapping the clause in the loan company's contract. "They can't have known you existed, otherwise they'd have sold it off and started again," mused Butler-Jones. "You're going to cost them billions," he laughed.

All the killings over the last few days were instantly explained and it was all to do with Scott. Some very rich men had discovered his existence and had tried everything within their power to kill him and save their precious investment. Scott couldn't have cared less about the money or the business but whoever was trying to kill him had killed the islanders and his father and he realised perhaps even his mother. They were not going to pay with their money but with their lives.

"Who?" asked Scott angrily. He was about to issue a few sanctions of his own.

"The largest privately owned corporation in the world, Transcon."

Chapter 63

The motorcade drew to a halt at the steps of the world's most recognisable aircraft, Air Force One. The heavily customised Boeing 747-200B was a symbol across the world of the power and prestige held by the leader of the world's last super power. President Sam Mitchum stepped out of his armoured Cadillac Limousine and began the walk towards the aircraft. Normally, he'd just stride across the tarmac and up the steps. However, that day was to be his last official trip aboard the aircraft before the election. It would be the last time he'd board the aircraft as the undisputed Commander-in-Chief and he was going to savour every last second.

As his photos were snapped, a car drew to a stop nearby and deposited Gerald Walters, the President's National Security Adviser and FBI Special Agent, Dwight Jennings. Walters wasted no time and walked directly towards the president, commanding Jennings to follow him.

"Sir, we need to talk."

"Right this second?" mouthed the president out of the side of his mouth maintaining his smile for his last chance photo session.

"Yes."

"OK, come on board, we'll talk on the way."

"I'm sorry Sir but we'd rather talk here."

"What here, on the steps?" asked the President, bemused.

"Well actually on the tarmac nearer the engine would be better," explained Walters walking back down the steps.

The President followed and the bizarre scene of the President, his NSA and an unknown man standing in front of one of the huge engines on the tarmac at Andrews Air Force Base unfolded. They seemed to be having an argument. This photo was guaranteed front page news the next morning.

There was, in fact, no argument. The gesticulation and raised voices were just an attempt to be heard over the noise of the idling jet engine.

"What is it Gerald? And it better be good!"

"Oh, it is," replied Gerald. "We got a few hits on tracing Hughes' calls."

"Go on," prompted the President.

"The first call was to a cell phone, registered to an elderly lady but it was a man who answered. His voice was sort of warbly so we couldn't run a trace. However he told him he'd call back following Hughes' revelation but never did. The cell phone has since been disconnected."

"So you're telling me we don't know who he called."

"Not exactly but earlier today, Hughes tried to call Max Ernst, an Executive Assistant at Transcon. He sounded desperate to talk to him but Ernst isn't taking his calls. Once he realised he couldn't get Ernst, he tried Henry Freeman."

The President immediately took note at the name Henry Freeman. He had been one of the party's largest contributors over his time in office and someone he regarded as a friend.

"What did Henry say?" he asked guardedly.

"Nothing. He didn't take the call either and made it quite clear through his secretary that he wouldn't accept any calls from Hughes."

"So what exactly do we know from this?" asked the President irritated.

"There's more," offered Jennings.

"Hughes got a call from a notorious bookie based here in Washington, big hitter. A man you don't mess around with. It seems our Mr Hughes is into him for a couple of hundred thousand. As soon as the call was over, Hughes phoned a bank in Panama to check on an account we knew nothing about. Seems it was emptied last night by some anonymous company based in Luxembourg."

"So we may be able to get him to talk?" interrupted the President.

"Sorry Sir, there's more." Jennings broke back in. "Hughes made a call just a short while ago, desperate, cut off and fearing for his life. He called…" Jennings paused for effect but succeeded only in irritating the President, "…Dan Baker!"

"Holy shit! You're saying Baker, Transcon and Hughes are all linked into this?" The President took a few seconds "Are you telling me the conspiracy is about to place a man in the most powerful job in the world?"

Jennings nodded enthusiastically, delighted the President had come to the same conclusion so quickly.

"So why the hell are we standing on a tarmac next to a fucking plane engine, instead of issuing arrest warrants?" demanded the President.

Walters took over. "Because we believe we are being bugged, we don't know who we can trust and we have absolutely fuck all proof."

"Hughes!" suggested the President.

"Just issue the order and we'll take him into custody, Mr President," smiled Jennings.

"Do it!"

Chapter 64

It had taken over an hour for Butler-Jones to detail his findings for Scott. The file he pulled from his bottom drawer was almost a foot thick and dated back almost 24 years. Butler-Jones it appeared was the diametric opposite of what Scott had initially believed him to be. It was clear from the detail and effort he had gone to, Butler-Jones was an exceptionally loyal, just and fair man. A man he felt sure would have been very similar to his own father.

"As you can see, Transcon has three CEO's and one CFO. They have been there from Day One and from the records I've tracked, they were the four who took charge following the death of your father."

Scott looked down at the four names, four men who thought they were on top of the world, untouchable, gods, deciding who should live or die. And four men who were about to die themselves.

"Charles Russell, Peter Astor, Andrew DuPont and Henry Freeman are going to be very dead men."

"But what about the company? I can go into court tomorrow morning and claim ownership, in accordance with the clause. It's airtight, you are the legal and rightful owner of Transcon. It's yours for the taking." Butler-Jones waved the contract in front of Scott.

"I don't care about the company, an eye for an eye is all I want right now. If I go to court, I can't then go and kill them. I'd be the number one suspect. No, I'm sorry, first things first. They die and then if we have time, we'll worry about anything else."

"Scott, I understand you want revenge but murder is a very serious path to take and knowing what these men have done, an extremely treacherous one at that!"

Scott had told Butler-Jones most of what had happened over the last few days but had not told him of his rather unique career.

"Don't worry, I know how to look after myself and anyway I've got some help meeting me later."

Butler-Jones gave up. It was obvious that emotions were running too high to waste time arguing. He'd try again once Scott had calmed down.

"Do you want to stay for dinner?" asked Butler-Jones, hoping he could tackle the subject later.

"No, I'm sorry I've got another meeting which I'll miss if I don't leave soon. But I'd love to come back and meet the family," said Scott pointing to the photos.

"Niece and nephew, I'm afraid," replied Butler-Jones sadly. "My wife and I tried but it wasn't to be."

"I'm sorry but I'd still love to come back and meet your wife and perhaps hear more about my father. And again, I'm so sorry about the rib."

"Not at all and I'd love for you to come back and please think about Transcon. Removing these men from the power they have would be as good as killing them. Trust me, powerful men fear failure more than death."

"I will but please don't mention this to anybody, not even your wife. I haven't been here, my very existence puts your life in danger. In fact," Scott took a thousand dollars from his back pocket and the papers and bank account details for the bank in Geneva and handed them all to Butler-Jones. "Consider this a retainer. You are now officially my lawyer and covered by lawyer-client privilege."

Butler-Jones smiled, the quick thinking and pragmatic approach to the situation reminded him of one man. "You are your father's son, Scott Kennedy." Butler-Jones patted him on the back as they walked to the study door.

Twenty minutes later and with the enemy names, he was on the train back to London and speaking to Ashley who, having just arrived back in Geneva, was searching for everything she could find on Eduardo Ramirez.

"Holy shit, Transcon? They're massive! Fucking hell!" she exclaimed as the information sank in.

"So don't worry too much about tracking Ramirez, we've got our bad guys," suggested Scott as a final thought.

"OK but it would be nice to find a link and just tie everything up neatly."

Scott couldn't disagree and tried to relax. He was not looking forward to the next hour. Somebody had sold him out and he just prayed it wasn't the Prime Minister.

At 22.13 the train drew to a stop in Marylebone and thanks to the underground, Scott was walking across Parliament Square in the heart of central London by 22.45., under the watchful gaze of two of the world's most proficient assassins.

Chapter 65

At precisely 22.40, the two cars pulled out from the underground garage of the Pimlico safe house. The cars were exact copies of two DPG, Diplomatic Protection Group, police cars that worked for the Royal and Diplomatic Protection Division of the Metropolitan Police Force and were responsible for the protection of the UK Prime Minister amongst other VIP members of the UK government and foreign embassies.

The two Metropolitan Police emblazoned red BMW's roared down the street and within two minutes were stationed just moments away from Downing Street. Should anyone take any interest in the two cars, however unlikely that may have been, the cars matched their real counterparts exactly, right down to registration plates and vehicle identity codes.

Ideally, they would have waited until almost 23.00 before arriving on site. However, a diversion had been arranged that was, unfortunately, out of their control and could mean up to a ten minute deviation in their plan. Although not perfect, the diversion was going to give them exactly the edge they needed.

***

With the time nearing 23.00, she checked her blackberry device. She had expected an update before then but nothing further had come through. The instruction remained the same, 23.00, London. She raised the magnifying scope and took another look through the top floor window, the lounge of Prime Minister Adam Smith came clearly into view, she scanned across the building and focused in on the bedroom. A large four poster dominated the room. However, both rooms were empty, with only two minutes to go, she was beginning to wonder whether something had gone wrong.

Chapter 66

"GO, GO, GO" shouted Jennings into his phone.

Ten miles South East, six members of the anti conspiracy team moved in on Stephen Hughes' Washington Apartment. Jennings had been confident the president would order his detention and had set up his men accordingly.

The portable battering rams made short shrift of the main door and the six flooded into the hallway and raced up the staircase towards his apartment door on the first floor. Again, the battering ram annihilated the door and within a minute of breaking through the first door, Stephen Hughes was being restrained and handcuffed.

The lead agent called Jennings.

"Got him and he's thanking us! He's acting like we've just saved his life."

"Excellent, take him back to the safe house and remember don't let anybody outside of our unit know we've got him. We're acting on behalf of the President himself. Even the Attorney General cannot know."

The instruction to his agent was irregular to the point of being illegal. The FBI reported to the US Attorney General, the highest ranking law enforcement officer in the government. However, if the conspiracy were centred around Transcon, the Attorney General was just as likely to be as dirty as Hughes was.

"Got you, we're on our way."

***

Ernst had just finished ripping the Metropolitan Police Chief a new anus when his phone rang. He excused himself from the office, comfortable in the knowledge that his priority was to assist in the capture of Eduardo Ramirez. As he walked into the corridor, he pressed the answer button.

"Ernst," he answered.

"Mr Ernst, hi. My supervisor suggested I call you direct. As per your instructions, we've been keeping an eye on Stephen Hughes."

"Yes," confirmed Ernst apprehensively.

"About two minutes ago, a bunch of guys, who I can only assume are Bureau, busted into his house."

"Fuck! Where are they now?"

"Still inside, no hold on…they're just coming out. He's cuffed and being pushed into one of their cars."

Ernst considered the risk. He knew Baker had thought it minimal but he couldn't agree. He made a decision. "Make sure he doesn't get where he's going alive!"

"What about the bureau guys?"

"Whatever, just don't get caught!"

***

The FBI guys didn't stand a chance. As they were making their way into their vehicles, the blue van that had been parked on the other side of the road, came careering towards them. The side door flew open and a wall of bullets crashed into them.

The two shooters had XM8 assault rifles, the newest rifles under development by Heckler & Koch, with a fire rate of over 750 rounds per minute. It did not take long to run through the 200-round drums on each rifle and for all movement to stop in the two cars. With a positive id on the body of Stephen Hughes, the side door of the van was closed and the wrecks of the two FBI cruisers left smouldering in the street. Job done.

***

The moment the phone rang, Ernst hit the answer button.

"Well?" he asked gruffly.

"Well what?" demanded Dan Baker.

"Oh sorry, I thought you were someone else. How can I help?"

"I should have mentioned before but didn't think it was important. However it probably is. Stephen Hughes called me earlier this afternoon."

Ernst felt as though he'd just been punched in the stomach.

"What did he say to you?"

"Nothing, he got my secretary but he may have left a trail."

If he had, it was a fluke. Hughes had no idea about Baker's connection to Transcon but with his demise, he wasn't going to be around to clear up any confusion. If he were being used as they suspected, his death would implicate an otherwise squeaky clean Baker.

"I'll call you straight back!" rushed Ernst, hanging up on his boss without so much as a goodbye.

Ernst redialled the previous caller and was hopeful when it was answered immediately.

"Hello?"

"Hi, it's Ernst, don't…"

"Job done Sir!" he interrupted.

"Shit!" Ernst hung up and called a very fucked off Dan Baker who was about to get even more fucked off.

Chapter 67

As Scott walked across the square, he began to sense that somebody was watching. He couldn't see anybody but knew someone was there. Leaving the relatively well lit square behind him, he continued onto Whitehall, darker and quieter. If anyone was going to try anything, they'd do it there. He scanned ahead and caught sight of one drunk leaning awkwardly against a wall, urinating and another slumped in the doorway obviously waiting for his friend.

Something didn't seem right, he knew nobody was expecting him but there was something about the drunks that just didn't ring true. For a start, there were very few bars in the area and certainly none that would allow patrons to become quite as inebriated as these two. Scott prepared himself as he drew closer, both appeared to be unaware of his presence but that could have been to draw him in.

With less then two meters between him and the closest drunk, both spun and jumped towards him. Scott was ready and jumped back, just keeping out of their reach, his fists up and ready to repel any attack.

"Shit, we nearly did it!" shouted the first drunk to the second.

On hearing the voices. Scott immediately relaxed. "Bastards!"

Kirk and Kyle, had got the message he had sent them. Their latest sanction had been in China and they had just come straight from there. Scott instantly knew from their playfulness that neither knew what had happened to the island and his family. The K Squad were a tight bunch and an attack on one of them was a declaration of war on all of them.

As Big Ben approached 22.50, Scott turned to them and asked them to sit down on the doorstep behind them. Scott brought them up to date on what had happened. Neither believed him to begin with but the sombre expression soon made them realise it was not a wind-up. A whole island and its community had been wiped out. Kirk and Kyle had been welcomed openly on the few occasions they had visited with Scott and both felt a huge loss. They took some comfort from the news that none would have suffered but like Scott, the grief was short-lived. Anger began to boil and the demand to know who was responsible soon bubbled to the surface. Vengeance was now the priority. Grief would wait until scores were settled.

Scott gave them the two minute version of what he knew, the link to Transcon and the belief that they were responsible and that ultimately, it was his fault. Both Kirk and Kyle reacted strongly to his guilt, asserting that the only guilty parties were those who had a hand in pulling the trigger. Scott had lost just as much as they had when the island was bombed. Their family was his family, their home his home.

Scott heard the first chime of Big Ben and realised they needed to get moving. As the second chime sounded, the three were up and walking towards the Downing Street entrance. They didn't hear the third chime. The explosions drowned out Big Ben and any other noise for the next ten minutes.

Chapter 68

The London Eye had been built to mark the new Millennium and stood over 135m tall. The wheel, on opening, was the largest observation wheel in the world. Standing on the banks of the Thames, it towered over the government buildings across the river and was only a few hundred yards from Downing Street. Originally planned to last only five years, its popularity had secured its permanency as a feature on London's skyline.

Although closing at eight during the winter months, the venue was available for hire for corporate events in the evening. The insurance company who had hired it that evening were celebrating the success of a recent merger between two competing organisations. Only three of the thirty two capsules were being used as with only seventy guests and each capsule holding up to twenty-five, the rest were superfluous. In any case the event was done on the cheap. The Champagne was really Cava. The food consisted of nuts, crisps and sausage rolls and the new MD had screwed the venue manager down to the barest minimum cost for the use of the Eye.

There were therefore more than a few surprised guests when two barges that were moored in front of the Eye began to let loose the most amazing firework display. None more so than their boss who just hoped he wasn't going to get stung for it. The fireworks were tremendous, lighting up the sky and booming across the city. The speed and ferocity of the show left hardly a second between bangs. With each flash of colour, a corresponding bang echoed across the skyline.

The duty manager at the Eye stared in disbelief. Nobody had told him they were going to let off fireworks. He didn't have a permit and it was going to cause all kinds of trouble. At the same time, however, it was absolutely the best firework display he had ever seen. Even the Millennium displays from around the world would have struggled to compete. Within seconds, his ears were ringing. The ferocity of the explosions were surely not normal, he thought as the sky continued to explode.

Of course, the insurance company had nothing to do with the fireworks. Mike Hunter had arranged it all as a diversion, no permit had been obtained and none would have been issued. The fireworks were way beyond the legal requirements allowed in the UK. There would most definitely be hell to pay but they would never find out who had arranged it. Everything was untraceable, even the barges which had been towed down earlier in the day were owned by a shell company that until that day hadn't existed. In any event, nothing could be done until the show was over and that would be ten minutes after it started and about seven minutes longer than the UK's PM had to live.

**

As the sky lit up, the two police cars burst into life, their blue lights switched on and both accelerating down Whitehall. As the explosions began to ring out, both cars raced towards the iron gate that secured Downing Street and flashed their lights to gain entry. As expected, the sight of the familiar cars did the trick, the gates swung open and the metal barrier that would stop a tank began to lower into the ground.

The confusion of the sudden explosions and the arrival of the speeding police cars had got them through the gates. The hard part was done.

As they sped past the first line of defence, the passengers in the cars shot the four policemen that had just let them in. The explosions overhead covering the spit of the silenced H&K MP5SD's. Within seconds, the two vehicles were at the front door of Number Ten and the two policemen covering the door were also shot. Five men poured out of the car and dispatched another two police guards, one of the men snapped open the boot of the first car and withdrew a small rocket launcher, flipped it onto his shoulder aimed and blew to smithereens the iconic symbol of the British government, the front door of Number 10. A further guard died in the blast while another three who had rushed to see what was happening were mown down before they even had a chance to raise their weapons.

All three of them paused as the flash lit up the sky and they saw the blue flashing lights career down Whitehall and turn sharply into Downing Street. Without thinking, they all began to sprint as the explosions literally pounded their ear drums. They knew the fireworks were not normal. As they reached the gate, the sight of the dead policemen confirmed their suspicions while the flash of light from the door up ahead told them they had to hurry. Whoever was attacking the PM had already breached the house.

Grabbing the standard MP5 issue weapons from the DPG officers, the three quickly but carefully made their way towards Number Ten. Two of the assassins stood guard, one holding an MP5, the other checking the skies with a stinger missile. The second Scott spotted the stinger, he knew the PM had not betrayed him. Obviously, someone had wanted to ensure the secret stayed exactly that. Scott added George Cunningham to his hit list. It was going to be a busy night.

Kirk and Kyle were slightly behind Scott and with no intention of waiting for them, Scott rolled out into the road, catching the attention of both assassins. He dropped the assassin carrying the MP5 first and smiled as he watched the second try to shoot him with the stinger. He waited longer than necessary as he let the assassin think he might just make it. Kirk, however, wasn't in on the joke and shot the stinger carrier with a three round burst to the head.

Scott signalled for Kyle to wait at the door and for Kirk to follow him inside. Once beyond the rubble of the front door, the house seemed eerily quiet despite the ongoing explosions overhead. Scott pointed for Kirk to take the stairs while he rushed towards the back of the house. An elevator had been installed recently which Scott hoped was sitting on the ground floor and would give him a chance to jump ahead of the assassins. As he opened the door, the door to the elevator was just closing. It seemed Scott wasn't the only person who knew about it. Just as the doors were about to close, Scott managed to force the butt of the MP5 into the gap. The doors immediately opened again. With his gun pointing the wrong way, Scott dived out of the way as a volley of bullets flew out of the small box.

Convinced he had shot him and seeing Scott's gun lying safely on the ground, the assassin advanced to finish the job.

Scott didn't hesitate. He needed to get to the PM. He spun and delivered a bone crunching punch to the throat of the assassin, the speed and power destroying the man's larynx and voice box before separating his spinal column cleanly from the base of his neck. His body dropped lifelessly to the ground. Scott pressed the button for the top floor.

The elevator travelled quickly but to Scott it felt like a lifetime. On reaching the top, the door opened to reveal the main door to the PM's apartment. It was shut. A good sign that the assassins had not yet made it to the top. Scott had thought as much. There were at least ten security stations within the house and as many men. They'd have to work their way through each of them if they wanted to make sure they got back out alive.

In between the fireworks, Scott could just make out the noises of small gun fire. As soon as it started, it stopped. The security men's pistols were being silenced by the assassins MP5s. Scott ran across to the door and found it locked. He banged on the door and prayed that the PM would hear him over the fireworks. Eventually, the door opened and a very frazzled and dazed PM stood before him. Scott pushed him down the corridor and told him to wait in the room at the end of the corridor before making his way back towards the staircase that would bring the assassins to the PM.

Scott stood to the side of the staircase, pushing himself as tight as he could against the wall and waited. The explosions from the fireworks continued to rock the building but Scott could feel the movement on the staircase. He was tuning out the explosion frequency and focusing on the footsteps edging towards him. With one step to go, he moved. Squatting and spinning, he threw his right leg out and almost removed the head of the first assassin with an upward kick that sent the man's body crashing into his colleague. The trigger of the second assassins gun was forced down and the first assassin's already lifeless body filled with bullets. Scott's move, however, wasn't finished. Following the momentum of the kick, he had literally leapt over the top of the two men and landing on the step to the rear of the second, crashed the point of his elbow into the man's temple sending him crashing to the floor and instantly stopping the flow of bullets. The man would be a vegetable for the rest of his life.

As the bullets stopped, Kirk appeared. All assassins it seemed were accounted for. Scott and Kirk walked back up the stairs and entered the PM's apartment and joined him in his bedroom.

***

As the explosions overhead had reverberated around the small bell tower, she had been caught in a dilemma. Muzzle flashes had been clearly visible within Number 10 and with no sign of the PM, she had considered whether she should abandon the post and get to Number 10 herself. However, she also knew that by the time she got there, it would all be over. The only viable option was to remain where she was and hope the PM would come into view.

She hadn't had to wait long. Not long after the shooting had started, the PM had run into his bedroom, extinguished the light and jumped behind his bed. She switched to night vision scope but still couldn't see him. However, she knew where he was. With the PM covered, she was comfortable she had made he right decision. No matter what happened, she had him in her sights.

The muzzle flashes continued to burst out of the windows and were now on the third floor, just one floor below the PM who scurried out of his room, her eye momentarily distracted by the flashes below. However, less than twenty seconds later, he was back and diving for cover behind the bed again. As the muzzle flashes stopped, she began to panic. There was only so much she could do. The glass between her and the PM was bullet proof and ideally, she'd have a .50 calibre rifle to ensure penetration. However, she had a slightly smaller calibre but hopefully just as effective. The L115A1 was a slightly modified version of the L96 Accuracy International sniper rifle and used an 8.59mm cartridge. The armour piercing rounds she had selected would be able to penetrate the glass and still have enough energy left to go straight through the bed.

With the muzzle flashes having ceased from below and the PM refusing to budge, she withdrew her blackberry device and selecting a number hit dial. She just hoped that he would hear the phone ring over the explosions from the seemingly endless firework display. Putting the blackberry on loudspeaker, she could just about hear the ring tone as she waited. The green glow began to appear in her scope and grow as the Prime Minister got up and walked to his phone on his bedside cabinet.

"Hello?" he asked tentatively.

"Mr Prime Minister. Don't move. I have you covered with a sniper rifle…"

The door burst open and Kirk and Scott flew in.

"Friend or foes!" she demanded as the two green figures shot into her view, as the Prime Minister turned to see who they were, a red dot appeared in the centre of Scott's head.

The Prime Minister didn't know what to say. If he said friend and she was with them, Scott would die and if he said foe to protect Scott and she wasn't with them, he'd die. The permutations of the situation were too much to be answered in a split second and the words of his mother from childhood popped into his head, 'now Andrew you must always tell the truth, bad things happen to people who lie.'

"Friend," he shouted into the phone.

Both Scott and Kirk looked at him in confusion as the panicking PM screamed 'Friend' seemingly randomly into the phone.

The PM closed his eyes as he shouted and waited for the shot to ring out but it never did, he opened his eyes and the red dot had disappeared.

"Sir, who's on the phone?" asked Scott, concerned by the Prime Minister's bizarre behaviour.

"A woman with a sniper rifle pointing at me," he answered.

"Not at you, covering you," she corrected over the phone.

"Sorry, covering me," he repeated for them.

Scott and Kirk smiled as they realised what was happening,

"Sir, will you tell Jasmin, to get her arse out of the Life Guards' tower and get it back over here," asked Scott.

As Jasmin made her towards them, Scott quickly explained.

"I sent a signal out on a communication channel suggesting a meet here tonight at 23.00. My island has been bombed and everybody killed. Jasmin has been on at us for some time that your security is lax. She promised the next time she was here, she could take you out and get away with it without any hassle. It seems she proved her point and thank God she's on our side."

The Prime Minister looked out his window and across to Life Guards Parade, the home of the Queen's ceremonial guards. The bell tower was clearly visible atop their barracks.

"Have I met Jasmin?" asked the Prime Minister, knowing he hadn't. In fact, he'd never met a female K Squad member.

"I don't believe so, Sir. She's relatively new, only been on the team for a few months. Joined us from MI6. We've needed a woman for a while but never had anyone with the skills until Jasmin came along. Exceptional shot Sir. "

Kyle rushed into the room. "We're clear, the cavalry's arrived," he announced. "The building's surrounded."

"OK, before I get swept out of here, who did this?" asked the PM angrily.

"I believe the same men who destroyed my island and I believe the Defence Secretary is working with them. They had to know where I was going before I got there to plan the bombing and I don't believe you told them."

The Prime Minister was a very intelligent man and didn't need to be convinced further. It all made sense.

"The little fuck. I'll get him picked up straight away!" the PM turned to the phone.

"No Sir, we'll deal with him." Scott placed his hand on the PM's arm stopping him.

"I can't sanction him, it's not possible," protested the PM.

"Nor needed. This is personal," replied Scott.

Chapter 69

They'd moved three times in the last eight hours but still they didn't feel safe. Streets that had not seen a police cruiser for years were littered with them. Crime in Anacostia for the first time in fifty years was down to almost nothing. If you so much as looked the wrong way, a cop was by your side and harassing you. The crackdown had been announced just a few hours earlier. The Chief of Police had called an unscheduled press conference and announced his plans. He had had enough of the crime ridden Anacostia. All leave was cancelled and the police would be taking the streets back with immediate effect.

His announcement was met with stunned silence and then a round of applause. For a long time people had been asking for this to happen but there was never the money, resource or whatever other excuse they could come up with. Then all of a sudden, out of the blue, every objection had been waved and a stream of police cruisers and riot teams entered the area; a mere ten minutes after the Chief's announcement, unheard of.

Questions rained down thereafter. Where were the funds coming from? What other services were going to be cut? Anger started to build as the reporters began to consider the implications of a huge resource being spent on those who contributed least. Were the hard working tax payers going to suffer because of the idle and lazy scum that inhabited the worst areas of Anacostia? As the questions flooded in, the Chief raised his hands to silence the mob. He had one more announcement to make.

"I received a call earlier today from presidential candidate Dan Baker. Mr Baker had recently driven through Anacostia and had been shocked by the deprivation just a stone's throw from The White House. He had asked what he could do to help and I told him it's nothing money can't fix. Mr Baker phoned me back an hour later. His fund raising dinner was an enormous success and he felt it was wrong, with everything that was going on, to just flush the money down the advertisers' toilet. He got into politics to do the right thing. Ladies and Gentlemen, Mr Baker is funding the additional resource, straight from his campaign fund. No services will suffer in Washington as a result of this clean up, none!"

The press went wild, rushing to the phones and news companies jumped to live feeds, interrupting news stories to break the news. Dan Baker was cleaning up Washington and he wasn't even elected yet.

Ernst was delighted, not only had they secured maximum police effort in helping find Ramirez but the publicity Dan would get from funding the operation would be ten fold what he would have achieved on a few shitty adverts that would have cost the same. Baker's call to the Chief had been carefully planned by Ernst. Calling just before he arrived and then just after he left with the offer to fund a high profile crackdown. Of course that was only part of what had swung it for the Chief, the million dollar bonus for finding Ramirez had been the clincher.

***

After watching the Chief's press conference, Vic knew they were dead. It wasn't if but when they found them. Dan Baker was letting them know personally how much Ramirez being caught meant to him. Vic Garcia looked at the three bodyguards, five was a big number to hide. He had been hunted many times before and had always made it but this time the stakes were much higher than a rival gang. The Ramirez family had given Vic a home when no one else would touch him and the dying wish of Eduardo was that he would protect his nephew. Vic was a man of honour and would die defending the young man but to do that he'd have to take whatever action was necessary. He turned to the bodyguards and told them to wait there. Vic got up and taking the now reclothed Eduardo by the shoulder led him out of the room. Vic closed the door and the two left their third hideaway behind. Five had become two, which had just made Mr Baker's job all the harder.

Part Five

Chapter 70

The news of the island's devastation was not well received by Jasmin. However, as with everyone else, the grief was soon replaced with a burning anger and a thirst for revenge. The information that there were a number of targets somewhat appeased her; at least she'd get the opportunity to claim one for herself.

As Scott laid out the plan for Russell and Cunningham in a basement room of Number Ten, his phone rang. It was 00.30.

"Scott?" asked Ashley.

"Yes."

"Thank God you're OK," said Ashley, relieved to hear his voice. "I've just seen the news about the attack, I can't believe they tried to kill the Prime Minister."

Scott could see the three sets of eyes watching him quizzically, all had heard the female voice and it hadn't taken long for Kyle and Kirk to put two and two together and come up with five.

"Is that the really hot bird we pulled off the plane?" asked Kyle.

Scott nodded and began to take on a slightly rosier complexion.

"I'm fine," Scott found it difficult to concentrate as his team mates described Ashley to Jasmin right in front of him.

"Can you not talk?" Ashley sensed something was wrong.

"Not really, can I call you back?"

"Yes but just one thing, I've tried everything, I can't get any link between Ramirez and Transcon."

"OK, I'll call you back." Scott hung up and stared angrily at the other three.

"Have we forgotten why we're here?" he snapped.

Kirk turned to Kyle and Jasmin and whispered loudly. "Definitely loved up!" all three smiled and apologised. The humour break was over and it was back to business.

"Kirk, Kyle, you stake out Russell's place while we take care of Cunningham."

***

Kirk and Kyle surveyed the mansion and its security as they arrived at the Regent's Park home of Charles Russell. He obviously took his security seriously. The men patrolling the grounds were exceptionally well trained and although looked unarmed, to the trained eye the way they walked and the clothing they wore suggested they carried sidearms. Two men manned the front gate while another four patrolled the grounds and that didn't include any that may be watching the multitude of security cameras which seemed to cover every square inch of the property.

"Well?" asked Kirk as they met up again after their scouting.

"Piece of cake!" replied Kyle.

***

In contrast, the home of George Cunningham Secretary of state for Defence, one of the UK Government's more senior posts lay relatively unprotected. With a list of enemies that included the world's more radical and high profile terrorist groups, Cunningham appeared to have no more than a high profile police car parked across the street from his home in very exclusive Belgravia. Scott shook his head, surely a home worth five million dollars would have rung a few alarm bells within the House Select Committee for Standards and Privileges, the body responsible for ensuring all members of parliament declared their financial interests.

Scott and Jasmin didn't bother worrying about the guards out front and simply entered the house from the unprotected rear. Jasmin made light work of the security sensors while Scott picked the lock. Within seconds, they were in the house and creeping silently through the darkened rooms in search of Cunningham. A phone ringing shattered the silence. Scott checked his watch, 03.00. A light came on, on the floor above them and was followed by heavy footsteps rushing across the floor and then down towards them. Scott had just stepped out of the study and assumed that's where the heavy feet were heading.

He hid in the shadows and signalled for Jasmin to step back into the lounge.

Cunningham, as Scott predicted, rushed past and grabbed the ringing phone in the study. It had taken all Scott's powers of restraint to stop himself from snapping the little fucker's neck there and then. Scott pressed his ear to the door.

"I'm sorry, I don't know what happened!" he protested.

After a short silence.

"I can't, he's not accepting my calls."

Short silence.

"No, he can't have guessed I was involved. He's probably asleep that's all."

Silence.

"Look, you planned the thing. This is your fuck up!" Scott heard the phone slam down. It was his cue. He opened the door and slid quietly inside. With his back to the door, Cunningham hadn't even realised until he turned round to go back to bed. The sight of Scott, the UK's secret assassin, an assassin he had helped to kill, standing in front of him instantly made his heart race and knees go weak. The feeling of dread began to rise from the pit of his stomach.

"You look like you've just seen a ghost," suggested Scott menacingly.

Cunningham recovered quickly. "No, not at all in fact. I didn't recognise you until just now. Sorry I don't often get intruders sneaking up behind me."

Scott shook his head. "This can go two ways, painful or quick. Trust me, you really do want quick." Scott's pupil's flared, a little trick he had learned that instantly unnerved people. His stare had gone from intense to insane.

"I don't know what you're talking about," replied Cunningham in his most arrogant and condescending tone, just as though he were shouting down a heckler in parliament.

Scott spun round, threw out his trailing leg and caught Cunningham perfectly on the nose, breaking it cleanly.

"Who?"

"Who what?" replied Cunningham, struggling to his feet.

Scott snapped out his foot and broke the arm Cunningham was using to push himself up, sending him crashing to the floor.

"You've not got it yet? I am going to kill you. I can make it quick which, thanks to you, was how most of my family and friends died or I can make it painful and punish you. The choice is yours."

Cunningham didn't hesitate and told Scott everything he knew which wasn't much more than Scott knew already. Although one surprise was the involvement of the US Secretary of Defence. The Unit and its existence was another, as was the name of its commander Mike Hunter. With two additional men on the hit list, Scott turned to the now trembling Cunningham.

"Anything else?"

A shake of the head sent a spray of blood from the broken nose across the cream carpet.

"Positive?"

"Yes!" confirmed Cunningham, praying that Scott's earlier threat was just that. He had told him everything knew and was hoping Scott would show some mercy.

Scott couldn't stand to be in the room with Cunningham a second longer. Every time he looked at him he just wanted to smash his face into a pulp. However, that would be too quick. Cunningham, despite Scott's earlier promise, would not die quickly.

Scott moved towards Cunningham and without another word delivered a crippling kick to his midriff. Cunningham was bent over double and desperately gasped for air, the pain was intense but bearable. Scott turned and left the room and with Jasmin at his side went back out the way they came.

Grabbing his stomach with his one good arm and struggling for breath, Cunningham hit his panic button and as he waited for his knights in shining armour to come to his aid, dialled Hunter back.

The pain started to get more intense as he waited for Hunter to answer. Eventually after the eighth ring he picked up.

"Hunter," he answered.

"It's Cunningham…" his speech struggled as he gasped for breaths. "We missed him, he got off the island…"

"What island? Who?"

"The target…he made it," Cunningham dropped the phone and bent over as a wave of pain passed through his intestines.

***

"You didn't kill him?" said Jasmin angrily as Scott explained what had happened before turning and walking back towards the house that was now bathed in light and had a number of blue lights flashing around it.

"Where the hell are you going?" he asked grabbing her arm.

"To kill that son of a bitch!"

"I said he wasn't dead, I didn't say I didn't kill him!"

"What?"

"I killed him slowly. He thinks I didn't kill him but all I wanted was to make sure he phones and warns them I'm coming."

"What the hell for?" shouted Jasmin stopping in her tracks.

"I want them to panic at every sound they hear and flinch at every sudden movement. I want them to shit themselves from now until we end their miserable fucking lives!"

"I can live with that," smiled Jasmin. "And him?"

"He's a bleeder, massive internal bleeding that even if they caught now would be too much to fix, he's dead. He just doesn't know it yet."

Chapter 71

Within seconds of Cunningham's call, the phone lines between The Unit, Transcon and Intelligence Agencies across the globe lit up. The level of security at each of the Transcon bosses was raised with their security detail instantly tripled and supplemented by the addition of heavily armed tactical response teams stationed nearby on 24 hour readiness.

Hunter's call to Ernst had spoiled what had already been a day of ups and downs. The success of Ernst's idea over the funding of the police crackdown had been a master stroke. Initial polls suggested a four point spike in Baker's already impressive approval ratings but this was marred by the killing of Hughes which Ernst had ordered. Although had Baker not been so fucking stupid and told him about the call, that wouldn't have happened. The news that the target was alive and well and on the warpath did not go down well and it was with some trepidation that Ernst picked the phone up to tell Baker.

"JESUS H FUCKING CHRIST!!" he screamed on hearing the news. "You have got to be fucking kidding me!!!"

"I'm afraid not," replied Ernst.

"What are we doing?"

"Everything we can, all agencies under our control are working on it as a priority."

"What about the girl, did she survive?"

Ernst hadn't even thought about her, but thought quickly enough on his feet to cover it off. "We don't know but we're looking for her as well," he'd have to phone Hunter the second he got off the phone to make sure she was added to the search.

Baker caught his anger and realised he needed to emphasise the danger Scott posed.

"Ernst, I can't tell you how important it is we find him and kill him. Eduardo Ramirez pales into insignificance compared to what this guy can do to us! We must find him and find him soon, time really is of the essence. He can take everything from us, everything."

With Baker's words ringing in his ears, Ernst phoned Hunter back and asked him if they had any leads on the girl. More honest than Ernst, he admitted he hadn't thought about her. Ernst went ballistic and told him to pull his finger out of his ass and do what he was exceedingly well paid to do, before slamming the phone down. A bit of anger motivation never hurt in a manhunt he thought.

The surprise death of Cunningham shocked the Transcon bosses. The stories of the UK Defence Secretary's last few hours filled the news headlines. The details of the excruciating pain all too relevant for each of them, a clear message to each of them from Scott, a professional killer was on their trail and it was personal.

The security at each of their homes was increased further and all high profile engagements cancelled.

Chapter 72

Kirk and Kyle had watched from their hideaway as the fleet of Range Rovers rushed through the gates and deposited their cargo of men throughout the property. The floodlights were switched on and the grounds blazed in a bright light more akin to a mid summer's day than 04.00. in the morning.

"Hmm little bit harder now!" exclaimed Kirk.

"Just a bit," agreed Kyle.

"Just a bit what?" asked Scott, startling the twins.

"Jesus, I wish you wouldn't do that."

"What?

"Sneak up so fucking well."

"So where are we?" asked Jasmin joining the group.

"I think someone tipped them off that we we're coming?" explained Kirk. "The place just filled up and lit up."

"Yep, it was me!"

"What the fuck did you do that for?"

"He wants them to shit themselves before we kill them," explained Jasmin.

Both the twins shrugged. "Fair enough," they said in stereo.

"So what's the plan?"

"Wait until sunrise and hit hard," replied Scott patting the kit bags they had brought from the flat in Bayswater.

Chapter 73

Charles Russell was a very worried man. The news of Cunningham's demise shortly after the failed attempt on the PM and the resurrection of Kennedy's son from the grave was a fucking disastrous scenario. When you added the fact that Kennedy's son just happened to be a prolific assassin who was a secret employee of the PM who they had just failed to kill made the worst even worse. It was highly likely that Charles Russell was at the top of the list of one of the world's most accomplished assassins who had just wiped out their team of highly paid and accomplished assassins.

Even with the wall of men around him, he felt uneasy and decided that Regents Park was just a little too public when Kennedy was on the rampage. A helicopter had been arranged for first thing in the morning. Charles Russell was going to spend some time visiting his various homes around the world. If he kept moving, he'd be harder to kill and at least that way, he wouldn't be top of the list. Freeman, DuPont or Astor could take the first bullet and draw the fucker out.

As the sun began to rise, Russell could hear the chopper coming in from the East. He grabbed his bag and almost ran towards the back door of the house, the sooner he was out the better. However, before he could reach the door, four members of The Unit's elite personal protection division blocked his route. Ex US Secret Service or Royal protection officers, the men took their duty as seriously as though the president or the queen herself were their ward. Charles Russell was going nowhere until the chopper was down and ready to leave. They would then rush him across the lawn, covering him with their bodies before bundling him into the chopper and accompanying him wherever he went.

The chopper suddenly appeared as though by magic from the glare of the rising sun on its final approach to the landing pad just metres from the back door of the house. With little or no view from the surrounding parkland, thanks to a high wall that surrounded the rear garden, the protection officers were comfortable with the exit route and were themselves glad of Russell's decision to get he hell out of dodge.

The first anyone noticed that something was wrong was when one of the protection officers saw a slight change in the landing pattern. The helicopter usually came in slightly further down the wall to allow a slow and easy approach into the pad. However, he initially put it down to speed. Russell wanted to get out quickly and they didn't have time for fancy flying. However, with this concern, he watched the helicopter more carefully than he would have otherwise and with only seconds to spare, he grabbed Russell by the cuffs and screaming to his colleagues, rushed him to the front of the house.

***

With the plan set and Scott just about to give the go, they heard the helicopter. Scott considered the options, let Russell board and get him as he left with the chance they may miss him. Or ensure he couldn't get out and kick things off in style.

"Kirk, Kyle take out the chopper pilots," he said into his small headset.

"Roger."

"Roger."

The four K Squad members were spread across the countryside, each having taken up sniper positions to cover the four corners of the house. Kirk and Kyle had the rear while Scott and Jasmin had the front.

Kirk and Kyle lined up their shots and fired. The suppressed 7.62mm SR25 sniper rifles hardly recorded a spit as the bullets tore through the air, straight through the glass of the helicopter, killing the pilots instantly. The power of the shot left no more than a bullet sized hole in each of the two front windscreens and to the outside world nothing had changed. However, the helicopter now had nobody to spin it around and land on the helipad. It simply kept going and crashed into the back of the house with a loud explosion.

"Now," said Scott calmly, as the helicopter hit.

All four began to pick off the men surrounding the property, the four semi automatic SR25's with 25 round magazines clicked away as each islander selected, aimed and shot, always selecting the man nearer the house, working their way forward. It took a few seconds before the guards realised what was happening and very few made it back to the safety of the house. With the numbers dwindling and shots raining in, Scott could almost smell the fear emanating from the house. It was almost time to move. A few more headshots to idiots looking out the window had all but discouraged the activity and offered them a fairly clear run in.

However, just before Scott issued the Go, the sound of two more choppers could be heard approaching.

"I've got them in my sights, a couple of Lynx gunships," announced Jasmin through their headsets.

"Can you take them?"

"Already on it."

"KK, go."

Jasmin had dropped the SR25 and moved over to a shoulder mounted Starstreak missile system. As she pressed the trigger, the missile fired and accelerated to Mach 3.5 before releasing its three explosive darts that were guided into its target by laser beam. The Lynx didn't stand a chance and with their tight formation, one missile proved more than enough as two darts singled out one while the third flew into the other, killing any hope for those inside the house that they might make it out alive.

Kirk and Kyle were up and moving. While one shot anything that moved in any of the windows, the other rushed forward and covered the other. Continuing this process until both of them were safely tucked up against the wall of the house.

Scott had lost his cover fire as Jasmin dealt with the incoming gunships. Loading a new magazine into his SR25, he ran and fired creating his own suppressing fire and was soon feeling the heat as the defenders threw down their own wall of bullets. Scott dived for cover and threw his body behind one of the bodies that now littered the once immaculate lawn. The body danced in front of Scott as the bullets tore it limb from limb as the defenders zeroed in on Scott.

Jasmine noted the change in noise from short bursts of fire to a continuous onslaught. With the Lynx choppers down, she spun round and spotted Scott just as the body covering him was about to disintegrate. She grabbed the AS50 Accuracy International sniper rifle from the kit bag and quickly brought it bear on the house.

Scott could feel each of the bullets move closer and closer as the body in front of him gave less and less resistance. Kyle and Kirk screamed for him to stay down but were powerless to help as bullets pinged just inches from their feet, pinning them to the wall. As the body gave way, Scott felt the first bullet strike his Kevlar vest. His body kicked as the force of the bullet lifted him off the ground.

Kirk watched as Scott's body kicked once and could wait no longer. He dived and rolled into the lawn with his finger pressed firmly on his trigger. Kyle could only watch as his twin brother fell to the ground, stopped in his tracks by the hail of bullets that surrounded Scott.

Jasmin felt the world slow as she brought the AS50 to bear and tried desperately to fire quicker as Scott's body flinched and Kirk's body stopped in mid air under fire from the house. She spotted the main protagonists and fired the massive 12.7mm bullets straight down their throats. The boom of the AS50 silenced the other weapons instantly as the defenders dived for cover.

Scott was up and moving as the first boom echoed out from the massive rifle, Jasmin was back in action. He sprinted across to the motionless Kirk and dragged his body towards the safety of the house wall. Kyle was beside himself as his brother's lifeless body was dumped at his feet.

"What the fuck!!!" screamed Jasmin through each of their headsets.

"I'm OK," replied Scott. "The vest caught the bullet. But I can't say the same for Kirk, he's been hit."

"Badly?"

Scott looked at Kyle who was checking on his brother's condition before answering.

"Five hits. One in the arm and another in the ass, both through and throughs. Three to his vest. He'll live!" replied a relieved Kyle, wrapping pressure dressings on each of the two wounds.

Jasmin continued to lay down suppressing fire as a groggy and pained Kirk came round.

"Thanks man," said Scott.

"Don't mention it," replied Kirk through gritted teeth.

"Don't mention it! What the fuck were you thinking about!" shouted Kyle.

"One of us had to step up and show some balls!" smiled Kirk.

"Prick!" said Kyle dropping his brother's head. "Let's go and get these mother fuckers!"

Kyle dropped his SR25 ,pulled his MP5SD from his back and prepared to enter.

"Scott?"

Scott winked at Kirk and grabbed his MP5SD and followed Kyle's lead

"Jasmin, stay on the perimeter and keep their heads down," commanded Scott.

"Will do!"

"OK, let's go."

With a flashbang grenade announcing his entry, Kyle burst in through the kitchen window, taking two guards down as he came.

Scott opted for a more dramatic entry.

"Jasmin any chance of a high explosive through the door?" asked Scott.

Less than a second later, the front doors were obliterated as the supersonic explosive shell literally blew them off their hinges. Scott followed up with a flashbang and was in the main hallway taking down three disorientated guards before they knew anything about it.

Scott could hear the sirens. The police had got the calls, probably from joggers or dog walkers who had called in on their mobile phones as World War III kicked off within the confines of the park.

"Come on guys, let's wrap this up quickly," he said into his headset.

The two seasoned killers worked their way through the house relentlessly. Every now and then the crack of the AS50 could be heard against the small weapons' fire as Jasmin picked off another guard stupid enough to have given his away position. Walls were as good as tissue paper against her AS50 and more than a few guards lost their lives thinking ducking behind the wall was safe.

With the ground and first floors cleared, only the second floor remained. Three flashbangs were tossed up into the hallway before another three a few seconds later. Only then did they advance. Scott predicted the guys closest to Russell would be the best and would be ready for Flashbangs but they wouldn't be ready for a second flashbang. Just when they were most alert after the first bang they'd hit them with another. It worked. The two men guarding the stairs took the full brunt of the second flash and were dropped like stones as Scott and Kyle charged up the stairs.

"Russell, come out, you piece of shit!" he screamed. "I'll spare the rest of your guards if you've got the balls to come out."

Much to his surprise, the door opened and an unarmed man appeared in the hallway.

"I'm Russell," said the man as he walked out his hands held high.

Scott stopped himself laughing. Russell was a businessman. This guy looked like action man, only a little older, even down to the square-top haircut. He obviously fancied himself as a fighter and probably had a knife or small handgun tucked into the belt of his trousers. Scott lowered the weapon. If they wanted to play he'd play. The sirens were getting closer but it wouldn't take long.

"OK," smiled Scott, handing his gun and sidearm to Kyle.

As Scott had expected, Action Man pulled a knife which immediately had Kyle raising his gun. Scott motioned for him to back off, which he did.

Action man lunged exactly as Scott had expected,. He dodged the move and threw a short but powerful punch against the man's impossibly square chin. Scott could see him buckle and he hadn't even hit him hard. Typical hard man with glass jaw. The man swivelled quickly and tried to catch Scott with his elbow but Scott had seen it coming and ducking under the elbow avoided the blow.

As the sirens grew even closer, Scott realised play time was over. With the man's head above him, he shot the palm of his hand up and under the bottom of the man's nose. The force of the blow sent thousands of slithers of bone cartilage into the man's brain shredding it as it went. The man's body slumped to the floor as did the morale of Russell's remaining guards who unceremoniously pushed the kicking and screaming Russell into the hallway to meet his killers. They quickly shut the door and prayed the offer of sacrifice would appease the attackers.

"Charles Russell?" asked Scott calmly of the man clawing at the door to the room he had just been thrown out of.

Russell didn't answer, his mind focussed on the safety behind the door.

"Charles Russell?" asked Scott again more loudly.

Russell realised the door wasn't opening and turned round.

"Whatever you want, however much you want, you can have it!"

"It's mine anyway," replied Scott.

Russell fell to his knees.

"Please don't kill me. Please," drool fell from his mouth as he cried and begged for his life. Urine soaked his trousers.

"Twenty-five years too late!" exclaimed Scott taking his sidearm back from Kyle and putting a bullet between Russell's eyes.

"What about them?" asked Kyle pointing to the door behind which the guards cowered.

"Let them be. Come on, let's go."

One down, three to go thought Scott, plus the extras of course but they could wait. Transcon were most definitely top of the list.

Chapter 74

"Sorry, did I wake you?" asked the caller.

"Who is this?" asked a dozy but awake Agent Dwight Jennings. It was not every morning somebody phoned at 03.00. Nor every day that half your team was wiped out in the middle of the day in a quiet and safe Washington neighbourhood. Jennings had spent most of the evening at the hospital. Two of his six agents had survived the attack. One, however, was critical with only a 20% chance of survival. The other had suffered only superficial wounds, although two bullet wounds seemed a little more than superficial to Jennings.

"President Sam Mitchum," replied the President.

Jennings sat bolt upright as though his commander and chief had walked into the room.

"Sorry Sir, how can I help?"

"Can you get down here right away Agent Jennings, we need to talk."

"Yes, Sir"

Forty minutes later, Jennings was being whisked through security at The White House. The President was waiting for him in the Oval office with his NSA, Gerald Walters. The door lay open as they stood waiting for Jennings to arrive.

"Good morning, Mr President, Mr Walters," offered Jennings as he entered the office.

"Good morning, coffee?" asked the President.

"No thank you, Sir."

"OK gentlemen, please sit. Dwight, Gerald just arrived so rather than repeat myself I thought I'd wait until you were both here."

Both Dwight and Gerald looked at each other, the tone of the President's voice was unlike any they had heard in a long time, grave and menacing.

"I've just got off the phone a short while ago from Prime Minister Smith in the UK. We had a very interesting chat. It seems they've been having a few problems themselves with a certain major corporation."

Both leaned forward as the President mentioned the prime minister and problems with a major corporation, both jumping to a similar question. Had Transcon tried to assassinate the PM of Britain?

"They have evidence to suggest that Transcon were in fact behind the assassination attempt on his life. However, the evidence at present is circumstantial and largely based on the testimony of the UK's Defence Secretary."

"But he died. What was it? A car crash they said on the news?"

The President shook his head. "No, it seems Mr Cunningham pissed off the wrong people. The PM's men took him out. The car crash is a cover up."

"What? They killed him?"

The President nodded. "That's not all though. I think the story's just breaking but Transcon's European Head, one of their shareholders, was executed just a couple of hours ago. I believe there was quite a battle and all hell broke loose."

"The PM's men?"

The President nodded.

"Can they do that?"

"I don't know but as far as PM Smith is concerned, Transcon declared war on the UK last night with the attempt on his life. They are a clear danger to the ongoing democracy of his nation and as such, he has let loose a team of specialists to resolve it. He's the same as us. He doesn't know who he can trust and who he can't. Apart, obviously, from his team for whom the matter was personal, whatever that means."

"So what can we do?"

"Nothing. It seems our Defence Secretary Todd Nielsen has been named as well. So I wouldn't even know who to approach to help us anymore. The list of people we suspect or know are involved just grows and grows. I'm beginning to think it's just the three of us who aren't in on it!"

"But we can't just let them get away with it. What about Baker?"

"I asked him about that, they have no evidence to suggest Baker is involved and we've not been able to tie him to Transcon either. I think that's a red Herring. Hughes was just probably trying to secure a job in the new administration."

"But we can't just sit on our hands and do nothing."

"You won't. The UK team may contact you if they need anything. As I said, as far as the PM is concerned, he is at war. We should be as well. The only problem is we don't know whether we can trust our soldiers to shoot in the right direction! So in the meantime, we give them whatever they want, whatever they want gentlemen. Our country is a democracy and will damn well stay one, at least as long as I'm sitting in this office."

Walters and Jennings nodded vigorously. The President switched on the news channel and they watched the pictures being beamed back from Regents Park in the UK. A helicopter crew had managed to get some aerial shots and the TV company was running them as a loop. The first thing they saw was the line of body bags laid out on the lawn. As they approached the rear of the house, the previously white house was blackened with a large hole through which the tail of a helicopter protruded. As the helicopter flew to the front of the house, huge holes seemed to have been punched through the wall and the front door was missing. A large blackened smouldering hole was left where it should have been. The cameraman then zoomed out and panned off to the right where two other helicopters lay smashed and crippled on the ground.

"Holy shit, what did they hit them with, a mechanized battalion?" exclaimed Gerald Walters as he took in the devastation.

The President shook his head, seeing the level of violence and the number of body bags, he was struggling to comprehend what he had been told.

"He told me there were just four of them."

Chapter 75

"Don't tell me not to fucking worry!" screamed Peter Astor. "Of course I'm fucking worried! Have you seen the pictures?"

The four remaining shareholders had been on a conference call since the news of Charles' demise had come in. Dan Baker was telling everyone to calm down. Security had been stepped up and as far as he was concerned, everything would be fine. Their main concern should be Kennedy's son. If he went to the courts, they'd lose everything.

"Of course we've seen the pictures, Peter," replied Henry testily. "But we're on the case and are tracking the killers down as we speak."

"Fuck off Henry. If they can get to Charles they can get to us. I've seen the body bags. He had a fucking army protecting him and they still got close enough to put a bullet through his forehead."

"So what do you propose?"

"Honestly, just now I'd rather give it all up, just give the kid the fucking company. I'd rather be alive and poor than rich and dead."

"Don't talk nonsense Peter. Anyway, we've the slight problem of being implicated in last night's assassination attempt on the PM to get round."

"Please tell me you are joking?"

The line remained silent as nobody spoke.

"Fuck! What fucking idiot decided to do that!" screamed Peter, his blood pressure reaching dangerous heights. They were either going to win this battle or die.

Andrew DuPont had remained silent throughout. Peter was expending enough frustration for both of them.

"So what are we going to do?" asked Andrew.

"In three weeks, I will win the presidency. After that, we're home and dry. After that, the lame duck President will be powerless. I'll start sorting things out. We just need to keep our heads down for a few weeks more."

"It's OK for you guys, we don't have the security you do. We're sitting ducks out here."

"Exactly," Peter threw in.

Baker thought for a second. "Well, that's easy to fix, come here. You can stay with Henry. We'll put a ring of men so tight around the three of you, nobody will get within a mile."

Both agreed.

***

As Baker put one phone down, another one rang. Bracing himself for more bad news, he picked it up. Nothing was going there way.

"We've got a hit on the girl," rushed Ernst.

"Where?"

"Geneva. We've picked her up on a street camera entering the Rocco Forte Hotel. I've got a team en route to get her."

"Don't kill her, we're going to need the leverage," replied Dan.

Chapter 76

The BAE 125 jet of the RAF's No.32 (Royal) Squadron touched down at Geneva airport just moments before the departure of a privately owned Airbus Corporate jet bound for New York. Although the airbus carried with it one of the main reasons for their visit, there was one other reason they had come to Geneva.

Medics had worked on Kirk during the short flight. Despite his injuries he refused to be left behind and demanded to be involved. Scott and Kyle had agreed; a one armed Kirk was better than most of the guys they'd come up against and the bullet in his ass, although funny, only seemed to be an issue when he wanted to sit down.

A car was waiting for Scott, Kyle and Kirk. Scott had decided that Jasmin should head off to the US. As far as he could gather, nobody even knew she existed and as such would not raise any warnings as she entered. The same could certainly not be said of Scott. He knew the moment he stepped on American soil, he'd be the most hunted man in the country. Jasmin would scope out the target and arrange any equipment they required, thanks to the President's offer of assistance. When Scott arrived in the US, he wanted to be ready to hit them fast. He'd only get one chance and he wasn't going to miss it.

The car drew to a stop at the rear of the hotel. Scott had upped the stakes dramatically that morning when he had executed Russell. Not only did they know he was alive, they now knew he was a much greater threat than they could have ever imagined.

Ignoring the questions as to who they were, the three marched through the service entrance and boarded the first elevator they came to. As the door began to close a hand shot in and stopped the door. The door re-opened to reveal a security guard, his hand resting on the pistol holster on his belt.

"Puis-je vous aider, Messieurs?" he asked.

"No but thanks for asking," replied Scott pressing the button again for the top floor.

The security guard put his free hand against the elevator door, stopping it from moving.

"I'm sorry but I'm going to have to ask you to leave," he replied, switching to English in response to Scott.

Kirk wasn't in the mood. In a blur of movement, he snapped his one good hand out and disarmed the security guard before he even had a chance to flinch. Holding the gun butt towards the guard to show he was not going to shoot him, said "Now fuck off and if you're a good boy you might even get it back."

As the guard tried to understand how the man with only one arm had managed to get his gun from him, Scott pressed the button and the elevator rose to the top floor.

Ashley opened the door on hearing Scott's voice and gave him a huge hug as he stepped into the lobby of the Royal Suite. Kyle and Kirk nudged each other like school children as they watched the unflappable ice cold Scott, seemingly melt into the woman's arms.

"You've met the gruesome twosome!" offered Scott as he noted the inane grins on the twins' faces.

"Yes... What the hell's been happening?" Ashley changed the subject quickly looking at Kirk's bandages and pointing to the huge plasma screen beaming the pictures from Regents Park.

"War!" replied Scott leading her into the lounge to bring her up to speed.

***

Ernst wasn't taking any chances. Normally, a couple of guys would have been sufficient to kidnap a woman. However, this one was fairly handy and had already killed two of the Unit's men. He therefore sent eight. He'd have sent more but with security around DuPont the priority, he didn't have anyone else to send and he didn't want to wait until DuPont had gone. They might have missed the girl.

Two cars and a van pulled up at the service entrance of the hotel and seven men piled out and into the corridor. The security man following his earlier scrape, took one look at the men and decided to stay put. His paperwork was much more important than seven very large menacing men, particularly when he was unarmed. Taking a similar route to the previous three, the security guard began to realise something was definitely not right. Looking at the clock he realised it was time for his break and couldn't think of a better time not to be there.

It had not taken long to track Ashley down. Every hot blooded male on the hotel staff knew where the American beauty was staying and it seemed she was alone. Somebody had been with her but they had left. The doorman had earned a $200 tip for his help and the men who had been sent to get the girl therefore knew exactly where she was.

The first of the group knocked on the door firmly. "Room Service!"

Scott had just finished telling Ashley what had happened the previous night when the knock came. "Have you ordered anything?" he whispered.

"No!" replied Ashley.

"Jesus, do these guys not watch TV. I mean, amateur hour or what? 'Room Service'!! Have you still got the 5.7?"

Ashley handed Scott the pistol. Kirk had the revolver from the security guard which he hadn't even bothered checking until then and found it was a useless replica.

Scott crept to the door and looked through the spy hole, one man stood with his back to the door, but he could see him motioning with his head. More men waited out of sight.

"Stall them," he whispered to Ashley.

"Just coming, sorry I was in the shower!" she shouted.

"Ashley you stay in there and lock the door. We'll keep them in the lobby area. That way we can control the situation."

Ashley shook her head but having seen the guys in action, they obviously knew a damn site more than her about how to handle these things.

With the lobby turned into a small enclosed arena, Scott, Kirk and Kyle took up their positions and at the nod of his head, Scott opened the door, standing back in anticipation of being charged.

They were. The men charged in with their weapons drawn.

The charger had thrown his full weight behind the door and with nobody behind it, it flew open easily and sent him crashing head long into the lobby. Scott delivered a crushing blow to the back of the man's head with his elbow as the man flew to the ground. Using the same arm. Scott threw a straight punch in to the next man, timed to perfection. His elbow locking just as impact was made, the man's jaw and cheek shattered from the force of the impact and his body stopped dead in its tracks.

As Scott's second man slumped to the floor, Scott looked around. Kirk and Kyle smiled back, two twisted bodies laying at each of their feet. Six armed men and not one had had the time to get a shot off. Not bad, thought Scott, just as the first bullet struck the door frame next to him.

"Shit, how many are there?" he asked in frustration at a bullet being fired

"More than six!" replied Kyle.

Scott grabbed a pistol from one of the men on the floor and dived into the corridor. The shooter was just a few feet from the door and had not expected anyone to come out. The Unit member scrambled to take the shot at the blur of Scott's body flashing out of the door but it was too late, Scott already had. The bullet struck him in the centre of the forehead and stopped any concerns about getting a shot off.

"Seven!" shouted Scott from the corridor.

"Nutter," replied Kirk.

"Grab Ashley, we need to go pay Mr DuPont a visit." shouted Scott, adding to himself as he covered the hallway. "Every time I think these fuckers can't piss me off anymore, they do just that!"

Chapter 77

As they sped out towards the Grand Chateau that lined the banks of Lake Geneva, Scott received a call from the Prime Minister which instantly changed their plans. News had come through to him that DuPont and Astor had fled back to the US and were, as they spoke, aboard Transcon jets on their way to New York.

Scott told the driver to head back to the airport while he tried to work out how they could get to the US without Transcon finding out. Commercial was out, every passenger entering the US would be under severe scrutiny and the moment they found which plane they were on they'd just shoot it down and Scott had no intention to make it that easy. The UK didn't have any long haul jets in the Royal flight. They couldn't trust anyone from the US. It seemed the President only had two people he could trust.

"We could charter a jet?" suggested Ashley.

"I could chip in $100, Kirk?" said Kyle.

"I could stretch to $200 if we get one I can stand in, Scott?" said Kirk laughing.

"I could maybe manage a bit more. $500," smiled Scott.

"Very funny, I'll pay for it," replied Ashley.

"Beautiful and rich, shame you found her first," whispered Kyle nudging Scott in the ribs.

"Wait a minute, I've got the accounts in Geneva, I never even asked what was in them."

Scott picked up the phone and dialled the Rothschild bank and asked for Herr Krauss.

"Good afternoon Mr Kennedy, how may I help you today?" asked Herr Krauss.

"Can you give me my balances please?"

"Of course, just give me a second."

Scott heard Herr Krauss tapping away on his keyboard.

"In the personal account 12 million 869 thousand 241 dollars and 98 cents, and in the savings account, 31 million 154 thousand 33 dollars and 2 cents."

Scott's arm began to shake, the most he had ever had in any account was about $8,000 and that was because he had been on an assignment where he couldn't spend anything for 3 months.

"OK and if I need to make a payment from the account,"

"Just phone me and I'll transfer the funds, we have a card being made for you and it should be ready for you in a few days."

Scott put the phone down, dazed at his new found fortune. Who needed Transcon?

"Well?"

"The flights on me!" he announced.

After a two hour wait for a jet to be prepared and the best part of $200,000 worse off, Scott, Ashley, Kirk and Kyle boarded the Bombardier Global 5000 for the eight hour flight to New York.

Chapter 78

With nobody looking for her, Jasmin slipped through the heightened security at JFK with ease. Her passport this time suggested she was from Singapore and her cover story was that she was there on a business trip for a few days. Not matching any of the four mug shots in the immigration officials special watch list, she was passed through.

Within an hour, she was standing on the corner opposite one of New York City's tallest skyscrapers, with TRANSCON emblazoned above its main entrance. The building although not the tallest was more stylish than most and most definitely more secure than any. Uniformed guards milled around the entrance while other less than discreet undercover security mingled with the public on the street. Inside the lobby large airport style scanners had been installed and every person had to go through the security control before access was gained through small tight corridors. If you did manage to get through the outer ring you'd have to run down the small corridors which Jasmin felt certain would have security gates at either end and shooting holes throughout. These corridors would become prison cells in an instant and coffins shortly after.

Frontal assault was most definitely ruled out and following a quick check of fire exits, it seemed that Transcon was going to be a very tough nut to crack.

Next on the list was equipment but with no plan to speak of, that wasn't going to be easy. However, the usual wouldn't go amiss and she called one of the numbers given to her by Scott. She detailed what she wanted and confirmed she would accept similar alternatives if need be. It wouldn't be easy he informed her but give him a few hours and he'd have them ready for her. With no plans but plenty of firepower, they could at least just go for it and die an honourable death she thought. Her phone rang.

"Hello?"

"It's me. How are you getting on?" asked Scott.

"Shit, it's a fucking fortress."

"Thought as much. The other two are going there too. We're on our way and should be with you in about three hours."

"Cool, see you then."

Both had been careful not to mention any names. Hopefully Transcon were still unaware of their imminent arrival.

Scott opened up one of the complimentary laptops and began to search. He had an idea how to land with minimum fuss but it wasn't going to be easy. After a few minutes, he made a phone call to one of the President's men who told him what he needed to do. Scott, under the watchful eyes of his co-passengers, went to speak to the captain to see how much it would take to buy his agreement. Scott was fairly certain he'd be able to cover it with his accounts.

It took more than he thought. Pilots weren't easy to bribe, particularly when they believed what they were doing would potentially destroy their careers. To assure him that was not the case, the President would probably give him a medal. That cost Scott double the amount, trying to use the President just made the pilot think it was even dodgier than he had initially thought. Rather than lose his licence, visions of imprisonment for drug running or worse flashed through his mind. However, for $500,000, the pilot was happy to do and risk whatever. All upfront and therefore after a call to Geneva and confirmation that the transfer was complete, the transponder was switched off and they took up position just above a nearby Jumbo Jet on course for JFK, close enough to hide their image from radar and just far enough not to alert passengers of their presence.

As they neared their final approach, the smaller jet began to slow and fall under the mass of the huge airliner. Just before they came into sight of JFK's tower and comfortably below its radar, they banked sharply to the East and lined up for their landing at New York's first municipal airport, Floyd Bennett Field, officially opened on the 23rd May 1931. Although closed for many years, thanks to recent airshows the runway was still maintained and with a runway length of just under 5000 ft, the Bombardier Global 5000 landed with plenty to spare and once refuelled would have just enough room to get airborne again.

Ashley, Scott, Kirk and Kyle stepped out of the aircraft and onto the tarmac and into the US. By the time the nearest police officer arrived on the scene, they were long gone. Leaving the pilot to bullshit his way out of trouble, a fuel truck had been arranged before they landed and fortunately the police officer didn't consider a fuel truck at an abandoned airport as out of the ordinary. The pilot explained how an engine leak had forced him down and how if he flew any further, he could have blown up over a populated area. Fortunately they bought it and left the pilot to tinkering with a spanner in the engine. As the cop left, the fuel truck finished and moved away. The pilot put the cover back on the engine and two minutes later was powering down the runway as the immigration officers came tearing down the runway after him. They were too late, his wheels were up and his next stop was Geneva. He had made it and $500,000 to boot.

Chapter 79

Jasmin gave the details of where to meet her. Fortunately, it wasn't far away. A small workshop in Brooklyn. On arrival, Jasmin whisked them through the door and into the large workshop area dominated by a black Chevrolet Suburban which had recently been delivered with all the weapons and equipment they had requested.

Scott didn't waste any time.

"OK, what have we got?"

Jasmin laid out a number of photos she had surreptitiously snapped of the building and highlighted the security she had seen.

"Shit, it's not going to be easy. Any sign of DuPont or Astor?"

"No, but there's a helicopter pad on the roof, it's highly unlikely they'd come by road," replied Jasmin.

"We could just fly a chopper onto the roof and come in that way," suggested Ashley.

"Nah, if they're that secure down here you have to assume they've got stingers up there. They had them in London," replied Scott. "Can we make it from the ground?" he asked.

"We may as well have flown the plane straight into the building. We'd definitely die but at least with the plane we'd have a chance of taking them with us."

"So we have to come from the top, without knowing what's up there."

Kyle and Kirk smiled. "Excellent! Helicopter tour."

"Yep," replied Scott.

Two hours later, the group were enjoying the highlights of the New York skyline although with high powered binoculars their focus was on one particular building. The security was just as they had feared. Tight. A small bunker sat on top of the huge structure next to the helipad and from the activity, it appeared there were at least ten men stationed there with heavy weaponry up to and including stingers. It was the tallest building in the area. No building overlooked it, other than the Empire State building and that was over a mile away. Even then, the bunker would offer excellent cover to any sniper good enough to shoot over that distance.

Back at the workshop, morale began to drop.

"There must be a way to get to them. The fuckers can't get away with what they've done," said Jasmin angrily.

"How about a Transcon helicopter? We'd maybe get in on that," suggested Kyle.

Scott considered the suggestion, it was one of the best so far but it was still too risky. Even in their own livery, if it wasn't expected, they'd probably shoot it down.

"Jesus, that's it. Guys get your kit ready, we're going tonight."

Scott picked up the phone and made a call. Afterall, he had said anything he could do to help. He then called John Butler-Jones with the instruction.

"Get the papers ready, tomorrow we go to court. I'm going to get my father's company back."

Chapter 80

Ernst took the call and passed it through to Freeman immediately before he left for the evening. He needed some space,. The three Transcon bosses were acting like scared little children and were doing his head in with their constant need for reassurance that they were safe.

Freeman took the call and immediately hushed his colleagues who were chattering in the background as he tried to hear the caller.

"Mr President, of course we'd be delighted to see you. I didn't know you were in town." After a few seconds of listening, he added "Yes of course that'll be fine, I'll see you in a few hours."

"Who was that?" asked Peter Astor.

"Sam Mitchum, he's in town and was devastated to hear what happened to Charles and wants to come over and pay his respects."

"Has he ever visited before?" asked a suspicious DuPont.

"A few years ago, fairly similar, dropped by when he was in town. We are his biggest contributor."

DuPont relaxed.

***

As the President replaced the receiver, he called through to his secretary, one of the few people he felt he could still trust.

"Janie, if anyone calls asking where I am, I'm in New York, OK? Anybody, oh except for Gerald or Agent Jennings."

"Will do, Mr President."

As she considered the request it was something that the man had suggested he'd be interested in. Any strange requests by the President, things that seemed out of the ordinary, any discussion involving other politicians, or presidential candidates. All she needed to do was text him the details and for that her mother would enjoy the benefits of one of America's premiere retirement homes for the rest of her life, all on him.

She withdrew her cell phone and making sure nobody was watching, typed in the message and sent it to the number. What harm could it do? Afterall, it wasn't hard to find out the President wasn't in New York.

***

Not knowing anywhere better, Scott arranged the meet at Floyd Bennett Field. With a fuming Ashley behind the wheel, they drew to a stop just two minutes before the allotted meet. Only Scott, Kirk, Kyle and Jasmin would be going on the mission. Ashley would stay behind, much to her disgust, and drive the car to the building just in case they needed her. She, of course, knew this was bullshit and it was simply because the other four were used to working with each other. Well that and the fact that they were much better fighters than she could ever hope to be but she certainly wasn't going to admit that to them. Those fuckers had also killed her parents.

As the lights began to descend towards them, they climbed out of the Suburban. All were dressed smartly in suits and wore shades, despite it being night time. Kirk's previously strapped arm hung limply, in an attempt to hide his injury. They each carried a H&K MP5SD sub machine gun and a Sig Sauer 229 pistol fitted with a silencer. As the VH3D Sea King helicopter came into land, the first thing they noticed was the livery, the familiar olive green body with white top and the United State of America written down the tail and the final clue to its occupant, the seal of the President of the United state of America was on the door. Of course this was one of nineteen such helicopters but then the only time people ever saw it was when the President was in it.

The K Squad boarded and waved goodbye to Ashley as the helicopter took off. The pilot turned round and asked for a destination. Scott explained. The nose dipped and within minutes, they were circling over the top of the Transcon Tower, as the pilot judged the wind direction and best approach to land.

With only seconds to go, Scott, Kirk, Kyle and Jasmin cocked there MP5's and hoped that none of the guards spotted that they were carrying SD models. The secret service would normally carry shorter KA4 variants. As the helicopter touched down, the four exited the aircraft and as would be expected from Secret Service agents, surveyed the location before allowing the President to exit.

***

The text came through not long after Ernst had left the building. Having missed the point of the President's call initially, it made no sense and he thought nothing of it. The woman was always sending useless information and he was beginning to wonder who was getting the better deal, him or her.

However, on a call to Baker a short while later, all became clear. Baker had told Ernst of the President's surprise visit and thought perhaps he should return to the office just to keep an eye on the three stooges. But when Ernst had broken the news of the text, it seemed obvious that the whole thing was a set up. Baker quickly explained what Ernst had to do. The opportunity was not one to be missed. Ernst immediately returned to the office and got everything in place and as Marine One was landing on the roof, he made his second exit of the day.

***

The guards did exactly what Scott expected, looked on as the four of them scanned the roof for threats. With a wave, the pilot much to the confusion of the guards, did exactly as instructed, took off and hovered a thousand feet above them.

As the guards' eyes followed the ascending helicopter, they shot the men where they stood. There was no time for mercy. All received double taps to the head. As the last four bodies were still falling to the ground, the four were off and moving, guns up, ready for any eventuality. As they made their way down the stairs, two more guards were taken out. The door onto the main reception area for the top floor lay ahead. Scott pulled it open slightly, three guards waited by the elevator doors. Scott held up three fingers and pointed the direction.

Three nods told him they were ready. He pulled the door wide open and Kirk, Kyle and Jasmin each dropped one each, Jasmin from a lying position, Kyle squatting over her and Kirk standing behind. The reception area was empty. Scott held his arm up, something was wrong. He held them back.

"If the president was coming to see you, would you wait in your office for him?" he whispered.

All three shook there heads in the negative.

Scott told them to cover him as he ran in the crouched position across the reception area. The door to the boardroom was closed and a Do Not Disturb sign was in place. Scott didn't like it. That was not how you prepared for a visit by the US President. Scott pulled out a small retractable mirror, normally used for looking round corners and placed it under the door. The wires attached to the door handle would ensure anyone turning it would have a seriously bad hair day. He couldn't see all the explosives but could see enough to know that the top floor of the building would be two floors lower after the explosion.

It also explained why so few guards were in position on the top floor. They knew they were coming. As Scott began to retract the mirror, the angle changed and he caught sight of a face sitting in one of the boardroom chairs. It was Andrew DuPont, only his tanned complexion had taken on a somewhat greyer hue. They needed to get into the boardroom, without triggering the explosive.

He signalled the other three over and explained the situation. They considered the options. Kyle considered more quickly than the others and after knocking the wall to the side of the door, broke the glass covering the emergency fire axe and proceeded to knock through the wall. Two minutes later, he had a hole large enough for Jasmin to squeeze through and another two minutes later, she had the explosives safely defused. On entering the room, all deflated. The three remaining shareholders had received one bullet each to the head. A pistol lay in front of each suggesting a ritual suicide. However, the shooter had been too highly trained. Each bullet had penetrated exactly in the centre of each of the men's foreheads. They had been executed and the explosion was set up to kill Scott and the others. Somebody was trying to cover their tracks.

Chapter 81

The judge had laughed Butler-Jones out of court when he had to admit he could not provide a birth certificate to authenticate Scott's age. Without that, the Judge declared that he couldn't possibly consider the merits of the case. Was he to believe that he didn't have one or that he had misplaced it because it proved his age to be beyond twenty five. He asked for something which proved when he was born and until then, not a chance.

Butler-Jones had scoured the local papers, national press, anywhere that a birth announcement could have been made but nothing. Scott advised him of the solicitor in Singapore but nothing, they still didn't even know the name of Scott's mother. The last people to see her alive were the islanders and they were all dead. They tried everything but to no avail. Butler Jones suggested contacting the widows of the dead shareholders and explaining the situation to them. Perhaps they would do the right thing. He had the evidence and just because their husbands were scum, didn't mean they were too.

Scott agreed and Butler Jones went to work tracking down the grieving widows.

***

Jasmin drove the rental car through the leafy suburbs of Washington and took the sign post for Bradley Farms, the house she was looking for was just a couple of miles down the road. A small park area came into view just before she reached the house. She pulled in, parking the car at the rear of the area, out of sight of the main road. She got out and made off on foot. The moonlight gave her just enough light to make her way through the small woods and she arrived at the back of the target house. She moved very slowly. The motion sensors would only come on if she moved too quickly and after some time, she reached the back of the house. A window was open on the second floor and shimming up the nearby drainpipe, gave her access to the house. Voices emanated from the bedroom. Not good. His wife wasn't supposed to be there. Her office had confirmed she was in California for a few days. However it soon became apparent that the voices were from the TV as it broke to the weather for the next day.

Jasmin edged forward and could just make out the mass lying on the bed through the gap. That was him, Todd Nielsen. The man who had bombed the island. She had begged Scott to allow her to deal with Nielsen. She needed this, she needed to feel she had avenged the islanders. With no objections from Kirk and Kyle who had already bagsied Mike Hunter, Scott agreed.

After confirming it was him, Jasmin stood and entered the room. Nielsen jumped up but on seeing the pretty girl, he relaxed. Somebody who knew him had obviously sent him a present. After all with Dan Baker about to become President, Todd Nielsen was on top of the world.

Unfortunately, the first thing Jasmin did was remove his tongue. She didn't want to listen to him screaming or begging for mercy for the next few hours, because that was how long it was going to last. Todd Nielsen, by the time he died, would wish he had never been born.

***

Kirk and Kyle took a slightly different approach with Mike Hunter, quick and easy. The man it seemed was rather nervous after his paymaster's demise and had taken to travelling with a significant number of guards. Trailing his vehicle in a plain white van, they simply accelerated, pulled in front, threw open the doors and fired an anti tank missile right into his Hummer. There wasn't enough left of him to put in an urn, let alone bury.

Chapter 82

Jennings had a team working full time trying to track down the leads to find out if, as Scott believed, there was someone else. They had tried Baker again but nothing came up, nothing linked him to Transcon. The discovery of Max Ernst's previous career as a KGB man put a new spin on things. The Russian Mafia may be involved and took the investigation off into a new direction as Jennings considered the possibility that the oligarchs of Russia had tried to control America.

Scott disagreed but Jennings, with little else to latch onto, went with it anyway.

***

As the days and weeks passed, Butler-Jones got nowhere with the widows. The lawyers at Transcon refused any contact and threatened him with injunctions if he continued to harass them.

Scott prepared for his twenty fifth birthday resigning himself to having lost any chance of regaining control of his father's company. It wasn't that he wanted the responsibility nor the money, its just that for the first time in his life, Scott felt as though he knew what his father would have wanted. His son at the helm of his company.

Scott's birthday would be celebrated at The White House. The squad, Ashley and the Prime Minister were to be guests of honour at a ball the President was throwing before the elections four days later.

They arrived in style, limos picking them up from their nearby hotel and driving them the short distance to the White House. The President met with them privately and thanked them again for their help in saving the democratic process before they joined the ball.

"Scott," interrupted the President. "I've got a gentleman here who wants to wish you a happy birthday."

"Hi, I believe you've just hit the ripe old age of twenty-five," smiled the man.

"Yes," replied Scott.

"A great age twenty-five, a great age!" he repeated.

Scott looked at the President as the man spoke.

"Sorry, I keep forgetting. Scott I should have introduced you, this is Dan Baker who is probably going to be our next President."

"Less of the probably, Mr President. Fifteen points ahead in the polls you know," he laughed.

"Well it was nice to meet you, Sir," said Scott turning back to his group.

"You too son, you too." Baker walked away smiling. Transcon was safe. Scott was no longer a threat. He'd enjoyed meeting the boy, after all this time. He'd always wondered what he looked like.

***

The morning after the party was not a pretty sight. It had been a heavy night and had resulted in them all falling asleep where they fell. They woke up to the NBC local news channel. Ashley checked the weather to see what she would do with the tourists for the rest of the day. Nobody wanted to do anything but sleep but Ashley was having none of it. They were in her home town and it was her duty to show them around.

As the weather report ended, the local news bulletin came on.

"Police are still hunting for Eduardo Ramirez in connection with a number of murders in the Anacostia area."

At the mention of the name Eduardo Ramirez, Jasmin's ears pricked up and she quickly turned to the screen. As did Ashley and Scott.

Scott spotted Jasmin's reaction. "What do you know about Eduardo Ramirez?" he asked.

Jasmin looked awkwardly at Ashley.

"Oh for God's sake, you can talk in front of Ashley."

"I sanctioned him about a month ago."

"You killed him?"

"Yes, he was trafficking young kids for paedophiles along with drugs. He had been warned but ignored the warnings," replied Jasmin.

"So it's a different Ramirez?"

Jasmin looked at him like he was stupid. She had just told him she sanctioned him. "But there is a family resemblance. They may be related, why?"

"He funded the loan that created Transcon. But we couldn't find any link between him and Transcon beyond the loan," explained Scott.

"Perhaps we should see if we can find this guy," suggested Kirk.

"Definitely," said Ashley. "Well at least we know what we're doing today then. The highlights of the worst and seedier areas of Washington tour."

Chapter 83

Election Day

The hunt for Eduardo Ramirez continued in vain. It seemed the young man had just fallen off the planet. The only information they had been able to glean was that Eduardo was on the run with a notorious local hoodlum Vic Garcia. Numerous comments had been made that as long as he was with Vic and didn't want to be found, they never would be.

Not long into another day's search, Scott received a phone call from Butler–Jones that put yet another spin on the whole matter. He had actually managed to speak to the widow of Charles Russell. It was in fact completely by chance. She had been to his offices as she had decided to get herself new representation. She was unhappy with how the Transcon legal team were treating her and wanted somebody with a bit of clout to back her up. Butler-Jones had been suggested. The fact that he worked for the Queen tended to impress most potential clients and she had been shown into his office.

Butler Jones had explained to Scott that the widows had not in fact inherited their husbands' shares. The shares had passed equally to the other shareholders. Scott had immediately jumped in, needlessly reminding Butler-Jones that they were all dead. Agreeing, he had also informed Scott that the widows would have had no objection whatsoever in talking to them. The lawyers were taking their orders from someone else. Someone was very much in control of Transcon despite every shareholder being dead. Scott speculated Ernst but Butler-Jones disagreed. The lawyers would only follow the legal owner's orders, not somebody who had executed the previous owners. No, the only conclusion he could come to was that Scott was right all along. There was somebody else.

***

The day passed quickly as election fever swept through the country. Dan Baker was well ahead in the exit polls, suggesting an even larger majority than predicted. It seemed his beleaguered rival was destined to lose by one of the biggest margins ever.

The writing was on the wall all day and it was only stubbornness that made him wait until after midnight to concede, calling Dan Baker at 00.01 to congratulate him on a well fought victory.

Dan Baker was to be the 45th President of the United States of America. His inauguration date was set for January 20th.

Epilogue

January 19th 2009

Dan Baker climbed the stairs of his Washington home for the last time. The next day would see him sleeping in The White House. He opened the door to his bedroom and was hit by a cold rush of air. He stomped across to the window and slammed it shut. He'd be glad to see the back of the housekeeper. How many times had he told her he didn't believe that fresh air helps you sleep nonsense?

The door to his room burst open and two Secret Service Agents rushed in, handguns drawn. Dan explained he had just slammed the window shut and suggested they calm down. He hadn't been in office yet to piss anyone off enough for them to want to kill him, yet, he added for comedic effect. Neither got it and left the room.

Dan went to the bathroom to brush his teeth. He didn't even notice the shower curtain move, nor hear the footsteps. He just felt a hand as it covered his mouth, a firm grip he couldn't move. He tried to scream but nothing came out. A face appeared in the mirror next to his and he recognised it instantly. He had seen it many times before and once even in person.

"Hello Mr President," said Scott.

Dan squirmed wildly but his body hardly moved. Scott's strength was far too great for him.

"I bet you're wondering why I'm here?"

Scott could feel the head try to nod.

"I found Eduardo Ramirez."

Dan Baker's eyes widened as the name and the information that name held registered instantly.

"In fact I found him some time ago, it seems you thought once you were elected, you could relax which is exactly what Eduardo's wise old friend Vic Garcia reckoned. It seems he was right."

Scott could see in the mirror the question in Baker's eyes.

"You're wondering why I waited 'til now? Simple really. I wanted you too taste it, to actually feel what you have murdered and cheated all your life to achieve. Just to stop you at the last second. You see you'll never be president. At your inauguration tomorrow morning, you'll be arrested. It's all been arranged. I'm not even going to kill you. You see if I killed you, you wouldn't suffer and I want you to suffer every second for the rest of your life. Every miserable second from now until you die in your prison cell. I want you to think of it as my gift to you."

Scott watched the life in Baker's eyes die as his dream came crashing to an end. His whole life had been geared for that one event and it was going to be a humiliation. Dan Baker, the President with the largest majority in the history of the USA, was going to be known for what he really was, a murdering, cheating, traitor.

"Close your eyes and don't move."

Baker did as he was told. He was sure Scott would kill him. He couldn't know about what he had done to his father without killing him for it.

"Come on, hurry up and get it over with!" he shouted.

Silence. Baker turned. Scott was gone. He walked back out into the bedroom, the window was open as it had been when he entered the room. He sat on the bed and thought of all that he had done to get where he was. How it would play out on the news. What would be the headline? Dan Baker arrested for murder and treason, not President Baker, just Dan Baker. He would be the embarrassment of the country, he'd rot in jail and be referred to as the man who nearly destroyed the country. He couldn't do it, he wouldn't let them do it.

Dan Baker, twelve hours from being named the 45th President of the United Sates of America, reached over to his bedside table. He noticed the picture frame was missing but thought nothing of it. As he removed the pistol from the drawer, he placed it in his mouth and died knowing he was still the president elect.

Scott heard the shot from just outside the perimeter of the garden and placed a call to Kirk.

"Well, did you get Ernst?" asked Scott.

"Nasty, very messy, cried, wet himself the lot. It's always the nasty ones that die with absolutely no dignity," replied Kirk.

Once they had Baker as the lynchpin, it had just been a matter of time before they found Ernst. They had been watching him for weeks waiting until they took Baker out to deal with him.

Scott hung up and looked at the family photo he had taken from Baker's bedside table. She was just as beautiful as she was in the picture with his father. How a man could do what Baker had done, he would never know. Power was a terrible drug but even drug addicts had limits. Scott had gone there to kill him, the arrest at the inauguration was all bullshit. If Baker had stuck it out, he would have been President. But after seeing his mother's face looking into her brother's eyes, he couldn't do it. Even if Baker had killed her, he couldn't kill him. Some killings were just wrong. The evidence from Ramirez was at best circumstantial but the look in Baker's eyes had proved it without a shadow of a doubt.

Scott picked up the phone and dialled Butler-Jones.

"Hi John, it's me. Terrible news. It seems my uncle has just committed suicide and I'm the only living relative. Transcon may well be mine afterall."

The End.

Please read on for an exclusive excerpt of America's Trust – available May 31st

America's Trust

by

Murray McDonald

Chapter 1

Present day
Tuesday 30th June 2015
Washington D.C.

It had been over three years since Jack had been able to walk down the street and open a bar door. The Raven Bar & Grill was just the type of place he needed: quiet, dark and grimy. The shabby exterior gave way to an even shabbier interior. This wasn't a place that was trying to look like something it wasn't. Its seventies décor was exactly that and not some hip designer's cool idea of what the seventies should have been. A line of booths filled one half of the establishment while the other was filled with a long wooden bar. Jack pulled up a stool and ordered a beer with a Scotch chaser. The barman looked at him like he knew him but poured the drinks without a word. Jack sipped the beer, his first real drink in a very long time.

In the three years since Jack's life had been no longer his own, he had lost both his wife and his purpose. Constantly under surveillance, he never had a minute to himself. Even at his wife's funeral, the shackles had not been loosened. What should have been a private occasion had been a very public event. Armed guards watched over his every move, cameras monitored his every step. He had wanted to jump in with her, go with her. He didn't want to go back. As the funeral ended, he had no choice. He had four years to serve, whether he liked it or not. That was his term. No time off for good behavior, that had been clear from the start. The federal government was a relentless beast and if it had you for four years, you gave it four years, no matter what.

Jack savored another sip. His wife had hated his penchant for dive bars but he loved the anonymity. Nobody knew him, nobody judged him. He missed her. He regretted every minute of the last few years when he had not been there for her. Her final breaths had been taken while he was hundreds of miles away. It was all his fault. Four years earlier, his actions had torn them apart. She didn't want him to do it but he had explained to her that he had to. It was a once in a lifetime opportunity. She had begged him not to. It wasn't like they needed the money. For Jack, it wasn't about the money, it was the thrill. Despite his actions, she had stood by him as a loyal wife and as the outcome was read out, she cried with him. Four years. It could have been worse. Some had served double that, but he had promised he wouldn't do it again. They had been the worst and last years of their marriage and he would never forgive himself.

He reached for his Scotch and downed it in one swift motion. It felt good. The heat of the alcohol burned the back of his throat and instantly cleared his thoughts. The TV was showing a round-up of the football and had the other six customers transfixed. Jack nodded at the barman and was rewarded with a refill. He allowed himself to relax, and began to appreciate his newfound freedom. He had walked along the street; he had entered a bar; he had ordered a drink. He was sitting enjoying the football with a bunch of guys who didn't care who he was or what he had done - all things that, for the last four years, had seemed a world away. For the first time in six months and probably in four years, he smiled, not a fake smile, not a smile for the cameras, but a genuine warm smile.

Jack was happy.

"Good whisky?" asked the drinker to his right.

"Great whisky," said Jack, raising the glass and looking at it before taking another drink. "Join me?"

"Don't mind if I do," accepted the drinker. "The name's Don."

"Jake," replied Jack. It was what his mother had called him, never wanting to name him after his father's father. He had been, she told everyone who would listen, the most unlikeable man one could ever have the displeasure of meeting. Jack's father had never once contested his mother's claim.

Jack nodded at the barman again and indicated for each of the other drinkers to be offered a Scotch. They all nodded and mumbled their appreciation and, almost as one, returned to the highlights.

"So what brings you to the Raven?" asked Don, nudging his stool nearer to Jack's.

Jack lifted his drink in answer. Don nodded acceptance and lifted his own, joining Jack in his drink.

After an hour and many Scotches too many, Jack stood up and wished his new friends goodnight. Those capable of responding mumbled a vague goodbye while Don also stood up.

"I have to head home too and face the music!" he said conspiratorially, dipping his head to the barman.

"Face the music?" asked Jack.

"Got laid off today," replied Don.

Jack had reckoned Don was mid to late fifties, around five to ten years older than himself, middle-management with a salary that allowed him few luxuries and a tough life. Jack had always been very good at reading people.

"God, I'm sorry to hear that," said Jack through the haze of alcohol. "What did you do?"

"Purchasing Manager for a government contractor, two hundred and fifty of us got canned today."

"Insignia DC?" asked Jack.

"How the hell did you know that?" asked Don, looking at Jack with some suspicion.

"It was on the news earlier, I recognized the number two hundred and fifty," said Jack, quickly covering his mistake.

Don continued to study Jack, unsure of him now. "You remind me of somebody." Don waved his drunken finger. "I just can't think who."

Jack shrugged and immediately got a response from Don. "The president! If it wasn't for your hair being thinner and wearing glasses, you could be his double!"

Jack laughed. If it weren't for the wig and the contacts he had to wear, he would have been a much more comfortable president.

Chapter 2

"Sorry," said Don, gently punching Jack's shoulder. "You're much too nice a guy to be confused with that scumbag president."

Jack managed to hold his laughter as the words hit home. "He's not *that* bad!"

"Son of a bitch cost me my job!" snapped Don, all joviality dropping from his voice. "Transferred it to China. Fucking *China*, can you believe it?!" he muttered as he staggered off towards his home.

Jack shook his head. "I'm sure he didn't!" he called after Don, knowing he damn well hadn't. He hadn't heard anything about Insignia on the news, he remembered the contract being discussed. Insignia had the contract for printing all federal brochures and documentation. There was absolutely no way Jack wanted that work going abroad in order to save a few bucks. He had made it clear that under no circumstance was the contract to be outsourced to a foreign company. He'd be asking a few questions the following morning, but he was going have to be careful as to how he came about the information.

Jack checked his watch as Don swayed off into the distance. He had been free for over four hours. Four hours and nobody knew he was missing. In his two and a half years as president, he had hardly had four minutes to himself, let alone four hours. Of course, he was assuming nobody knew. With no Blackberry or method for anyone to contact him, they may have been turning the White House upside down to find him. Mind you, if he were missing, he had to assume there would be helicopters and police cars scouring the city. He picked up the pace as he headed south back down 16th Street, NW. There was no point ruining a good thing by being greedy on his first outing. He covered the two miles much more quickly than the outward leg. At midnight there were far fewer people around to watch and analyze.

He hung a left on K Street NW and a right onto Vermont, and as midnight signaled the start of a new day, Jack walked towards the entrance of the Daniela Center. As he withdrew the key to open the security door before him, it flew open, knocking him backwards onto the street.

A man paused briefly before him, recognition registering instantly on the stranger's face as to who Jack really was. However, before Jack could say a word, the street was bathed in flashing blue lights and the scream of sirens as the street filled with police officers and FBI agents in what, to Jack, looked like full riot gear. The police rushed forward, and Jack anticipated being rushed into a car and being sped back to the White House and most likely given a severe dressing down by the Secret Service and his senior staff. However, he was brushed aside as the focus appeared to be the stranger who had almost knocked him over. The man, who Jack estimated to be in his late forties or early fifties, was thrown unceremoniously to the ground before being handcuffed and marched past Jack towards a waiting sedan. As they rushed past, a young female FBI agent holding one of the stranger's arms, brushed past Jack.

"No need to be alarmed, sir," she said. "Just a routine operation. We'll be out of your way momentarily."

Jack was frozen to the spot. Although they were the words that she would have used with the president, the way she had delivered them was exactly how she would have calmed a member of the public, which is exactly how she had seen him - a member of the public. The operation wasn't about Jack, it was about the stranger. Jack looked across as the man was being directed into the back of the sedan. The stranger caught Jack's eye and winked a wink that told Jack the stranger knew exactly who he was.

Jack continued to watch as the young female agent looked around the street and, satisfied with what she saw, circled her finger in the air. Sirens and lights instantly stopped and with one last look back towards Jack but looking straight through him, she disappeared into the sedan. No sooner had she closed the door than the car screeched away. By the time Jack looked back towards the door of the Daniela Center, it was hard to believe what had just occurred. Not a police officer was in sight.

He stepped once again towards the security door and, a little more tentatively than earlier, he entered the apartment block. Checking that nobody was around, he walked towards the end of the corridor and removed another key from his pocket. This one was far older and the door in front of him was far heavier than the security door at the entrance to the building. The key turned easily, far easier than on his exit. He opened the door and entered the apartment where time had stopped over 60 years earlier. The décor was upmarket fifties. The appliances in the small kitchen were museum pieces, as was the TV set. The dust that had settled suggested, like the furniture, that Jack was in fact the first living soul to enter the apartment since its previous occupant had vacated. Jack looked again at the simple note from his predecessor.

> *If you are reading this note and have come from beyond the park, enjoy the freedom it allows, I know I did! HST*

Jack instantly recognized the initials 'HST'- President Harry S. Truman, the man who had rebuilt the White House in the late forties. Obviously, his building had gone beyond the confines of the White House. Jack pulled back the rug and, lifting the hatch, he reentered the hole that led down to a subterranean tunnel. He shut the hatch and pulled the cord that ensured the rug would slip back into place. He climbed down the ladder and mounted the small bike that he had ridden what he guessed to be around a quarter of a mile from the White House. As he neared the end of the tunnel, he once again entered the coffin-sized vertical capsule and, by turning the handle at his waist, wound the small capsule up, by some hidden mechanism, back into his private office, previously his wife's dressing room.

Stepping back into the room, he noticed a small note on the floor of the capsule. He looked around the dressing room; it definitely hadn't been there when he left. He had searched every inch of the capsule when it had appeared earlier that evening. It wasn't something he had ventured into lightly. It wasn't every day that a decorative column which had stood *in situ* for the three years you had been in residence spun round and revealed itself to be an elevator of sorts. Jack had spent a long time looking at every detail and it had been with great trepidation that he ventured in and moved the lever that had lowered him to the tunnel below.

He bent down, retrieved the slip of paper, and read it.

Mr. President, if you are reading this and have not spoken with me, they have me. I must speak to you urgently. Our country and our very way of life as Americans depends on it.

Find me and beware The Trust.

Tom Butler

Jack's memory flashed back to the face of the man being arrested in front of him and the recognition on his face. He had known Jack was the president. It was Tom Butler he had witnessed being taken away. Tom Butler knew about Jack's escape route. Tom Butler had a key to Harry Truman's apartment. The apartment had been locked when Jack had returned. Tom Butler was a man the president wanted to talk to but Tom Butler was a man the president couldn't possibly know anything about.

Jack stepped back from the column and watched in panic as the column spun back to reveal its original and more normal decorative façade. His escape route had gone without him fully understanding how it had ever really appeared. He stepped forward in the hope that walking towards the column would elicit a response, but nothing happened. He shook his head. It wasn't that simple, otherwise his wife would have found it many years earlier. Not to mention every cleaner that had ever worked in the private apartment. He studied the column in great detail. Nothing, certainly nothing visual, suggested any hint of the hidden mechanism.

Jack crossed the small room and sat staring at the column. The alcohol had dumbed his senses, he wasn't thinking straight. He was missing something obvious. He must be.

Daylight hit him like a sledgehammer. The small room took the full brunt of the sun's early morning reveille. Jack covered his eyes desperately but the ache in his brain failed to dissipate. It wasn't the light. The memories of the previous night came flooding back. The beer and the whisky had taken their toll. He wasn't as young as he used to be and certainly wasn't used to drinking anything like the quantities that had so easily slipped down in the past.

He opened his eyes and found himself staring at the column, just as he had been when the fatigue and alcohol had ended any chance of uncovering the secret. He stood up unsteadily; the pounding in his head was going to take some getting used to. Hangovers had been a thing of the past. The President of the United States did not drink to excess and did not gamble - just two of the long list of his previous behaviors that were absolutely forbidden in his current office. *Forbidden is perhaps too strong a word*, thought Jack, *'not expected' is perhaps more accurate.* The expectation levels of a president were, to say the least, extraordinary. The expectations of a president who had lost a wife were inconceivable. He had to be strong at all times, even by her graveside. Weakness was not an option. Bollocks, it was all bollocks. His strength had never been doubted. It was exactly why he was where he was. After years of poor leadership, the country had been desperate for a strong and capable leader to take control. General Jack King, former Army chief of staff and former chairman of the Joint Chiefs of Staff, offered that in spades. Jack was exactly what the country had craved, a politician who they could believe in, a man of his word, a man who put his country and its strength above all else. The Republican nomination was secured even before Super Tuesday, with every other candidate unwilling to add to the humiliating defeats they had already suffered at the hands of the country's clear favorite.

With debt spiraling, unemployment out of control and what seemed no end to the downturn, Jack King had won the 2012 election by one of the clearest margins in modern history.

Jack was ready. His presidency was going to be one of legend, one of resolve. He was going to turn the country around in four years. In and out. That was his motto throughout his military career. Hit the problem hard and fast. He had promised his wife just that. His country had needed him and he couldn't say no. Four years was all he needed.

That was until the day of his inauguration and the revelation that was about to be bestowed on the new president, America's Trust.

Chapter 3

When the key turned in the lock at 4:00 a.m., Tom Butler knew he was about to die. After his arrest by the FBI, he had been marched into the local office and watched as the lead female agent had gesticulated wildly on the phone. When she had ended the obviously angry exchange, she had subsequently kicked a wastepaper basket clear across the room. "Put him in a fucking cell!" she had shouted before storming out of the building. Tom knew then he was in trouble. The tentacles of The Trust had reached far deeper than he thought possible.

The door opened to reveal two immaculately dressed men in suits, one standing well over six feet in height while the other barely cleared five feet.

"Mr. Butler?" the smaller of the two asked.

Tom feigned tiredness and nodded sluggishly, rising slowly from the narrow bench that doubled as a bed.

"How can I help you, Agent?" asked Tom stretching and yawning.

"Special Agent Wen Chan. There's been a terrible mistake but I'm pleased to say it's been resolved," smiled Chan.

"Excellent, so I'm free to go?" asked Tom, knowing it was the last thing they planned for him.

"Yes, Mr. Butler," replied the other agent.

Tom smiled. "And I suppose you're Agent John Smith!" said Tom, referencing the man's European features versus Chan's Asian heritage. Wen and Chan were the two most popular first and last names in China and the equivalent of Western society's 'John Smith'.

The American agent smiled and nodded. They knew Tom Butler would not fall for their bullshit cover story but the show wasn't for Tom Butler, the show was for the FBI.

"So what's the plan guys, get me out and offer me a lift home?"

Chan nodded.

"Airline ticket bought in my name and a look-a-like to use my passport and make the trip? I'm guessing South America or South East Asia?" added Tom, shaking his head. He knew exactly how effective the plan would be.

Smith smiled. "Quit stalling and start walking!"

"Hmm, I think I'll just hang out here, thanks."

"I would advise against that, Mr. Butler," countered Chan sinisterly.

"Or what? You'll kill me?" laughed Tom.

Chan's sinister smile didn't waver. "No, we'll simply extend our area of operation. Who knows what you may have divulged to that pretty little niece of yours?"

Tom's anger exploded and he charged across the room. Before he reached Chan, Smith's massive hands grabbed him and held him back.

"Let's just calm it down," Smith suggested to both Chan and Tom. "Creating a scene does none of us any favors."

Tom struggled against Smith's grasp but soon realized it was futile. The man was like a rock, a solid mass of muscle covered his already inflated frame.

"Stay the fuck away from her!" hissed Tom as he accepted his fate.

"All you need to do is walk out of here a happy bunny and she'll be fine, that's a promise," offered Smith in a conciliatory manner.

Tom nodded his head in acceptance and followed Chan out of the room. The sight of the three men would have raised some sniggers during the day, a real small, medium and large offering. Each stood a good head taller than the next. Tom at 6 feet had never felt taller while Chan led the way and never smaller when Smith took over as they neared the front door of the all but empty Washington field office.

"Smile for the camera!" whispered Chan as they neared the door that would lead them to the main entrance.

Tom was finding it hard enough to take his last few steps, never mind throw a smile to the inanimate cameras that followed and recorded their every move as they walked silently in a death march towards his last breath.

"Special Agent Chan!" came a shout from behind. One of the few FBI agents on duty at 4:00 a.m. stopped them all in their tracks.

Tom turned and noticed Chan's hand move slowly and carefully towards the bump on the inside of his jacket. Chan refused to look back.

"Yes?" he asked, shouting behind him towards the onrushing agent, his hand nearly touching the handgrip of his pistol.

"You left your ID card when you signed out, Mr. Butler."

Tom watched as Chan spun and in the blink of an eye, removed his hand from his pistol grip and held it out to the helpful agent who placed his ID safely in it. The movements, Butler noticed, were exceptionally fast and left the helpful agent blissfully unaware of Chan's previously deadly intent towards him.

As the agent walked away, Tom couldn't resist. "Tsk, tsk, imagine leaving your fake ID behind," he chided quietly.

"Who said it was fake?" questioned Chan so straight-faced that Tom realized he had seriously underestimated his foe.

The final door buzzed open and the coolness of the early Spring morning flooded into the vast entrance hallway. Tom looked around, desperate to scream for help but unwilling to sacrifice his niece. He knew it was likely to be an empty threat. They knew she had nothing whatsoever to do with his work but it was a threat he nonetheless took seriously. She was the only person on the planet they could have used against him. The fact they knew that was more than enough to make him take his fate with as much dignity as he could possibly muster.

He could see the car sitting waiting for them. Its engine was running and a third agent, or whatever the hell they were, was ready and waiting behind the wheel. Just a few steps and the sidewalk separated him from his imminent death. The moment he was in the car, they'd probably put a small caliber gun to his head and end it quickly. The last thing they'd want was a struggle or a fight in a confined space.

He recognized the National Building Museum directly ahead as he stepped outside. He'd never had a chance to visit but had always wanted to. Another thing to add to the quickly filling list of things he had always wished he had done. With each step, it seemed he had done less and less with his life. He tried to remain strong. He thought of the people through the ages being marched proudly to their deaths. Fighting for what they believed in, dying for their cause. *Fucking idiots*, he thought angrily while trying to remain ramrod straight and defiant to the last.

As he neared the top step, his resolve began to waver. Less than ten yards separated him from the ominous black car, its engine humming in the silence of the night while its tail lights emitted a bloody glow that cut through the early morning haze. Agent Smith stretched out and guided Tom down the stairs, his powerful hand bearing more weight than either he or Tom would acknowledge. As Smith helped Tom, Chan raced ahead and opened the rear door. There was no interior light. Great care had been taken to ensure the light had been extinguished. Another sign that Tom's fate was imminent.

As they neared the car, Smith's hand moved from near Tom's waist to his head, gently guiding it lower and lower as he maneuvered Tom into the back seat.

***

"What the fuck do you mean he's been released?!" screamed Special Agent Jane Swanson.

She hung up in disgust and punched the steering wheel in frustration. She wasn't interested in listening to the agent's groveling bullshit of an excuse. He should have fucking well checked with her. She was a rising star but a blighted one. Her anger issues were legendary, as was her profanity. Her ability to solve cases and get her man was surpassed only by her ability to piss off every member of her team and most of the command structure. Luckily for her, she was hated slightly less than she was feared.

She had been promoted and demoted with regularity and was in a current positive trend - the promotions outweighed the demotions. There was very little doubt that her successes were all that stood between her and the unemployment queue. She was a handful and a loud one, but she was also usually the smartest and quickest in the room. Conformity was most definitely not her strong suit. A trait the FBI craved in 99% of its agents, the 1% being the acceptable tolerance of brilliance. There was no disputing Jane's brilliance; it was just whether one day her behavior would outshine it. When that day came, she and the FBI would part company, more than likely, not amicably.

She floored the accelerator and her Audi RS4 station wagon exploded to life. The 450bhp of power bit down into the four-wheel drive train and powered the family size car as though it were an Indie racecar. Jane Swanson loved the wolf in sheep's clothing and the RS4 rocketed in a matter of seconds to over 100 mph. The roads, at 4:00 a.m., were empty. She hit the switch and ignited her blue strobes just in case, and had the added security of knowing the ceramic brakes would ensure she stopped quicker than she accelerated, should the need arise.

The RS4 wasn't cheap, but with no plans for marriage or kids and an inheritance from her grandparents burning a hole in her pockets, she had taken one look and thought what the hell? If ever a car had been built for Jane, it was the RS4. They were just meant to be together.

She called the office back. The adrenaline rush from the acceleration had calmed her mood.

"Don't let them leave before I get there!" she demanded.

"They've already gone. One of the agents had left his ID and I just gave it back to them as they left the building," offered the helpful agent nervously.

"Shit!" she yelled, more in frustration than anger. "I'm heading East on G, were they pointed North or South on 4th?"

"North in a Chrysler 300," replied the agent, watching the car pull away on the CCTV system that covered every inch of the building and its perimeter. "Jesus!" screamed the agent jumping out of his seat.

**

Tom was forced in beside the smiling Chan, his hand resting close to the pistol that he had so nearly utilized just moments earlier. As the door shut behind him, Tom feared the worst and sucked up every piece of courage his body could muster, which was very little. The front door opened and the large frame of Smith folded itself into the cramped front seat.

No sooner had the door closed, the car began to glide away from the curb. Smith swiveled around in his seat and facing Tom, revealed a small, almost ludicrously sized pistol poking out of his right hand. Of course, in Chan's hand, the gun would have looked almost normal. In Smith's hand, the small .22 caliber pistol just looked wrong. However, at close quarters, it was an excellent kill weapon, causing only a small entry wound, no exit wound and enough power in the bullet to rattle around in the brain cavity ensuring a fairly quick and painless death. Tom knew he wouldn't even bleed much. The heart would just stop pumping and the blood would remain in situ. As clean a kill as you could get with a gun.

Tom braced himself for the bullet's impact and closed his eyes. Being thrown forward and realizing he was being thrown forward was the last thing he had expected.

Chapter 4

"Just what in the fuck do you guys think you're playing at?!" screamed Swanson, jumping from her car. She had driven straight towards the Chrysler as it had attempted to exit 4th Street. Her ceramic brakes had been the difference between emergency braking and an emergency call out.

"What are *we* playing at?!" screamed the driver in response, rising shakily from his seat, pointing at her car just an inch from his bumper. "You nearly killed us all!"

"Don't be a fucking drama queen!" she chided, brushing past the driver towards the rear of the car and pulling open the door.

"Mr. Butler?" she asked stretching out her hand.

Tom opened his eyes for the first time and looked into the eyes of his savior. Unrestrained by a seat belt, he had hammered into the back of the front seat. He shook his head in an attempt to understand exactly what had just happened. Agent Chan, it seemed, was in a similar condition. He looked on in a daze as he also had hammered into the seat in front. However, whereas others were simply dazed, Agent Smith poured blood. His lip and nose had split due to the small .22 caliber pistol slamming into his face as his unrestrained body had also been thrown forwards in the car. The windscreen barely restrained the giant form of Smith as his outstretched hand containing the small pistol finally caught up. The irony was not lost on Tom as he began to fully understand the picture in front of him. The small weapon chosen for its lack of bloodletting had created a geyser in Smith's nose.

Tom smiled and accepted Swanson's outstretched hand.

Chan was quick to recover. "He has been released, Miss Swanson!"

"Not by me!"

"It is not your decision to make," answered Chan authoritatively.

"In which case he is free to go with you or come with me, right?" asked Swanson cuttingly. Something was amiss and she had every intention of finding out what exactly it was.

Chan grabbed Tom as Agent Swanson began to pull Tom out of the vehicle.

"Hit it!" screamed Chan.

The driver reacted quickly and began to move but with Swanson's Audi RS4 to negotiate, it wasn't the sudden acceleration that Chan had been hoping for. Swanson removed Tom with a smirk while Chan looked on in frustration as the driver eased beyond the RS4 and then hit it.

Tom and Swanson watched Chan spin around in his seat and could almost hear the screams of anger as he vented at his colleagues while watching Tom and Swanson fade into the distance.

"So, Mr. Butler," said Swanson turning to Tom. "Are you going to tell me what the fuck is going on?"

Tom shook his head, and Swanson took him by the elbow and led him back towards the FBI field office.

"I thought as much," she said despondently.

"I've been released!" Tom said, struggling gently against Swanson's grip.

"Perhaps, but I've a funny feeling I just saved your ass and for that you are going to tell me something before you go anywhere."

Tom looked at the surprisingly perceptive agent. He guessed she was mid-thirties at most, and from her confidence and the way in which she carried herself, she was an exceptionally capable one at that. She was right. He likely *would* be dead now if it were not for her instinct and, of course, her maniacal driving. He looked back towards her abandoned car, a station wagon, but a very butch looking station wagon.

"Should you not move that?" he asked, motioning his head towards her car and changing the subject.

She looked around. She wanted to get Butler back into protective custody. Her alarm bells were ringing on full alert. The streets were empty and Chan and his colleagues' Chrysler were a dot on the horizon.

"You don't mind?" she asked.

Butler shook his head and she changed direction and led him back to the Audi.

"How many kids you got?" asked Butler taking the passenger seat.

"Not married."

Butler smiled. He knew she wasn't married before he asked. "This car has a kind of family exterior but inside it's all business." He tried to move in the seat but it had devoured him with its sporty snugness. "It's so you!" he added with sincerity.

Swanson looked at him for some hint of sarcasm but Butler looked deadpan and straight ahead. She shook her head and turned the ignition key. The engine's bass-like roar announced its readiness to leap forward. Swanson eased the straining beast towards the garage entrance just a few yards ahead. The automatic doors began to rise at the click of her remote, and she looked again towards Butler and smiled. He reminded her very much of her father.

She turned the wheel sharply and floored the engine, the tires screeched and strained as the full power of the engine took them all by surprise. The car rocketed away from the FBI building and hurled its passengers across Washington.

Butler suddenly considered the prospect of a double bluff and instantly panicked.

"Have you eaten?" asked Swanson nonchalantly, taking a corner meant for 20 MPH at 60 MPH.

Butler relaxed mentally, at least as much as the G force being exerted on his body would allow. "Room service wasn't due 'til seven!"

"Excellent, I'm famished and technically you are free."

Butler was no fool; the informality and lack of prying eyes was exactly what Swanson wanted. His already excellent opinion of her increased even further. She was a very smart young woman and one that would require him to be on top of his game. The last thing he'd want on his conscience was knowing he had gotten her killed.

Chapter 5

Jack woke up on the morning that would see a new America - an America that had spent four years in almost constant turmoil was coming to an end. He offered a new choice for America, a strong and proud America that rewarded those who worked hard and believed in the founding fathers' principles. Nobody could deny that the last president had had the unenviable task of trying to recover from the global financial crisis, but one poor decision after another had been more than the public could stomach. Change was needed and President Jack King was the man chosen for the job. It wasn't quite a landslide victory but not far from it.

It would be an uncharacteristically quiet inauguration; the twentieth fell on a Sunday and law dictated that the president must be sworn in by the twentieth. An official ceremony would be held the following day.

President King took the oath of office in a small ceremony conducted by the Chief Justice attended by his wife and senior staff. His speech, safely tucked in his inside pocket, a month in the making, would have to wait until the public ceremony the following day. It was a speech that would never see the light of day. A speech full of hope and determination to work hard, pay down the debts of a wasteful government and ensure the generations to come wouldn't have to pay for the generations in the past.

"Mr. President?"

Jack continued his discussion with the Chief Justice. He had a list of deeply unpopular laws passed by the previous incumbent to overturn as a priority and took the opportunity to discuss his plans with the Chief Justice.

"Mr. President?" asked Kenneth Lee, this time more firmly.

Jack turned, expecting to see his predecessor, but Kenneth was staring directly at him.

"Mr. President, we have a meeting scheduled."

Jack looked over his shoulder before pointing to himself questioningly, much to the amusement of those gathered in the Oval Office.

Kenneth Lee had been Jack's Chief of Staff from the moment he had entered the race. In fact, Kenneth Lee was the reason Jack King had entered the race at all.

Before Kenneth had approached Jack, he had taken an almost unheard of governor of Wyoming, America's least populous state and made him the frontrunner for the Republican nomination. Overnight, the photogenic Wyoming governor was the answer to every Republican's prayers. Swing voters loved him and with a Hispanic grandmother, another huge block of votes was in the bag. In both ability and stature, he soared above his contenders throughout the televised debates. The Republicans were back in a big way. There was little doubt in anyone's mind that he was their man. By the time November came, the race was down to three.

Jack's first meeting with Kenneth had been on a cold winter's evening. A knock at his door at 9:30 p.m. was not unheard of but certainly not common. Kenneth Lee stood before him with a look of desperation on his face. Jack recognized Kenneth instantly. Jack was a staunch Republican supporter and had been a vocal advocate of the Wyoming governor's plans to rebuild America from the ground up. Inviting him in, Jack was totally unprepared for the conversation that was to ensue.

In short, Kenneth Lee had made it abundantly clear that his country needed him to serve again, only this time in a slightly enhanced role. Two hours earlier, the governor of Wyoming had died of a massive heart attack. The announcement would be made within the next hour and with the pitiful display of the governor's Republican contenders and the rock bottom approvals for the current Democratic incumbent, it was feared the impact of the news and the lack of hope it offered would send the country spiraling into a major economic depression. A phone call from the chairman of the GOP had sealed the need for Jack to 'step up and take the reins'. The party was on the brink of meltdown, they needed somebody the country could look up to, a man of stature, a man of leadership, a man the country could respect and follow. General Jack King, former chairman of the Joint Chiefs, was their man.

His country needed him. Jack had never been found wanting when his country called. He stood up and helped the country through the mourning of a president who would never be and gave them the president they all dreamed could save them.

Kenneth Lee had been by his side from that day, an ever constant. He was a political warrior who ensured he was one step ahead and never ambushed. Money had never been an issue. Kenneth Lee had secured the largest war chest ever to be collected to fight a campaign. When more funds were needed, he doubled and trebled whatever the requirement was. Despite the election being almost a certainty from day one of Jack's nomination as the Republican candidate, Kenneth took no chances. For every dollar the Democratic incumbent spent, Kenneth spent two on Jack.

"We need to go, Mr. President," prompted Kenneth.

It was the simple act of Kenneth calling him Mr. President rather than Jack that made the realization of what he had achieved really hit home.

Jack realized then just how much his and his wife's lives were really about to change.

After a small applause from the rest of the room, Kenneth led Jack with purpose towards the Cabinet Room. An elderly gentleman, immaculately presented, awaited their arrival.

"Mr. President, may I introduce you to Mr. Warren Walker. Mr Walker, the President," said Kenneth.

He stood and bowed his head slightly, shaking hands with President King. "Delighted to meet you, Mr. President and please accept my congratulations on your superb victory."

"Thank you," replied Jack looking to Kenneth for some indication as to why they were meeting with Mr. Walker.

"I can see Kenneth has not warned you of our meeting," said Mr. Walker, correctly reading the situation.

"No he hasn't," replied Jack honestly while staring at Kenneth. He turned to face Mr. Walker.

"I asked him not to. All he knows was that it was imperative I met with you on the twentieth of January 2013. 'You' being the president of the United States, not necessarily you, Jack King, if you understand my meaning."

"Yes," replied Jack. "If I hadn't won, my opponent would be sitting here meeting with you."

"Before I begin, I must note that my instructions are to discuss this with the president of the United States only. If you choose to include your Chief of Staff that is your choice."

Jack looked back at Kenneth, his mind racing. What was the old guy going to hit him with? Was this the Area 51 alien chat or some other secret that you only became aware of when you were president?

"I didn't catch which arm of the government you represent, Mr. Walker?" asked Jack, prying for some clue.

Mr. Walker smiled warmly. "Oh, I am not from any part of the government, Mr. President."

Jack looked again at Kenneth for some clue about what was happening. Kenneth shrugged his shoulders, in an 'I don't know, your call' fashion.

"We're in this together, it's his fault I'm here!" said Jack jokingly. However, his mind continued to race, and one question was stuck in his mind.

"Actually, would you mind excusing us for a moment, Mr. Walker?"

"Not at all, Mr. President," he answered, not moving.

After an awkward second, Jack got up and motioned for Kenneth to follow him. They exited the room into Jack's PA's office.

Before Jack could ask, Kenneth was on the defensive. "No idea, I was just informed that the meeting was scheduled."

"By whom?"

"Your PA informed me it was in the diary when we came into office."

"What, we're taking meetings arranged by the previous government?!" he asked, incredulous. "How many more have they left?"

"None, this was it. We tried to clear it but it wouldn't delete. It was like it was hard wired into the system. I was sure it was a glitch until half an hour ago when I got the heads-up that your 1:00 p.m. had arrived!"

"Well I'm not going back into a meeting arranged by my predecessor," concluded Jack.

"But that's the strange thing, according to the system, it wasn't the previous government that arranged the meeting."

Jack waited for Kenneth to reveal who had, but he remained silent; it was obviously too big a deal to just tell him outright.

"So who did then?" Jack played along halfheartedly, much to Kenneth's disappointment.

"William Howard Taft. As in President Taft!" revealed Kenneth.

Jack could barely hide his incredulity that a president had allegedly arranged a meeting 100 years in the future.

"Are you mad?" he asked.

"That's not the best part, the meeting was at the request of JP Morgan, who died less than a month later."

"Bullshit! Why on earth would a meeting arranged a hundred years ago be in a modern computerized diary system?"

"I thought the same. I can only assume the meeting was noted in each of the presidents' subsequent diaries and passed onto each subsequent PA until it was computerized. Thereafter, it must have just been coded in and the code has been there ever since," Kenneth surmised, facing the door to the Cabinet office that held the answer.

"How on earth did they know it would be a Mr. Walker?" asked Jack, facing the same door, finding the weak link in Kenneth's summation.

"There's no name listed, it just states 'a representative of America's Trust'."

They looked at each other and it was clear both were desperate for more information.

Jack walked towards the door and opened it. Kenneth remained standing. He, as Mr Walker had pointed out, was not invited.

"You don't mind if Kenneth joins us do you, Mr. Walker?"

"Not at all, Mr. President, that is your choice."

As they sat down, Mr. Walker cleared his throat. Both the president and his Chief of Staff were on the edge of their seats.

"Gentlemen, how much do you know about compound interest?" began Mr. Walker. It was only thanks to their exceptional poker faces that Mr. Walker failed to notice just how underwhelmed his audience was by his question.

Chapter 6

Butler pulled himself gingerly out of the Audi. The relief at reaching the diner in one piece was slowly sinking in. He felt as though he should bend down and kiss the sidewalk but felt the gesture, although warranted, a little melodramatic.

"You know there is a brake on the car, right?" he offered helpfully, with a soft dose of sarcasm.

Swanson didn't even justify his criticism with a response. She merely smiled politely and led the way into the diner.

"Clever name!" added Butler with yet more sarcasm. Swanson shook her head.

"You know it's a diner, so what better name than 'The Diner'?" explained Butler to the uninterested Swanson.

Swanson dismissed Butler by simply pointing towards a booth while she caught the waitress' eye. A simple two fingers raised by Swanson received a nod of understanding from the waitress, along with a warm, welcoming smile.

Obviously a regular, thought Butler as he took his seat. The subsequent look of disapproval from the waitress to Swanson when the waitress eyed Butler, did not go unnoticed by him.

Swanson pulled herself into the booth. "Calmed down yet?" she asked sternly.

Butler caught himself. She was right, he did have to calm down. How many people, however, had met their executioner, stared down the barrel of the gun about to kill them, only to be saved at the last second? The vision of Smith beginning to pull the trigger with a smile on his face was not one Butler would forget, nor did he ever wish to remember. He realized Swanson was staring at him, reading his every thought. She was an FBI agent trained in the art of reading every nuance, every movement and action of their suspects. He had to change the subject.

"Not a fan?" he asked, motioning towards the waitress.

Swanson looked bewildered for a second. "No, no, she's been trying to set me up for some time and you're the first guy I've ever brought here. She put two and two together and came up with about eighty seven," she laughed. A little too much Butler thought. Although who was he kidding? He was old enough to be her father. At least it had lightened the mood. She was studying him again.

"Do they have a menu?" he asked, keen to have something to do other than be under her gaze.

"Already ordered. Now are you going to tell me what the fuck is going on or not?"

"I don't know what you mean," he said unconvincingly.

"Okay, let's do it the hard way," said Swanson, noting Butler moved back slightly in his seat. "Full name?"

"Remember I've been released."

"On you go," said Swanson. She had seen the fear in Butler's eyes. She knew he was going nowhere.

"I think we both know I'm not going anywhere, although do you mind if I just nip to the restroom before we get started?" he pleaded, a little too pathetically.

Swanson wasn't quite buying Butler, something was amiss. He came across meek and mild, but his eyes told her something different.

"Fine, but don't do anything silly."

Butler got up and found the restroom. The pay phone sat next to the entrance of the restrooms just as he had hoped. He dialed the number and was pleased to hear the voice on the other end. "Six?"

"Negatori," was the slightly panicked response.

"Scatter!" he said quickly and hung up, a huge weight lifted from his shoulders. He made his way back to the booth and pulled himself in.

"Thomas Franklin Butler," he said.

Swanson noticed his change in demeanor.

"Occupation?"

"Retired."

Swanson smiled without any warmth. Butler understood.

"Retired analyst," he added with a hint of a grin.

Swanson remained silent.

"Honestly, I *was* an analyst!" he replied indignantly.

"Retired?" she questioned, unconvinced. She knew Butler was fifty-four from the APB that had been circulated for his arrest. Other than his name and age, the APB had been bereft of any other information. Fifty-four was not an age you retired willingly unless monies allowed, and from what she could see, certainly from his clothing and wristwatch, money was not overtly displayed.

"Downsized," admitted Butler reluctantly.

"From where?"

"My firm on Wall Street," replied Butler.

"So you were a financial analyst?"

"Yes," lied Butler.

Swanson did not miss the lie, the telltale movement of his eyes giving him away. Before she could challenge him, the waitress arrived with their two coffees and two of the largest mounds of pancakes Butler had ever seen. He stared at them in disbelief.

"Seriously, half that would still be far too much!" protested Butler, looking around his mound to the lithe and athletic figure of Swanson.

Swanson missed little. "I've got an extremely fast metabolism," she said in response to his quizzical look.

"I'll gain three pounds just looking at this," murmured Butler as Swanson tucked in.

She washed down her first mouthful and picked up where she had left off. "So, what was the name of your firm?"

Butler took a mouthful just as she began to speak. He took his time masticating the melt-in-your-mouth pancake, not an easy task as he desperately tried to stall long enough to work out exactly what he was going to tell Agent Swanson.

"Well?" she prompted.

"I worked for…" the sight of the Chrysler pulling to a stop at the curb stopped him in his tracks. Swanson followed his gaze out of the diner's window and calmly reached for her cell phone.

Butler's reprieve had been short lived. They knew he was with a senior FBI Agent. Whoever was pulling the strings had obviously decided this was no longer an issue and Butler's removal was worth that level of fallout. He knew Swanson was a dead woman, her intervention had sealed that. He thought he'd have time to work out a way to save her. The arrival of Chan and Smith so publicly was an extremely worrying turn of events. Such an overt display would suggest the timescales were even less than Butler had feared.

"Don't!" warned Butler. Despite the early hour, the diner had a number of patrons taking advantage of their 24/7 operation.

"Don't what?" replied Swanson angrily lifting the cell to her ear.

"Call for backup. They've already decided we're collateral, no point adding others."

Smith and Chan exited the Chrysler and took up station at the curbside. The Band-Aid on Smith's nose proudly displayed Swanson's earlier intervention.

"What in the fuck are you talking about?" Swanson was beginning to get seriously pissed off with his cryptic approach to whatever was going on. She began to move from the booth but was stopped by Butler, his hand snapping across and firmly pinning hers to the table.

"I said don't!"

"Take your hand the fuck off mine," she hissed angrily. Her body continued to move despite her hand being left behind, leaving her in the bizarre situation of leaning towards Butler while trying to get away from him. "I'm going to speak with those two assholes and find out what they want."

"Fine," Butler released his grip and let her walk two paces away before adding, "but they're going to kill you."

Swanson laughed but saw nothing in Butler's face to suggest that he was being anything but sincere. She looked outside. Her smile dropped slightly and she noticed that her movement had resulted in a readying of Chan and Smith. Their jackets had been opened and their handguns visible. The FBI standard issue weapon was a Glock. Years earlier it had been possible to use a personal weapon but those times had long since gone. Every FBI Agent who wished to remain one carried a Glock. From what Swanson could make out at the distance between herself and Smith and Chan, neither carried a Glock. Not good.

Noticing her hesitation, Butler went on. "They won't come in here, too many cameras. One above the till, one in the corner on the way through to the restroom and if I'm not mistaken, that smoke detector is a fish eye camera," he said without looking at any of them. "It's a twenty-four seven joint, lots of drunks and brawls. They'll have a direct alarm to the police and the cameras will be linked to the web. They can't simply steal the tapes. We're safe for now."

Swanson sat back down. She had a feeling Butler was finally revealing himself.

"Analyst?" she asked sarcastically.

Butler shrugged his shoulders. "I analyze situations," he offered with a smile.

"For who?"

"For whom," he corrected.

"Fuck, whatever!"

"Formerly the CIA."

"So you were downsized?"

"Hmm, I think fired would be more appropriate."

"That doesn't sound good," she said with some concern, wondering whether Chan and Smith really were the good guys.

Butler watched as she looked at Chan and Smith. "Trust me, I'm not your problem here."

"Are they CIA?" she asked watching the two become twitchier. Her sitting back down had unnerved them.

"I'm not sure. Hired assassins, probably," mused Butler, refusing to look at them.

"So they were going to kill you?"

"Right about the time you drove your car at them. Smith was about to pull the trigger when we had to brake."

"Holy fuck!" she exclaimed a little too loudly and caused a number of patrons to turn and look at them.

Butler threw a look towards the other patrons that resulted in them all suddenly finding whatever food lay before them far more interesting than anything else.

"I do therefore owe you a very heartfelt thank you," said Butler.

Swanson looked deep into the eyes of a man she had arrested the previous day, just spent the last hour with, and it seemed had just met in the last few seconds. The man before her bristled with confidence, sat straighter and sounded far more commanding than the man she had arrested.

"Who exactly the fuck are you?" she asked again.

"A great friend and a truly terrifying enemy," he replied while watching another Chrysler pull to a stop.

"And how should I view you?" she asked, her hand moving towards her Glock. She was going to have to choose sides. She had noticed the other car draw to a stop and three men had exited. It was five against two and Butler was unarmed.

"If your hand moves any closer to your gun, I'll be your killer but if you hand me the gun, I'm your only hope!"

"I thought you said they wouldn't come in?" she asked, the tension was palpable.

"I was wrong!" he replied simply. "But if we don't move now, a lot of innocent people are in danger!"

Swanson considered the threat and Butler's concern for the other diners and made an instant decision that she'd have to live with for the rest of her life, however long that would be.

"Run!" he said.

"What the fuck do you mean run?"

"Back door, hit it and run for our lives."

"You have got to be fucking kidding me," she said as they both stood up and Butler led the way towards the restrooms. They watched as the five men, as one, moved towards the diner's entrance. Chan raised his hand to his mouth. He was communicating with someone, whoever was covering the back, Swanson thought.

Before she had a chance to tell Butler, he swept past her, hit the emergency bar on the fire escape with his back and turning through one hundred and eighty degrees, raised his hand, and in one swift and seamless move, removed Swanson's Glock from her holster and shot the two men waiting for them in the alley to the rear. Swanson stood helpless; her backup weapon was in her Audi parked out front.

The noise of the Glock was followed quickly by the front door of the diner crashing open. All hell had broken loose.

Swanson was not unaccustomed to firefights but was used to a significantly larger force than the opposition and usually benefitted from having her own weapon.

Butler grabbed her free hand and catapulted her through the door with him. The two ambushers were down. Butler handed Swanson her weapon while retrieving one from the ground as they sprinted down the alley. The first shots rang out just as they cleared the corner.

"Fuck!" screamed Swanson, her adrenaline pumping to levels she had never before thought possible.

Butler just kept running. He wasn't kidding, she thought, his plan is exactly what he said, run.

"I'll call for backup!"

Butler shook his head. "You don't understand, we can't trust anyone!"

"We can trust the FBI," she replied indignantly.

"The same guys that handed me over to two killers!"

Swanson was about to reply but two bullets zipping past her head stopped any further discussion. Butler skidded to a stop, spun and dropped down to one knee, again all in one fluid motion. The shooting position allowed him to fire off four accurate shots that stopped the two pursuers in their tracks. They both slumped to the ground. From a distance, it was hard to tell how badly they were hurt but from the lack of screams, Swanson could only assume the hits were fatal.

"Who the fuck *are* you?" she asked in awe. He was fifty-four but ran faster and shot better than anyone she had ever trained with, and she had trained with some seriously tough guys.

"Let's go, and will you please lose that cell phone - they're tracking it!" he asked firmly but politely.

"Shit!" Swanson threw the phone towards the pursuers without a second thought. This shit was real.

After another ten minutes of running, Swanson was ready to drop. She could run a half marathon with ease but not at the pace at which Butler ran. He eased up, and she bent over, emptying the contents of her stomach onto the ground.

"Sorry about that," said Butler, "but I wanted to be sure we'd lost them. I assume two followed on foot while the others retrieved a car. We probably lost them when we ditched your phone."

Swanson looked up at him briefly. Her breath was slowly coming back and her stomach had relaxed.

"Now can you please tell me what the fuck is going on?" she struggled between breaths.

Butler looked around again. They were in the middle of a park under a bandstand; even from above they couldn't be seen. They were as safe as they were going to be anywhere.

"You've heard of America's Trust?"

"Of course, everyone has."

"Two years ago, when I was working a case, I stumbled across something. Two months later, I was fired. I've been looking into it ever since. America's Trust is a sham. America as we know it is on the brink of extinction."

Please go to Amazon to continue reading America's Trust – Available May 31st

Other Books by Murray McDonald

Critical Error

Divide & Conquer

America's Trust

Young Adult – *The Billionaire Series*

Kidnap

Assassin

Printed in Great Britain
by Amazon